MIDNIGHT PATRIOTS

An Einstein-Chaplin Thriller

PAUL LEVINE

BOOKS BY PAUL LEVINE

JAKE LASSITER SERIES
To Speak for the Dead
Night Vision
False Dawn
Mortal Sin
Riptide
Fool Me Twice
Flesh & Bones
Lassiter
Last Chance Lassiter
State vs. Lassiter
Cheater's Game
Early Grave
Lassiter's Ghost (coming soon)

SOLOMON vs. LORD SERIES
Solomon vs. Lord
The Deep Blue Alibi
Kill All the Lawyers
Habeas Porpoise

LASSITER, SOLOMON & LORD SERIES
Bum Rap
Bum Luck
Bum Deal

EINSTEIN-CHAPLIN SERIES
Midnight Burning
Midnight Patriots

STAND-ALONE THRILLERS
Illegal
Ballistic
Paydirt
Impact

PRAISE FOR "MIDNIGHT BURNING"

"Aside from Einstein, the genius in this book is Paul Levine, who uses real people and true events to weave an intricate thriller tapestry and to enhance a tale that has more plot turns than a spiral staircase." —*Bookreporter*

"Levine has carefully crafted an intriguing and in many ways timely historical thriller that immerses readers in the world of 1930s Los Angeles." —*Booklist*

"Levine does an excellent job capturing the atmosphere of Golden Age Hollywood as well as the spirits of two of the most important figures of the era." —*Library Journal*

"This series promises to mix fun capers with serious societal commentary and is one to watch out for." —*First Clue Reviews* (Book of the Week)

"Einstein and Chaplin are phenomenal main characters. The cast of characters is rich and varied, and the author easily blends fiction with fact to create a compelling, well-researched novel." —*Historical Novel Society*

"Best historical thriller of the year." —*Best Thriller Reviews*, 2025

"A captivating narrative filled with richly developed characters who evoke powerful emotions...a compelling story set against a backdrop of intrigue and suspense that is truly unforgettable." —*Coffee Pot Book Club* (United Kingdom)

"Paul Levine brings the snappy humor of his terrific Jake Lassiter series to the ingenious pairing of real-life friends Charlie Chaplin and Albert Einstein on a roller coaster ride to save America from a fascist threat within its borders." —Jacqueline Winspear, *New York Times* bestselling author of the Maisie Dobbs series

"JAKE LASSITER" SERIES

"Jake Lassiter is great fun." —*New York Times Book Review*

"Lively entertainment. Lassiter is attractive, funny, savvy, and brave."
—*Chicago Tribune*

"Mystery writing at its very, very best." —*USA Today*

"Jake Lassiter is the lawyer we all want on our side, and on the page."
—Lee Child

"Clever, funny and seriously on point. Top-notch stuff from Paul
Levine. His Jake Lassiter is my kind of lawyer." —Michael Connelly

"One of the best mysteries of the year." —*Los Angeles Times*

"Levine's prose gets leaner, meaner, better with every book. And Jake
Lassiter has a lot more charisma than Perry Mason ever did." —
Miami Herald

"Another enjoyable, breathless thriller." —Oline Cogdill, *South
Florida Sun-Sentinel*

"Filled with smart writing and smart remarks." —*Dallas Morning
News*

"Enough courtroom shenanigans to please even the most stalwart
John Grisham fan." —*Lansing State Journal*

"Paul Levine is one of Florida's great writers, and 'Lassiter' is his
greatest creation." —Dave Barry

"An extraordinary hero stars in a legal tale as believable as it is
riveting. The ending courtroom battle sears with intense and realistic
turns and builds to an unforgettable closing scene." —*Kirkus Reviews*

"SOLOMON vs. LORD" SERIES

"Remarkably fresh and original with characters you can't help loving and sparkling dialogue that echoes the Hepburn-Tracy screwball comedies. A hilarious, touching and entertaining twist on the legal thriller." —*Chicago Sun-Times*

"The barbed dialogue makes for some genuine laugh-out-loud moments. Fans of Carl Hiaasen and Dave Barry will enjoy this humorous Florida crime romp." —*Publishers Weekly*

"Some of the juiciest and funniest lingo I've read in a thriller in a long time." —*Connecticut Post*

"The writing makes me think of Janet Evanovich out to dinner with John Grisham." —*Mystery Lovers*

"Hiaasen meets Grisham in the court of last retort. A sexy, wacky, wonderful thriller with humor and heart." —Harlan Coben

"Levine writes some of the funniest – and most wickedly accurate – courthouse dramas you'll ever read." —Carl Hiaasen

"The repartee between Solomon and Lord is some of the greatest dialogue I have read in years, and is reminiscent of the very best of Dave and Maddie in the early episodes of Moonlighting." —*Bookreporter*

"A sexy read. Set in hot, hot Miami, the sexual tension flies off the page." —*Word Museum*

"A risqué version of the classic bickering of Tracy and Hepburn, *Solomon vs. Lord* is a humorous, fast-paced legal romp, the dialogue crisp and often wickedly barbed." —*Blogcritics*

Charlie Chaplin and Albert Einstein at the premiere of *City Lights*
January 30, 1931

MIDNIGHT PATRIOTS

An Einstein-Chaplin Thriller

PAUL LEVINE

HERALD SQUARE PUBLISHING

AUTHOR'S NOTE

Dear Readers,

Midnight Patriots is the second novel in my series featuring real-life friends Albert Einstein and Charlie Chaplin. Midnight Burning, first of the series, was named "Best Historical Thriller of the Year" by Best Thrillers Book Review. Both novels stand alone, so you can read them in any order—no homework required. If you'd like to sample *Midnight Burning,* the opening chapters follow the Afterword of this volume. The excerpt can be found on page 335.

Midnight Patriots unfolds in November 1940. Europe is in flames. Germany occupies much of the continent, and the Luftwaffe rains terror on London. Fritz Duquesne, a German spy straight from the history books, schemes to steal America's nuclear secrets and hatches a plan to kidnap Einstein. Enraged by Chaplin's mockery in The Great Dictator, Adolf Hitler dispatches an SS assassin to silence the man who weaponized laughter.

You won't want to miss the forthcoming Jake Lassiter novel, *Lassiter's Ghost.* Eight years after Early Grave, Rodrigo Pittman is a newly minted lawyer in need of clients. Penelope Claypool, a Miami television personality, wants him to overturn her father's murder conviction on the ground that Lassiter, suffering from CTE, botched his case. Rodrigo gets advice from the spirit of his deceased godfather...or are those just voices in his head? Here's a sneak peek:

Rodrigo slumped into his chair and closed his eyes.

"Do you need my help, partner?" Jake asked.

"Yeah, could you stick around for awhile?"

"I'm all yours 'til 6 o'clock. Then it's Texas Hold'em with my old teammates."

"Where are you? Heaven?"

"Doubt it."

"Hell?"

"Maybe. It's as hot as Miami but less humidity."

###

The first three chapters of *Lassiter's Ghost* are included in this volume and can be found on page 347. For more information, please visit Paul Levine's website at www.paul-levine.com and sign up for Paul's newsletter at www.paul-levine.com/newsletter/.

Paul Levine

Santa Barbara, CA

CONTENTS

For Marcia. Then…now…forever.

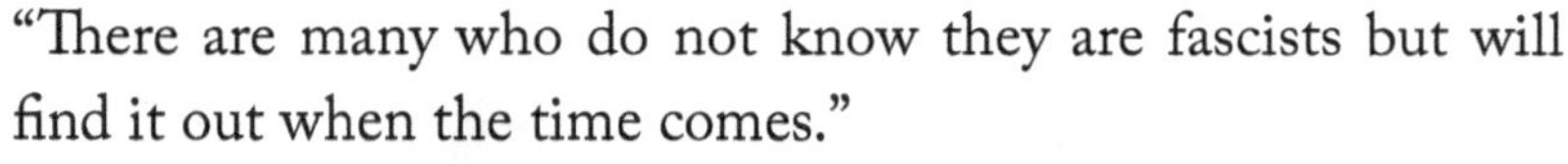

"There are many who do not know they are fascists but will find it out when the time comes."
—*For Whom the Bell Tolls* by Ernest Hemingway

PART ONE

PASSION AND PATRIOTISM

ONE
FRIGHT NIGHT
Thursday, October 31, 1940

It was a Halloween night filled with passion and betrayal, patriotism and treason, threats and treachery...and a sucker punch to the gut.

The Waldorf Astoria stood like a titan against the Manhattan skyline, its glimmering windows masking a thousand secrets within. In one bedroom of a luxurious suite, Albert Einstein was tangled under the sheets with a Russian woman he failed to realize was a Soviet spy. In another bedroom, his friend Charlie Chaplin made love to a woman he knew very well to be William Randolph Hearst's mistress.

On the Starlight Roof, a handsome man in his early sixties named Fritz Duquesne passed his wristwatch to a portly man with a bushy beard glued to his face with spirit gum. Known to intelligence agencies on three continents as "The Duke," Duquesne was a German spy, and his watch contained seven frames of microfilm.

In a private dining room adjacent to the Norse Grill, FBI Director J. Edgar Hoover let his royal squab go cold as he pontificated on the likely saboteurs behind a recent munitions plant explosion in New Jersey, a disaster that had claimed fifty-one lives.

In his spacious forty-first floor apartment, Cole Porter hosted a Halloween party, playing piano as Bing Crosby and Ethel Merman took turns improvising risqué lyrics to his tunes.

Downstairs in one ballroom, the Eagle Squadron—volunteer American pilots soon bound to England to fight the Luftwaffe—partied on Chaplin's dime. "You have the heartfelt thanks of all Brits, including me," the famed actor had told them earlier, raising a glass in salute.

In an adjacent ballroom, raucous German American Bund members drained kegs of Dortmunder beer. Passionate nationalists—their nation being Germany—they belted out the Horst Wessel song, roaring the lyrics, "Millions look to the swastika with full hope." Between the two ballrooms, twenty uniformed NYPD officers formed a picket line, alert for a fracas.

In the lobby, Mickey Cohen, a short, stocky man with dark hair plastered with Brilliantine, confidently strode toward the elevators, feeling the comfortable weight of his .38 revolver beneath the contours of his bespoke pigeon gray suit. Cohen, a former prizefighter who had turned to crime, was feeling chipper. Two weeks earlier, the bookmaker, extortionist, armed robber, and hired killer had married LaVonne Weaver, a red-headed twenty-three-year-old part-time prostitute. The only wedding guests were a few L.A. gangsters and Cohen's bulldog Toughie. Ben (Bugsy) Siegel had wisecracked that Toughie resembled his master with his stumpy body, pug nose, and hang-dog expression.

Earlier in the evening, Cohen had dropped a wad of C-notes on LaVonne and guided her to the jewelry store in the hotel lobby. She pecked him on the cheek and chirped, "Diamonds is a girl's best friends."

Now, riding an elevator to the forty-third floor, Cohen was troubled. He didn't want to shoot Charlie Chaplin. He liked the guy, did business with him, underwriting his fire insurance policy. Nothing on paper, but the movie star paid the gangster not to burn down his movie studio. The problem was William Randolph Hearst. The big tub of lard had asked for a favor from Cohen and had promised one in return. Do the media mogul's bidding and Cohen would get his own reporter from the *Los Angeles Examiner*, a scribbler who'd follow his night crawling on the Sunset Strip. Unlike most hoodlums, Cohen craved publicity.

As for Hearst, jealousy had driven the publishing magnate to violence. Chaplin had been having an on-again, off-again affair with Marion Davies, Hearst's mistress of two decades.

"Just wound the little Cockney clown," Hearst had said. "A gunshot to the leg."

But this ain't a movie, Cohen thought grimly. A gunshot to the leg could kill a guy if you hit the wrong blood vessel.

The elevator chimed. Cohen stepped out, catching a whiff of grilled sweetbreads from a room-service cart. At the door to Chaplin's suite, he deftly worked a hook-and-rake lock pick, a treasured Bar Mitzvah gift, and stepped inside, quiet as a feather on a breeze. The living area was dim, just a shimmer of light from a window over Park Avenue. He approached the bedroom door, a Persian rug muffling his footsteps. He inched the door a crack, peered into the darkness. Sheets rustled. A duet of sighs and heaves and gasps.

Oh, Chaplin, you dirty dog. Caught you in the act!

Cohen drew the .38, aimed at the wall four feet above the bed, and fired three times. A wake-up call.

In the enclosed space, the gunshots thundered like cannon fire. A woman screamed. A man shouted. Cohen flicked on the lights, revealing two terrified faces.

"*Chyort poberi!*" the woman screamed in Russian.

"*Gottenyu!*" the man yelled in a German accent.

"What the hell?" Cohen's eyes settled on the woman, a decent looking brunette in her forties with a dimpled chin who clutched the bed sheet to her chest. Not as modest, the man was about sixty with a pale, soft body, a head of wild white hair and a bushy mustache.

"Is that you, Professor?" Cohen asked.

Albert Einstein squinted, recognizing the flattened nose and three-inch facial scar of a pugilist. Mickey Cohen, one of Chaplin's gangster friends.

"Mr. Cohen, are you *meshuga*?" Albert Einstein demanded.

Cohen had pistol-whipped men for lesser insults than calling him "crazy," but this was Einstein, the biggest brain in the universe, and more important, someone respected by Bugsy Siegel, the gangster's boss. "Whadaya doin' here, Professor?"

"Until a moment ago, *shtupping*."

"Sorry, get back to it."

"Now? My *schmekel* has shriveled like overcooked kugel."

"I thought you were Chaplin," Cohen said, slipping the gun back into its holster.

"What! Charlie's your friend. He gave you a wedding present not two weeks ago."

"It was very thoughtful," Cohen admitted. A custom piece of Waterford crystal, shaped like a revolver. While it didn't fire bullets, Cohen thought it could be a useful blunt instrument if anyone gave him lip in his Highland Avenue bookie joint. "This ain't personal, Professor. It's business."

"It's about Marion, isn't it?" Einstein said. "Mr. Hearst sent you."

"Well, it don't take a genius, but yeah."

Einstein's eyes flicked to the door, and Cohen followed his gaze. In his business, you never missed a gesture unless, as Siegel liked to say, you wanted to wake up dead.

"There's another bedroom here, ain't there, Professor?" Cohen said.

Charlie Chaplin sat up in bed, his ears perked. "Were those gunshots?"

"Probably a Halloween party down the hall," Marion Davies replied, her tone breezy.

Their bed bouncing completed, Charlie and Marion were naked, sprawled contentedly under the comforter in the suite's second bedroom. The day had been a triumph. Chaplin's new motion picture, *The Great Dictator*, which savagely ridiculed Adolf Hitler, had premiered at two Manhattan theaters to thunderous applause and rave reviews. He had dined with Einstein, his dear friend, and they discussed America's ill-preparedness for the all-but-inevitable war with Germany. Fourteen months earlier, Hitler had invaded Poland, and just four months ago, hapless France had collapsed like a soufflé in a cold draft. For the past eight weeks, the *Luftwaffe* had blitzed London with its inhumane bombing runs.

Einstein, despite a lifetime of pacifism, had twice written President Roosevelt, advocating a vigorous program to produce an atomic bomb. Chaplin admired the physicist's resolve, though he dreaded the future they'd foreseen over dinner: a war for the survival of civilization.

This night, however, was reserved for personal pleasures. Chaplin had rumpled the sheets with Marion, the charming, guileless petite blond actress who never demanded anything from him. Both parties felt more than a little guilt about sneaking around behind Hearst's back.

Marion was barely nineteen and kicking up her heels in the Ziegfeld Follies when she met the fifty-three-year-old married newspaper mogul. When Hearst traveled on business, leaving Marion alone and antsy in the beachfront home he had built for her, she craved Chaplin's company.

Chaplin had warned her about Hearst's private investigators trailing her to his Beverly Hills estate, but she didn't care. Perhaps it was Marion's way of making Hearst jealous, Chaplin thought. Pushing him to divorce Millicent, mother of his five sons, which no one expected him to do.

"Hey, Charlie! Grab your long johns and c'mon out here," growled a voice from the living room, rough as gravel.

"Is that...?" Chaplin whispered, trembling.

"Mickey," Marion said, calmly.

"Cohen?"

"Well, it ain't the mouse."

"C'mon you little rascal!" Cohen boomed. "Don't make me come in there."

Chaplin leapt out of bed, pulled on his boxer shorts, padded barefoot to the window, and paused to consider his options, of which there was only one. He opened the window and looked straight down to Park Avenue four hundred feet below.

"Cholly, don't jump!" Marion implored him.

But Chaplin had already climbed onto the narrow ledge. The familiar Manhattan symphony—honking taxicabs and wailing sirens—played beneath him. Overhead, a DC-3 droned toward New York Municipal Airport. A stiff breeze rustled the curtains as Chaplin, graceful as an acrobat, inched along the ledge, the autumn wind whipping at his thin frame.

Cohen strode into the bedroom, trailing the citrus scent of Jean Marie Farina cologne, which he specially ordered from France. He found Marion lounging on the bed in a red satin negligee trimmed with delicate French lace. Sucking on a Chesterfield, her legs crossed, she flashed a generous portion of ivory thigh.

"Hello Mick." She lifted her chin and exhaled a puff of smoke, holding the pose like the actress she was.

"You're a naughty girl, Marion, and W.R. is steamed."

"Tell the big galoot to divorce Millicent, and I'll never look at another guy."

"Not my business, sweetheart."

She took another drag and exhaled a long plume of smoke. "Funny thing is, I love that silly old man. Not because he's so wonderful in the sack. I could find a better lay any Wednesday. But Willie makes me feel I'm worth something."

"You're stalling, kiddo. Where's Chaplin?"

She shrugged her bare shoulders. "Dunno, Mick."

Cohen glanced at the open window, the curtains waving like a ghostly shroud and thought it could be a diversion.

Chaplin was a slippery little fellow.

The gangster checked under the bed, inside the closet, and finally the bathroom.

No dice.

He moved to the window, stuck his head out and looked both ways along the ledge. His eyes adjusted to the darkness, and he caught a fleeting glance of Chaplin's white boxers. The actor appeared to be suspended in air six feet from the building.

What the hay? An impossible sight.

Then Cohen saw that Chaplin was climbing one of the metal flagpoles that rose from concrete sockets in the ledge, trying to reach a higher floor.

"Chaplin! You nutjob! Get back in here!"

Cohen heard the crunch of stones cracking and saw the flagpole socket spitting chunks of concrete. The pole dipped like a see-saw in slow motion, Chaplin hanging on with both hands, his feet dangling into space. No where to go but straight down...to certain death.

"Aw, hell, I ain't here," Cohen muttered, turning away from the window, already crafting his alibi.

TWO
THE DUKE AND THE PHARMACIST

Fritz Duquesne masked his irritation as his guest ordered a Brandy Alexander—a frothy concoction fit for a woman's palate—but certainly not the booze of soldiers and spies.

What's next for the second round? A Pink Lady?

Duquesne sipped his customary martini, always made with Plymouth gin, despite his utter disdain for the British. He had honed his craft across decades and the far corners of the world—South Africa, England, the Americas—his craft being espionage. Apart from his work as an intelligence agent and saboteur under a dizzying array of aliases, he was a crack rifleman who had once served as Theodore Roosevelt's hunting guide in East Africa. Now he masterminded a German spy ring of thirty operatives, headquartered in New York City.

Broad-shouldered, physically fit at sixty-three with wavy brown hair, thin lips and a strong chin, Duquesne wore a nondescript gray suit, white shirt, and gray tie. No savvy spy would wear flashy attire that could be remembered by a curious observer.

He sat at a table in the shadow of a decorative pillar on the Starlight Roof of the Waldorf Astoria Hotel. On warm summer evenings, the roof opened, and couples in swanky duds waltzed under the stars. On this brisk Halloween night, the roof was closed, and white-coated, gold-buttoned waiters scurried about, ferrying platters of cherrystone clams, cold salmon in aspic, and guinea hens galantine to the well-heeled diners. His guest, a portly man in his forties whose name was Klaus but called himself Bill, wore a teal double-breasted suit, a red patterned tie, and two-tone shoes. Bill's beard and mustache were ludicrous fakes, but thankfully the lighting was dim, and no one gave him a second look. Bill sipped his foamy drink, a stripe of crème de cacao studded with nutmeg coating his faux mustache.

A rank amateur!

Bill's primary task was to collect scraps of information from various American university laboratories researching nuclear fission.

"How are things in the Ivy League?" Duquesne asked.

Meaning physicist Enrico Fermi's lab at Columbia University.

"The tablet's not yet in the mortar," replied Bill.

Meaning no functional nuclear reactor...yet.

On the bandstand, Xavier Cugat's orchestra throbbed through a rumba, the conga drums pounding so loudly that Duquesne, deaf in one ear from a cannon blast in the Second Boer War, strained to hear his companion's whispers.

"Handsome wristwatch, Fritz," Bill said, ignoring instructions to never mention Duquesne's real name.

Lunkhead! Pharmacist by day, covert operative by night. A volunteer from the German American Bund.

"Yours, too, my friend." Duquesne removed his watch and placed it on the table, and Bill of the fake beard did the same. Identical Gruen Curvex wristwatches with black dials, crafted in Switzerland and modified in Berlin. Each watch had a removable caseback, a tidy compartment for holding microfilm.

Wordlessly, the two men exchanged watches, and the orchestra swept into *Chica Chica Boom Chic* with Carmen Miranda in a red sequined bodice and a white turban rather than her usual fruit headdress, singing in Portuguese, one of five languages Duquesne spoke fluently.

His watch, now on Bill's wrist, held seven frames of microfilm with classified information filched from the National Defense Research Committee's headquarters at Fort Meade. The subject matter: the latest information on America's nuclear fission research.

An espionage coup!

Bill's secondary duty was as a courier, the middleman between Duquesne and an agent who would take Pan Am's Yankee Clipper flying boat from the Marine Air Terminal in Queens to Lisbon in a brisk twenty-seven hours with stops in Newfoundland, Ireland, and the Azores. From Lisbon, an easy flight to Hamburg and the headquarters of Abwehr, the German counterintelligence agency. It would be an espionage triumph that Duquesne's rivals at Schutzstaffel, the SS, would envy.

"Make sure you're not followed to the terminal," Duquesne instructed. "Employ transit switching and doubling back."

"I know, I know. I use buses and taxis, and when I get to Bowery Bay Boulevard, I go into a grocery store and come out the back."

"Don't use the same store twice."

"Sure thing," Bill the pharmacist said. "Don't worry so much."

But you're lazy and sloppy and undisciplined, and I trust you as far as I can throw a Panzer tank.

"I'm damn impressed you got documents out of Bullfrog," Bill said, using the code designation of the NDRC. "How the hell did you do that, Fritz?"

Again, my name! The dummkopf!

"That's tradecraft you need not know," Duquesne snapped, steel edging his voice, "and if you speak my name once more, I will jam a steak knife through your tongue."

The pharmacist looked crestfallen, as though a customer had complained that his lumbago medication gave him diarrhea. But he was relentless. "Jeez, pal, I'm just complimenting you. Security at Bullfrog is tighter than a miser's wallet. They search every employee coming and going. You can't sneak a camera in or smuggle a document out. And yet..." He tapped his watch with a pudgy finger.

If Bill hadn't been such a total nincompoop, flapping his gums like a ventriloquist's dummy with a broken jaw, Duquesne would have suspected he was a double agent, fishing for information. But he knew the pharmacist was just an aspiring spy with a half-baked devotion to his forebears' German homeland.

Duquesne shot a look at a nearby table where a fortyish man in a white dinner jacket, his dark hair slicked back, leaned close to a twentyish woman in a green silk cocktail dress, her blond hair pinned in an elegant French twist. Clearly not FBI, but it paid to be cautious.

"It took me well over an hour to get here tonight," Duquesne said. "From Yorkville on the Upper East Side?"

"Why so long?"

"I went the opposite direction. North to 110th Street, across the Park, and down Columbus Avenue, doubling back a couple times."

"I take your point," Bill said. "Evasive maneuvers because of the feds."

"It's been years since they had me under surveillance, but you never know when they decide to open an old file."

Bill stiffened as if something unpleasant just occurred to him. "Could they be watching us now?" His eyes scanned the room with a look as guilty as a grave robber with muddy boots and coffin splinters in his palms.

"It's possible," Duquesne replied evenly.

"Can they tie you to that explosion in New Jersey?"

"What explosion is that?"

"Aw, c'mon. You know. All those dead workers at the munitions plant."

"I've heard nothing about that," Duquesne said, his tone as innocent as the mewing of a newborn fawn.

THREE
WHAT A SWELL ORGY THIS IS

Fighting the fear that bearhugged his chest and quickened his breaths, Chaplin clung to the flagpole bearing the French flag—a bitter irony given that France was now occupied by Nazi bastards flying swastikas from every corner. The pole creaked downward like a railroad crossing gate, betraying his plan to climb up and leap to a higher floor. Instead, he was descending, arms outstretched, looking like his neighbor Harold Lloyd dangling from a clock face in *Safety Last*. But that was a trick of camera angles and hidden platforms. This was no illusion—just a high-wire act without a net, and only bone-crushing asphalt below.

Stay calm! You've jumped off buildings into moving trucks. You've flown a trapeze. You can do this.

The pole mount crumbled further, tilting below ninety degrees. Chaplin calculated his distance from the ledge two floors below his suite.

Eight feet? Ten? It doesn't matter. I have to fly!

He kicked back and swung forward, folding his body, his hands nearly touching his toes, like a diver doing a jackknife off the three-meter board. He thrust his arms overhead, seeking forward momentum while pumping his legs as if running on air.

Fly, Charlie, fly!

His toes landed on the building window ledge, but his weight was behind him, and he was about to topple backward into space. He windmilled his arms and fell forward into a window, gripping the outer sill, his heart hammering like Gene Krupa pounding the drums in *Sing, Sing, Sing*.

He was outside the windows two floors below his suite. No sign of Mickey Cohen, who surely wouldn't have followed him. Music streamed from an open window twenty paces away. Shivering in his boxers, Chaplin carefully soft-stepped in that direction.

A piano melody floated out as he approached the window, where a tall, handsome man in cowboy garb stood smoking a stogie, the smoke curling into the frigid night air. Chaplin eased closer to the window, not two feet from the cowboy, who said, as casually as discussing the weather, "Evening, Chap."

As if it were no surprise to see one of the biggest Hollywood stars undressed and clinging to a skyscraper like Batman in the Detective Comics.

"Good evening to you, Coop."

"Nice costume," Gary Cooper said, taking in Chaplin's undershorts. "Beats the hell out of all the tin men and scarecrows and wicked witches inside."

Cooper, in a cowboy hat, faded plaid shirt, soiled vest, and a prop six-shooter in a holster, looked every bit the saddle tramp in *The Westerner,* which had opened a few weeks earlier. He gestured over his shoulder where a Halloween party was in full swing. "C'mon in and have some of Cole's champagne."

Aha! Cole Porter's six-bedroom apartment on the forty-first floor.

Chaplin smiled with relief. He was among friends.

"Thanks, partner," Chaplin said, climbing through the open window. He made his way to the living room where a dozen familiar faces broke into smiles, and a uniformed waiter offered champagne, which he declined. Porter, resplendent in a green velvet tux and bow tie, played one of his lighthearted tunes on the piano, *Well, Did You Evah?* Ethel Merman and Bing Crosby, stationed just behind him and a little sloshed, chimed in, substituting "orgy" for "party" in the line, "What a swell party this."

Noticing Chaplin in the room, Merman, costumed as the Wicked Witch of *The Wizard of Oz,* belted out:

"Have you heard...that poor old Chap...lost his pants in a slight mishap?"

Crosby, in a Tin Man getup, crooned:

"Well, did you evah?" Together, they sang:

"What a swell orgy this is!"

Chaplin forced a smile and walked past the piano, Porter winking at him, apparently approving of his costume by Fruit of the Loom.

But there's no time for revelry. I need a telephone!

Chaplin headed down a marble-floored corridor and stopped at the open door to a sitting room. Inside, half-a-dozen guests looking gloomy surrounded a Philco floor-model radio.

"This is London," Edward R. Murrow's somber voice declared, his voice as distinct as if he were in the room.

Chaplin froze. For weeks, he had been listening—first in disbelief, then in horror—to Murrow's broadcasts from rooftops and air-raid shelters. Under assault from Germany's barbarous bombing raids, London was burning.

When will America get off its arse and join the fight against the monstrous Reich?

"The raid, which started about seven hours ago is still in progress," Murrow intoned with the gravitas that came with hoisting a million Brits on his shoulders. Chaplin pictured the correspondent in his trench coat, a cigarette dangling from the corner of his mouth, bearing witness to Hitler's savagery.

"I'm in a ditch dug into a lawn of a London park," Murrow continued. "Inside are half-a-hundred people, some stretched out on hard wooden benches. The rest huddle in their overcoats and blankets. Dimmed electric lights glow on the whitewashed walls, and the cannonade of anti-aircraft and the German bombs rattle the dust boards underfoot."

A partygoer, a man in his fifties in a Buck Rogers spaceman costume, shouted "Dammit!

We need to send ships and planes to the Brits before it's too late."

"That's hokum," countered a mustachioed man in tan breeches, riding boots and a long tailored coat, apparently going for the Rhett Butler look. "Let the Europeans kill each other, and we'll tend to our own business."

Chaplin had no time to enter the argument. He continued down the corridor and entered Porter's book-lined study. A stocky fortyish man in a gray suit with padded shoulders sat at a desk, yammering into the phone at a staccato pace: "Giggle water flowed freely at tunesmith Cole Porter's Halloween bash," rasped newspaper columnist Walter Winchell. "Perched like a robin on a tree limb, a budding starlet wore an off-the-shoulder shred of cellophane that wouldn't pass the Hays Code."

Winchell continued dictating to the rewrite man at the *Daily Mirror*. "I won't name names, but she's been in more laps than a napkin."

"Walter, I need the phone," Chaplin interrupted.

Winchell shot him a glance. "On deadline, Charlie. Hold your horses."

"It's an emergency."

"A matter of life and *breath*?"

"Yeah, Mickey Cohen's trying to kill me. And don't print that!"

"Hello, rewrite," Winchell said into the phone. "Gotta scram. A headliner wants the phone. I'll call you back."

Winchell picked up his charcoal fedora, ran two fingers down the center dent, and tugged it onto his head. "Who you gonna call, Charlie?"

"A guy with a bigger gun," Chaplin said.

"I saw your new flicker," Winchell said, starting for the door. "You didn't just skewer Hitler and Mussolini—you carved them up like a Sunday roast. And how about that review in the *Times*? 'Perhaps the most significant film ever produced.'" He let out a long whistle. "Just be careful, Charlie. If Mickey Cohen doesn't ace you, some Nazi might. Either way, I want your last words."

When Winchell was gone, Chaplin picked up the phone. "Operator, long distance. Hollywood 5151."

Moments later, a voice answered: "Brown Derby, Vine Street."

"Ben Siegel's table," Chaplin said. "And don't call him Bugsy."

FOUR
GANGSTER VS. NAZI

Unperturbed by the evening's chaos, Marion Davies slept peacefully in Chaplin's suite. Margarita Konenkova, still fuming, left Einstein's bed and returned to the apartment she shared with her husband. Sergey Konenkov, a renowned sculptor, had earned fame with works depicting Jesus Christ and his apostles. His most recent creation, a bust of Einstein, was now displayed at Princeton's Institute for Advanced Study. Which is to say, Einstein, a widower, was having an affair with his sculptor's wife.

It was nearly midnight when Mickey Cohen and Albert Einstein rode an elevator down forty-three floors to the lobby. "Professor, do you mind being my hostage 'til I find Chaplin?"

"I can't think of a more interesting fellow to spend the evening with."

"That's the ticket," the gangster said. "And I got a favor to ask."

"*Nu,* what would that be?"

"Would you teach my bride to be smart?"

"How do you mean, Mr. Cohen?" Einstein asked.

"She ain't had much schooling, unless you count the school of hard knocks. Maybe you can teach her some five-dollar words. Polish her to a shine like my alligator wingtips."

"Your bride as Eliza Doolittle," Einstein mused.

"What?"

"*Pygmalion.*"

"Watch your mouth! LaVonne ain't too bright, but she's no pig."

"No, no, no. Mr. Cohen, I was referring to a play."

Einstein had seen the first production of his friend George Bernard Shaw's *Pygmalion* in Vienna more than twenty-five years earlier. "You want me to be Professor Higgins to teach Eliza, or LaVonne in this case."

"Yeah, if that's the way you wanna look at it."

They stepped into the lobby, a huge open space with wood-paneled walls, soaring black pillars, and intricate plaster ceiling reliefs. Partygoers in elaborate Halloween costumes streamed past, and music from a swing band put a hippity-hop in everyone's step.

"Wouldn't hurt me none to learn a few fancy words, too, Professor," Cohen added. "They hauled my ass into reform school when I was nine for holding up a movie theater with a baseball bat."

Einstein made a soft *tut-tut-tut* sound.

"Only thing I learned was how not to cry when they slugged me with a bicycle tire."

"Mr. Cohen, did you know that Charlie was in and out of dreadful workhouses in London as a child? The guards would beat him with sticks."

Cohen boomed a laugh. "I know what you're doing, Professor. Psychotic warfare."

"Psychological warfare? No, sir. I'm appealing to your humanity, your empathy."

"Uh-huh. Thing is, I'm on a job for Mr. Hearst. Just like my jobs for Ben Siegel, I don't welsh on a deal."

They spotted a phalanx of uniformed NYPD officers at the bottom of double staircases that ascended to the ballroom floor. The cops seemed intent on separating two groups of men scrambling down the steps. A sergeant blew his whistle then shouted, "German Bund to the left, American flyboys to the right!"

"Hey, Flatfoot!" Cohen called to a young cop a foot taller than his own five-feet-five, elevator heels included.

"Yeah?" the policeman said, eyeing Cohen warily.

"What's the rumpus?"

"Hotel booked the Bund and the Eagle Squadron into adjacent ballrooms, and the flyboys decided to settle some fascist hash."

"How's that, Officer?" a puzzled Einstein asked.

"The German American Bund is boozing it up, singing Nazi songs, preaching overthrow of the U.S. government, and what-not. Next door, the American pilots volunteering for the RAF are partying before shipping out. They decided not to wait to fight the Krauts."

"Bless them fellows," Cohen said. "You agree, Professor?"

"I'm a committed pacifist," Einstein said, "but where Nazis are concerned, there is a moral obligation to fight."

On the Bund side of the police line, a stocky man in a toothbrush mustache, not unlike his hero, turned to the American pilots. "The Luftwaffe will send you and your Spitfires down in flames!" he taunted.

Two pilots tried to get at him, but the police held them back. Cohen and Einstein threaded their way through the crowd and spotted LaVonne, Cohen's bride of two weeks. Two men towered over the petite redhead, who wore a burgundy velvet cocktail dress, seamed stockings, and T-strap shoes. Around her neck was a double strand of pearls, courtesy of a gambling debt Cohen had collected from a jeweler's assistant manager.

"C'mon, doll," the larger man said. "Fess up. If you're married, where's your hubby?"

"Right here, crum-bum!" Cohen said, his voice the hiss of a snake.

The larger man snorted a laugh. He was a hair over six-feet tall with a wind-burned face, burly neck, sloping shoulders, and thick wrists. The husky physique of a working man, but with a belly that hung over his belt. Maybe a spiker, pounding metal spikes through railroad ties, or a rivet buster, hammering red-hot carbon-steel rivets on construction crews. In a wrestling match, Cohen knew, the big man could break him in two with a bear hug. And a well-timed punch from the big bozo could bust his jaw.

I gotta strike first...and second...and third.

The big man's companion was tall and gangly with a chicken neck and an Adam's apple the size of a baseball. Both men wore brown shirts with epaulets and red-and-black swastika armbands, agog as they were with notions of their membership in the Master Race.

The big man looked at LaVonne and hooted. "You're married to this shrimp?"

"*Oy vey,*" Einstein said.

"Mickey, don't," LaVonne pleaded, sensing where this was headed.

"What's with the swastikas?" Cohen demanded. "You a coupla Nazi numbskulls?"

"We're bringing fascism to America," the gangly man said.

"Little fellow, you look like a Hebe." The big man wagged a thick finger at Cohen.

This would never happen in L.A., Cohen thought, where he was well known, his photo appearing in Hearst's *Examiner* with regularity, usually in a nightlife column.

Mickey Cohen dining here, drinking there, avoiding assassination attempts here and there.

Legs spread at shoulder width, his left foot ahead of his right foot, with his right heel off the floor in the "crushing grapes" position, Cohen was in the proper stance to throw any number of combination punches. The two men did not notice his stance or his clenched fists or the scar tissue under his left eye, a relic of dozens of prizefights where, bloodied or not, Cohen had gone the distance. They didn't notice his utter fearlessness, didn't realize he was a *shtarker*, a Yiddish word with several meanings, one of which was "tough Jew."

Cohen's face was as placid as a moonlit pond. Imminent violence calmed him. Three years earlier, he'd visited the set of *The Last Gangster* to collect protection money from MGM, and he'd met Edward G. Robinson, a fellow *landsman* who was born Emanuel Goldenberg and was playing the title character.

"Hey, Eddie, don't curl your lips and snarl," Cohen told him at the lunch break. "That don't scare no one but a pansy. Whisper. Trust me, it's scarier."

But Robinson said the director wanted him to "play it large."

That's Hollywood for you! Phony as a three-dollar bill.

Cohen unbuttoned his suit coat and bounced on his toes, but before any punches could be thrown, Einstein said, "Perhaps we should talk with the gentlemen."

"About what?" the big man demanded.

"You two look like intelligent men," Einstein lied with a straight face. "Last month, a German U-boat sunk the *Benares*, which was carrying four hundred civilians, including ninety children being evacuated from England to Canada because of Germany's barbaric bombing. Now, considering that, would you perhaps be inclined to alter your political beliefs?"

"So they sunk a ship." The big man turned toward LaVonne. "All's fair in love and war, ain't it sweetheart?"

Faster than a hummingbird's wings, Cohen dug a right hook deep into the diaphragm of the big man who *whoomphed* air from his lungs and doubled over at the waist. Then the left-right combination came so fast it seemed to be one punch. The left shattered the orbital rim of the man's right eye with an audible *cru-u-nch*. The right uppercut caught the man flush on the chin, buckling his knees and sitting him down.

The other man, the gangly one, stood motionless, paralyzed. Cohen couldn't resist the bullseye of the man's prominent Adam's apple. The punch splintered his thyroid cartilage and sent him into a gagging fit.

"Hitler's only got one nut," Cohen said to the big man who was heaving breaths, still on the floor. "That's one more than you'll have if you say another word to my wife."

"My goodness," Einstein murmured.

"Aw, Mickey, didja have to do that?" LaVonne said, trying to sound exasperated, but admiration leaked through.

"I purposely didn't hit 'em in the nose 'cause I didn't want blood spraying your new dress," Cohen said, establishing his chivalry.

An NYPD sergeant in his forties, a beefy black man with prominent sideburns, walked slowly toward them, gold buttons gleaming. The big Nazi was on his knees, as if in church expressing reverence for the Eucharist. His skinny pal was holding his throat, croaking unintelligibly. The sergeant sized up the swastika armbands, frowned, and said, "What's going on here?"

"These mashers were putting the make on my bride," Cohen said, cool as ice.

"And this being our honeymoon and all," LaVonne added, pouting.

"What's your name, sir?" the sergeant asked politely.

"Meyer Cohen, Sergeant," he answered respectfully, giving the man's stripes their due. "Of Los Angeles."

"And what brings you to our fair city?"

"The Twentieth Century Limited," Cohen replied with a straight face.

"Okey-dokey, wise guy. Why are you in New York?" *Nyoo Yawrk.*

"Business travel. I'm the West Coast representative of a New York corporation."

The sergeant snorted a laugh. "Would that corporation happen to be Murder, Inc., the outfit run by Meyer Lansky and Lucky Luciano?"

"I don't know nothin' 'bout that," Cohen said.

The sergeant chuckled and said, "My wife goes to the picture shows twice a week and reads that magazine, *Photoplay.* I seen your picture there...*Mickey* Cohen. You and Bugsy Siegel invested in some movies."

"Is that a crime, Sergeant?"

"Not in my precinct. Neither is beating the tar out of Nazis." He lowered his voice. "I fought the Hun at St. Mihiel in 1918, and my sons will probably be fighting them again. I got no beef with you, Mr. Cohen, but maybe you should call it a night."

"Ain't gonna say a word to no more Nazis," Mickey promised. "I'm going completely incom-avocado," which the sergeant took to mean "incommunicado."

"As for you two stupes," the sergeant growled, "get the hell back to Yorkville before I book you for disorderly conduct."

He doffed his cap toward LaVonne, and said, "Evening, Ma'am." Then he walked back toward the row of officers.

The two beaten men hobbled away, the larger man muttering, "*verdammter Schwarzer.*"

Cohen introduced Einstein to LaVonne, then said, "The Professor's gonna be teaching you about books and how to act with important people and what spoon to use with your chicken pot pie."

"Well, ain't that peachy?" she replied, hands on her hips. "And who's gonna teach you, Mick?"

Cohen ignored the jab and said to Einstein, "Me and LaVonne are going to our suite. You tell Chaplin he ain't off the hook. Either we have a sit down, or I catch him on the Super Chief and throw his bony ass off the train outside San Berdoo."

Thirty feet away, two men watched the abbreviated fight and its aftermath. "Do you recognize the little man with the quick fists?" Fritz Duquesne asked.

"Never saw him before," said Bill the pharmacist, scratching at his fake beard.

"Did you notice that when his suit coat flapped open, he had a gun in a shoulder holster?"

"Must have missed that."

Of course, you did. You wouldn't recognize a Jew at a Bar Mitzvah.

"A little man with a gun and the swagger of a gangster," Duquesne mused.

"The other man is Albert Einstein," the pharmacist said proudly, as if identifying the most famous scientist in the world was worthy of its own Nobel Prize.

"Indeed. Out here in the open for all to see. Does that give you any ideas?"

The pharmacist appeared puzzled. "I suppose he's just a regular fellow, despite all the hullabaloo."

"Do you comprehend that your sacred task is to convey America's nuclear secrets to the Reich?"

"You betcha."

"And standing before us is the man whose discoveries about energy and mass made nuclear fission possible."

"So?"

"So you will do your job as a messenger boy, and I will orchestrate the most breathtaking espionage operation in the history of warfare."

The pharmacist stared at Duquesne, who clearly enjoyed milking the moment. Finally, the spymaster leaned in and said, "My friend, I will kidnap Professor Einstein and deliver him to Berlin trussed and bound like a Christmas ham."

FIVE
THE GANGSTER, THE COUNTESS, AND THE MOVIE STAR

Ben (Bugsy) Siegel was slicing into his broiled calf's liver, plated with breaded tomato, mushrooms, and allumette potatoes—a hearty square meal for a buck—when the telephone rang. One of the perks of celebrity at the Brown Derby, a phone on your reserved table.

"My apologies," Siegel said politely to his companions and picked up the handset. For a moment, he listened, his blue eyes narrowing as Charlie Chaplin's frantic voice crackled through the line. Pressing the phone to the lapel of his bespoke charcoal silk suit, the gangster said, "Chaplin says Mickey Cohen's trying to kill him."

"Mickey must have his reasons," said Countess Dorothy Di Frasso, munching on her sautéed Catalina sand dabs.

"For real or in a picture?" asked Cary Grant, leaning forward. The actor had already polished off his creamed Turkey Derby, a house specialty. Broad-shouldered and debonair in a double-breasted, glen plaid suit he'd worn in *His Girl Friday*, Grant epitomized Hollywood charm, his every movement elegant. Leaning closer, the actor spoke into the phone. "Hello, Charlie. How's the lad from Lambeth?"

Recognizing the distinctive voice of his fellow Brit, Chaplin replied, "Not as chipper as the boy from Bristol."

"Would you two Limeys stop jerking each other off?" Siegel growled, reclaiming the line. "So, talk to me, Charlie."

"Ben, you gotta tell Mickey to stand down," Chaplin implored, the line hissing with static.

"Calm down, Chap. If Mick wanted you dead, you'd be in a New Jersey swamp by now."

"Yeah? He burst into my hotel suite firing a gun!"

"If he missed, he was just getting your attention." Across the table, the Countess' eyes sparkled with delight at the dangerous tenor of the conversation. At fifty-two, the married millionairess had a weakness for gangsters and actors, and Siegel, with his athletic build, strong jaw, and easy smile, was certainly the former and desired to be the latter. Officially, the Countess was his entrée into Los Angeles society. Unofficially, she was sharing his bed. Meanwhile, Siegel's wife Esta stayed home in Beverly Hills with the couple's two daughters.

Siegel had come a long way since extorting pushcart peddlers on the Lower East Side as a twelve-year-old. A thug with a temper, he earned the nickname "Bugsy," as in "crazy as a bedbug." Once a hit man for Murder, Inc., Siegel now considered himself a businessman, his business being the rackets. Meyer Lansky and Lucky Luciano, his boyhood friends, sent him to Los Angeles three years earlier to muscle in on gambling operations. Now, the thirty-four year old was a wildly successful bookmaker, loan shark, and extortionist with ownership interests in racing wires, casinos, and the numbers games.

"Charlie, it's your own damn fault," Siegel said. "You been playing with fire in a gas station."

"You know? You know about Marion and me?"

"Everybody in town knows. How could you do that to a friend?"

"I was stupid. And selfish. W.R.'s always been kind to me."

"I'll tell you this, Chap. If you'd cockeyed me instead of Hearst, I'd have plugged you myself."

Cockeyed? Surely, Siegel meant "cuckolded," Chaplin thought. Sitting in Cole Porter's study, he wondered why the gangster had expressed not the slightest surprise at the turn of events.

"Ben, did you know Hearst sent Mickey after me?"

"Of course, I knew!"

"Why didn't you warn me?"

"'Cause I'm not a rat."

"Cohen's your enforcer. You could have told him to stand down."

"Mickey's entitled to freelance. That's our deal."

"Then tell him I'll double what Hearst is paying."

"No can do. Hearst ain't paying cash, and Mickey don't need the dough."

"Then what...?"

It took Siegel a few minutes to explain, in which time his calf's liver had turned cold and unappetizing. Hearst had promised that a nightlife reporter would accompany Cohen on his nocturnal escapades where he dipped his beak into the till of Sunset Strip nightclubs and ate and drank gratis in return for not pistol-whipping the bartenders. A newspaper photographer would tag along so that the newspaper wouldn't run old mugshots where Cohen resembled a Jewish Al Capone.

"I thought you guys paid reporters *not* to put your names in the paper," Chaplin said.

"Mickey would rather sit in a booth at Rhum Boogie and chat up the socialites than whack guys," Siegel said. "Plus he loves the spotlight."

Not unlike you, Chaplin thought.

Siegel's star had dimmed somewhat as he was currently out on bail, facing a first-degree murder charge for the slaying of a mobster-turned-informant named Harry "Big Greenie" Greenberg. Siegel did not seem perturbed by the pending trial, confident that the state's eyewitness would never make it to the courthouse.

Siegel signaled a waiter to remove his uneaten entree and bring him a thunderbolt cocktail, a potent mix of gin, whiskey, and brandy. "Mickey might rearrange your pretty face, but he's not gonna kill you," he said into the phone. "Apologize to Hearst and promise to stay away from his squeeze, and this will blow over."

"You can broker that?" Chaplin asked.

"It'll be done tomorrow."

"I'll tell W.R. I feel like a louse, which I do."

"Attaboy, Charlie. Be humble, prostate yourself." *Prostrate*, Chaplin figured.

"Hang on, Charlie. Cary wants a word." Siegel handed the phone to the actor.

"Just screened *The Great Dictator*, Charlie," Grant said, enthusiastically. "It's a masterpiece."

"Thanks, pal," Chaplin said.

"Meanwhile, I'm churning out fluff, light as dandruff."

"Nonsense, Cary! You're a great entertainer."

"I'm not sure *My Favorite Wife* will be remembered once the popcorn goes stale."

"Don't sell yourself short, Archie," Chaplin said, using the diminutive of Grant's birth name, Archibald Leach.

"In any event, there are bigger fish to fry, Charlie. London's ablaze and I'm worried sick."

The two men shared mutual respect, forged by their similar hardscrabble English childhoods. That the undernourished urchins would become wealthy and famous more than five thousand miles from home...well, it was so damn unlikely that it left both men in states of wonder.

"Same here," Chaplin said. "The Blitz is never far from my mind."

"Except when you're *yentzing* Marion!" Siegel cut in.

Chaplin said, "Cary, I've been talking to Professor Einstein about what we can do to get America off the dime and send military aid to Britain without strings attached."

"'Can you get a print of *The Great Dictator* to FDR?" Grant asked.

"He's screening it tomorrow. It's the damn Congress that's the problem."

"Kissing Lindbergh's ass," Grant agreed.

"Isolationism is just another name for cowardice, Cary. Those America Firsters don't understand that Hitler won't stop."

For a moment, neither man spoke, and the only sounds were the *hums* and *hisses* of the long-distance line. Then Grant said, "Charlie, just watch your back. Taking on Hitler is damn dangerous."

"Gimme that!" Siegel said, grabbing the phone. "Charlie, are the fascists threatening you?"

"A few anonymous phone calls and letters. Somebody threw a stink bomb over my gate. Those clowns who call themselves Silver Shirts have been driving by the studio, yelling in German."

"Rat bastards," Siegel said.

"When the picture goes wide next week, I suspect there'll be more. I'm hiring additional security for my studio."

Siegel was quiet a moment, then added, "I could round up a few of the boys."

Chaplin said softly, "To do what, Ben?"

"You know."

"On second thought, I'm not sure I want to know."

"Just thinking out loud. Maybe I'll call Whitey and Frankie and Al. We see some palookas wearing swastikas anywhere near Sunset and La Brea, we'll make wiener schnitzel out of their kidneys."

Chaplin, who had not been born yesterday, knew that Whitey Krakow, Frankie Carbo, and Albert Tannenbaum were torpedoes tied to multiple murders. "Is that a good idea, Ben?"

"Aw, probably not. I get caught packing, my bail will be revoked. But I'm worried about you, Charlie."

"I'll be fine, Ben."

"Really? Traveling with Professor Einstein. An enemy of the state, according to Hitler."

Again, there was silence on the line. After a moment, Siegel said, "Tell you what, Charlie. I got a new job for Mickey. He's gonna be your bodyguard."

SIX
FOREIGN PRINCES AND POTENTATES

Special Agent Brian Sullivan did not relish the prospect of a private dinner at the Waldorf Astoria with FBI Director J. Edgar Hoover and Associate Director Clyde Tolson.

There were several reasons for Sullivan's discomfort, one being that he was simply too tall. Not when he played college basketball at St. Joe's in Philadelphia, averaging a respectable eleven points a game and earning the sobriquet "Sharp-Shooting-Sully." And not when he married his childhood sweetheart Bridget Deasy who at five-feet-ten towered over every girl at Hallahan Catholic Girls School.

But at six-feet-three and appearing taller with his sandy-hued, high-rise flat top, Sullivan was too tall for Hoover.

The FBI Director was five-feet-seven but looked shorter, perhaps because of his fireplug body, which went quite well with his heavy jowls. Tolson, Hoover's handsome constant companion at work and on pleasure trips to Florida, was perhaps two inches taller. For whatever reasons—insecurity, jealousy, paranoia—the Director surrounded himself with diminutive agents in the Washington D.C. headquarters.

"Shorter agents are better for surveillance because they don't stand out in a crowd," Hoover once told a reporter, unconvincingly.

On train rides between New York and Washington, Sullivan often escaped into Raymond Chandler's detective novels. He'd laughed aloud at a line from *The Big Sleep*: "Tall, aren't you?" a woman asked Philip Marlowe. "I didn't mean to be," the private eye replied.

Same with me, and if my height puts a ceiling—Ha!—on my career, so be it.

At thirty-six, Sullivan was content in the New York office where his degree in accounting proved useful in bank and stock fraud cases. Usually the distance from Washington was enough to insulate him from Hoover's personal vendettas against labor union leaders and socialists, as well as writers, intellectuals, and celebrities he deemed to be subversive. That had changed four weeks earlier when Sullivan suffered through the most embarrassing assignment of his career.

At Hoover's personal direction, Sullivan had traveled to Trenton, New Jersey, to observe Albert Einstein's naturalization ceremony. His task? Ensure the physicist recited, verbatim, the oath to "renounce all allegiance to any foreign prince, potentate, state, or sovereignty."

Einstein had spoken the words, his eyes welling with tears. Afterward, he'd declared to reporters, "American democracy is not just a form of government but a great tradition of moral strength."

Nonetheless, Hoover continued to snoop on Einstein's mail due to his association with the International Relief Association, which assisted refugees fleeing Germany. Hoover believed the group had communist ties, despite Eleanor Roosevelt being one of its charter members.

Sullivan considered his surveillance of the naturalization event to be ludicrous busy work. Three weeks earlier and sixty miles away, a catastrophic explosion of three hundred thousand pounds of gunpowder killed fifty-one workers at the Hercules Powder Plant in Kenvil, New Jersey.

I should be hunting saboteurs, not socialists!

Now, seated in a private dining room off the Waldorf's Norse Grill, with no leads in the Hercules investigation, Sullivan hoped he was being assigned to the case, albeit belatedly.

"My first inclination was sabotage by a communist cell," Hoover said, slicing into his royal squab.

Of course it was. You see Reds under every bed, except the one you share with Tolson.

"But our informants ruled that out," Hoover continued.

"The plant supplies explosives to the British," Tolson said, between bites of his roast sirloin Richelieu, "so sabotage by fascists seems to be a logical conclusion."

As it would have been on September 12, the day of the explosion, seven weeks ago!

"We need to infiltrate the German American Bund, the Silver Legion, and the other fascist groups in the Northeast," Hoover said. "I'm assigning our best men in the New York office to handle the probe."

"With you in charge, Special Agent Sullivan."

That's what Sullivan thought he would hear, yearned to hear. But not what he heard. "While they're beating the bushes, Agent Sullivan, you'll go deeper into the Einstein investigation," Hoover continued.

"Sir? I thought there were no further questions about Einstein's loyalty," Sullivan said.

"Mouthing a few words doesn't change decades of his anti-nationalism and pro-pacifist rhetoric," Hoover said. "Or his ties with subversives."

"Like Charlie Chaplin," Tolson said. "Thirty years in this country, and he still hasn't become a citizen. What does that tell you?"

"A couple of fellow travelers," Hoover said. "They were spotted in the Men's Bar earlier tonight, toasting those damn fool pilots going to fight with the RAF. And Einstein claiming to be a pacifist."

"Respectfully, sir," Sullivan said, "Professor Einstein wrote a letter to FDR last year, warning that Germany was working on a powerful new bomb, and that we needed to jump start our own nuclear fission program."

"And just who would benefit from an American nuclear program?" Hoover asked.

"Sir?"

"Standing up to Germany is just what Joe Stalin wants!" Hoover thundered. "Whether Einstein knows it or not, he's a handmaiden of the Soviet Union."

Sullivan realized he hadn't touched his poached cod, and he was rapidly losing his appetite. He barely noticed when Tolson placed a folder on the table and began sliding 8x10 black and white photographs toward him.

"The woman is Margarita Konenkova." Tolson tapped an index finger on the head shot of a short-haired, attractive woman in her forties.

Hoover broke in, "She's a suspected Soviet spy and a possible nymphomaniac."

Sullivan wondered, *Which is the more grievous sin to the prudish Director?*

"We have proof of her sexual relationship with Einstein, and we suspect she's dallied with this fellow here." Tolson tapped the photo of a man who looked to be in his mid-thirties. Neatly trimmed dark hair, serious expression, heavy eyebrows.

"J. Robert Oppenheimer, a so-called boy-genius physicist at Berkeley," Hoover said, "with more commie contacts than a dog's got fleas. Clyde?"

"Oppenheimer's brother-in-law, landlady, ex-girlfriend and his almost-wife are members of the Communist Party or were before they bailed out," Tolson said.

"Almost-wife?" Sullivan asked.

"He's marrying a biologist named Kitty Harrison tomorrow in Nevada," Tolson continued. "She's getting divorced in the morning and by afternoon, Oppenheimer will be her fourth husband. Oh, she's also pregnant with his child."

"The immorality is staggering," Hoover said.

The FBI Director as our Puritan preacher, a Cotton Mather of the Twentieth Century.

"On Tuesday," Tolson said, "Oppenheimer and Einstein are holding a debate at Princeton. Something about gravitation."

"And my role in this?" Sullivan asked, trying not to sound disappointed or mad as hell.

"You'll be there, Sullivan," Hoover informed him. "Take notes. Pay close attention to anything touching on national security."

"Yes, sir."

"We expect Margarita Konenkova to be there, probably with her Soviet handler," Hoover continued.

"So you think that Oppenheimer and Einstein are Russian spies?" Sullivan asked, barely masking his skepticism.

"Perhaps not knowingly," Tolson said. "They could be hapless dupes. Or just..."

"Jewish sex maniacs," J. Edgar Hoover said.

SEVEN
THIS IS LONDON

"This is London. I'm standing again tonight on a rooftop looking out over London, feeling rather large and lonesome. In the course of the last fifteen or twenty minutes there's been considerable action up there, but at the moment there's an ominous silence hanging over London. Straightaway in front of me the searchlights are working. I can see one or two bursts of anti-aircraft fire in the distance. Just on the roof across the way I can see a man wearing a tin hat, a pair of powerful night glasses to his eyes, scanning the sky. In the opposite direction, there is a building with two windows gone. Out of one window there waves something that looks like a white bed sheet, a window curtain swinging free in this night breeze. It looks as though it were being shaken by a ghost. There are a great many ghosts around these buildings in London."

– Edward R. Murrow, CBS Radio

EIGHT
AGAMEMNON CALLS ACHILLES...LONG DISTANCE

It was nearly two a.m. in New York when Chaplin placed a second call to Los Angeles, Mickey Cohen sitting at his side.

"W.R., I am so damn sorry," Chaplin said when Hearst came on the line. "You've given me nothing but friendship, and I betrayed you."

The line buzzed for a moment, Hearst keeping quiet, perhaps wondering if Chaplin was sincere or merely playing a part. Then Hearst said, "You're a libertine, Charlie. A Lothario, a Casanova. You can't help yourself. It's who you are."

"I'm filled with regret," Chaplin replied. "As Agamemnon confessed to Achilles, 'Mad, blind I was! Not even I deny it.'"

Cohen, who had been polishing his obsidian and diamond cufflinks with a silk kerchief, let out a low whistle in appreciation of Chaplin's performance.

"It will never happen again," Chaplin promised. "And I hope I haven't forever lost your friendship."

"I understand what drives you, Charlie. An alienist would say it was your hardscrabble childhood. Underfed and underloved. Now, with everything in the world at your disposal, you can't keep your hands out of everyone else's candy jars, including mine."

"Never again, W.R."

Hearst harrumphed and, like a presiding judge, pronounced sentence. "You're barred from San Simeon for four months, Charlie."

"I understand," Chaplin said, though it seemed like an odd period of time

"I'm going to throw a helluva party for my seventy-eighth birthday next April, and I want you there."

Aha! The big shindig is in four months.

"It would be my pleasure, W.R."

When the call was over, Cohen said to Chaplin, "Just now, Charlie, your eating crow. Was you acting? Or was that real?"

Chaplin shrugged. "How would I know?"

NINE
PUSHING A PACIFIST TOWARD WAR
Monday, November 4, 1940

Major Leslie Groves switched off his radio in the middle of a Pepsodent commercial—"Removes stains with absolute safety"—and placed a phone call from his office in Washington to the Institute for Advanced Study in Princeton, New Jersey. He had sparred with generals, corporate titans, even the U.S. President without breaking a sweat, but this phone call made his nerves jump. The major's mission was to persuade a man he deeply admired for his towering intellect and commitment to social justice to do something he was philosophically opposed to do.

"What is it, Major?" Albert Einstein asked when he took the call. "Now that I'm a citizen, am I being drafted?"

Major Leslie Groves smiled to himself. He'd heard about the professor's sharp sense of humor, and sure enough, Einstein was already blending dry wit with the gravity of current events. Less than two months earlier, Congress had passed the first peacetime draft in American history.

"Actually, Professor," Major Groves said into the phone, "I wanted to invite you to meet with Professor Richard Tolman of Caltech. I believe you know the gentleman."

"A brilliant chemist," Einstein said. "Used general relativity to develop his concept of relativistic mass."

"And with Professor Vannevar Bush as well."

"An equally brilliant electrical engineer," Einstein said, his voice tinged with curiosity. "*Nu*, what have you got up your sleeve?"

Groves cleared his throat and readied his pitch like Bob Feller winding up to unleash his fastball. "The meeting will also include the Presidents of Harvard, MIT, and the National Academy of Sciences, as well as Brigadier General George Strong."

"The National Defense Research Committee. But what would they want with an *alter kocker* like me?"

Employing the jocular Yiddish term for an old fogey.

"There would be no nuclear fission program without your special relativity, Professor."

"Frankly, Major, because I introduced relativity to physics, the world now greatly overrates my scientific abilities."

A sense of humor and modest, too.

"You postulated that a huge amount of energy could be released from a small amount of matter," Groves pressed. "That's our foundation for a new type of bomb."

"I'm a theoretical physicist. I can't build a toy airplane, much less a bomb."

"Your guidance would be invaluable, Professor, and you needn't muscle a wrench."

"My dear Major, I've made it quite clear I want no part in developing an atomic bomb."

Groves had anticipated this and knew the moment of confrontation would be fraught.

How to proceed? Confront or cajole?

Groves was an engineer by training, not a debater or public speaker. Forty-four years old, son of an Army chaplain, fourth in his class at West Point, Groves believed in logic, not verbal gymnastics. He also knew better than to try to outsmart the smartest man in the universe. Still, he had to persuade.

"Professor, last year, after German scientists had split the uranium atom, you wrote a letter to FDR, urging him to start a program to develop atomic weapons. Seven months ago, displeased with the scant progress, you again wrote the President, pointing out more German advances. One month later, you wrote Lyman Briggs at the Uranium Committee, pleading for greater urgency and work on a larger scale. In short, Professor, not only did you theorize that energy equals mass times the speed of light squared, you've also been the foremost proponent of atomic weapons, however reluctantly."

Silence on the telephone line.

Did I push too hard?

"Major Groves," Einstein finally said, "I may have pointed out that giant stags roam the forest, but that does not mean I will load the rifles to shoot them."

"And yet, others will. And if the Nazis have the bomb first..."

He let the thought dangle, knowing the weight of it required no elaboration. Again, silence.

Groves pressed on. "Professor, Alfred Nobel, whose prize you won, intended that his brainchild be used for mining and construction, not war. But it was inevitable that dynamite would make its way to the battlefield. Experts tell me that the same is true for atomic power, once its secrets are unlocked."

"Even if I wanted to help," Einstein countered, exasperated, "I could never get security clearance. The FBI reads my mail and listens to my phone calls. J. Edgar Hoover equates pacifism with communism. Surely, you know this."

"I know he's harassed you ever since you sought your first visa to come to the States. But the Army has no reason to question your loyalty."

"Careful, Major. Mr. Hoover might question yours for even talking to me."

"We'll need scientists of all stripes for a project this immense, and I don't care if they joined some commie clubs in college or if they're parlor pinkos today. And I don't care if we give Hoover a heart attack as long as we get the job done."

Einstein chuckled. "So, if you don't mind my asking, how is it that a lowly major is in charge of this atomic bomb project?"

"Sorry to say, Professor, but there really isn't a project yet. This is Washington, and there has to be a song and a dance before anything gets done. For what it's worth, in two weeks, I'm due for a pair of silver eagles on my tunic. Until then, my day job is to construct a pentagon-shaped building for the War Department in Virginia. Almost seven million square feet, according to the latest plans."

"Good heavens, Major. That will take years."

"If it takes more than sixteen months to build, they'll bust me to corporal and hand me a mop for latrine duty."

Einstein laughed, a warm sound, and Groves felt a flicker of hope. "Professor, would you at least consider visiting the Committee?"

"You are persistent and seem like a fine fellow. But I must respectfully decline. Now, I need to prepare for a symposium tomorrow. There's a young physicist named Oppenheimer who will run circles around me if I am not ready."

"J. Robert Oppenheimer, the *wunderkind* at Cal," Groves said, flaunting his knowledge. "Graduated from Harvard in three years, *summa cum laude*. Ph.D. from Göttingen in theoretical physics under Max Born. Full professor at Berkeley at thirty-two. Widely published. Chain smoker. Recuperated from a bout of tuberculosis at a ranch in New Mexico."

"You've done your homework, Major."

More than you know.

Groves had compiled files on European scientists who had fled the Nazis, each a potential contributor to the atomic bomb project. Without the newcomers to our shores, he knew, America would be even further behind Germany. There was Leo Szilard, the Hungarian physicist who had helped Einstein draft the first letter to Roosevelt. Enrico Fermi, an Italian, had achieved nuclear fission in a Columbia University lab by bombarding uranium with neutrons. Then there were Hans Bethe and Rudolf Peierls, both German-born, and Edward Teller and John von Neumann, both Hungarians. Oppenheimer, an American, was the outlier, though his education in Germany made him part of the intellectual diaspora. Groves also kept tabs on several female scientists he believed brought critical attention to details that men often overlooked.

"Professor," Groves said, "would you not love to see the look on Hitler's face when Jewish scientists he chased from Europe develop a bomb that could reduce the Reichstag to smithereens?"

"Not only persistent, you are also persuasive. Alas, I must still respectfully decline."

Groves felt deflated but not defeated. They said their goodbyes, and Groves calculated just how long it would take to drive to Princeton. An unbridled optimist, he was never thrown off course by minor setbacks. He got things done, built Army bases from the ground up, never took no for an answer, be it from a steel mill owner or, in this case, the genius who upended mankind's understanding of the universe. Groves took Einstein's "no" to mean "maybe," and believed with all his heart that securing a "yes" was for the greater good of the country he loved.

TEN
SURVEILLANCE

Einstein, Chaplin, and Cohen were having lunch at a corner table in Danny's Diner, just outside Princeton, New Jersey. The building gleamed with polished chrome, its curved lines evoking the silhouette of a streamlined passenger railroad car. Red and blue neon lights trimmed the perimeter of the building, glowing day and night since the diner never closed. Inside, the sharp aroma of burgers sizzling on the flat top grill mixed with the unmistakable scent of frying bacon and just a whiff of freshly brewed coffee.

"You're flat-out wrong, Albert!" Charlie Chaplin declared, gesturing with a fork dripping with mashed potatoes.

"My moral position is neither right nor wrong," Einstein replied calmly. "It is simply my position." He had told Chaplin about turning down Major Groves, and the actor wasn't happy about it.

"Isn't it true that the Germans are far ahead of us in developing an atomic weapon?" Chaplin asked.

Einstein blew on a spoonful of steaming tomato soup and said, "Unfortunately, true. Werner Heisenberg, who I'm sorry to say is a first-rate physicist, directs their *Uranverein*, the Uranium Club."

"Sounds like a Mickey Rooney movie," said Mickey Cohen between bites of an egg and sausage sandwich. "Once they build the uranium clubhouse, Mickey starts dancing with Judy Garland."

Cohen, Chaplin's duly appointed bodyguard, had chosen the table, which had a clear view of the front door as well as the parking lot through oversized windows. Ben Siegel's orders had been clear:

"Keep your eyes peeled for Nazi bastards. Anybody looks cross-eyed at Charlie, take 'em out of the game."

Just this morning, Chaplin's studio on La Brea Avenue in Los Angeles had been hit with Molotov cocktails. There had been no damage as the bottles hit the parking lot asphalt. Then there was the swastika painted on the exterior fence and a handwritten note promising to "gut that Jew Chaplin like a possim," getting his religion wrong and misspelling the marsupial.

Chaplin stabbed at his overcooked meatloaf as if it were Hitler's chest. "Dammit, Albert. Your moral obligation is to fight fascism. You pushed FDR to get off the dime, but that's only the beginning of what you can do."

"Please, Charlie," Einstein said. "Respect my wishes."

"Every night, I listen to Murrow on the wireless, and I get sick to my stomach. London is burning, my friend. If not for the Atlantic Ocean, New York would be, too. And if those bastards get their hands on a super weapon..."

The diner's brass bell chimed as a man in his sixties entered, wearing a well-cut gray suit. He made a casual survey of the room, his gaze brushing past their table. He slid into a booth twenty feet away. After unfolding his newspaper and ordering coffee from a passing waitress, he absently touched his false mustache with a knuckled finger. The carefully trimmed goatee and horn-rimmed glasses completed his disguise.

Cohen had been studying the man through the window since he got out of his car, a late model Packard Super 8. He had parked next to what looked to be a Ford delivery van, but there were no names on the side. What also caught Cohen's attention were the two people inside the van. They just sat there. A man in a coat, tie, and wide brim fedora that shielded his eyes. And a dark-haired woman. Both appeared to be in their thirties. The man with the newspaper had glanced their way as he walked up the three steps to the diner's front door.

Are you two bozos working with Newspaper Man? Cohen wondered.

The waitress delivered the man's coffee, and Cohen watched intently as he raised the cup to his lips. The movement revealed a bulge in the man's suit coat.

Son-of-a-bitch is toting iron!

Cohen reflexively moved his elbow toward his chest, making sure his .38 was there. Of course it was. He scanned the patrons on the counter stools. Civilians. He hoped none would leap into the line of fire when he opened up. He kept one eye on Newspaper Man and another on the van. If the man and woman came in the front door, they likely weren't in on it. If one came in the front and the other went around the back—fire regulations required a rear door—Mickey would light the place up.

Fritz Duquesne made a show of reading the *Newark Star-Ledger* but also kept an eye on Einstein and the other two men at the table.

Always surveil your target. Know his habits and his movements and learn his vulnerabilities.

Admiral Canaris at Abwehr had approved Duquesne's plan to kidnap Einstein, leaving the details to his most experienced operative. Duquesne had not yet decided time or place or the method of transport from the States to Berlin.

A headline caught Duquesne's attention: NAZI SABOTAGE SUSPECTED IN HERCULES BLAST THAT KILLED FIFTY-ONE. The New Jersey munitions plant supplied explosives to the British, so obviously, the authorities blamed Germany for the massive blast.

But try and prove it!

The evidence disintegrated with three hundred thousand pounds of gunpowder. More than twenty buildings were leveled, cars were bounced off roads, and the impact registered on a seismograph at Fordham University fifty miles away. Duquesne's alibi was solid, a German-American friendship lunch in Summit, New Jersey. Twenty miles from the blast, the concussion wave poured over the Heidelberg restaurant like rolling thunder. Startled, guests bolted from their chairs as if stung by wasps. Duquesne calmly buttered his Parker House roll and smiled to himself. His role had been minor, dispatching a few operatives to scout the plant and provide security for the saboteurs dispatched from Germany.

As for those fifty or so Americans incinerated...well, that's a preview of what's to come.

Now, Duquesne was troubled. He had followed Einstein from his office at the Institute for Advanced Study to the diner where he was joined by the other two men. One was Charlie Chaplin, the little bastard who was going to make another million bucks or more from his calumny against the Führer. The other diners didn't seem to recognize the movie star. Off screen, with a shock of silver hair and intense eyes, he bore little resemblance to his screen persona. Everyone recognized Einstein. There were nods in his direction, but no one pestered him. So close to his Princeton office, he was probably a regular here, Duquesne figured.

Would any civilians leap to your aid if I snatch you from the parking lot? Some Yank who fashions himself Hopalong Cassidy?

The third man at the table complicated matters. Duquesne recalled his punches, snapping like whips at the hapless Bund bullies in the Waldorf Astoria lobby. Remembered, too, the gun under his suit coat. The man had a scarred face and cold, reptilian eyes. Looked like a pro, a button man, but what was he doing with the two big shots?

And what about the man and woman in the unmarked Ford van? Still just sitting there.

Who the hell are you two?

Ten minutes earlier...

Inside the van in front of the diner, Milagros Vazquez said, "So you're saying the little guy with Chaplin and Einstein is a gangster?"

"Meyer Cohen, goes by Mickey," Brian Sullivan replied. "FBI File Number 755912."

"Showing off your memory with numbers."

"Accounting degree," Sullivan said. "Before your time in the field, Millie, Cohen was a thug for Murder, Inc. About three years ago, he headed west to hook up with Bugsy Siegel's rackets in L.A."

"So what's he doing with Chaplin and Einstein in New Jersey?"

"No idea."

Special Agent Sullivan and his female companion were on surveillance, the law enforcement equivalent of watching paint dry...in the rain. They had followed Einstein from his office at the Institute adjacent to Princeton University and watched him join Charlie Chaplin and Mickey Cohen for lunch.

So far, they had spotted no Soviet agents among the truck drivers, plumbers, businessmen, and assorted locals who were chowing down on burgers, grilled cheese sandwiches, and chicken-fried steaks.

What a shit assignment, Sullivan thought for the umpteenth time.

Sitting behind the wheel, Sullivan wore one of his several off-the-rack, pin-striped gray three-piece suits, a white shirt and burgundy tie. Next to him, Milagros Vazquez, whose friends called her "Millie," wore a green crepe sheath dress, a cropped, boxy jacket, black pumps and beige seamed stockings.

Dress like you're working the cosmetics counter at Macy's.

That's what the Special Agent in Charge of the New York office had told her. Milagros Vazquez was not a special agent, as the FBI had no "G-Women." Not one. Officially, she was a radio operator in the New York office. But six years earlier, during the "Uprising of '34," as the textile workers' strike was called, she was assigned field duties. The strike lasted only three weeks but stretched from Maine to Georgia, and with heavily armed National Guardsmen handling the mill owners' dirty work, eighteen workers were killed.

Believing that the textile workers' union was riddled with communists, FBI Director Hoover orchestrated an undercover operation in which Sullivan posed as a reporter for the *Daily Worker* to get access to union leaders. As several organizers and shop stewards were Puerto Rican, and no special agents in the New York office spoke Spanish, Vazquez was sent along to pick up any conversations Sullivan couldn't understand. The granddaughter of immigrants from Spain and the daughter of a high-school social studies teacher who preached perfect diction, Vazquez spoke unaccented English and could eavesdrop on Spanish speakers while appearing oblivious. While no communist plots were uncovered, Vazquez overheard a plan to firebomb a textile mill warehouse, and she received a special commendation for her work.

At the Agent in Charge's suggestion, Vazquez soon began accompanying Sullivan on surveillance assignments. He looked less like a G-Man with an accompanying girlfriend or wife, the reasoning went.

At thirty-one, Vazquez was a tall, lanky woman with dark hair and a cinnamon complexion who stayed calm in potentially dangerous situations. The two grew close, Sullivan fond of her in an older brother sort of way. They both had spouses—Bridget and Mario—and the foursome would occasionally double date.

Over the past few years, Milagros Vazquez developed other skills useful to the Bureau. She had exceptional eye-hand coordination and could aim a cigarette-pack camera at precisely the right angle without looking at the target. She also set up electronic devices—some lawful, some not—used by the Bureau. A movie buff, she perked up the moment she recognized Chaplin.

"How nifty is this assignment," Vazquez gushed.

Sullivan rolled his eyes. But he remembered his early days as a special agent, when opening a target's mail seemed exciting, even when it turned out to be a Sears Roebuck catalog.

"Mario and I saw *The Great Dictator* last night," Vazquez said, her face lighting up. "Chaplin dug Hitler a new rectum, pardon my French. And here's the thing, Brian. The movie was hilarious."

Sullivan watched a man in his sixties park his Packard Super 8 next to the van, climb the steps into the diner, then take a seat at a table with a direct view of Einstein, Chaplin, and Cohen.

The man opened a newspaper and began reading.

"I sure as heck don't know how a movie about fascists can be hilarious," Sullivan said, happy to pass the time.

"That's Chaplin's genius," Vazquez said. "His real-life wife, Paulette Goddard, is his love interest, and their relationship provides the movie with warmth."

"She's a dish," Sullivan allowed. "But in real life, they barely speak."

"And you know this, how?"

"Everyone knows. It's in all the movie magazines." They sat in silence a few more moments.

"I've got a movie for you, Brian," she said, continuing her small talk. "You being from Philadelphia and all."

"Something shot on the banks of the Schuylkill?" he ventured.

"It's called *The Philadelphia Story*. Comes out next month."

Looking through the window, Sullivan had a profile view of the man who had parked his Packard next to them. He watched the man drink his coffee and thumb pages of his newspaper.

Under his suit coat…is that the bulge of a gun?

"Millie, do you recognize the man at the corner table with the newspaper?"

"Never saw him before, but he's packing."

Sullivan shot a look at her. His partner, as he'd come to regard her, had given no indication that she even noticed the man.

"Millie, they oughta make you a special agent."

"Never gonna happen, Brian. Not unless I learn to pee standing up."

Sullivan squinted in the direction of the gun-toting man. Good physical condition for someone his age. Broad shoulders, wavy hair, a strong, prominent nose.

You look vaguely familiar. But who the hell are you?

"It stars Cary Grant, Katherine Hepburn, and Jimmy Stewart," Vazquez said.

"What does, Millie?"

"*The Philadelphia Story*. It's a comedy about divorce."

"Sounds even less plausible than a comedy about Hitler." Sullivan kept his eyes on the lone man with the newspaper. "Millie, you need to use the ladies' room."

"I do?"

"Take your Lucky Strikes. Get a head shot of the mystery man."

Vazquez understood. She carried what looked like a pack of cigarettes—"It's Toasted"—under the Lucky Strikes red-and-black logo. Pushing down on what appeared to be a cigarette extending from the pack would trip the shutter. There was no viewfinder, so the photographer had to be adept at aiming blind.

She took a moment arranging herself, checked to be certain the cigarette pack camera was in her purse, and said, "Sure thing, Brian. But you owe me two tickets to *The Philadelphia Story.*"

Mickey Cohen watched as the dark-haired woman stepped from the van and into the diner. She walked toward Newspaper Man's table, pulled a pack of Lucky Strikes from her purse, paused and said something to a waitress who pointed toward the rear of the diner. The woman never glanced at Newspaper Man but simply headed in the direction the waitress had pointed. The restroom.

Nothing odd about that, Cohen thought, except the way the woman stopped in front of Newspaper Man seemed a bit off. Most people would have walked to the counter to ask the waitress for directions. And the cigarettes? The dark-haired woman slid the pack back into her purse without shaking one loose.

Cohen shifted his gaze back to Newspaper Man, who had given no indication of knowing the young woman in need of the toilet. But then, professionals would be stone-faced. Cohen took a forkful of Boston cream pie, half-listening to Einstein and Chaplin, who were blissfully unaware of any potential assassins lurking just feet away.

Einstein was reminiscing about his late wife Elsa, his voice tinged with melancholy. Chaplin remarked that he already missed Marion. "But I've learned my lesson," he said. "You could try being faithful to Paulette," Einstein said, his tone gentle, though the words were sharp.

"Too late, Albert. When we were shooting *Dictator*, she wouldn't even speak to me off the set."

Minutes passed. The woman was still in the restroom. That left the driver behind the wheel of the van and Newspaper Man, sipping coffee at his table. Could they all be working together? Cohen had been around long enough to know that women, particularly gangsters' molls, could handle heaters. Machine Gun Kelly's wife Kathryn, Baby Face Nelson's wife Helen, and Buck Barrow's wife Blanche all came to mind. Not to mention Ma Barker and Bonnie Parker. Let your guard down with one of them, and a sawed-off shotgun would cut you in half.

If this is a setup, there are two men and one woman outflanking me. I can take two of them, but three?

He pushed his plate aside and leaned in. "Fellows," he said, his voice low but firm, "let's get the hell out of here. This place is giving me the heebie-jeebies."

ELEVEN
STUBBORN AS AN ARMY MULE
Tuesday, November 5, 1940

Major Leslie Groves stood before the bathroom mirror in his hotel room, trimming his salt-and-pepper mustache. He squinted critically, considering whether he was getting jowly. The radio was on, Charles Lindbergh preaching about world affairs in his self-assured tone, as if he were a seasoned statesman, instead of a know-it-all blowhard.

"I am not pleased with either choice for President," Lindbergh said. "Both Roosevelt and Willkie speak of neutrality, but their thinly disguised support for England is readily apparent."

"Because they're both good men!" Groves shouted, pointing his scissors like a saber at the radio.

It was election day, and Franklin Roosevelt was heavily favored to win an unprecedented third term over Republican Wendell Willkie, a corporate executive with no government experience.

"Scratch the surface of Roosevelt, and an interventionist peeks out," Lindbergh continued.

"Scratch your surface and a swastika peeks out!" Groves railed.

"A saner course would be to negotiate a neutrality pact with Germany," Lindbergh said. "If all of Europe falls to the Reich, that is none of our concern."

"Appeaser! Defeatist! Moron!" Groves bellowed, his voice echoing off the bathroom tile.

Fed up, Groves switched off the radio just as the hotel room telephone rang. Wrapped in a towel, he snatched the receiver from the night stand. A woman's crisp voice instructed him, "Hold for the Director."

Not even a "please," Groves noted.

After a ten second wait, a man's gruff voice said, "You going back to school, Major?"

"No, sir. Why would you ask?"

"Because you're in Princeton! Want to tell me why?"

"I'm sure you know, Mr. Hoover," Groves said.

You probably also know I ate eggs-over-easy for breakfast.

"Darn right I know!" J. Edgar Hoover boomed. "You're planning to invite Einstein to infiltrate the National Defense Research Committee."

"He's already declined my invitation. Now, I intend to badger him into accepting."

"Einstein is an extreme radical, a subversive with communist tendencies. I sent General Miles all the evidence."

"I read your letter, Mr. Hoover. You said Einstein attended a World Congress Against War in Amsterdam eight years ago, a shindig organized by communists. But the Army's investigation showed he refused to attend, specifically for that reason."

"There's more evidence than that. His so-called pacifism is nothing but thinly disguised communism."

"And yet," Groves countered, "he set aside decades of preaching pacifism when he urged the President to develop an atomic bomb before the Nazis can do it."

"Don't be a child! Our ultimate war will be with Soviet communism, not fascism."

"But it's Germany that has seized half of Europe and firebombs London."

"There is much you don't know, Major. Security issues I cannot disclose."

Playing the old I-know-secrets-you-don't game, Groves thought.

"This is not the time to let a Trojan Horse through the gates," Hoover continued.

"I appreciate your concern, Director, but I don't believe Professor Einstein is a security risk."

"No? Why do you think he became an American citizen?"

"Oh, I don't know," Groves replied dryly. "Maybe because he loves America for welcoming him when he fled Germany."

"Or maybe so we can't deport him, ever think of that?"

"With all due respect, sir, that reasoning is as solid as a latrine dug in quicksand."

"Don't you sass me, Major."

Picturing Hoover at his desk, his pudgy face turning red, Groves couldn't resist snapping the man's garters. "If Einstein turns me down, I'll just invite J. Robert Oppenheimer in his place."

"The hell you say! He's a bigger commie than Einstein!"

"I'll take your opinion into account," Groves said, "but the Army is not bound by a civilian agency's recommendations."

"You insolent nobody! I know all about you. Stubborn as an Army mule, always thinking you know more than your commanding officer. No wonder you spent fifteen years as a lieutenant. Not exactly a meteoric rise. Your only skill is building barracks for the Quartermaster Corps, and now some idiot in the War Department attaches you to a secret weapons project. Hear this, Major. If you cross me, you'll never see silver eagles on your shoulders, much less silver stars. And I say that, both as Director of the Bureau and a colonel in the Army Reserve."

"*Lieutenant* colonel," Groves corrected him. "Pretty much an honorary title handed to you after the Great War, which you sat out with a deferment thanks to your civil service job. But I appreciate your career advice."

"Why, you pissant! I'll see to it that you..."

Hoover ranted on, but Groves had already hung up the phone.

TWELVE
THE GREATEST LIVING PERSON

Ten minutes before the symposium was to begin, Major Groves entered the anteroom of Fuld Hall in Princeton, New Jersey and introduced himself to Charlie Chaplin, J. Robert Oppenheimer, and Albert Einstein.

"Professor Oppenheimer, I enjoyed your paper on the gravitational collapse of stars," the major said.

"I hope you're not siding with Albert on the concept," Oppenheimer replied. Tall and lanky in a baggy gray wool suit, the physicist looked older than his thirty-six years. His angular face and intense eyes gave him an air of perpetual weariness.

"I'm not sure what to think about giant black holes in outer space," Groves said. Unlike the gaunt physicist, the major looked like a man who never skipped a meal.

With a twinkle in his eye, Einstein said, "So, Major, you drove all the way from Washington to learn what happens when a star runs out of fuel?"

"Actually, I was hoping my spiffy uniform and winning smile would change your mind about the NDRC."

Einstein regarded the stocky major in his belted olive coat festooned with ribbons, gold oak leaves on his shoulder straps. "You cut a dashing figure, Major, but my answer remains the same."

Chaplin, quick to catch on, grew agitated. "Albert, old friend, your country needs you."

"So says the man who refuses to become an American citizen," Einstein fired back.

"I'm a citizen of the world," Chaplin said. "You, my dear Yankee Doodle Dandy, turned down a simple request to chat with your fellow eggheads."

"I did my part with my letters to the President."

"But is that enough?" Oppenheimer interjected, a cigarette dangling from the corner of his mouth.

Einstein shot a sidelong look at Groves. "Perhaps you should invite my young friend Oppie to schmooze with the Committee."

"I've been considering that," Groves said, his tone thoughtful.

"And I would accept," Oppenheimer said, taking a long drag on his cigarette, his cheeks hollowing into dark shadows. "But not on my honeymoon."

The symposium at the Institute for Advanced Study was billed as a discussion of Oppenheimer's newly published paper, "On Continued Gravitational Contraction." Those on the Princeton University campus called it the "Oppenheimer versus Einstein Debate."

The audience was a who's who of intrigue: a German spy, a Russian spy, two FBI agents, an Army major, a dozen Institute researchers, several university professors and a smattering of students. Chaplin stood on the stage at the lectern, Einstein sat in a wing chair on one side, Oppenheimer on the other.

Unseen by the audience, Mickey Cohen sat on a stool behind the curtain, peering out at the crowd. Bugsy Siegel had called that morning to tell him that vandalism at Chaplin's studio and threats on his life had increased every day since the premiere of *The Great Dictator.*

"The Silver Shirts have teamed up with the American White Guard, the German American Bund, and the American Nationalist Confederation," Siegel said. "Nazis coming out of their rat holes everywhere, so don't let Charlie out of your sight."

With Chaplin about to begin the introductions, Cohen scanned the audience and saw a familiar face: the dark-haired woman from Danny's Diner. She had stepped out of the Ford van, walked inside, headed toward Newspaper Man, who was packing, then detoured to the restroom. Now, she took a seat next to a fellow in his thirties in an off-the-rack navy blue suit, a *schmatte* that cost far less than Cohen's two-tone alligator shoes. Probably the driver of the van, Cohen figured. The woman was mildly attractive, not in a flashy way. The man had what passed for Irish good looks, bland as sand.

Cohen's intuition and experience told him the pair were not gangsters, as he'd first thought.

Gumshoes, private dicks, maybe. But who would hire them? And who were they tailing? Einstein? Chaplin? Me?

Usually a shamus works alone. Leaving open the possibility they were coppers.

Plainclothes detectives work in twos. But I haven't committed any felonies recently…at least not in New Jersey.

Brian Sullivan's gray fedora sat on his lap, and Milagros Vazquez's green felt pillbox hat sat atop her head. The two FBI operatives sat dead-center in the auditorium. On instructions from the Director, they were there in case either Einstein or Oppenheimer showed any signs of disloyalty.

As if one of them might leap to his feet and sing L'Internationale.

Margarita Konenkova, Einstein's sometimes lover, sat in the back row, wearing a long, flowing silk dress with geometric prints, a chunky red Bakelite wrist bracelet, and a matching beret tilted at a jaunty angle. An artistic look. Her Soviet spymaster, known as a *rezident,* had instructed her to be there in case nuclear secrets overflowed like a boiling *rassolnik* soup.

Assigned "special tasks," as the agency called them, she had already introduced Einstein to her *rezident* at a cocktail party in New York where the man posed as an arts patron. The spy asked a few questions about nuclear fission, but Einstein steered the conversation to the refugee crisis in Europe. Margarita quickly concluded that her lover had no inclination to share America's nuclear secrets, even if he knew any.

Margarita's husband, Sergey Konenkov, the famed sculptor, greeted well-wishers outside the auditorium where they paused to admire his bronze bust of Einstein, smiling under crinkly eyes, his wild hair frozen in high metallic waves above his head. Konenkov, white-bearded and craggy faced at sixty-six, knew nothing of Margarita's adventures, romantic or political.

Fritz Duquesne sat in the front row dressed in a navy tweed sport coat with leather patches on the elbows, and gray wool slacks. His mustache and full beard were fake, but indistinguishable from the real McCoy. Round tortoiseshell glasses completed his makeover. A slightly altered look from the diner, perhaps that of a tenured professor.

The Nazi spy had two reasons for attending the debate. Just as with Margarita Konenkova, he would be alert for any leaked nuclear secrets. But more important to him, as it would be to Werner Heisenberg's *Uranverein*, he wanted to know as much about Einstein as possible. He had seen the scientist emerge from an anteroom with a stocky Army major who now sat in the auditorium.

Just what are you doing with the American military, Professor? Surely, when I have you shackled in leg irons, you will tell me.

Chaplin had barely begun the introductions when a fair-haired young man wearing a herringbone jacket and Princeton tie emblazoned with orange and black shields rudely interrupted him. "I saw your new picture, Chaplin! What gives you the right to besmirch the reputation of a great world leader?"

The room erupted—half gasping, half applauding.

"An expert on the Reich are you?" Chaplin replied smoothly.

"Berlin is like a finely tuned clock," the young man said, a sneer on his lips, "and the trains run on time...unlike the Pennsylvania Railroad."

In the audience, Fritz Duquesne stroked his faux beard and smiled. The boisterous young fellow was likely a Princeton student. Duquesne knew that the uneducated and unwashed of America embraced fascism. Now he entertained the delicious possibility that the pampered sons of bankers and corporate titans, robber barons and captains of industry, might also don the swastika when the revolution came to American shores.

"What else do you like about Germany, other than those punctual trains?" Chaplin asked.

"I was a coxswain on our mixed pairs in the '36 Olympics. The Germans' love of country was invigorating."

Chaplin did not miss a beat. "Coxswain, eh? You like barking orders and having others do the heavy work."

"*C'est la vie*," the callow fellow said with a shrug. "In life, there are leaders and laborers."

From behind the curtain, Cohen watched the smirky blond wiseacre. The gangster didn't know a coxswain from a cockroach, but if he ran into this punk, he'd slap him silly.

Chaplin kept his tone even. "I assume you're one of those bright lads at the university who answered that student survey, 'Who's the Greatest Living Person in the World?' Professor Einstein, my dear friend, came in second." He paused for effect. "Adolf Hitler finished first."

Murmurs swept through the audience, and Chaplin continued, "*The New York Times* expressed shock, but why? Princeton is a university with no Negro students, no women students, and so few Jews they'd have a hard time gathering a..." He turned to Einstein. "What's the word, Albert?"

"*Minyan*," Einstein said.

"Ten or more Jews in a communal prayer," explained Oppenheimer.

"You naifs know nothing of the world!" Chaplin boomed. "Nurtured like orchids in your estates in Newport and Oyster Bay, your mansions in the Hudson Valley and on the Main Line, your silver spoons dipped in caviar, you are woefully ignorant of life. Of men scratching out a living with their hands, of children in tenements going to bed hungry."

The cocky coxswain was stunned into silence, and anxious whispers rippled through the auditorium like an incoming tide. Just where would Chaplin go with this? But the man who had once been a starving boy in London had said his piece and set about the business of introducing the sixty-one year old genius and the brilliant young upstart.

From his spot in the first row, Major Groves paid close attention to the two men with towering intellects. Though their presentations did not involve nuclear fission, he daydreamed about having one or both of them help the NDRC undertake research on an atomic bomb.

"When a star exhausts its nuclear fuel, it will contract due to its own gravity and approach a state of infinite density," Oppenheimer said to the audience. "Spacetime curves infinitely, wrapping time, space, and light around itself. Nothing, not even light, will escape. Professor Einstein disagrees, but it is his general relativity that predicts these gravitational collapses."

In rebuttal, Einstein said, "My mathematical prediction is one thing. Physical reality is quite another. Without observational proof, you ask us to believe that the universe is filled with what…dark holes vacuuming up the detritus of dead stars?"

They went on for a while and then took questions.

A studious looking young man who had been taking notes asked, "Professor Einstein, it's been thirty five years since your *annus mirabilis.*" Showing off his knowledge of Einstein's miracle year when he produced four papers, including special relativity.

The lad continued, "Given all the young physicists like Professor Oppenheimer with new ideas, has time passed you by? Should you be put out to pasture like an aging racehorse?"

The crowd grumbled disapproval, and Oppenheimer aimed a finger at the questioner.

"That's damn impertinent!" The mild expletive made the crowd gasp, as moviegoers did one year earlier when Rhett Butler allowed as how he didn't give a damn.

Einstein merely smiled beneath his mustache and said, "Put out to pasture? Perhaps. Is there a brood mare in this retirement plan?"

Laughter rolled through the crowd. Oppenheimer, perpetually serious compared to the slyly humorous Einstein, still scowled at the questioner. "Lest there be any mistake, I stand on Professor Einstein's shoulders."

"And I stand on Isaac Newton's who stood on Galileo's," Einstein chipped in. The crowd applauded, both speakers winning over the audience.

Fritz Duquesne raised his hand, adopted a Boston Brahmin accent, and said, "Professor Einstein, do you think it's possible to create an atomic bomb by splitting the atom?"

"I wish the answer were no," Einstein said, "and while 'splitting the atom' is a misnomer, a self-sustaining nuclear chain reaction is almost certainly possible, and German scientists are said to be close to doing it."

Oppenheimer said, "Professor Einstein is too modest to say that his special relativity predicts such a chain reaction."

"Embarrassed, not modest," Einstein said.

"If you placed enough uranium in a stack of graphite," Oppenheimer continued, "you'd have a good start on a nuclear reactor of fissionable materials."

A young man in rimless eyeglasses piped up, "Question for both of you. If the government asked you to roll up your sleeves and make such a bomb, would you?"

"My pacifism argues against it," Einstein said.

"This isn't a case of opening a lab on Monday and walking out with a bomb on Friday," Oppenheimer said. "You're talking about hundreds, perhaps thousands of physicists, chemists, metallurgists, mathematicians, engineers, technicians, construction workers, mechanics, and support staff mastering equipment and facilities that do not yet exist, at a cost of untold hundreds of millions, perhaps more than a billion dollars. They would undertake the most complicated tasks of science and engineering ever attempted by mankind, not to mention the risks. In comparison, the pyramids of Egypt were a sandcastle on a beach. But to answer your question, if asked, of course I would take part. I believe it is an American citizen's duty."

The auditorium exploded in applause, and Major Groves appraised the serious young physicist. So thin as to appear frail, he didn't look like a leader who could rally troops.

But there's something compelling about you, Oppie. Just how the hell am I going to get you past J. Edgar Hoover's paranoia?

Einstein also considered his passionate and brilliant colleague. He thought of the other physicists who were intellectually capable of taking on nuclear fission. Teller, Peierls, and Bethe were in their early thirties, Fermi not yet forty and Szilard forty-two.

At sixty-one, am I the old racehorse headed for the pasture...or the glue factory? Nein, noch nicht. *No, not yet.*

There was a spirit of competition among scientists that had never appealed to Einstein. And yet, at this moment, he found himself toying with an unfamiliar impulse: he didn't want to be left behind. Oppenheimer's exuberance was contagious, and Einstein felt a sudden surge of energy in himself. He made eye contact with Major Groves in the front row, smiled and nodded.

I won't light the fuse on a bomb. But I'll chew the fat with those fellows—the eggheads, Charlie calls them—at the NDRC. What's the harm in that?

THIRTEEN
THE LONDON FIRE BRIGADE

"This is London, ten minutes before five in the morning. Tonight's raid has been widespread. Bombs have been reported from more than fifty districts. I've spent a night with the London Fire Brigade. For three hours, I shivered in a sandbag crow's nest atop a tall building near the Thames. It was one of the many fire observation posts. A German bomber came boring down the river. We could see his exhaust trail like a pale ribbon stretched straight across the sky. Half a mile downstream there were two eruptions and then a third, close together. The first two looked like some giant had thrown a huge basket of flaming golden oranges high in the air. The third was just a balloon of fire enclosed in black smoke above the housetops."

– Edward R. Murrow, CBS Radio

Wednesday, November 6, 1940

The day after the debate, Fritz Duquesne drove from Princeton to the small town of Kenvil, New Jersey. Eight weeks had passed since the explosion at the Hercules Powder Plant, and he wanted to see the aftermath firsthand. With the saboteurs safely out of the country, his remaining duties were less espionage than disinformation. He seeded rumors in the press, pinning the blame on the Irish Republican Army. It was a plausible diversion as munitions from the plant were bound for England, and some IRA factions had flirted with the Reich as means of undermining British rule in Northern Ireland.

Duquesne felt a pang of jealousy that his own role hadn't been larger. Still, pride swelled in his chest at the results.

The long arm of the Reich can strike anywhere.

Americans clung to the illusion that the Atlantic and Pacific Oceans rendered them untouchable.

So naive, these Yanks!

Duquesne knew of the Reich's *Amerika Bomber* project, a scheme to develop long-range bombers that could strike the States. Once England fell, Germany would turn its sights to Greenland, establishing Luftwaffe bases within reach of New York. The prospect thrilled him. He had nursed a grudge against America for siding with the Entente Powers in 1917, but it paled next to his hatred for the British. Born in South Africa, he had fought the English during the Second Boer War and later honed his skills as a saboteur in the Great War.

Now, standing near the shattered ruins of the Hercules plant, the full scale of the destruction left him momentarily awestruck. Two dozen buildings had been obliterated, their skeletal frames scattered across a wasteland of scorched concrete, blackened timbers, and mangled rebar. Perhaps it was his imagination, but he thought he smelled the lingering acrid tang of explosives over the desolate expanse.

Driving back through the tiny burg, he noted the lingering scars on the community. Homes bristled with scaffolding as carpenters and roofers patched roofs and walls. Most windows had been replaced, but the Methodist church still wore plywood where stained glass once depicted Jesus. Sacred panes weren't something you picked up at the local hardware store.

He spun the radio dial, but every station offered some variation of the same story: Roosevelt's landslide victory over Wendell Willkie, sweeping thirty-eight of forty-eight states. Duquesne had little interest in the election, though he would have preferred Joseph P. Kennedy—recently resigned as Ambassador to Great Britain—in the Oval Office. Such an odd appointment by Roosevelt, Duquesne mused. Kennedy had been openly anti-British and quietly sympathetic toward Berlin. He had scandalized the British by fleeing to the countryside during the Blitz, and outraged Americans with his dour pronouncement that democracy was likely finished on both sides of the Atlantic.

Duquesne thought ahead to 1944 and toyed with a pleasant fantasy.

President Joe Kennedy and Vice President Charles Lindbergh. Or vice versa. Now, there's an Administration the Reich could work with.

Duquesne stopped at a diner outside Newark, ordered meat loaf and a cup of coffee and used the pay phone. With the assistance of the operator and two nickels, he reached a tavern on Second Avenue in Yorkville, the center of German-American life in Manhattan. He asked Lukas the bartender if there were any messages for Frederick Fredericks, one of his many aliases, admittedly a rather uninspired one.

"East Quogue called," Lukas said. "Am I pronouncing that right, Frederick?"

"Close enough. What time?"

"Maybe three hours ago."

Duquesne hung up and called a number in the Long Island town of East Quogue. "How's the weather in Portugal?" Duquesne said when a man answered.

"The package never arrived," came the reply.

Duquesne squeezed his eyes shut and grimaced. The man in East Quogue used powerful shortwave telegraphy equipment that communicated with Germany. The message was clear. The courier carrying microfilm from the NDRC had not been on board the Yankee Clipper when it arrived in Lisbon.

"Hamburg demands your explanation," the man said.

As if it's my fault!

Duquesne placed another call, this one to the New York pharmacy where Klaus worked when he wasn't Bill the Spy with the ridiculous beard. He had been given the simple task of delivering microfilm to the courier. What had happened?

"Klaus didn't come into work today," the store manager said on the phone. Duquesne hung up and tried Klaus at home. No answer.

The lazy dummkopf must not have taken an evasive route and never shook his tail! Doubtless he led the FBI straight to the courier, and now both men were in custody.

The saving grace was compartmentalization. Neither man knew the identity of the agent inside Bullfrog—the NDRC–or how the documents were obtained.

Our agent on the inside is safe and can continue working.

Duquesne called the man in East Quogue a second time and put the best spin he knew on the situation, explaining it was a minor setback involving only couriers and not Abwehr's intelligence agent. He could hear a pencil scratching paper at the other end of the line.

"Your agent inside Bullfrog just called," the man said.

"What?!" The breach of protocol sent a chill through the aging spymaster. The agent was only to communicate with him. The mission, which had once seemed so promising, had come a cropper. "And the message?"

"U.S. Army Intelligence interrogated everyone at Bullfrog," the man said. "Hooked them up to something called the Berkeley Psychograph that's supposed to detect lies."

Duquesne felt a tightness in his chest, as if the words themselves had weight. The mission was not intended to be one-and-done. If undetected, the German agent who worked inside the heavily guarded walls of the NDRC could purloin military secrets for years. But if caught, the entire operation failed.

"Passed with flying colors," said the man on the phone. "*Gott sei Dank!*"

Thank God, indeed! A Psychograph! Americans and their love of technology. So many more reliable interrogation techniques, from freezer compartments to thumbscrews.

"One more thing," the man in East Quogue said. "Bullfrog expects two visitors today. One is of great interest to Abwehr and the other to Schutzstaffel."

Duquesne would have preferred being told straightaway who was of interest to both the intelligence agency and the SS, but then it occurred to him.

"Einstein and Chaplin!" Duquesne gasped. "Both at the NDRC?"

"That's the information."

Duquesne knew that Admiral Canaris at Abwehr was salivating over his plan to snatch Einstein. But the SS and Chaplin? It could mean only one thing: Hitler's loathing for the comedian's mocking portrayal in *The Great Dictator* had evidently escalated to an assassination order.

A less experienced operative would have been thrilled by this fortuitous event, two missions intertwined. But Abwehr and the SS often worked at cross purposes with territorial jealousies and conflicting priorities. Kidnaping Einstein and killing Chaplin in the same venue at the same time presented logistical complications the *Schreibtischhengste*—desk jockeys— would never comprehend.

The man in East Quogue provided an address in Laurel, Maryland, where Duquesne was to meet an SS agent, an assassin, no doubt. They would travel together to Fort Meade, site of NDRC's offices.

"Who's the ranking officer?" Duquesne asked.

The man chuckled. "Hamburg would say you. Berlin would say the other fellow."

Duquesne accepted the non-answer as the truth. The rift between Abwehr and the SS spanned more than the 300 kilometers separating the two cities.

"Any idea who this fellow is?"

"SS wouldn't say, but I'd wager he's half your age and twice as ruthless."

"I wonder if you've just insulted me," Duquesne said.

"Not at all. The SS recruits sociopaths. You are many things. Clever. Bold. Strategic. A lifelong soldier, not an assassin. If I were you, I'd exercise extreme caution."

"That's how I've stayed alive all these years," Duquesne said, hanging up the phone.

FIFTEEN
JOY RIDE

The midnight-black Rolls-Royce Phantom III limousine reminded Mickey Cohen of a hearse, which made him edgy. Facing the rear, he sat in the passenger compartment, all burgundy cloth and mahogany trim. His bride, LaVonne, was at his side, with Einstein and Chaplin seated across the fold-out table, facing forward. The setup was so genteel it seemed as if they were playing bridge, rather than en route to Fort Meade, thirty miles northeast of the nation's capital, where the NDRC's temporary headquarters awaited.

"It's my honeymoon, Mickey, and you're taking me to an Army base," LaVonne had complained that morning. "You gonna enlist?"

Cohen didn't bother telling her that he had registered for the draft several months earlier, as required by the new Selective Service Act, then failed his physical exam on account of a perforated eardrum from his boxing days. Cohen was happy about that, but not the doctor's scribbled notation that he was a "criminal type with chronic antisocial tendencies and morally unfit for service."

Across the table, Einstein was buried in a copy of *Nature*, a magazine that, to Cohen's disappointment, did not feature photos of wild animals. Instead, the scientist was reading an article entitled "Reactions Produced by Neutrons in Heavy Elements" by a fellow named Enrico Fermi. Chaplin, meanwhile, skimmed *The New York Times*. Up front, the chauffeur kept the giant limousine humming along at a steady fifty miles per hour, the passenger compartment sealed off by a closed glass window.

They were talking about yesterday's presidential election, Einstein still giddy from voting for the first time barely five weeks after becoming a U.S. citizen.

"Today, I feel like a true American," the scientist said as they left Princeton.

"I hope you voted for the winner," Chaplin prodded him.

"Of course, I did! Mr. Willkie seems like a nice fellow, but Mr. Roosevelt has the experience and the moxie to face the world's perils."

From his perch, Cohen kept a watch out the rear window, trying to spot any cars following them. So far, nothing suspicious. Bugsy Siegel had telephoned again that morning with a warning. William Dudley Pelley, head of the Silver Legion of America, a crackpot who called himself the "American Hitler," had offered a ten-thousand dollar bounty on Chaplin's life.

Not on my watch, you Nazi bastard.

One year earlier, Cohen had been part of a crew that had busted up a Nazi meeting hall at Alt Heidelberg in downtown Los Angeles. The Kraut lovers were celebrating Germany's invasion of Poland, home to three million Jews. A young rabbi from Boyle Heights had asked Siegel to gather some *shtarkers* who knew how to swing lead pipes. "Broken bones are jake, but no killings," the rabbi said.

You never knew when you might need a character witness, so Cohen abided by the rabbi's instructions. That night, the gangster used his fists, armed with brass knuckle-dusters, and cracked several Nazi jaws. He wouldn't mind doing it again.

They were an hour south of Princeton when Cohen heard a roar, like MGM's lion at the start of a picture. Through the rear window, a sky-blue convertible loomed, closing the distance. Its skirted fenders dipped and rose like ocean waves, its streamlined body poised like a cheetah about to pounce. The horn blared—a brassy, insistent call.

Einstein turned to look. Chaplin stirred from his reading to glance as well. The convertible, with darkened windows and the top up, hung six feet off the limo's bumper.

"What the hell, Mick?" LaVonne's voice rose with alarm.

"A Bugatti 37 Cabriolet," Cohen said.

"Helluva motor car," Chaplin said, "almost impossible to get."

"I tried to buy one but got out-bid by an oil millionaire," Cohen said. "Damn thing will do a hundred-thirty easy."

With the Bugatti's horn still blasting, Cohen rolled down the window to the driver's compartment and spoke to the chauffeur. "Jazz it up to sixty-five and keep her there. And don't shit a brick if you hear gunfire."

"*Oy vey*," Einstein said.

The Bugatti's horn blared again as it pulled up alongside the limo, inching closer. Its spoked wheels came perilously close to the limo's fat whitewalls.

"He's trying to run us off the road!" LaVonne shrieked.

"He'd be an idiot to sideswipe us." Cohen knew that the slender Bugatti would bounce off the four-ton limo, but that didn't mean the chauffeur would stay calm. He wished Three-Finger Monty were at the wheel, the best damn getaway driver in the City of Angels.

The darkened passenger side window of the Bugatti rolled down, and an arm appeared holding a flag that whipped in the wind. Bright red with a white disc, and in the center, a swastika, black as death. The flag of the Third Reich.

"Nazis!" LaVonne screamed.

Einstein and Chaplin exchanged worried glances. It had been three years since they'd both been targeted in Operation Hollywood, a plot by American fascists to assassinate them. They had escaped, but the movement hadn't weakened; if anything, it had grown stronger as Germany bulldozed its way across Europe.

Cohen cranked down the window facing the convertible and pulled out his .38. He could easily take out a tire, but he didn't trust the Bugatti's driver to avoid a collision. He could focus on the extended arm and approximate the location of the flag-waver's chest and plug him. He was considering his shot as the flag disappeared, and a head popped out of the open window.

The smug blond Princeton brat who took umbrage at Chaplin's mocking of Hitler! A rich prick, undoubtedly the son of a bigger rich prick who spoiled the kid rotten.

The dumb cluck was laughing. Then the unseen driver floored the accelerator, and the Bugatti shot forward, engine screaming. In thirty seconds, it was out of sight far down the road.

Chaplin nudged his friend. "Just a college prank, Albert, but admittedly with dark overtones."

Einstein stared out the window, his brow furrowed. "This country that took me in when I fled the fascists," he said softly. "This country that I love. What is happening to her?"

An hour later, with the limo still heading south, Einstein was tutoring LaVonne, at Cohen's request—or demand—that the Professor "smarten her up." Chewing a wad of Juicy Fruit gum, she frowned and said, "I don't get it. Tell me again."

"My happiest thought," Einstein said patiently, "was when I imagined myself in a free-falling elevator and concluded that I wouldn't feel my own weight. I wouldn't feel gravity."

"I coulda told you that," LaVonne said. "When I was a kid, we'd jump off the rocks into the water at a limestone quarry. You didn't feel nothing 'til you hit the water."

"Then you already understand the foundation of general relativity," Einstein said smiling.

"I toldya I wasn't stupid, Mickey," she said, tossing a triumphant look at her husband. "Let's talk about American history," Einstein said. "I learned a great deal while preparing for my naturalization exam."

"Shoot, Professor."

"What is the supreme law of the land?"

"The tommy gun," Cohen blurted out.

"Shush, Mick!" LaVonne scolded. "I'm thinking." Buying time, she patted the coil of the fiery red mane at the nape of her neck. A fancy French twist, thanks to a visit to a swanky New York salon. "Possession is nine-tenths of the law," she ventured at last.

"Actually, it's the Constitution," Einstein said. "Let us move on. What did the Declaration of Independence do?"

"I declared my independence the week I set up shop in L.A.," Cohen said. "Knocked over a bookie joint run by Johnny Roselli and Jack Dragna."

"Hey, Mickey! The professor asked me, not you," LaVonne complained.

"Clipped the Eyetalians for twenty-three large," Cohen continued.

"How about that?" Einstein said. "Almost exactly the same amount of money I received for winning the Nobel Prize." He turned back to LaVonne. "Do you know the answer, dear?"

"Gimme a minute." LaVonne smoothed the folds in her silk, tea-length dress in muted gray silk. Marion Davies had taken her on a Manhattan shopping spree that ended at the elegant Hattie Carnegie store.

"You look like a librarian," Cohen had told her that morning.

"Like you've ever been in a library," she fired back.

"Mrs. Cohen?" Einstein prompted, his tone encouraging.

She pursed her lips, wrinkled her brow and said, "The Declaration of Independence is what allowed my Momma to leave my Pop with everything she could fit into our Model B."

They were on a bridge crossing the Delaware River when Cohen, looking out the rear window, said, "Whatta we got here?"

"What is it, Mick?" LaVonne asked.

"That green Hupmobile has been ducking in and out of traffic, trying to look like it ain't following us."

"Not again," Einstein said.

"Probably too far south for more college boys," Chaplin said.

Cohen snapped the brim up on his homburg and squinted to get a better look. "Two people up front, can't make them out from here."

He tucked his left elbow against his chest, checking that his .38 was back in its holster.

They were across the bridge now, in Delaware, and the Hupmobile had allowed one car to get between it and the limo. They stayed that way for the next several miles. Then Cohen lowered the window partition again and told the chauffeur to pull off the road as soon as the shoulder was wide enough to accommodate the bulky vehicle.

Moments later, the big whitewalls kicked up dirt as the limo rolled to a stop off the roadway. Cohen watched through the side window as the Hupmobile passed them. In the passenger seat sat a dark-haired woman, her face carefully angled away, as if she'd suddenly developed an interest in the car's dashboard.

"That's her," Cohen muttered. "The woman who hit the restroom at the diner and showed up at the Institute. The driver's gotta be her pal from both places." His eyes took in the license plate as the Hupmobile passed them. "U.S. Government."

Back at the Institute, Cohen had pegged the pair as plainclothes detectives, but he realized now he'd been wrong. The truth was as obvious as Al Capone's scar.

Feds. G-Men. FBI. But who were they after—and why?

SIXTEEN
STANDOFF AT THE FORT

A military policeman waved the limousine through the Perimeter Security Point, and it continued toward the Fort Meade guardhouse. The plan was to drop off Einstein and Chaplin at the base, after which the chauffeur would take Mickey and LaVonne Cohen to a nearby town. LaVonne wanted to shop for a new hat. Mickey? He asked about a sporting goods store, and not for a squash racket. He wanted a crossbow.

"Take your average security guard at a warehouse," Cohen explained to Einstein and Chaplin. "He's an ex-cop who's had a few guns waved in his face and don't scare easy. Now, give one of your men a pistol and another a crossbow. The guard can't take his eyes off the arrow, which, by the way, is called a bolt. Scared stiff, imagining what it would feel like to have the damn thing puncture his liver and come out the other side."

The limo slowed to a stop and Einstein asked, "*Was ist das?*"

A commotion. The green government Hupmobile sat sideways in front of the barrier arm, barring entry. Major Groves stood nearby, deep in a heated argument with a tall man in a suit and gray fedora. Two Army jeeps flanked the Hupmobile, and six military policemen carrying sidearms watched the hubbub. A woman lingered a few steps away, observing the exchange.

"All's not quiet on the Eastern Front," Chaplin said wryly.

Einstein and Chaplin stepped out of the limo and approached Major Groves, who gave them a brief nod but didn't stop arguing. Cohen noticed the woman. She was unmistakably the same one from the Institute and the diner. The troublemaking pair, Mr. and Mrs. FBI.

Major Groves was losing patience. The couple had announced themselves as FBI special agent Brian Sullivan and investigator Milagros Vazquez, a *woman.* That was a first in Groves' experience. He thought it was high time the Bureau hired full-fledged female special agents but supposed Hoover would have to retire or die before the Bureau took that path.

"If you two don't move your car," Groves snapped, "I'll have it towed to a heavy weapons range and when our howitzers are done with it, I'll ship the scrap metal to J. Edgar Hoover."

"That's not in the cards, Major," Sullivan said calmly. "The Bureau forbids Professor Einstein from entry to the National Defense Research Committee by direct order of the Director."

"Agent Sullivan, you can tell Hoover he has no jurisdiction over a military base."

"The security breach changes that equation," Sullivan countered. "Once top-secret materials leaked, it became an FBI matter."

"Security breach?" Einstein whispered to Chaplin, who offered only a shrug.

"Professor Einstein has never set foot inside the NDRC and obviously has nothing to do with any leak," Groves said.

"He has graciously offered his time to help his country in a race for a weapon that might determine the fate of all mankind."

That took Einstein aback. He had not considered an atomic bomb in terms writ so large, but of course, that's exactly what was at stake. For better or worse.

"May I say something, Agent Sullivan?" Milagros Vazquez asked, her voice deferential.

"Of course, Millie. What is it?"

She turned to the major. "*Para el FBI, Commandante Groves, este es nuestro terremoto en Nicaragua,*" she said.

Groves' eyes widened, a flicker of recognition crossing his face. "*Ondas de choque en Washington.*"

"What the heck's going on?" Sullivan asked.

Groves cracked a smile. "Investigator Vazquez obviously knows that I led our engineering team in Nicaragua after that horrible earthquake in '31." He turned to Vazquez. "And yes ma'am, I understand that the security breach at NDRC is causing 'shock waves' in Washington. A nice play on words, evoking the quake. But regardless of the fuss your boss is making, the Army won't cede command and control of a military base to a civilian agency, not even the FBI."

Sullivan glanced at Vazquez who returned the look with raised eyebrows that seemed to say, *I tried.*

"So go tell Hoover," the major continued, "that a better use of his time would be tracking down Nazi saboteurs."

Sullivan tried and failed to suppress a smile, which Groves caught. The major could read facial expressions the way Cole Porter could read music.

The FBI agent agrees with me! He thinks Hoover sent them on a fool's errand.

"Now, agent Sullivan and investigator Vazquez," Groves said, steel in his voice, "you've followed your orders as far as they can take you. If you'd like, I'll write a note to your mommies—or the Director—that you've been a good boy and girl, but if you don't move that green puke-mobile in the next sixty seconds, you'll be walking back to D.C."

SEVENTEEN
THE SPY AND THE ASSASSIN

Peering through binoculars, Fritz Duquesne watched the Rolls-Royce limousine drop off Einstein and Chaplin. Then something peculiar caught his eye: a civilian car blocking the fort's entrance. A man in a navy blue suit and a dark-haired woman stood beside it, arguing with an Army officer.

"The Achilles' heel of America," Duquesne muttered. "No clear lines of authority."

"What's happening?" asked Reinard Schmidt, seated beside him.

"The man and woman—police of some sort, I assume—have been shadowing Einstein and Chaplin. Now they're interfering with their entry to the base."

Duquesne sat at the wheel of his Packard Super 8 coupe, parked just off the access road to the fort. Schmidt, an SS assassin by profession, occupied the passenger seat. Tall, rangy, and roped with muscle, Schmidt was the picture of Aryan perfection: corn-yellow waves of hair, glacial blue eyes, and cheekbones sharp enough to cut stone. A living poster for *Volk und Rasse*—People and Race—the propaganda magazine. In the Packard's luggage trunk, the assassin's prized Karabiner 98k sniper rifle lay nestled in its leather case, complete with a 4k Zeiss scope.

Schmidt glanced at the trees lining the road. The few remaining autumn leaves barely rustled. "No wind," he said approvingly.

"What difference does that make? You're not taking the shot here."

"Unless I change the plan."

"You have no such authority." Schmidt smirked.

"*Mit perfekten Bedingungen ist es ein Kinderspiel.*" Saying the conditions were perfect and the shot would be child's play.

Schmidt was perhaps thirty years old and wore his arrogance as if it were an Iron Cross, Duquesne thought.

I have known you only an hour and hate you already.

"So there is no mistake," Schmidt said, for what felt like the third time, "the assassination of Chaplin takes precedence over the kidnaping of Einstein."

"Show me those orders, Herr Schmidt," Duquesne said coolly.

"*Verdammt!* You know very well there are no written orders."

"Then perhaps you imagined them," Duquesne taunted.

Schmidt barked a laugh. "As you imagined guiding the U-boat that sank the Hampshire and killed Lord Kitchener in the Great War. At Schutzstaffel, they say you are a teller of tall tales."

"Whereas the Abwehr says nothing of you. They've never heard your name."

Like much of what Duquesne said every day of his life, the jab was false. The assassin's reputation preceded him: a ruthless sniper who had eliminated resistance leaders in Poland and France, as well as a dozen Germans deemed insufficiently loyal to the Führer. Rumor had it Schmidt was also tasked with dispatching German operatives who displeased Heinrich

Himmler, the ruthless Reichsführer of the SS. It was not a comforting thought.

Schmidt's mission was clear—kill Chaplin for his calumny against the Führer. Hitler loathed the actor's mocking portrayal of him in *The Great Dictator*, a blustering buffoon with cowardly and effeminate mannerisms. The insult cut deeper than Churchill's condemnation of the Führer as a "monster" or Roosevelt's denunciation of his "reign of terror." To Duquesne, the mission was a strategic blunder.

Provoking sympathy for Chaplin and drawing more attention to his film? Asinine! Alienating American politicians being cultivated and paid by Abwehr? Inane!

The Packard was parked a half kilometer from the Fort Meade sentry station. A man in gas station coveralls had pretended to replace a perfectly fine rear tire. His Ford pickup, adorned with freshly stenciled lettering—Miller Sunoco Gasoline and Service—completed the ruse.

A passerby would likely not notice the polished Oxfords on the mechanic or the breathing holes in the oversized toolbox in the truck bed. The latter was designed to hold Einstein, somewhat uncomfortably, for the short drive to a waiting airplane.

The faux mechanic was one of Duquesne's agents. Sitting in the truck's cab was a second man in coveralls, a fellow who had boxed as a heavyweight under the name "Berlin Bruno." Max Schmeling he was not, as Bruno lost twenty-one bouts while winning eight, but he was large and had a fearsome demeanor. Duquesne doubted he would need the full team to subdue Einstein, but he believed in preparing for the unexpected.

Schmidt sat massaging his right hand, some kind of sniper warm-up. The gesture irritated Duquesne, as did everything about the SS man. What grinded at Duquesne like a dentist's drill was simple. The *Schweinehund* was a swaggering upstart. It took no courage to hide in bushes and put a bullet through a man's skull at six hundred meters, as Schmidt supposedly had done.

Whereas I prefer to kill up close where I can see fear in the man's eyes, and he can see the cold determination in mine.

Duquesne notched his first kill when he was twelve years old at his family's trading post in South Africa, using a spear to impale a man who had attacked his mother. In the five decades since, he had killed with guns, knives, and bombs, and on one occasion, a sword. He had worked as a big game hunting guide, a newspaper reporter, a novelist, a spy, and a saboteur. He knew the world.

These days, he was bored by the administrative duties involved in running a spy ring of thirty operatives, many of them rank amateurs. He frequently clashed with his superiors at Abwehr and knew many considered him a *wandelndes Pulverfass*, a "walking powder keg," or as the Americans might say, a "loose cannon." Still others thought he was over the hill. More recently, his *residenturleiter*, the station chief, was not impressed when he came up with the plan to kidnap Albert Einstein.

"What will we do with that old man?" the station chief demanded.

I am two years older than Einstein, so what does the station chief think of me?

"It's Einstein who roused Roosevelt from his stupor to start a nuclear program," Duquesne had said. "If he were a useless old goat, would their new Defense Committee have invited him into their secret chambers?"

Thankfully, Admiral Canaris, who had known Duquesne for decades, overruled the station chief and gave his blessing to the kidnap mission. Duquesne knew from newspaper stories that Chaplin and Einstein were scheduled to be in Chicago in two days for the second debate with Oppenheimer. Logic dictated that, after leaving the NDRC, the two friends would begin their journey by train. While nearby Portland station was a possibility for travel on the Baltimore and Ohio line, Duquesne would wager that the limousine would take them to Union Station in D.C. to catch the Capitol Limited. Either way, the Packard and the pickup truck would follow them. The moment to strike would be when the pair stepped from the limo. The plan was simple and clean, though it required cooperation and timing. And that meant no freelancing from Reinhard Schmidt.

At the railway station, there would be perhaps ninety seconds to act, just enough time for the dual mission. The targets would exit the limousine. There would be luggage to turn over to porters, good-byes to be said, and possibly a cash tip for the chauffeur.

Schmidt's first gunshot would take out the pint-sized bodyguard, and in that long second where everyone freezes in shock and disbelief, the second shot—preferably to the head— would end Chaplin's life. In the pandemonium, Berlin Bruno would snatch Einstein and stuff him into the oversize toolbox of the pickup truck with the faux mechanic at the wheel. Duquesne and Schmidt in the Packard would follow the truck—customized with an oversize engine—to the Potomac River where a Consolidated 28 long-range seaplane waited at the dock. The seaplane would fly to Bald Head Island, North Carolina where a German American Bund official owned a marina and service dock. After refueling, they would fly to Havana where a German freighter would be waiting for the trip across the Atlantic to Hamburg.

Through the binoculars, Duquesne saw movement. The green Hupmobile had cleared the path. Einstein and Chaplin climbed into an Army jeep and were driven into the fort.

"Two hours, I'm guessing," Duquesne muttered. "Then no more than thirty minutes on the road to Union Station."

He felt the tingle of excitement that still accompanied every dangerous mission. And why not? This would be the greatest coup of his career.

EIGHTEEN
THE LOCKED ROOM MYSTERY

A military policeman, sergeant's chevrons sharp on his sleeve, guided the jeep through the bustling Army post. Major Groves sat ramrod straight in the front passenger seat, while Chaplin and Einstein shared the back, gawking at the hustle and bustle of an active military base. Soldiers streamed past at double-time, Army trucks chugged to and fro, and the post had the feel of wartime, even though America was at peace, for now.

"What was that about a security breach?" Chaplin asked.

"Last week, Leo Szilard gave a classified presentation to the Committee behind closed doors," Groves replied. "Then microfilm copies turned up inside the wristwatch of a Nazi courier intending to hop onto a flight to Portugal."

"Blimey!" Chaplin exclaimed.

Einstein shook his head, his wild hair ruffling in the breeze. "Poor Leo must be bereft."

"Indeed. Until we plug this leak, we can't expect Szilard or his colleagues to share their research with the Committee. We have both the courier and his contact in custody and they're being questioned."

"The last I heard," Einstein said, "Leo was working on chain reactions in uranium and carbon systems."

"That was earlier this year," Groves said. "Now, he's onto something new and breathtaking."

Einstein turned to Chaplin. "See, Charlie, I told you I was behind the times." To Groves, he added, "So what was Leo doing here?"

"His project needs additional funding, so he traveled to the source of the Nile, or the Potomac, as the case may be. Szilard presented a top secret slide show to the Committee."

"Who was in the room?" Chaplin asked, much as a detective might.

"The Committee members, each with one aide," Groves said. "Two committee secretaries, one running the projector and the other taking notes. Everyone was thoroughly searched going into and out of the room."

"Where were the slides made?" Einstein asked.

"Excellent question," Groves said. "Szilard's team at Columbia made them and sent duplicates to MIT's Radiation Laboratory where parallel research is ongoing."

"Then the security breach could have happened at either location before Leo ever got here."

"Not possible. The leak could only have originated from this building."

The jeep pulled up to a concrete structure that resembled a pillbox minus the gun ports. Two MP's stood guard at the entrance.

Major Groves said, "The microfilm contained seven typewritten pages that were quite nearly verbatim reproductions of the material on the slides. A word was missing here and there, but strikingly, three complete lines of type were absent on page five. That corresponded with a projector mishap during the presentation. The bulb blew and obliterated three lines on one of the slides, the same missing portion on the microfilm."

"And the slides at Columbia and MIT are intact," Einstein said, his quick mind connecting the dots. "Hence your certainty about the leak."

"Precisely," Groves confirmed. "If the slides had been duplicated prior to being placed in the projector, there would be no missing lines. I personally destroyed the slides after the presentation, so they couldn't have been duplicated after they were shown."

"Any transmission equipment in the building?" Chaplin asked. "Shortwave radio, that sort of thing?"

"Not even a telephone," Groves said. "We've considered everything, even the possibility of documents being attached to helium balloons and sent up the chimney, with conspirators tracking the wind patterns outside the base perimeter."

"Rather farfetched," Chaplin observed.

Einstein stroked his mustache thoughtfully. "Occam's razor suggests the simplest, most straightforward explanation is usually correct."

"Then perhaps fresh eyes will see something today," Groves said hopefully.

Once inside the building, Einstein underwent a thorough search conducted by two enlisted men with corporal's stripes on the sleeves of their service shirts. He surrendered his meerschaum pipe, a pouch of Turkish tobacco, and the fountain pen and notepad he always carried in case inspiration enveloped him like the scent of a beautiful woman's perfume. Finally, he turned over his wallet.

"My pockets haven't been so empty since I worked in the Swiss patent office," he quipped.

Since Chaplin lacked security clearance, he waited in an anteroom manned by two armed MPs. He would not be allowed into the inner sanctum.

"They showed your new picture at the base theater last night," one MP said. "Laughed my arse off."

"Made me angry," the other MP said.

Chaplin waited, uncertain of the man's meaning.

"When we get into the war, we'll make Hitler pay for what he's doing to the Brits," the second MP said. "It'll take time, but we'll smash Berlin into rubble."

Warming to the young soldiers, Chaplin suggested a game of penny pinochle while they waited. He was several dollars in the hole—intentionally—when a lieutenant with a buzz cut and a serious demeanor stepped into the anteroom.

"Mr. Chaplin," the officer announced, "you're wanted in the Provost Marshal's Office. I'll accompany you, sir."

"Have I been drafted?" Chaplin asked with a smile.

"No, sir. You have a telephone call."

"Who could possibly know I'm here?" Chaplin wondered aloud.

"Apparently President Roosevelt," the lieutenant said.

NINETEEN
THE PRESIDENT NEEDS YOU

"Bravo, Mr. Chaplin," Franklin Roosevelt's patrician voice flowed through the receiver, each syllable steeped in that unmistakable Hyde Park drawl. *Brah-voh, Mistuh Chahp-lin.*

"They screened *The Great Dictator* for Eleanor and me last night, and it's damn brilliant. You made Hitler look like a pompous dunderhead." *Pahm-pus dun-dah-head.*

From somewhere in the fort, Chaplin caught a voice on a loudspeaker, the words barely discernible: "Artillery range."

"Kind of you to say so, sir," Chaplin replied.

The loudspeaker screeched again, louder this time: "Artillery range, live."

"And congratulations on your re-election, Mr. President," Chaplin continued.

"About that, how would you like to come to Washington and speak at my inauguration dinner in January?"

"Oh. Well. I..." Like the Tramp himself, Chaplin found himself speechless. "I wouldn't know what to say, sir."

"Your monologue at the end of *The Great Dictator* will do nicely. Your plea for democracy, for the end of tyrants and dictators, for the cause of brotherhood among men and nations." Roosevelt paused, then recited Chaplin's words from memory: "'Jew, gentile, black man, white. We all want to help one another. We want to live by each other's happiness, not by each other's misery.' Well said, Mr. Chaplin. Well said, indeed."

"Some of the critics didn't care for my sermonizing."

"To hell with critics! Now, will you come to Washington and speak at my dinner?"

"I'd be honored, Mr. President."

The line went quiet, and all Chaplin could hear was the distant echo of artillery rounds. He knew more was coming from the White House but had no idea what. Finally, FDR spoke again. "Is it true you're friends with Charles Lindbergh?" *Lind-bugh.*

"More like bickering acquaintances. He's naive and given to simple solutions to complex problems. Most of all, he can't see the depth of Hitler's evil."

"It's worse than that, Charlie. *Cholly.* Lindbergh admires Hitler for his ruthless efficiency, for flattening Poland and cowing France into surrender, for subduing Denmark, Norway, Belgium, Luxembourg, and the Netherlands without breaking a sweat. Fact is, Charlie, Lindbergh's either mendacious or simply stupid."

Chaplin thought of Einstein's quip: *The difference between genius and stupidity is that genius has its limits.*

"Lindbergh railed against our swapping fifty obsolete warships to Britain in the Destroyers-for-Bases deal," Roosevelt continued. "He lobbied against Cash-and-Carry, and now that England's running out of gold, he's preparing to assault your homeland's only hope."

Chaplin waited, the President milking the moment for suspense.

"In a few weeks," Roosevelt said in a low, deliberate tone, "I'll be proposing Lend-Lease. It will allow England to borrow ships, aircraft, tanks, and munitions to stave off invasion by the Nazi hordes."

Chaplin understood: Lend-Lease would sidestep the Neutrality Acts handcuffing Roosevelt. "And you think Lindbergh will publicly oppose it?"

"I know it!" Roosevelt boomed, his voice competing with distant explosions. "He says 'America First,' but he means 'Germany First.' Lindbergh has a national radio address planned for next week to oppose Lend-Lease and advocate a neutrality pact with Germany."

In Chaplin's mind, he saw Edward R. Murrow atop a London rooftop, flames licking the night sky. "That would be the end of England, sir."

"Which is why your countrymen need your help."

Chaplin froze. "What can I possibly do?"

"On Saturday, you and Professor Einstein are traveling on the Super Chief from Chicago to Los Angeles."

Chaplin didn't bother asking how Roosevelt knew.

"Lindbergh will be on the train as well," the President continued.

Chaplin wondered...with his wife Anne or one of Lindy's many female admirers? Not that Chaplin held the moral high ground on fidelity. He was just irked that his indiscretions appeared in Hedda Hopper's column while Lindbergh's were hushed up.

"Anne won't be with him," Roosevelt added, as if reading Chaplin's mind. "Which is fine and dandy. They feed off each other's worst instincts."

Chaplin mumbled his agreement. He had read Anne Morrow Lindbergh's bestseller, *The Wave of the Future*, which practically cheered the rise of totalitarianism.

"Charlie, you've gone from London workhouses to becoming one of the richest men in Hollywood," Roosevelt said. "Lindbergh admires self-made men. You won't change his mind about the big picture, but if you could convince him to sit this one out—like Bill Dickey in the second game of a doubleheader—it would be a huge help to your homeland."

Chaplin rubbed his temples. "What makes you think he'd listen to me?"

Roosevelt chuckled. "You're Charlie Chaplin. Your films are testaments to orphans, immigrants, and the working class. You stand for the triumph of kindness and humanity over cruelty and indifference. If Lindbergh won't listen to you, he's a lost cause."

"I'll do my best, sir."

"And maybe get an assist from Professor Einstein. The two of you are a formidable team."

Roosevelt was like a great film director, Chaplin thought, skilled at coaxing the best performances from his cast of characters. After their goodbyes, Chaplin sat for a moment, grappling with the enormity of the task. Lindbergh had spent years convincing America that Roosevelt was a warmonger, that Jews were Bolsheviks, and that Britain was a decadent, dying empire. He painted Germany's conquest of Europe as inevitable—and irrelevant to America.

How do I convince Lindbergh to change his mind or just clam up for a while?

Short of having Mickey Cohen toss him off the train between Albuquerque and Gallup, Chaplin hadn't the faintest idea.

TWENTY
SZILARD'S PROGRESS

Vannevar Bush puffed at his pipe, the faint aroma only deepening Einstein's longing for his confiscated meerschaum. They sat in the windowless office of the National Defense Research Committee's chairman, discussing the work of physicists Leo Szilard and Enrico Fermi at Columbia University—and speculating how far Werner Heisenberg's team had progressed in Berlin.

Bush, a lanky sixty-year-old in rimless glasses and a gray flannel three-piece suit, was an engineer and inventor by training, and the director of the Carnegie Foundation by vocation. Four months earlier, President Roosevelt had appointed him chairman of the newly formed NDRC.

"We know we're behind the Germans," Bush said, his tone measured, "but Szilard's work is giving us real cause for enthusiasm."

Einstein waited for him to elaborate.

Bush glanced left and right, lowering his voice as if Nazi spies might be lurking along the wainscoting. "Combining the work at Columbia and Princeton, Szilard discovered that after two beta-decays, uranium-239 forms plutonium."

Einstein's bushy eyebrows shot up. "Which is likely as fissile as uranium-235."

"So you would agree this is a significant development," Bush said, with the practiced understatement of an academician.

"Indeed. It suggests that the loss of neutrons to resonance absorption in uranium-238 won't be an impediment to criticality, and the uranium-plutonium breeding cycle could convert most of natural uranium to power." Einstein absently patted his jacket where his meerschaum would have been. "It's a major advance."

"And for now, America is alone in this knowledge. Thankfully, the secret hasn't left our shores—though it was a close call."

"I would like to see Szilard's calculations," Einstein said. "Then perhaps I could share an idea or two about his work on a fast neutron breeder reactor."

For the moment, Einstein's scientific curiosity eclipsed his lifelong pacifism. He wasn't thinking of nuclear fission as the precursor to a weapon of unimaginable destruction but as a theoretical puzzle, one to be unraveled by the elegant interplay of physics and mathematics.

"Nothing would please me more, Albert."

Einstein's curiosity was piqued. "Then, over a cup of tea, please tell me more about this 'close call' of yours."

TWENTY-ONE
THE DAMNATION OF FAUST

The sun had sunk to the horizon, casting long shadows over the landscape, and the air carried a November chill. But Fritz Duquesne refused to roll up the window of the Packard. The car still sat five hundred meters from Fort Meade's sentry post, the spy and the assassin waiting in silence for Einstein and Chaplin to emerge.

Duquesne wouldn't show the slightest weakness in front of Schmidt, who lounged in the passenger seat wearing a short-sleeved khaki shirt that showcased his biceps. The assassin, a man of few words, seemed perfectly at ease in the chilly silence, his sniper's world one of solitary surveillance and nondescript quarters. Duquesne, though not naturally loquacious himself, found the quiet oppressive. It took all his restraint to keep from speaking first.

Finally, Schmidt broke the stillness with a single word: "Glasses."

Duquesne handed him the binoculars. Schmidt raised them to his eyes, focusing on the fort's front gate. "Darkness complicates the shot," he said. "Temperature changes, too. And the wind is picking up."

Duquesne made a scoffing sound. "Up close with a Luger erases those concerns."

"But snarls the getaway. Particularly at a railroad station."

"Not if you've planned your escape with two alternatives."

"Don't tell me my job, *alter Sack.*"

Old sack? The impertinence! The sheer arrogance!

"Fine, Schmidt. You do your job, and I'll do mine."

A sudden chill crept into Duquesne's bones. He turned the ignition key, pulled out the choke, punched the starter button, and depressed the clutch while giving it a little gas with the gearshift in neutral. As the engine growled to life, he gradually eased the choke in, then turned on the heater fan and the radio. Edward R. Murrow's calm, steady voice filled the cabin, accompanied by the distant wail of air-raid sirens.

"Once I saw *The Damnation of Faust* performed in the open air at Salzburg," Murrow was saying. "London reminds me of that tonight, though the stage is so much larger. Earlier, an anti-aircraft battery fired just as I drove past. The hot wind lifted me from my seat. The streets of London now resemble a ghost town in Nevada—not a soul to be seen."

Schmidt reached over and snapped the radio off. "I don't need to hear an American weeping for his British friends."

"Whereas I enjoy hearing of our triumphs over the Tommies," Duquesne said.

"Hah. All we do is burn down a row of flats, kill a few old ladies. Göring brags about his Heinkel bombers, but they never hit munitions factories or aircraft plants. This war will be won by men on the ground with rifles. As it always has been, and as it always will be."

The young fool, Duquesne thought. Clueless about strategic aerial bombardment, let alone the potential of atomic bombs. And while Duquesne hated to agree with anything Winston Churchill said, didn't the old lush complain that generals were always fighting the last war? The French and their Maginot Line—deftly sidestepped by the Germans—were proof of that particular bloody pudding.

"As for you," Schmidt said, "skulking about, stealing scraps of supposed enemy intelligence, most of it useless, some of it outright misinformation. Thirty aliases, isn't it? Boris Zakrevsky. Piet Niacud. Colonel Beza. And your tradecraft? Deceit, trickery, lies. It's almost...what is the word...*weibisch*. Feminine." Schmidt's laugh was the growl of a Doberman Pinscher. "In Berlin, they make sport of you, say you're nothing but a poseur."

Duquesne's jaw clenched so tightly his muscles danced. "Herr Schmidt," he said, voice taut, "I killed men before you were born—and close enough to feel their final breaths." He tilted his chin toward the man, their faces inches apart. The threat was unspoken but unmistakable.

"If you sneak up on me while I slumber," Schmidt sneered, "your creaking bones will wake me, and I'll slit your throat with the Nahkampfmesser that sleeps beside me."

Referring to a wood-handled combat knife, Duquesne knew.

"Such big talk, Schmidt," the old spy said, voice icy.

Twenty years ago, I'd have jammed a Luger into your mouth, shattered your teeth, and splattered your brains across the uphol-stery.

He killed the engine. The two men sat in a silence that deepened as the darkness wrapped around them like a suffocating shroud, and the cold night seeped in.

Schmidt's mockery had left a mark.

Am I a laughingstock in the Reich's highest circles?

The microfilm debacle had done him no favors. Schmidt's insolence, though infuriating, served as a sharp reminder:

Duquesne needed to redeem himself. Kidnaping Einstein and delivering him to Germany took on even greater importance.

As he often did, Duquesne visualized the mission, step by step. Then his thoughts veered off course, like a locomotive onto a side spur. He imagined Einstein shackled in his seat on the seaplane to Havana. Across the aisle sat Schmidt, tipsy from *Kornschnapps,* boasting of his perfect shot that felled Chaplin. When the sniper closed his eyes, lost in dreams of Cuba's *putas*, Duquesne would signal Berlin Bruno who would crush the *arschloch*'s skull with a lead-filled sap.

Oh, the delicious cr–a–ck!

They'd open the aft door and toss Schmidt's limp body out, watching his arms flail and legs churn before the ocean swallowed him whole.

A delicious fantasy. But would he do it?

Oh, yes. And enjoy every moment.

TWENTY-TWO
ALL THE BLINTZES IN BROOKLYN

After an hour poring over Szilard's calculations, Einstein told Vannevar Bush that he was very encouraged with the progress being made at Columbia University. He then reviewed reports from Princeton, the University of Chicago, Berkeley, and Caltech, and the importance of the NDRC—its very *raison d'être*—dawned on him.

Harmonious cooperation. Coordinating teams of physicists and chemists and engineers so that their collective work was greater than the sum of their individual efforts.

Bush invited Einstein into the conference room where the Committee was gathered. The members resembled portraits from the walls of a Philadelphia country club: old white men in gray three-piece suits. There was the president of MIT, the president of Harvard, the head of Bell Telephone Laboratories. A rear admiral, a brigadier general, the Commissioner of Patents, a Caltech physics professor—and another visitor, Major Groves.

Groves unpacked his briefcase and launched into a presentation. "When a full-fledged atomic bomb project begins in earnest, we'll need dozens—no, hundreds—more scientists.

Women are a tremendous untapped resource, and we need to bring them into the fold." A few Committee members grumbled, but no one raised a discernible objection.

Groves began listing names. "Leona Woods, a young physicist working with Fermi at the University of Chicago."

Einstein nodded.

"Maria Goeppert Mayer, a Columbia physicist who fled Hitler."

"Brilliant," Einstein said. "An expert on double beta decay."

Groves flipped a page in his notes. "Lise Meitner. Discovered protactinium-231. Eighteen months ago, she replicated nuclear fission in her lab."

"The German Marie Curie," Einstein said. "But I've spoken with Lise, and she refuses to work on anything connected to nuclear weapons."

Murmurs rippled around the table, but Groves continued for several more minutes, highlighting women scientists. As the afternoon waned, the Committee adjourned for a break.

Bush introduced Einstein to a woman seated at her desk outside the room, fingers clacking her typewriter's keyboard. "Professor, this is Hannah Spears. She was my secretary at MIT before joining me here."

"Very pleased to meet you, Miss Spears," Einstein said.

"*Guten Tag, Herr* Einstein." *Ein-shtein.*

"I did not expect to hear German spoken inside these walls," Einstein said, chuckling.

"I was born in Zurich and grew up speaking French, German, and a little Italian," Hannah Spears said. "Please forgive me for continuing to type. I like to transcribe while my memory is fresh."

Einstein raised an eyebrow. Her shorthand pad lay open, the notes intact. So why the hurry? He studied her: forties, blond hair streaked with gray and pulled into a neat bun. She wore a pinstriped charcoal dress and rimless spectacles, fitting seamlessly into the Committee's conservative aesthetic.

"A beautiful city, Zurich," Einstein said. "I studied at the Federal Polytechnic there."

"You must have been an extraordinary student."

"*Ach*, as a student, I was no Einstein."

Hannah chuckled at that, and Bush said, "A late bloomer, but what a bouquet."

Einstein said, "Which neighborhood was yours, Hannah?"

"Center city," she replied.

"Lovely." Einstein noticed that she was still typing without consulting her shorthand pad, but rather maintaining eye contact with him. "Whenever I had a few francs," he continued, "I'd visit a tavern across the street from Grossmünster Church. Cheap beer, fat sausages, and the rowdiest students."

"Oh, how I wanted to go," Hannah said, smiling wistfully, "but my father said it was not a place for a young lady."

"Quite right, now that I think about it. And what did your father do?"

"He owned an amusement park."

"What fun it must have been for you as a child," Einstein said.

Hannah stopped typing. "When I was in my teens, I worked all the rides and sideshows, but my father was afraid I would run off with a midway barker or roustabout, so he sent me to a British finishing school to learn English and manners."

"You succeeded on both counts," Einstein said.

Bush beamed with pride as Hannah resumed typing. Her eyes flashed to her notepad and back again quickly.

"Hannah translates our German documents," Bush said. "Some of our émigré scientists still write in German, and once in a while, our allies come up with a document from Kaiser Wilhelm Institute. The Norwegians seem particularly good at espionage on our behalf."

"Those are the exciting moments," Hannah said. "Usually, I just take notes of the meetings and transcribe them."

"Hannah was working the projector during Szilard's presentation," Bush said, "so you can imagine the War Department investigators and the Military Police gave her the third degree."

"It was quite harrowing to be suspected of treason, for goodness sake!" she said.

"And ridiculous!" Bush said. "Hannah took no notes, and as I told you, I destroyed the slides immediately after the presentation. How a nearly verbatim transcript appeared on microfilm in the hands of a spy is a baffling mystery."

Hannah flipped several pages of her shorthand pad, as if skipping them, and continued typing. Einstein processed the information, came to his conclusion, and wondered just how to break the news to Vannevar Bush.

Ten minutes later, Einstein was back in Bush's office enjoying tea and scones when he posited his theory. Bush's teacup stopped halfway to his lips and his look was incredulous. "Albert, are you saying Hannah is German and not Swiss?" Bush asked.

"Not at all. Her English is accented in a way consistent with that of the Swiss whose first language is German. I spent enough time in Bern and Geneva to recognize that."

"Then what? Her father didn't own an amusement park but was a German spy?"

"The two are not mutually exclusive. I venture to say that he did own such a park and that Hannah indeed worked there but did not disclose the sideshow she worked on."

"Sideshow? Please, Albert. You're speaking in riddles."

"Let's start with this. That tavern I mentioned across from Grossmünster Church—the one she wanted to patronize—doesn't exist."

"A trifling thing. Perhaps Hannah didn't want to admit she was unaware of a tavern in her neighborhood."

"Of greater importance, she typed up her notes from Major Groves' presentation today from memory, only pretending to consult her pad while keeping eye contact with me."

"Blast it, Albert," Bush said, annoyed. "A good memory is an excellent attribute for a secretary."

"My theory is that Hannah, when she got home after Szilard's presentation, typed nearly verbatim the information on the slides, except of course the lines that had been obliterated by the blown bulb."

"You're suggesting she has a photographic memory?" Bush asked, incredulous.

"Eidetic memory," Einstein corrected. "Very rare, but trainable. I would bet all the blintzes in Brooklyn that Hannah recalls in vivid detail visual images and documents that she has only seen briefly, and that she discovered her talent at a young age."

"How? Where?"

"A memory sideshow at her father's amusement park. No tricks or sleight of hand. Fifty or so people write their names on a tablet, and after only a few seconds of studying, with music and fanfare, the performer calls the names in perfect order. My guess is that Hannah realized she was better at it than the sideshow performer and took over the job. If her father was a Nazi sympathizer, she was likely sent to Hamburg to train with intelligence agents at Abwehr."

Bush's face darkened. "If you're right, she's an ongoing threat. We need to have the Army lock her up."

"Or," Einstein said, "bring Major Groves into the conversation. He may want you to keep Hannah close. Feed her fabricated reports. Disinformation to mislead the Reich."

Einstein didn't elaborate, but the meaning was clear. What would have been an intelligence disaster had the Nazi courier not been arrested could yet be turned into a triumph of counter-espionage.

TWENTY-THREE
THE SPY'S SECOND MISSION

Reinhard Schmidt retrieved the leather case from the luggage trunk and slid into the passenger seat next to Fritz Duquesne, whose eyes remained fixed on the sentry station at the entrance to Fort Meade. Schmidt opened the case and carefully assembled his prized Karabiner 98, fastening the two-piece stock, inserting the barrel, and tightening the band. He had one hand on the bolt assembly when Duquesne, brow furrowed, broke his silence.

"What the hell are you doing, Schmidt?"

"You've spent too long sitting on park benches feeding pigeons," the SS assassin said, his voice dripping with condescension.

Go ahead. Insult me all you want. My memory is long, my vengeance swift.

"This is a rifle," Schmidt said, a schoolmaster explaining a crayon to a child.

"I can see that. Why now? Why here?"

Schmidt picked up an mm Mauser cartridge, rolling it between his fingers as though communing with it.

Putting on a show, Duquesne thought. *Flaunting his supposed expertise, as if he can tell one cartridge from another.*

"The spotlights at the sentry station guarantee I can see my target." Schmidt nodded toward the fort. "But I can't be sure of the lighting at the train station. And if it's Union Station, with all the congressmen and dignitaries, it will be crawling with police."

"Look around you," Duquesne snapped. "There are ten thousand soldiers within spitting distance. Don't even think about taking your shot here."

"I have full authority of the Schutzstaffel to alter plans as required."

"Einstein and Chaplin will be coming out in a jeep, same as they went in. If you shoot Chaplin, a dozen MPs will blanket Einstein and haul him back into the fort."

"Chaplin's death is Schutzstaffel's highest priority."

"And kidnaping Einstein is Abwehr's highest priority."

"Reichsführer Himmler will not step aside for Canaris' *umhang und dolch,* cloak and dagger games, which frankly carry the whiff of melodrama."

So that's it! The longstanding feud between Admiral Canaris, a true military man, and Heinrich Himmler, a true weasel, has come to a head.

Three years earlier, Himmler's thugs broke into Abwehr headquarters, purloined secret files related to German-Soviet military cooperation, and torched the building. Himmler made no secret of his desire to wrest control of counterintelligence from Canaris.

Political infighting will be the death of the Reich!

"I will kill Chaplin," Schmidt declared, his tone final. "Then you can do as you please."

"*Gott verdammt!* What do you think the soldiers will do after you fire? Sing campfire songs?"

"Peacetime soldiers!" Schmidt spat the words. "Confusion will reign. I'll take out the highest ranking officer I see through the scope. Probably the one who escorted the two of them inside. You'll have time to pull forward and snatch the Jew scientist, then drive away. You know how to do a U-turn and a power slide, don't you Frederick Fredericks?"

Taunting me with one of my aliases, his sarcastic tone dipped in poison.

"Or if the gunfire frightens you," Schmidt said, not letting up, "drive off and wait for another day."

"I'm not your getaway driver or your valet."

"Alas, today you are both if you're nimble enough not to be captured or killed."

The impudence! The lack of respect! So typical of the SS. What haughty fools! Hitler's personal vendetta, fueled by Himmler, taking precedence over an earth-shattering espionage coup.

Just ask Werner Heisenberg if he'd like to add Einstein to his team at Uranverein.

Duquesne's thoughts churned as he considered the motives of the rat-faced Himmler. It struck him then. It wasn't enough just for the SS's mission to succeed.

Abwehr's must fail!

Bringing Einstein to Berlin would polish Admiral Canaris' image, something Himmler could not abide. If the bloodless bastard could not claim credit for such a triumphant operation, he would sabotage it!

Schmidt's goal was to malign Admiral Canaris' reputation beyond repair and to dismantle Abwehr so that Himmler could usurp counterintelligence, sabotage, and espionage for himself.

A chill crept down Duquesne's spine as he considered just what that would entail.

Schmidt's mission isn't just to assassinate Chaplin. It's also to kill me.

TWENTY-FOUR
TO PERSUADE A MOLLUSK

Chaplin was delighted to learn that Einstein was giving advice to the NDRC and amazed that he had just scored a counterintelligence victory, figuring out the source of the leak. The old genius still had what it took. At the same time, Chaplin felt inadequate. His homeland was bombed nightly, civilians incinerated in their homes or buried in the rubble of direct hits on underground stations.

My wealth and celebrity are meaningless if I cannot help my countrymen survive. But the more he thought about, the more daunting the task assigned by the President. *I'm an actor and writer and director...not a statesman or debater.*

Lindbergh's views were as rigid as reinforced concrete, bolstered by a pigheadedness Chaplin couldn't imagine cracking.

These thoughts played in Chaplin's mind as he rode in a jeep with Einstein from the NDRC building to the front gate. It was a chilly night, all the more so in the open vehicle. The Rolls limo awaited to take them to Union Station in D.C., where they'd board the Capitol Limited, the overnight train to Pittsburgh, then onward to Chicago. After that, the second Einstein-Oppenheimer debate, followed by a forty-hour journey on the Santa Fe Super Chief to Los Angeles.

Forty hours to put a dent in Lindbergh's bullheaded certitude.

Major Groves drove in a mini-convoy, one jeep in front of them and one behind, each manned by four MPs carrying sidearms. "So Major, while I was shooting the breeze and losing at pinochle to a couple of bored enlisted men," Chaplin said, "Albert revolutionizes your atomic bomb program and catches a Nazi spy."

"I revolutionized nothing," Einstein corrected him. "I recognized the ingenuity of Szilard's work, and I have an idea for him, which may or may not be useful."

"But the Professor *did* uncover the spy," Major Groves said. "Army Intelligence is searching her apartment as we speak and has already uncovered incriminating evidence."

Chaplin clapped his friend on the shoulder. "I'm so proud of you, Albert."

Groves said, "The Secretary of War will decide whether to lock up Hannah Spears or get her to work as a double, knowingly or not, to feed disinformation to Berlin."

"Albert makes me feel so irrelevant," Chaplin said. "I've done nothing for England's survival."

"You're too hard on yourself, Charlie," Einstein said. "You've given money. You've supported the Eagle Squadron."

Chaplin shook his head. "A couple months ago, I heard Churchill on the wireless. 'Never in the field of human conflict was so much owed by so many to so few.'"

"Saluting the brave lads of the RAF," Groves said.

"Since the Blitz began, I've been thinking that I'm one of the many doing so damn little."

"You're not suggesting you fly a Spitfire against the Luftwaffe," Einstein said.

"Actually," Groves said, "I believe Mr. Chaplin has some news to share with us."

Chaplin was startled. "You *know*! You know the President called me."

Groves smiled but said nothing.

"*Nu*, Charlie? FDR called you?" Einstein asked in wonderment.

The convoy slowed as a line of olive-green trucks emblazoned with white stars rumbled past, their cargo beds stacked with heavy ammo crates. The acrid smell of gasoline and motor oil filled the air, punctuated by the distant crackle of rifle fire.

"Hold on," Chaplin said, his suspicion rising. "This was your idea, wasn't it, Major? This impossible assignment?"

Still, Groves was silent.

"What are you two talking about and not talking about?" Einstein asked.

As the jeeps started moving again, Chaplin relayed his conversation with FDR. There was work to do on the train, both for him and for Einstein.

"I'll help any way I can with that *momzer* Lindbergh," Einstein said, using the Yiddish term for "scoundrel" or "bastard."

Chaplin turned to Groves. "Albert's peeved because he sent Lindbergh the letter about beefing up an atomic bomb research program, asking him to deliver it to FDR, and the grease monkey didn't do it and never replied."

"Were you unaware of his politics?" Groves asked.

"Foolish of me," Einstein admitted. "I thought his patriotism might trump his isolationism. Turns out Lindbergh has the intellectual velocity of a mollusk—and that might be an insult to mollusks."

The three jeeps slowed again, this time to allow half-a-dozen open trucks to pass. Their cargo was human, the first draftees under the new Selective Training and Service Act. The young men were still in civvies, hair not yet shorn, eyes darting to and fro, nervous as caged chickens on the way to the slaughterhouse.

"This will be a most interesting train ride," Einstein said.

"Your compartments will be in the same car as Lindbergh's," Groves said, "and there's something else I need you to do."

Chaplin cracked a grin. "Listen for heavy breathing if Lindy gets lucky and picks up a chippy at the stop in Dodge City?"

"Not far off the mark. Pay attention to all his visitors, especially chippies. Keep an eye on the club lounge. See who he drinks with or plays cards with, and certainly note any guests to his compartment."

"I think I follow you," Chaplin said.

"Do you think you can operate a miniature camera the boys in Army Intelligence have put together?"

"I can operate any camera on Earth," Chaplin said.

"Major, you think Lindbergh is consorting with German spies?" Einstein asked, puzzled.

"It's unlikely, Professor."

"Then why would we be watching and listening and photographing if—"

Chaplin interrupted him. "You don't get it, Albert. If we can't get through to Lindbergh with our powers of persuasion, Major Groves is going to play hardball."

"Now I am really lost."

"Sharp elbows," Chaplin said. "Get down and dirty. Hit below the belt."

"Charlie, could you be more specific?"

Chaplin gave a knowing look. He enjoyed a plot with intrigue. "Albert, the Major won't say it, but we're looking for a particular woman. Knowing Lindy, she's a tall, svelte blonde in her thirties, perhaps with a German accent."

Groves allowed himself a small chuckle. "Nice work, Mr. Chaplin, though sometimes she affects a French accent, just for variety."

"I don't understand," Einstein said. "How do you two know about this woman?"

"Just guesswork on my part," Chaplin said, "but I suspect the Major has more detailed information."

"Army Intelligence kept tabs on Lindbergh on his visits to Germany," Groves said. "He's involved with several women, two of them sisters."

"Goodness," Einstein said. "But how can you use such personal matters?"

Groves wouldn't answer, so Chaplin did. "Albert. If we can't persuade Lindbergh to back down, Major Groves wants to blackmail him."

Einstein harrumphed and said, "That's so unsavory. Charlie, how can you be a party to such a thing?"

"Please don't lecture me, old friend," Chaplin fired back. "The Germans indiscriminately slaughter women and children. What they're doing is inhumane and barbaric. I can live with 'unsavory.'"

TWENTY-FIVE
WHEN TO FIGHT AND WHEN TO TAKE FLIGHT

Fritz Duquesne wondered if paranoia had convinced him that Himmler had dispatched Reinhard Schmidt to kill him.

Am I inflating my significance to a level bordering on delusion?

Still, prudence demanded preparation. His left hand brushed his right forearm, just below the elbow, confirming the spring-loaded sleeve-blade hidden beneath his shirt. A sharp snap of his arm at a forty-five-degree angle would unleash the stiletto into his waiting palm. Lethal efficiency at a moment's notice. But here, in the Packard's claustrophobic front seat, would it even work? Schmidt was younger, stronger.

Would he disarm me and carve his initials into my neck before I could strike?

The evening chill seeped through the Packard, and the straight-eight engine thrummed in neutral, the heater fan showering them with oily air from the engine compartment. Both men kept their eyes on the sentry station at the fort's front gate. Nearby, the Rolls-Royce limousine sat parked, its chrome grille gleaming faintly in the mist. Duquesne spotted the short man in the suit—the one who had thrashed the Bund goons at the Waldorf and reappeared with Chaplin and Einstein at the diner. A human terrier, bristling with aggression.

Through binoculars, Duquesne scanned the scene. The little man was showing something to three MPs. Duquesne shifted his view and picked up the chauffeur leaning against the front fender of the limo, smoking a cigarette, and a young woman, a redhead, chatting with two soldiers off to one side. She had been with the bodyguard in the lobby of the Waldorf.

Movement at the front gate drew Duquesne's attention. The barrier arm lifted, and three jeeps rolled out of the fort, stopping just beyond the gate. The first carried four soldiers, the second an officer driving Chaplin and Einstein, and the third another four soldiers.

"What the hell is this, the American Expeditionary Force?" Duquesne said.

"Afraid, master spy?" Schmidt taunted him.

"I've stayed alive for forty years knowing when to fight and when to take flight," Duquesne snapped. "Only a fool shoots here."

"*Halt den Mund!*" Schmidt barked, commanding Duquesne to shut up. That's it. Duquesne's thoughts blazed like fire through dry brush.

It's not paranoia! Schmidt wouldn't dare treat me this way if I lived to report his conduct to Berlin. He's going to shoot Chaplin—then turn the rifle on me.

Duquesne cursed himself for leaving his Luger in the glove box. He had been in tight spots before and had always escaped. Now he considered all possibilities, from a preemptive attack to a hasty retreat.

Calm. Stay calm and think!

Through the evening mist, Duquesne watched Chaplin and Einstein alight from the jeep and speak to the officer who had driven them out of the fort. Perhaps saying their good-byes.

Duquesne had only seconds to conceive a plan and execute it.

The Luger! Did I lock the glove box?

He couldn't remember.

Schmidt quickly exited the passenger door, carrying his Karabiner. Resting his left elbow on the hood, he raised the weapon, the stock snug against his shoulder, and sighted through the scope. Duquesne considered the glove box. Schmidt would sense his movement if he fumbled for the Luger. He needed another option.

He raised the binoculars and saw the chauffeur toss away his cigarette and open the rear door, but his two famous passengers made no movement to enter the limo. The bodyguard was still talking to the small circle of soldiers.

Schmidt drew back the bolt and slammed it forward to strip a cartridge from the magazine and into the chamber.

Chaplin turned and was facing the Packard. A stationery target.

"Clear shot at Chaplin as soon as the officer moves," Schmidt said, his voice cold and mechanical.

Insanity, Duquesne thought, envisioning the MPs roaring toward them in jeeps, weapons firing.

"Turn off the engine," Schmidt ordered from his perch outside the car. Duquesne did nothing.

"*Gottverdammt*! Kill the engine! The bonnet's hopping like a jumping bean."

With the clutch depressed, Duquesne gunned the accelerator, the straight-eight roaring like an oncoming storm, the big Packard trembling. Then he clicked on the radio. Comedian Jack Benny was wisecracking with the announcer on *The Jell-O Program.*

"*Give me golf clubs, fresh air, and a beautiful partner,*" Benny's voice crackled, "*and you can keep the golf clubs and fresh air.*"

"The engine!" Schmidt yelled. "Turn it off."

Duquesne cranked up the volume on the radio.

"Two men are in a bar," Benny continued. *"One says to the other, 'Do you know what I got for my wife yesterday?'"*

"No, what did you get for your wife?" the announcer asked.

Schmidt banged a fist on the hood. "Do it!"

"I got a poodle," Benny answered.

"I wish I could make a trade like that," the announcer dead-panned.

Laughter came from the radio, and Duquesne smiled through the windshield at Schmidt.

Enraged, Schmidt leaned into the open passenger window, his rifle in one hand. *"Arschloch!"* Turn off the—"

Duquesne jammed the shift into first gear and floored the accelerator. The Packard shot forward, the window pillar slamming into Schmidt's left temple with a bone-jarring thud. Duquesne threw the car into reverse, the Packard lurching backward, and the front pillar smashed into the right side of Schmidt's skull. The assassin crumpled to the ground, his rifle discharging skyward, the gunshot echoing like a cannon blast in the cold night air.

Duquesne shifted back into first gear and muscled the steering wheel hard to the right. The four-thousand-pound Packard surged ahead, its tires crunching over Schmidt's midsection with a grotesque finality. If the man screamed, Duquesne could not hear him over the laughter and applause on the radio.

Behind him, the Ford pickup with its faux service station lettering roared to life. Berlin Bruno and the so-called mechanic, both loyal to Duquesne, fell into formation. They would support whatever story he chose to spin about Reinhard Schmidt's unfortunate demise. The Packard and the Ford executed tight U-turns, their engines roaring as they sped away from the fort and into the darkness.

No one mistook the sound for a backfiring car or a cherry bomb tossed by some young hooligan. To soldiers accustomed to the crack of rifle fire on the range, the gunshot was unmistakable.

A soldier shouted "Incoming!" Major Groves threw his arms around Einstein, shielding the scientist and turning him away from the direction of the sound. Chaplin dropped into a crouch, poised like a wrestler about to tangle with an opponent. The MPs drew their sidearms in unison.

Cohen had been demonstrating his newly purchased "Ye Atom Smasher" crossbow to three soldiers. The handsome weapon with its walnut stock and metal trigger was capable of piercing a Manhattan phone directory from A to Z. Cohen wheeled around, instincts honed by years of close calls, and spotted the Packard screeching into a turn. He raised the crossbow and fired from the hip, the motion as smooth and natural as wielding a "Chicago typewriter," the tommy gun of his past.

The steel spring uncoiled with the speed of a striking viper, the bowstring snapping in a sharp *thwip*. The arrow arced upward, soaring to its apex before gravity asserted itself—just ask Einstein—and sent it plunging in a graceful parabolic curve toward the Packard.

The arrow whistled through the open passenger window and *thowmped* into the tan leather upholstery six inches from Duquesne's right thigh. He flinched, staring in disbelief at the vibrating shaft, which wagged back and forth like a schoolmarm's admonishing finger.

In his decades as a soldier and spy, Duquesne had been shot at by rifles, pistols, and cannons. He had dodged hand grenades, hatchets, and sticks of dynamite. But an arrow? Never. Letting out a long, relieved breath, he laughed—an almost unhinged sound.

Duquesne shifted into third gear and hit the accelerator, the Ford pickup close behind. North into Pennsylvania, that was the plan. As always, he had escape routes memorized for when missions derailed. He knew every highway and byway, every promising turnoff in the unfamiliar terrain. A motor lodge outside Gettysburg came to mind. Safe, discreet, isolated. He could rest there for the night and continue west to Chicago on Route 30, the Lincoln Highway, in the morning. The thought struck a chord.

Gettysburg and Lincoln.

Two enduring lessons from Cemetery Ridge and Ford's Theatre: Stake out the high ground, and always watch your back.

In two days, Einstein would be in Chicago for another of his debates with Oppenheimer. There would be ample opportunity to snatch the old scientist, and now there was one less complication: no Reinhard Schmidt to interfere.

TWENTY-SIX
THE IRON BROOM
Thursday, November 7, 1940

"I would have preferred Wilkie over Roosevelt, but I'm not fulminating about it," J. Edgar Hoover said. "Neither one has the balls to meddle in Bureau business."

"FDR has to know that you have the goods on him and Lucy Mercer," Clyde Tolson said.

"Of course he does. Not that I blame him for fooling around. Eleanor's a parlor pinko with a big ass and a bigger mouth."

"Still, I didn't think the cripple would win in a landslide," Tolson said.

Hoover and his associate director, both gray-suited and severe, were in a small conference room in FBI headquarters. The Director was purposely keeping Agent Brian Sullivan and his female assistant waiting to show irritation with them. After several minutes, Hoover jabbed a button on the intercom. "Mabel, tell that tall drink of water to haul his Irish ass in here. The woman, too."

Milagros Vazquez felt invisible. Twelve minutes into the meeting, neither Hoover nor Tolson had acknowledged her presence. No greeting, no smile, not even a glance. Brian Sullivan, bless him, used the inclusive "we" when discussing their assignment and even praised her performance at Fort Meade.

"Miss Vazquez knew that Major Groves spoke Spanish, and she cleverly used his experience in Nicaragua to make a point," Sullivan said.

"So what?" Hoover shot back. "We're judged on results, not effort. And this was your responsibility Sullivan, not hers. Your job was to keep Einstein out of Fort Meade, and you failed."

The Director would rather have a spy case unsolved than let others get the credit, Vazquez thought.

She had read the non-classified portions of the Einstein file. There was no evidence of disloyalty. Quite the opposite— Einstein seemed to love America for its freedoms. The Bureau had investigated his late wife Elsa and found nothing suspicious. The same went for his son Hans, an engineer working for the U.S. Department of Agriculture in South Carolina.

Hoover kept grilling Sullivan and ignoring her. She felt like the ghost in that Cary Grant movie, *Topper.* Maybe it's my outfit, she thought. A brown wool jacket with padded shoulders and a cinched waist matched the walnut conference table almost too well. But in her heart, Millie Vazquez knew that she was invisible because she was a woman and Hispanic to boot.

Hoover's disdainful voice broke her thoughts. "Albert Einstein enchants an audience of so-called intelligentsia at Princeton, takes the time to vote, travels to Fort Meade and uncovers a Nazi spy? Is that your report, Agent Sullivan?"

"All in a day's work." Sullivan aimed for humor, but Hoover's face remained granite.

"Who'd he vote for?" Tolson asked. "Norman Thomas, the socialist, or Earl Browder, the communist?"

"I wouldn't know, sir," Sullivan said, fiddling with his tie. "I was stationed outside the polling place."

Minutes dragged by as Tolson skimmed Sullivan's report on the NDRC security breach. When he finished, he sighed. "Jesus H. Christmas."

"What's the bee in your bonnet, Clyde?" Hoover asked.

"The Bureau vetted Hannah Spears for the NDRC and found zilch. Then, in fifteen minutes, Einstein nails her as a spy."

Hoover grumbled like an unhappy bulldog. "What muttonhead cleared her?"

"Special Agent McNutt," Sullivan said, quickly adding, "from the D.C. office."

Hoover grumbled louder. Tolson thumbed a few pages and said, "Thirty-one years old, finance degree from Rutgers. His father's a Republican congressman from New Jersey. Family's Episcopalian."

"Suitably raised, suitably educated," Hoover said.

Suitably short, Sullivan thought. He had debriefed the unfortunate Malcolm McNutt who was about five-feet-six when the interview began and seemed to shrink with each line of questioning.

McNutt had been distraught, apologizing profusely for giving Spears security clearance without digging deeper. He'd confirmed her father owned an amusement park in Switzerland but failed to discover that he was an outspoken member of the National Front, a pro-fascist political party.

Tolson summarized grimly: "Her father wrote glowing articles about Hitler for *Der Eiserne Besen*."

"Translation!" Hoover barked.

"The Iron Broom," Milagros Vazquez said.

Hoover finally looked at her. "You speak German, too?"

"*Ein bisschen*. A little, sir, from high school courses."

Hoover mumbled an acknowledgment.

Tolson said, "Hannah Spears' father wrote under his actual name, which makes the intelligence failure even more grievous."

Sullivan kept quiet, but he thought McNutt's report the single most appalling error he had witnessed inside FBI headquarters.

The Federal Bureau of Investigation is supposed to stand for Fidelity, Bravery, and Integrity. But with politics, cronyism and chicanery, was it becoming the Fiefdom of Buffoons and Incompetents?

Thumbing through Sullivan's report, Tolson summarized what Agent McNutt missed: While Hannah Spears wasn't listed as a member of the fascist party, she attended meetings, handed out flyers, and typed her father's articles. She also worked a ticket booth and drove a miniature train at her father's amusement park. Then at age fifteen, wearing the embroidered silk tunic and fake-jeweled turban of an Indian maharani, she performed in a sideshow as *Fräulein Gedächtnis*, Miss Memory.

"Is it possible this is some commie trick?" Hoover asked. "An insidious plan to set up this Spears girl and blame the Reich for the security leak?"

"I don't see how, sir," Sullivan said. "There's a two-year gap in Hannah Spears' personal history, and Army Intelligence believes she spent the time at Abwehr in Hamburg undergoing advanced memory training."

"Army Intelligence!" Hoover spat the words. "Clowns."

Yeah, except they're the ones who pounced on the courier and stopped Szilard's report from making its way to Berlin!

"Sullivan, where would you least want to be assigned, Butte or Bismarck?" Hoover said.

Oh shit! Am I taking the fall for this?

"I wouldn't know, sir," Sullivan said. "I've never been west of Cleveland."

"Butte's higher and colder and gets more snow," Tolson chimed in.

Hoover slammed an open palm on the conference table. "Enough said. Clyde, re-assign this McNutt to Butte. Give him a pair of snowshoes as a going-away present."

Sullivan let out a long sigh of relief.

"So where are Einstein and Chaplin headed after this dog and pony show they're doing in Chicago?" Hoover asked.

"Back to Los Angeles on the Santa Fe Super Chief," Sullivan said.

"The lap of luxury," Tolson said.

"Pack your bags, Agent Sullivan," Hoover said. "Report on everyone Einstein meets from the moment you leave Dearborn Station until you arrive in Los Angeles. And don't run up a bar tab in the lounge car." Chewing over a thought, he turned to Tolson. "Clyde, how close does the Super Chief get to Mexico?"

"Albuquerque," Tolson said. "Maybe three hundred miles from the border."

"Sounds about right."

Hoover turned to Sullivan. "We've had reports that some of Trotsky's people have been crossing into the States since the assassination."

It had been less than three months since Joseph Stalin had an NKVD agent chop Leon Trotsky to death with an axe near Mexico City, Sullivan knew. An intramural communist squabble. But he had no idea where Hoover was going with this. "Internationalists," Hoover said sharply. "Like Einstein."

"Sir?" Sullivan said.

Did Hoover just equate Einstein, an avowed pacifist, with Trotskyites who preached international revolution?

"Keep your eyes on Chaplin, too," the Director said. "He's not a citizen, and if he consorts with subversives, we'll deport him to his beloved England. Let him dodge the Luftwaffe's bombs."

Sullivan gritted his teeth and forced himself to remain silent.

"Take the young lady with you," Hoover continued, likely not knowing Milagros Vazquez's name. "See who comes aboard in Albuquerque speaking Spanish. If they contact Einstein, get photos and ID's."

"Our cover, sir?" Sullivan asked.

"Married couple."

Sullivan and Vazquez exchanged glances. Worried glances. One of them had to speak up. "And the accommodations, Mr. Hoover?" Vazquez said. "On the train."

"Oh, right. Well, you can't have two single roomettes if you're married. A two-bedroom suite should do. You'll figure out how to use the bathroom."

Tolson chuckled. "Like Clark Gable and Claudette Colbert in *It Happened One Night*."

With not the slightest glimmer of a smile, Hoover ended the meeting with a brusque, "But no monkey business."

TWENTY-SEVEN
GO WEST, OLD SPY

In the morning, over a diner breakfast of flapjacks and coffee, Duquesne asked the waitress where to pick up Route 30 to drive west. She wiped her hands on her apron and said if you're going as far as Pittsburgh, take the new Pennsylvania Turnpike that had opened five weeks earlier.

"Why go through every podunk town in P-A when you can cruise at seventy halfway across the state?"

Taking her advice, Duquesne drove north to Carlisle under a gunmetal gray sky, then merged onto the smooth, modern turnpike. The limited-access roadway stretched ahead like a ribbon of promise, ending twenty miles southeast of Pittsburgh. From there, the Lincoln Highway would take him straight to Chicago.

As he drove, he thought about the helpful waitress.

The Yanks are a friendly people, and they don't want to fight another European war.

The problem was FDR, who was ordering hundreds of millions of dollars of new aircraft and naval vessels. Itching to rescue his pal Churchill who could give a rousing speech but didn't have the men or materiel to withstand a German land invasion. The *Hakenkreuzflagge* would be flying over the Palace of Westminster by summer of next year...unless Hitler's idiotic advisers, including his Swiss astrologer, tell him to attack the Soviet Union instead.

Duquesne turned on the radio and was greeted with the lively pulse of Glenn Miller's *In the Mood*. An invigorating tune. How regrettable that the Reich scorned American jazz a s*entartete Musik*, "degenerate music."

Had Hitler ever heard Miller's trombone glide across those velvet waves? Of course not. The Philistine Führer, accustomed to the garish and gaudy, likely found the Mona Lisa's enigmatic smile insufficiently grandiose.

Ride of the Valkyries. That was Hitler's speed. The stormy clash of brass and timpani, conjuring celestial warriors barreling through tempestuous clouds. An anthem for Panzer tanks flattening the French countryside. It wasn't in the Führer's nature to appreciate the languid sweetness of Miller's *Moonlight Serenade* or Benny Goodman's *Moonglow*.

Rain sheeted down, the wipers *ker-thumping* steadily. Duquesne's thoughts turned to Schmidt's demise.

The blood. The arrow. I have a splendid idea.

He had kept the arrow as a souvenir. At the motor lodge, he had wiped the front seat clean of Schmidt's blood, though he now noticed a few missed drops. He would smear a dollop on the arrow's bullet-point head and craft his story: an American soldier, part of a secret archery squadron, had killed the SS assassin. The U.S. Army must be training for stealth warfare. Crossbows made virtually no noise. Clever, no?

The absurdity of it made him smile, reminding him of the improvisational jazz he loved, where melodies wandered into unexpected yet harmonious places. He was already drafting the report in his mind.

"While it is tragic for the Fatherland to lose a patriot of such skill and vigor, Schmidt's death was not in vain for it revealed a heretofore unknown tactic of an enemy's war plans."

At Abwehr, Admiral Canaris, who had known Duquesne for decades and was well aware of his dark humor, would chuckle when he heard that. Not that the Admiral would believe it for a moment, but his disdain for the SS would make for a delightful conversation over brandy on Duquesne's next trip to Hamburg.

But as the Packard hummed along the rain-slicked turnpike, Duquesne's earlier confidence began to wane.

Himmler, for all his flaws, is not a fool.

An assassin he trusted with a mission close to the Führer's heart—if that's not an oxymoron—winds up dead by bow and arrow. Himmler might toy with the notion of American archery squads, but only briefly, before turning his thoughts to darker suspicions. And Himmler, being Himmler, would act.

Duquesne tightened his grip on the steering wheel, the realization settling over him like the damp chill of the rain.

Himmler won't hesitate to send a second *Einsatzmann* to kill Chaplin...and to exact revenge against me.

"I don't know what you're complaining about," LaVonne Cohen said. "This sleeper is right as rain."

"It don't compare to the Santa Fe Super Chief," Mickey Cohen scoffed. "Wait'll we get to Chicago and change trains. Our accommodations will be the cat's pajamas."

LaVonne cocked her head seductively and said, "The bed looks cozy as a hayloft, and that's all I care about."

They were aboard the Capitol Limited, an all-Pullman train from Washington D.C. to Chicago. Their sleeper compartment had a comfortable drawing room and newfangled bathroom, and the Limited, with its streamlined diesel engine and modern cars, was a fine mode of travel.

But Cohen, who wore bespoke suits, Italian silk ties, and handmade shoes, was a snob where the finer things in life were concerned. Maybe selling newspapers at age seven on street corners—and beating up other kids to take their spots— had ignited the lust for all things elegant and refined. And true enough, the Santa Fe Super Chief was newer, faster, and more plush—a favorite of Hollywood celebrities and gangsters alike.

Cohen's orders from Bugsy Siegel hadn't changed: stick close to Chaplin on the Capitol Limited, shadow him in

Chicago during the Einstein-Oppenheimer debate, and escort him to Los Angeles on the Super Chief.

"Don't worry your pretty haircut, Ben," Cohen had told him. "I'm gonna protect Chaplin and Einstein, too, like they was my brothers." Before retiring to their sleeper, Cohen had done his rounds. He checked on Chaplin and Einstein in their compartments, then walked the entire length of the train: through the sleeper and club lounge cars, the dining car, and finally the baggage-dormitory car. Fifteen minutes later, he did it again. If a restroom was occupied, he waited to see who came out. He spotted two cinder dicks—railroad detectives—doing a poor job of blending in. Their identical baggy blue suit coats barely hid their shoulder holsters. Each nodded and smiled, but their eyes stayed sharp and watchful. For once, Cohen was happy to see John Law in his proximity.

Cohen was still trying to make sense of the gunshot outside the Army base. It was impossible to tell who had been the target, but it sure as hell wasn't a deer in the nearby woods. The dead man found on the access road had a sniper rifle and a torso squashed like he'd been run over by an Army tank. No identification, the soldiers said. Cohen figured Chaplin was the likely target, but it could just as easily have been Einstein, the Army major—or even himself. He wouldn't put it past Jack Dragna or Johnny Roselli to put out a contract on him.

The Capitol Limited was cruising through Martinsburg, West Virginia when LaVonne tried on the braided straw skimmer hat she'd bought on their excursion into Laurel, Maryland, a little town she'd declared "Hicksville, USA." The

Cohens had shopped there while Einstein and Chaplain visited the NDRC. LaVonne had been looking for silk hostess slacks for entertaining at home but could only find denim ranch pants. "Sure ain't no Bullocks in this burg," she had complained, referring to the department store on Wilshire Boulevard.

Mickey, on the other hand, had been pleased with the sporting goods shop where he bought the crossbow, fifty bolts, and fifty rounds of .38 caliber ammunition. Not that he was low on ammo—he just had a thing about *fresh* ammo. Just as he washed his hands multiple times a day and changed his socks at least twice a day, he had a compulsion about his cartridges.

Now, in the sleeper compartment, admiring her reflection in the mirror, LaVonne played with the brim of the straw hat and pursed her lips, painted cherry red, a shade popular in speakeasies fifteen years earlier.

Watching her, Mickey said, "I don't like to *kvetch*, but this train's got a rougher ride than the Super Chief." He wiggled his hips in rhythm with the shimmy of the car.

"Honey bun," LaVonne said with a sly smile, "that's just gonna make shaking the sheets more fun tonight."

TWENTY-NINE
HANDMAIDENS OF THE REICH
Saturday, November 9, 1940

Hours before boarding the Super Chief, while exiting the elevator in Chicago's Parker House hotel, Chaplin had a flash of inspiration.

If Einstein and Oppenheimer can debate, why not Lindbergh and me?

Haranguing Lindy over drinks in the lounge car wouldn't work. If the argument became heated, the ever-polite pilot would simply excuse himself and retreat to his sleeping compartment, likely with some adoring cutie in tow. But a debate with rules and procedures would force Lindbergh to stay engaged. If the press covered their skirmish, newspapers might editorialize that isolationism was the wrong tack and that Lend-Lease was an absolute necessity to save democracy. Public opinion would be swayed, perhaps even nudging Lindbergh to pull his big fat head out of the sand. At least, that was Chaplin's optimistic theory.

So, let's go, Lindy. Like Lincoln and Douglas. Like Einstein and Oppenheimer. Let's debate tonight.

Then as though scripted by fate—or a Hollywood screenwriter—there he was. Crossing the hotel lobby, Charles Augustus Lindbergh. At thirty-eight, he was tall, rangy, and handsome, though his once blond hair was retreating like the British Expeditionary Force at Dunkirk. He was with two men Chaplin instantly recognized.

Henry Ford, white-haired and gaunt at seventy-seven, bore the long, solemn face of a man who had never laughed in his life. He and Lindbergh shared the ignominious honor of having accepted the Grand Cross of the German Eagle, the Nazi regime's highest award for foreigners. Both blamed Jewish conspiracies for stirring anti-fascist sentiment and dragging America toward war. The other man was Colonel Robert McCormick, the sixty-year-old owner of *The Chicago Tribune*. With his heavy eyebrows and brush mustache, he resembled a stern headmaster. His newspaper regularly decried FDR's New Deal as old communism and beat the isolationist drum from sea to shining sea. A trio of handmaidens of the Reich.

Chaplin watched Lindbergh heartily shake hands with his two pals, who exited the lobby toward a waiting limousine on Monroe Street. Lindbergh headed back toward the elevators where Chaplin intercepted him.

"Hey Slim," he called out.

"Charlie! I heard you were in town. Are you on the Saturday night Super Chief?"

"All the way to the City of Angels."

"Great! Me, too. Say, you'll never guess who I lunched with."

"I'll take a stab. Two titans of business ready to march us proudly into the nineteenth century."

Lindbergh chuckled. "Aw, c'mon Charlie. You can't be against the America First Committee."

"Sure I can because they're fascism first and America second."

Lindbergh shook his head and gave Chaplin his aw-shucks grin. "Don't tell me you want to send our boys overseas to prop up the British Empire."

"I want us to give England the means to defend itself."

"A lost cause, my friend."

Chaplin jabbed a finger at Lindbergh's chest. "You think Hitler's going to stop at England?"

"That's as far west as he can go! Why do you think God gave us the Atlantic Ocean?"

"So you'd have someplace to fly overnight."

"I'm serious, Charlie."

"Then how about that mutual defense pact Hitler just signed with Japan? You think the Japanese will stop with French Indochina?"

Lindbergh laughed. "That's horse hockey, Charlie. The Pacific Ocean's wider than the Atlantic. We simply can't be attacked over water."

Chaplin flashed his movie-star smile. "Slim, this is invigorating. The two of us jawing over important events."

Lindbergh nodded. "We can agree on that."

"Then let me tell you my idea to make this train ride a lot more interesting."

PART TWO

THE SUPER CHIEF

THIRTY
THE FRED HARVEY GIRLS

All nights should be so crisp, the sky so clear, the moon so majestic.

At Chicago's Dearborn Station, the Warbonnet locomotive—sleek and resplendent in red and yellow, its design inspired by a Navajo headdress—pulsed with quiet power, poised to chase the horizon. Behind it stretched a line of gleaming stainless steel carriages. Their interiors boasted satinwood and mahogany paneling, brilliant turquoise and lustrous silver upholstery. The Santa Fe Super Chief radiated elegance from its drawing rooms to its club cars—a palace on wheels.

That morning, Einstein and Oppenheimer had debated at the University of Chicago, presenting their positions on gravitational contraction. The audience was rapt, the atmosphere congenial, and not a single mention of nuclear fission or atomic bombs darkened the discussion. At lunch in the Pump Room of the Ambassador East Hotel, they were joined by Leo Szilard, the physicist who had conceived of the nuclear chain reaction and co-authored Einstein's first letter to Roosevelt urging a robust atomic program. Over cherries jubilee and brandy, Oppenheimer and Szilard affirmed their commitment to building a nuclear weapon if called upon.

"To that, I wish you godspeed," Einstein said, "by which I mean the speed of light." Now, at six p.m., Dearborn Station hummed with its usual pre-departure bustle.

Passengers mingled on the platform, exhilarated by the promise of their journey. Already on board were the porters and stewards, chefs and sommeliers, all trained to pamper the travelers. There were well-dressed businessmen, collars stiffly starched, prosperous families with squirming children, retirees who had saved for years, now in their Sunday best, freshly barbered young men, hair pomaded, cheeks tingling from cologne, starry-eyed newlyweds, their luggage redolent of supple leather, card sharks in pencil mustaches who had outstayed their Midwest welcomes, tourists from here and there, heads swiveling like searchlights sweeping for celebrities: "Is that Clark Gable?"

Striding across the platform were Mr. And Mrs. Mickey Cohen. Always meticulous about his appearance, Cohen wore a worsted wool double-breasted charcoal suit, a crisp white cotton shirt with a subtle sheen and heavy gold cufflinks. His shoes, also custom made, were black, cap-toe oxfords. Not the ones with the special steel plates, suitable for stomping deadbeats who welshed on their bets. Those days were over.

LaVonne wore a figure-hugging, emerald green silk crepe dress with a sweetheart neckline that accentuated her décolletage, seamed silk stockings, and T-strap heels in black patent leather. Her chandelier earrings sparkled as she turned her head.

Throughout the station, railroad detectives scanned the crowd for troublemakers.

Alexander Gorky, a former Pinkerton detective turned railroad bull, stood on the platform, still as a rocky island, watching passengers move around him like currents in a stream. A portly man of fifty-five in a three-piece suit, Gorky was chief of security for the Super Chief. Thus far, nothing untoward caught his eye.

Mickey Cohen could spot a copper the way a birder spots a sage-grouse, and he had pegged Gorky as a cinder dick at the station's Fred Harvey restaurant. Parking his butt at the counter where he could watch the door, Gorky had been chowing down pork chops with apple rings, never giving Cohen so much as a second glance. A realization came to the gangster.

I'm just a guy hitting the feedbag with my wife. But if I'm sitting with torpedoes like Pug Carbo or Whitey Krakow, half the Chicago P.D. would be here to sweat me.

Marriage was a good cover, Cohen concluded, at least when out of town. In Los Angeles, his mug was too well known to go unnoticed. Having finished their main courses, hot roast beef sandwich with gravy for Mickey, chopped sirloin steak for LaVonne, Cohen signaled their Harvey Girl and said, "Sweetheart, how 'bout some stewed pears for dessert?"

"She ain't your sweetheart," LaVonne berated him.

"No kidding, hon. She looks like a friggin' nun."

All the Harvey Girls wore their hair tied back under a net and were draped in black, ankle-length dresses topped by white aprons with bows at the waist, black shoes and opaque black stockings. Their server had a complexion as white as the mashed potatoes she served alongside the beef sandwich. Being white, as in Caucasian, was also a job requirement, along with being unmarried, wearing no makeup at work and honoring a ten p.m. nightly curfew.

"I'm just saying, don't be flirting with no girls on our honeymoon, for Pete's sake," LaVonne said.

Mickey grunted something unintelligible, then chewed silently, having sunk into a funk. LaVonne was a fun broad, and the sex was tip-top, but you could say the same for the dames at the House of Francis on Sunset Boulevard where he was comped by Lee Francis, the madam.

Married life, he realized belatedly, had more rules than a gangland sit-down.

"Let's board," Cohen said. "I gotta keep my eye on Chaplin."

THIRTY-ONE
THE MYSTERIOUS SCHÖNE FRAU

I must be slipping!

Fritz Duquesne silently berated himself as he sat in a swivel chair by a wide window of the Super Chief's observation car at the rear of the train. He had boarded early precisely for this vantage point, where he could survey the platform as passengers approached. Yet here he was, castigating himself for allowing a porter to carry his reddish-brown leather suitcase.

The suitcase looked innocuous enough. But it did not contain a shaving kit or a change of underwear. It housed his wireless radio: a transceiver, power supply unit, antenna, headphones, and telegraph key, all secured in custom-fitted compartments to prevent any jostling. The case was heavier than it appeared, a fact the porter—a graying Negro man of perhaps fifty-five—realized the moment he picked it up and let out a surprised *oomph*.

"Books," Duquesne said quickly. "I'm quite a reader."

"Yes sir," the porter replied, as he had doubtless said to passengers a thousand times.

I always carry the case myself. What was I thinking? And why the defensive "books" remark? The porter couldn't care less if I was toting bricks or gold bullion.

Duquesne chalked it up to fatigue. Even with the Pennsylvania Turnpike chewing up half the drive, it had been a slog, and now he felt all of his sixty-three years. He had earned his fatigue. After all, he had been fighting battles since the Second Boer War at the turn of the century.

When Britain falls, when Churchill swings on the gallows, perhaps I shall take my leave. But am I fated to always sleep with one eye open and my hand near the hidden blade?

Through the window, Duquesne surveyed the platform, forcing himself to concentrate. He looked for familiar faces: an Abwehr agent sent to assist—or replace—him, an SS assassin sent to kill Chaplin, himself, or both. An FBI agent whose face might have appeared in an Abwehr dossier.

Nothing alarming caught his attention. Perhaps the SS didn't even know he was here. With luck, the details of his mission to kidnap Einstein had stayed within the sturdy walls of Abwehr's General Kommando in Hamburg.

Then he spotted them: Charles Lindbergh, towering over Chaplin, both men in three-piece suits, walking toward the Super Chief and deep in conversation.

What is the Reich's favorite American doing with one of its enemies of the state?

It wasn't an idle question. Through intermediaries, the Führer had courted Lindbergh, attempting to persuade the aviator to run for president against Roosevelt. Lindbergh had politely declined, but the Reich kept meticulous records on him. Every public utterance, every private whisper they could capture, was cataloged, and his future remained promising. Four years from now, Lindbergh would only be forty-two, and surely the cripple Roosevelt would not run for a ridiculous fourth term.

There is more than one way to conquer America.

Three paces behind the pair of celebrities was Chaplin's pint-sized shadow, the thug who seemed to follow the actor everywhere. Just as in the lobby of the Waldorf and at Fort Meade, he was with a petite redhead, and from their body language, they might have been squabbling.

That's when a tall, slender, striking woman sashayed into his line of vision. She looked to be about thirty. Her blue eyes were wide set, her cheekbones carved from ivory, her nose straight and delicate. Her full lips were set in a slight smile more imperious than friendly. The waves of her honey blond hair cascaded to her shoulders, bouncing with each step. All in all, the woman shimmered like polished gold.

She wore a form-fitting red silk dress with a sweetheart neckline, capped sleeves, and a cinched waist, the hem brushing just below the knee. Draped over one arm was a full-length black cashmere coat. She held the hand of a boy of about five, with neatly trimmed hair the color of straw. He wore a charcoal wool blazer, navy trousers, and a red bow-tie over a white shirt.

They look as if they'd stepped out of one of those Astaire-Rogers pictures, dressed to the nines.

The woman's movie-star glamor didn't escape Chaplin. As she crossed diagonally toward the train, mother and son in perfect step, the actor's head snapped to the side as if punched by Max Schmeling. Stutter-stepping, Chaplin nearly tumbled into a pratfall. He recovered, elbowed Lindbergh, and said something Duquesne couldn't hear but guessed to be along the lines of "Get a load of that dish."

Lindbergh glanced that way and quickly looked back toward the train. Too quickly. No comment, no smile, no flicker of interest. Duquesne considered himself an expert on human behavior, part of his tradecraft in counterintelligence. He didn't know who the woman was, but one thing was certain.

Charles Lindbergh knows you, schöne Frau, *but doesn't want to appear to. So, who are you beneath that dazzling facade? What secrets do you possess?*

With a sea of passengers streaming across the platform toward the train, Duquesne vowed to uncover the truth long before they reached Los Angeles.

THIRTY-TWO
THE USEFUL IDIOT

Happy to oblige Chaplin's request, the Santa Fe Railway erected a small wooden stage draped with red, white and blue bunting on the platform adjacent to the Super Chief. Chaplin's studio publicists worked the telephones, and a gaggle of reporters and photographers from Chicago newspapers showed up, PRESS cards tucked into the bands of their bowlers and trilbies. Five newsreel crews were on hand—Pathé, Movietone, Hearst Metrotone, March of Time, and Paramount News—ensuring that moviegoers would see several minutes of the debate the following week.

Chaplin, Lindbergh, and Einstein climbed the three steps to the stage. Buzzing with excitement, passengers crowded close.

"Ladies and gentlemen, it is our great fortune to hear from two of America's great men," Albert Einstein announced to the crowd, though he believed one of the men to be a dunderhead. "Charlie Chaplin and Charles Lindbergh will each make brief remarks, stating their positions on this country aiding Britain in its defense against the savage Nazi regime of the Third Reich." He paused, allowing the tension to build, then quipped, "There, I think I've given away my position."

The crowd chuckled and clapped politely. Passengers who had already boarded stepped off the train to witness the spectacle. Among them was Fritz Duquesne who stood on the top of the stirrup steps of the observation car, scanning the crowd for anything—or anyone—out of place.

Chaplin took the microphone first, his voice impassioned. "I'm not advocating we send our boys to fight a European war. And I'm not advocating giving away ships and planes and armaments. But for mercy's sake, Germany is dropping thousands of pounds of bombs each night on London, killing innocent civilians in their homes. We have a moral obligation to sell or lend or lease Britain weapons and munitions under President Roosevelt's plans."

A few in the audience applauded. The reporters scribbled in their notebooks, and the movie cameras whirred, the film whining through the gears.

Chaplin turned to Lindbergh, who smiled amiably before addressing the crowd. "I don't blame Charlie, who's a Brit, or Professor Einstein, who's a Jew, for their positions. But we can't allow the natural passions and prejudices of other peoples to lead our country to destruction. England is an ossified empire, a hapless relic, and we cannot prop her up, only prolong her agony."

Chaplin raised his voice. "Despots and dictators will only grow bolder if we throw up our hands and declare there is nothing to be done."

Undeterred, Lindbergh said, "We must not permit ourselves to be drawn into a foreign war simply because agitators, well meaning as they might be, use subterfuge and propaganda to arouse our sympathy for one side."

"It's not propaganda," Chaplin fired back, "when people are buried alive in tube stations, when women and children are incinerated in their flats."

"Don't be swept away by emotion," said the pilot who had a reputation for stoicism, even when his infant son was kidnaped and murdered. "Logic, rather than sentiment, must control our actions. We should not antagonize Germany but rather focus on problems at home. We should preserve our inheritance of European blood and guard ourselves against dilution by foreign races."

The crowd shifted uneasily. A few scowled, while two or three men clapped hesitantly.

Chaplin, however, was delighted. Lindbergh had stumbled into the minefield of his belief in eugenics, a topic sure to alienate many in the crowd.

From his perch, Duquesne took in the scene. He knew that most Americans sympathized with Britain but were staunchly against sending troops overseas. Roosevelt's Lend-Lease proposal hung in the balance, and Berlin's strategy depended on keeping America on the sidelines. That was the purpose of the Tripartite Pact signed six weeks earlier in Berlin. It pledged mutual defense among Germany, Italy, and Japan. If the U.S.A. awoke from its torpor and attacked any of the three, the other two vowed to respond with force. Yet Duquesne harbored doubts about the pact's wisdom. Hitler might control Mussolini, but Japan? No one in Berlin even knew who called the shots in that enigmatic country.

Emperor Hirohito? Prime Minister Konoe? Minister of War Tojo?

Duquesne caught a glimpse of the glamorous blonde with the little boy. She was near the front of the crowd, less than six feet from the speakers' platform. Chaplin was reciting civilian casualty figures and detailing damage to St. Thomas Hospital and the House of Commons by German bombing. But the woman was intensely focused on Lindbergh. Her body was still. Her head never moved. A statuesque statue.

Duquesne processed various possibilities. The blonde was one of Lindbergh's stable of thoroughbreds he saddled up when wife Anne wasn't around. Or, the woman wanted to be. Or, given Abwehr's desire to exploit Lindbergh's personal life, she could be a German agent. But that seemed farfetched, especially since she's carting around that little boy. Duquesne let the thought simmer like a stew pot of goulash and came up with a disturbing possibility. Maybe the cute little *Junge* is her cover, and she's an SS assassin, sent to replace Reinhard Schmidt. Raising once again the possibility that the assassin's assignment was twofold.

Kill Chaplin...then kill me.

As a trained agent, she would not reveal her interest in Chaplin, hence the distraction by focusing on Lindbergh.

A flashbulb went off, and Duquesne's vision was momentarily filled with a constellation of luminous specks dancing behind his eyelids, shimmering like celestial bodies. Only then did he realize he was in the field of view of both the still cameras and the thirty-five-millimeter newsreel cameras.

Damn, I am slipping!

He imagined a photo of Chaplin and Lindbergh appearing in *The Chicago Tribune* the next day with his own face clearly visible in the background. If the photo ran on the wires and was seen at Abwehr...well, it was such an amateurish breach of tradecraft, he didn't want to think about the consequences.

Lindbergh's demeanor turned serious and he said, "FDR has asked Congress for one billion dollars to build fifty thousand warplanes. I repeat, one billion dollars!"

A murmur rippled through the small crowd, and a man in a blue blazer called out, "That's a lot of clams."

Another man looked toward Chaplin and said, "Is that on the level, Charlie? A billion bucks?"

"It's true, and I'll tell you why it's the right thing to do. Because—"

Lindbergh broke in, saying, "And who's gonna pay, fellow? You are. Main Street paying so Wall Street bankers and internationalists can live on Easy Street."

Duquesne smiled to himself. *Wall Street bankers and internationalists?* Nazi code for Jews.

"And why the heck do we need those weapons of war?" Lindbergh asked rhetorically.

Chaplin jumped in. "Because six days before FDR told Congress the country needed to beef up its air power, Germany invaded France, Belgium, Luxembourg and the Netherlands. And now, England is in flames. That's why the heck we need weapons of war." He turned to Lindbergh with a look of sadness. "Honestly, Slim, what would you have us do?"

"Mind our own darn business!" Lindbergh boomed, his voice uncharacteristically loud. "America first!"

"Like it or not," Chaplin said, "the world has become our business. Eight weeks ago, the *City of Benares*, a passenger vessel, set sail from Liverpool carrying British civilians and unaccompanied children away from the horrors of the Blitz to safety in Canada. A rescue ship. A refugee ship. A mercy ship. In the treacherous waters of the Atlantic, a German submarine sank the *Benares*, killing nearly three hundred people, including seventy-seven children. Children!"

"A regrettable mistake of war," Lindbergh replied coldly. "The U-Boat captain could not be expected to know the passenger manifest."

Duquesne stifled a smile. Lindbergh was such a *nützlicher Idiot*, a useful idiot. What a glorious notion that in four years he could be president. Duquesne toyed with the image of a state dinner at the White House, Lindbergh hosting Hitler, Goebbels, and Göring.

And perhaps me, too. Surely, I will no longer be in the field but perhaps a position at the Embassy, masterminding counterintelligence from behind a grand mahogany desk.

Duquesne shot a look at the blonde. She was off to the side, with her back to the cameras. No photos of her in tomorrow's newspapers.

Is this schöne Frau *a more meticulous agent? Is she laughing at me, mocking my sloppiness, confident that she can dispatch me with a poisoned cocktail or a stiletto hidden in her garter belt?*

He squinted, trying to determine if she was looking his way. Even though his eyes had stopped blinking, little black dots floated across his view like gnats over a summer pond, impossible to swat away. Was it his imagination, or was she regarding him with a knowing smile?

Duquesne's thoughts were interrupted by the conductor, a strapping man with a lush handlebar mustache perfectly suited for the baritone in a barbershop quartet. Standing outside the observation car, he rang the locomotive's brass bell six times, each clang echoing like cannon fire. As the echoes died, the conductor bellowed, "All A-a-a-board!"

The passengers ascended into the sleeping cars. The twin diesel-electric locomotives spooled up with a resonant *whum,* the air brakes released with a sigh, the horn blared its warning, and the sleek, stainless steel train eased forward. As it gathered speed, the engines drummed with the timeless rhythm of westward destiny.

Duquesne went to his drawing room, his mind focused on the mysterious woman. His instincts told him there were complex layers beneath her alluring feminine exterior.

Friend or foe?

But of course there would be no reason for the *Reich* to send a friend.

THIRTY-THREE
BEDROOM SPECULATIONS

Charlie Chaplin, whose father was an alcoholic, was a teetotaler for much of his life, but tonight he needed a drink. Changing Lindbergh's mind about isolationism seemed as likely as convincing the tides to ignore the moon. And the backup plan—gather evidence of infidelity to blackmail the pilot—well, that wasn't Chaplin's cup of tea. Upon reflection, it rankled his sense of decency.

With my marital track record, I'm hardly one to cast the first stone or snap the first tawdry photo. But I promised Major Groves, so there's that.

Chaplin strolled down the sleeper car's corridor, the train's cushioned springs making for a comfortable, gently swaying ride. The wheels clicked rhythmically over the rails, a soothing counterpoint to the day's frustrations. Through an open door, he caught the strains of *Le Rouet d'Omphale* and the opening line of a hit radio program: "Who knows what evil lurks in the hearts of men? The Shadow knows."

Chaplin smiled, recalling his friend Orson Welles, who had voiced the Shadow before leaping into films. The twenty-five-year-old *wunderkind* was now hip-deep in a hush-hush project at RKO. Over lunch at the Brown Derby, Welles had whispered that the picture was a thinly veiled jab at William

Randolph Hearst. Dangerous business, Chaplin thought. Ridiculing Hearst on film might be riskier than romancing his mistress.

Chaplin stepped out the door of the sleeping car onto the gangway, the steel wheels *clacking* over rail joints, the cars bucking like dancers jitterbugging. From the flexible vestibule, he entered the club lounge car, passed the barber shop through a spicy cloud of Pinaud Clubman cologne, and strolled into the bar, a space of warm woods, golden-hued ceiling, and carpet the color of desert sand. The chairs were upholstered in turquoise and orange, a southwestern motif, and Navajo-inspired art decorated the walls.

Behind the bar stood a trim, handsome man with a pencil mustache and a complexion of warm mahogany. His white tunic was starched to perfection, his bow tie crisply knotted. Two overweight middle-aged men in vested suits leaned against the zebrawood-paneled bar, each clutching a cocktail in one hand and a Partagás cigar in the other. They looked like central casting's picks for heartless bankers foreclosing on family farms. Wisps of cigar smoke, scented of leather and spice, curled upward, bluish in the overhead lights.

Several tables were occupied by lone businessmen, and a young honeymooning couple sat so close they might well have merged into one shadow. But it was the lone woman at a corner table who nearly took Chaplin's breath away.

She was slender, with almond-shaped eyes, high cheekbones, and a honey-colored complexion. Her dark hair was swept into an elegant updo, and she wore a silk blue dress that nipped at the waist and padded at the shoulders, paired with white gloves that reached her elbows. When she turned and dimpled a small smile in Chaplin's direction, he responded with his best Klieg-light grin.

"Miss Horne, I believe?" He stopped short, bent at the waist with a flourish, head tilted forward like the prow of a ship.

"Mr. Chaplin," Lena Horne replied.

"May I sit?"

"You'd better...before you topple over."

"Is my affliction that obvious?"

"It's flattering." She motioned with a gloved hand, and Chaplin took the chair next to her. He checked the nearly empty coupe glass in front of her and said, "Another?"

"Champagne cocktail," Her voice lilted like a melody over moonlit waters.

A white-jacketed, bow-tied waiter appeared, and Chaplin ordered two of the same. "I saw you sing at Café Society in the Village just last week," Chaplin began as the waiter disappeared.

"You frequent Negro clubs?"

"Whenever I can. Your *Stormy Weather* nearly made me cry."

"You should have come backstage to say hello."

Was there a hint of flirtation there? Chaplin hoped so. "Aw, I'm not a stage door Johnny," he said.

Lena flashed a smile bright as a sunburst. "Perhaps you were occupied with another woman."

"Not that night. Flying solo."

"Ah, but I saw you at a table near the stage chatting away with a gorgeous redhead."

Puzzled, Chaplin shrugged. "I don't think so."

Lena's smile was taunting. "Black fishnet stockings, low-cut fire-engine red bodice. So classy and demure."

"Ha! The cigarette girl!"

"You spent enough time to clean her out of Lucky Strikes and Chesterfields." Lena's tone was teasing, her eyes twinkling.

The waiter returned with their cocktails. Outside the window, the Super Chief sliced through coal-dark Midwest farmlands, its air horn blasting as they approached a crossing.

"You're a sassy gal with personality to spare, Miss Horne." His voice was playful.

"Please call me Lena. Do you never tire of it, Mr. Chaplin?"

"Call me 'Charlie.' Tire of...?"

"Chasing skirts."

"Ah, my reputation precedes me."

"Like the locomotive pulling the Pullman cars."

She sipped her cocktail, her gloved hand delicate around the coupe glass. At the next table, a well-dressed couple in their fifties stared at Lena, disapproval in their narrowed eyes. The man, hair the color of a nicotine stain, parted in the middle, pince-nez spectacles perched on his nose, might as well be wearing a sign that said, "Kansas City. Insurance." The woman, her lips pressed into a tight line, whispered something, and the man frowned.

"Are you between marriages?" Lena asked, ignoring the couple.

"More like between affairs."

"Then you're still married to Paulette Goddard?"

He hesitated, then said, "Separated on account of illness."

"Oh, my. How so?"

"Paulette got sick of me."

She raised her elegantly arched eyebrows. "I think I understand you, Charlie. You simply can't help it."

"Help what?"

"Being a heel. A rake. A tomcat. It's who you are."

He shrugged, unrepentant. "I just haven't met the woman who can nail my foot to the floor."

"Now you're looking for a taste of the exotic."

"Lena, I simply love women. Slender, petite women and ripe, full-bodied women. Tall women and short women. White, black, brown, any shade you can name. And if she's also smart and talented, well yes, I make bedroom speculations."

She drilled him with her luminous eyes. "Just out of curiosity, how old are you?"

He ran a hand through his wavy white mane and flashed the devilish smile that had weakened the knees of starlets, chorines—and cigarette girls—on both coasts. "Fifty-one and feeling fit."

"I'm twenty-three."

"Perfect! You know what I'm thinking, Lena?"

She smiled over the rim of her coupe glass. "I'm pretty sure I do."

"You oughta be in pictures."

Her laugh bubbled like the champagne. "And I'll bet you have a role just waiting for me."

"Not yet, but I'm thinking of adapting the musical *Show Boat* into a movie."

"And I suppose I'd be Julie." She put a sad note in her voice and sang, *"Can't help lovin' dat man o'mine."*

At the next table, the fiftyish woman stood up abruptly and loudly commanded, "Carl, let's go!" Her husband complied, and they scurried off.

"What got her girdle in a twist?" Chaplin said.

"Oh, I think you know, Charlie."

"That's the thing, Lena. *Show Boat's* really about racism and social justice. It's a show for the greater good."

"Oh, please. The show's filled with racial stereotypes." She sang again, "*Tell me he's lazy Tell me he's slow. Tell me I'm crazy, maybe, I know.*"

"Yes, but that's to make a point, Lena."

"'Old man river keeps on rolling?'" she said, making it a question.

"That's the metaphor for racism. An endless, unfeeling river. Joe the stevedore toting the barge, lifting the bail, getting drunk, landing in jail. Then there's the social taboo of the interracial love story. Rich, layered themes that movie audiences have never seen. We could make music and history together."

"If you're serious, Charlie, I'll think about it." She cocked her head to one side and gave him a smile both winsome and captivating. "But I'm not coming to your drawing room tonight."

"It's a two-night trip," Chaplin said, undaunted.

THIRTY-FOUR
THE EAVESDROPPER

In the club lounge car, his face hidden behind a newspaper, Fritz Duquesne savored the byplay two tables away. Charlie Chaplin, Hollywood's notorious cocksman, had been stopped cold by the beautiful Negress. Duquesne ordered a gin and tonic and turned his thoughts to this man despised by Hitler and his cronies.

Earlier in the day, with time to kill, Duquesne had caught *The Great Dictator* at the Oriental Theatre in Chicago's Loop. He found the film hilarious—a satirical masterstroke puncturing Hitler's pomposity. That it ridiculed the demigod who paid his wages didn't trouble Duquesne in the least.

I do not so much work for the Reich as against England. And I can do my job without idolizing Hitler or his thuggish sycophants.

Chaplin's talent as writer, director, and actor was undeniable. The call for peace and brotherhood at the end was maudlin, of course—pure Chaplinesque sentimentality—but it didn't diminish Duquesne's enjoyment. Who knew humor could cut sharp as a saber?

Now Duquesne buried himself in *The Chicago Tribune*, brimming with news to his liking. The British were apoplectic over the sinking of the *Jervis Bay*, an armed merchant vessel laughably outmatched by the German heavy cruiser *Admiral*

Scheer. The article deliciously detailed how the British ship had found her final berth on the ocean floor, along with her captain and crew.

Another story reported that Neville Chamberlain was near death from cancer, spending his last days at his home in Hampshire. Duquesne wondered if the former Prime Minister realized what a patsy he had been for Hitler.

Then there was a strongly worded editorial denouncing President Roosevelt's efforts to aid the British with ships and weapons as the "dangerous stepping-stones to war."

"Keep America neutral," the editorial said.

Music to my ears, Duquesne thought.

Duquesne was able to read and eavesdrop at the same time. He was rooting for Chaplin to achieve his conquest. The more time he spent with the woman, the less time he would have for Einstein. The more Einstein was alone, the easier he would be to kidnap. If the Super Chief ran on time, as it almost always did, they would be pulling into the Needles, California station around 2 a.m. Monday morning, roughly thirty hours from now.

The plan was simple, as the best plans were. At the railway station, Einstein would be lured to the Western Union telegraph office, where Duquesne's men would abduct him. From there, it was a five-minute drive to the Colorado River and the waiting Consolidated 28 seaplane. The itinerary mirrored the earlier botched attempt at Fort Meade, with the addition of a refueling stop in Tampico, Mexico, before the five-hundred-mile flight to Havana. There, Einstein would be hauled onto a German freighter for the crossing to Hamburg.

Einstein was not to be harmed, at least not yet. In Germany, his old friend Werner Heisenberg would try to enlist him in the

Uranverein at Kaiser-Wilhelm. If Einstein refused, as he surely would, his friends and loved ones, still trapped in occupied Europe, would die one-by-one in increasingly horrific ways until he complied.

The denouement a tad messy, but at its essence, simple.

Now, just before dinner, it was time for Duquesne to repair to his compartment, set up the wireless, and make sure all the pieces were on the chess board for the coming gambit. He stood, smiled in the direction of Chaplin and the beautiful woman who had thus far spurned the actor's advances, and carrying his newspaper, headed out, happy to still be in the game.

THIRTY-FIVE
SAVE THE CHILD

Oblivious to the man with a rolled-up newspaper slipping out of the lounge car, Charlie Chaplin had eyes only for Lena Horne. A sudden realization struck him.

She's not just beautiful. She's smart and poised, talented and self-confident. And she's going to make it!

He worried about all the young women flocking to Hollywood, chasing dreams of stardom. Acting, singing, and modeling were the Pied Piper's calls, but most of those women ended up working soda fountains, cocktail lounges, and dance halls. Or worse. They arrived with new cardboard suitcases or canvas grips. When the money dried up and dreams died, the return trips by Greyhound to Kansas City or Wichita or a thousand tiny burgs were dismal affairs.

Failure, so often predicted by friends and family, left a taste as bitter as regret and twice as hard to swallow.

Chaplin had met Paulette Goddard, his third wife, at a Hollywood party when she was twenty-two and he was forty-three. Goddard, born Marion Levy, was a bit player in movies, but he had seen a diamond in the rough and taken her under his wing—as was his wont. He convinced her to ditch the platinum blond tresses and go back to her natural brunette.

He sent her to acting classes, had her move in, and eventually married her. His appraisal had been correct.

She proved to be a talented actress, becoming his leading lady in *Modern Times* and *The Great Dictator*, and barely losing out to Vivien Leigh for the role of Scarlett O'Hara in *Gone With the Wind*. The marriage, however, foundered on the rocky shoals of his infidelities.

Lena Horne's voice interrupted his thoughts. "You're going about it all wrong with Lindbergh."

Chaplin blinked as if slapped in the face. "What?"

"I watched your little debate. He already knows about the barbarity of the German bombings. You told him nothing new."

"So how can I do better next time?" Chaplin asked, genuinely puzzled. "What's the major premise of his argument?"

"No American boys in foreign wars."

"And he's probably right that aiding the British will drag us into war. While you and I may believe such a war is just and necessary, Lindbergh and his supporters do not. And you won't change his mind with generalities about German atrocities."

"Generalities!" Chaplin sputtered. On movie sets where he owned the studio and employed all the actors and crew, his judgment was rarely questioned. Lena's criticism caught him off-guard. "For goodness sake, I invoked the sinking of the *Benares*. Seventy-seven innocent children dead!"

"That's just a number. A rational argument, but not an emotional one."

"Really? I thought a theme of 'Save the Children' hit the right note. Jewish, Gypsy, Protestant, Catholic. All the children in Europe. A universal plea."

"But not a personal one."

Chaplin threw up his hands. "I don't know how to make it personal."

"Lenny Grimmond," she said.

"Who?"

"The five-year-old son of Hannah and Edward Grimmond. After their home in Brixton was bombed, they sent Lenny on the *Benares* for the safety of Canada. His body was not recovered."

Chaplin felt grief envelop him like a thick fog, pain for a child and a family he did not know and would never meet. "How do you know all this?"

A waiter came by with hors d'oeuvres on a silver tray. Chaplin examined the toast points with caviar and dollops of crème fraîche but declined. Lena did the same.

"I read three newspapers a day and listen to Mr. Murrow on the radio at night," Lena replied. "A dead child with a name and photograph tends to stick in your mind."

The train rounded a curve without slowing down, the carriage tilting just enough to be noticeable. Chaplin leaned back, considering Lena's advice. "I see where you're going. Make it personal. Little Lenny Grimmond. Murdered. A real person, someone we can picture in a flannel shirt and knickerbockers, a shaggy haircut his mother gave him during the blackout."

"And...?"

"And what, Lena?"

"Something you don't say but strikes common ground nonetheless."

It only took Chaplin a few seconds, and the realization hit him. "Blimey! Lindbergh's son, Charles Junior. Murdered. You want me to trigger Lindy's empathy with the subconscious connection between the two atrocities. Save the *child*. Not anonymous children." He thought it over, nodded, and repeated the phrase, "Save the child."

"Plus four," she said.

Again, Chaplin was puzzled.

"Four of Lenny's siblings were also on the *Benares*," she continued.

"Oh, Lord no! Did they...?"

"All dead. Gussie, Violet, Connie, and a little boy whose name I can't remember."

"I have a staff that can find out. Names, ages, hobbies, photographs. I'd like to try again with Lindy." He looked at her, unabashed admiration in his eyes.

Lena rewarded Chaplin with a warm smile. "You are a rapscallion, Charlie Chaplin, but one with a good heart."

THIRTY-SIX
WHITHER THE DUKE?

Am I getting soft? Has time passed me by?

Those were the questions buzzing in Fritz Duquesne's mind as he unlocked the latches on his suitcase wireless. The pleasant buzz he had experienced in the club lounge car had drifted off like the last wisp of steam from a cooling locomotive.

Tonight's task was a simple one. Check in by wireless with an Abwehr agent in Missouri who would transmit the message to the operator in East Quogue who would contact Hamburg by shortwave, thanks to a sixty-foot antenna disguised at the upper reaches of a water tower.

A well-trained monkey could accomplish my task.

He had started to question his usefulness.

A lifetime as a soldier and spy.

He had slept in the jungle during monsoons, had tromped through muddy trenches that ran red with blood, had sucked on icicles on a pillbox roof for drinking water. And now, in his plush Super Chief drawing room, wearing bedroom slippers for his bunions but still in a suit and tie, he felt a mixture of ennui and melancholy.

Twenty minutes earlier, Duquesne had made his way from the club lounge car to his sleeper car, stumbling on the gangway, the vestibule between shimmying cars, his balance not what it used to be. In the past, he had stayed in shape. Hitting the heavy bag in the gym, running up stadium stairs, using a chair in a hotel room for dips and elevated push-ups. But lately he had let himself go, had developed a paunch. Yesterday, at the hotel in Chicago, he had carried his suitcase wireless while a bellman handled a larger piece of luggage. They both stepped lively to get into the lobby elevator.

"You're looking spry, sir," the bellman said, intending it as a compliment.

"Spry?" Isn't that what you call an elderly gent who can still amble, despite a cane, the gout, and creaky knees?

His mind flickered to an image of Reinhard Schmidt, so young and strong. But so arrogant, he never saw Duquesne's sneak attack coming. Had it been a fair fight, the two of them on firm ground and unarmed, Duquesne knew he would not be here in the warm glow of subdued lighting, perfectly crafted cocktails, and a delicious dinner awaiting in the dining car.

Just look at this place!

The sofa was upholstered in a rich red fabric, and the walls were paneled with golden yellow satinwood. There was, of course, a modern and private toilet.

How could an old soldier not be spoiled and weakened by such extravagances?

How long had it been since he had been admiringly dubbed "The Duke" by the brass at Abwehr? How long since a counterintelligence triumph? It had been nearly four decades since he had impersonated a British officer and plotted a successful assassination in Cape Town. In the Great War, he had sabotaged British merchant ships off the coast of South America and created havoc with the King's interests in multiple countries. He was captured three times—once each by the British, Portuguese, and Americans—and had escaped from prison three times.

And now?

Gone were the days of strolling into DuPont headquarters in Delaware, posing as a visiting chemist, and leaving with the formula for a new incendiary reagent. Now, as a colonel in Abwehr, he ran an outfit of more than thirty agents in the States, mostly recruited from the German American Bund. But he felt more like an administrator than a field operative. And on many days, just a clerk, coding the field agents' reports, tapping out endless messages in Morse code on the shortwave.

Not that he wished to be in the field doing their grunt work. Photographing aircraft plants and shipbuilding factories, purloining specifications for new torpedoes, rifles, and gas masks.

Scouring public records for blueprints of factories and maps of sewer systems. It was all rather mundane.

He remembered how that bastard Schmidt had belittled his work, called him a poseur, "stealing scraps of supposed enemy intelligence, most of it useless, some of it outright misinformation."

Now, in a rare moment of self-doubt, Duquesne admitted to himself that his work these days would hardly tilt the outcome of a war. But that only made the Einstein mission even more important. With its success, he imagined admiring glances and endless kudos.

"There walks the man who brought Albert Einstein to Berlin in chains!"

A tale that would be retold for as long as the Reich existed, one thousand years, if you believed the Führer. The thought pepped him up.

I could become as legendary as General Epaminondas who crushed the Spartans at the Battle of Leuctra nearly four centuries before Christ was born.

Those doubts? Unwarranted. His skills had not diminished. On his way out of the club lounge car, he had walked past the crew quarters and, without even pausing, noted the passenger manifest on a clipboard hanging from a partition. The name of the elegant and mysterious blonde was "Margaret Jones."

As likely true as my *"Frederick Fredericks" moniker.*

Margaret Jones. A bland, forgettable name one he might have chosen for a female agent whose real identity was likely more along the line of Gisela von Weimar. He had passed close to her in the corridor earlier that day. She was asking a sleeping car porter when dinner would be served. He detected only the slightest accent, which he identified as a native German speaker who learned English from BBC broadcasts, a common method at military intelligence schools. The porter told her that a steward would announce dinner by walking through the train, delicately hitting notes on a bell chime. That seemed to surprise her, which indicated this was her first trip on the Super Chief. Most likely a meaningless tidbit of information, but tradecraft demanded the accumulation of random facts.

Duquesne had taken the streamliner to Los Angeles one year earlier to meet with American fascist William Dudley Pelley. The mission was to ascertain whether the founder of the Silver Legion of America was a serious man or a lunatic. Pelley openly boasted he would overthrow the U.S. government with an armed militia, and Duquesne decided he suffered from delusions of grandeur. But then, so did you-know-who in Berlin.

Duquesne used a key to unlock his suitcase wireless and went to work. He removed the transmitter, the receiver, and the power unit, and set about connecting wires to the Morse key. He attached the crystal and the tank coil to the transmitter, plugged in the headphones, and fastened the flexible antenna into place, then strung it along the wall and window, hanging it with tape. He cracked the window, felt the rush of cold night air, the sound of wheels on tracks louder, and taped the loose end of the antenna to the exterior of the train. Ah, the wonders of shortwave wireless, bouncing signals off the ionosphere, the greatest intelligence tool since Aeneas Tacticus devised coded messages in ancient Greece.

He hit the power switch and...nothing happened. *Verdammt! I didn't plug the unit into the power outlet.*

He fixed that problem and went to work. It was tedious, tapping out espionage code in Morse code, but within a few minutes he had transmitted a message to the agent in Sugar Creek, Missouri, asking if the operatives and the airplane would be in place in Needles, California for the snatch and flight. He then described "Margaret Jones" and requested Abwehr reply with any information.

"*Is she one of us?*" Meaning Abwehr. "*Or is she SS?*"

Or, Duquesne wondered, is she really just Margaret Jones, a lovely woman with a five-year-old son?

Ordinarily, Duquesne would have set up the time for the next transmission, but tonight there was no need. The Super Chief had a ten-minute stop in Kansas City at 2:35 a.m., and the agent from Sugar Creek would be waiting on the platform as Duquesne made a point of getting some fresh air, stretching his legs...and confirming all details of his mission.

He carefully dismantled and re-packed the wireless, locked the leather case, then hit the buzzer to summon the sleeping car porter. Another gin and tonic before dinner felt just about right. Plymouth gin and Schweppes tonic water.

Oh, damn you, Brits! I hate your decadence, but love your cocktails.

THIRTY-SEVEN
THE ON-THE-FLY PACKAGE

Near the Chillicothe railway station, where the Illinois River meandered through the prairie, a postal clerk hefted a fifty-pound canvas mail sack onto the metal arm of a trackside crane. The Super Chief's whistle pierced the air as it thundered toward him at eighty miles per hour. He swung the crane arm out, and seconds later a clerk in the passing mail car extended a J-shaped catcher arm through the open door. With a sharp *whoosh*, the arm snatched the canvas sack filled with letters, magazines, and newspapers, yanking it cleanly into the postal car.

The on-the-fly mail pickup—a daily ritual of the railway postal service—had gone off without a hitch. Ten minutes later, a porter in the sleeper section delivered a package to Brian Sullivan and Millie Vazquez in their drawing room, where they were registered as Mr. Bruce Dawkins and Mrs. Mildred Dawkins of Williamsport, Pennsylvania.

Sullivan opened the FBI dossier on Fritz Joubert Marquis Duquesne, known to intelligence agencies worldwide as "The Duke." Sitting on the edge of a plush lounge chair, Sullivan leafed through the hundred-page file and whistled. "Millie, that photo you snapped in the diner was pure gold. Look what the New York office came up with."

She peered over his shoulder at a photograph dated March 1900 and labeled "Captain Duquesne." The man in his twenties was ruggedly handsome in khakis and a slouch hat, a bandolier of 7 millimeter Mauser shells crossing his chest, sleeves rolled to expose thick, veined forearms. A Boer soldier fighting the British, then a German spy and saboteur in the Great War.

Now, forty years after taking up arms against the Brits in South Africa, he was still waging his private war.

The pieces were falling into place, Vazquez thought. When Lindbergh and Chaplin held their impromptu debate on the platform at Dearborn Station, she noticed a man of about sixty who looked familiar. Now she realized he had been in the front row of the Einstein-Oppenheimer debate in Princeton, looking like a professor in a tweedy sport coat with elbow patches and a Princeton tie. Same mustache, same glasses, though he'd had a full beard. He had raised his hand and asked Einstein whether it was possible to create an atomic bomb by splitting the atom.

Two appearances might have been coincidence—except he was also the man with the goatee at the New Jersey diner, hiding behind a newspaper while studying Einstein, Chaplin, and Mickey Cohen at lunch. A man who kept changing his appearance. Vazquez had captured his image in the diner with her Lucky Strike camera, sending it to the FBI's New York office. The Super Chief's passenger manifest listed Duquesne as Frederick Fredericks, an alias so absurd it revealed the spy had a sense of humor.

The on-the-fly package revealed what had happened in their absence. FBI agents had arrested a German American Bund member, a pharmacist by day, attempting to pass NDRC microfilm to a German agent at the Marine Air Terminal in Queens. The FBI had held him seventy-two hours without access to counsel, or anyone else for that matter.

FBI interrogators had told him, falsely, that he was a suspect in the Hercules Powder plant explosion that killed more than fifty workers, and he cracked like a soft-boiled egg.

Sweating profusely, the amateur spy—a mule, really—swore he knew nothing about the explosion but admitted delivering a Gruen Curvex wristwatch to a man about to board Pan Am's Yankee Clipper. He denied knowing what was inside the watch, which he said was given to him at the Waldorf Astoria Hotel by a man in his sixties he knew only as Fritz. Broad shoulders, an accent not quite British but close.

The agents showed him the photo taken by Millie Vazquez in the New Jersey diner, and courting their favor, he joyously shouted, "That's Fritz! He's a super spy!"

Aidan Murphy, the FBI agent in charge, looked at the photo, put two and two together, and realized that "Fritz" was the German operative Fritz Duquesne. Murphy had been there in 1932 when the New York office arrested Duquesne for sabotaging a British ship during the Great War, killing three sailors. The British ultimately decided that their fifteen-year-old case lacked evidence, and Duquesne walked free to resume his espionage career.

A few hours after fingering Duquesne, the pharmacist was allowed to see a lawyer and immediately recanted. He never heard of a "Fritz" and only delivered the watch to the port because a stranger on Fifth Avenue offered him a hundred bucks to do so.

Skimming the Duquesne dossier, Sullivan said, "In the Great War, Duquesne claimed he impersonated a Russian Count named Boris Zakrevsky and joined Lord Kitchener on the *HMS Hampshire*. Somehow, Duquesne signaled a German U-boat, which torpedoed the British ship. Kitchener was killed, and Duquesne escaped in a lifeboat."

"That sounds about as likely as *Hell Below*," Vazquez said, dismissively.

"How's that?"

"A fanciful submarine movie starring Robert Montgomery."

"You're probably right. The dossier says 'unconfirmed.' But it also says Duquesne is still working counterintelligence for Abwehr."

"And now he's here." Vazquez said.

"Who's his target? Einstein or Chaplin? And why?"

"Hard to tell." Vazquez gazed out the window where moonlit cornfields flowed past. "Could be planning to assassinate Chaplin or pump Einstein for nuclear research details."

Sullivan frowned. "He could have killed Chaplin in New Jersey. Why chase him cross-country? And as far as the Bureau knows, Einstein isn't involved in any atomic projects."

"But Major Groves brought him into the NDRC's inner sanctum." Vazquez turned from the window. "Brian, I have a plan that might appeal to your passion for intrigue."

He chuckled.

THIRTY-EIGHT
THE UNION MAN

Ezra Jefferson loved his job. Loved it, despite the grueling schedule, despite being on his feet on a twelve-hour shift, despite being away from his precious Althea for three weeks out of four. Loved the gleaming, luxurious streamliner itself, the deep and steady hum of the diesel-electric locomotives, so unlike the hissing and chugging of the old steam engines. Loved the glide through the heartland of America, the rhythmic clatter of steel wheels against rail joints, a peaceful lullaby in those precious few hours of sleep in the dormitory car.

Most of all, Jefferson loved being a union man, earning a decent salary and looking forward to a pension, all thanks to A. Philip Randolph, founder of the Brotherhood of Sleeping Car Porters. Because of the union, porters received overtime when they worked more than two-hundred-sixty hours a month, and their pay was no longer docked when a passenger stole a towel or ashtray.

And that pension! How many Negroes who hadn't finished high school had that easy chair waiting for them at the end of the line?

Jefferson was fifty-two with a neatly trimmed mustache and salt-and-pepper hair at regulation length. His blue uniform was neat and wrinkle-free, his black leather shoes polished to a high gloss, the gold buttons of his tunic wiped of any fingerprints and his blue cap perched at the specified angle. Paid for by the Santa Fe...thanks to the union. When he started work, before the Brotherhood days, porters were required to buy their own uniforms.

With twenty-seven years on the rails, Jefferson performed every duty of a sleeping car porter with care and cheerfulness. Carrying luggage, making beds, tidying compartments, fetching drinks, newspapers, and snacks, shining shoes, answering endless questions about schedules, stops, menus, and the views from the observation car.

"Yes, ma'am. That's the Mississippi River."

"That's right, sir. We've crossed into Iowa."

"No, sir. We won't be able to see the Grand Canyon."

Althea Jefferson, Ezra's wife of twenty-six years, taught history at Jordan High in the Watts neighborhood of Los Angeles. Their twin sons were now juniors at San Francisco State College. All this good fortune—achieved through hard work and playing by the rules set by others—combined to make Jefferson one happy man.

He found the celebrities on the Super Chief remarkably down-to-earth and polite. Errol Flynn trusted Jefferson to feed his beloved schnauzer, Arno, and take him for quick walks at stops along the run. Jefferson delivered strawberry milkshakes on more than one occasion to Judy Garland's compartment and an old-fashioned or two to Clark Gable's quarters. Gable enjoyed a game of gin rummy in the club lounge, and Jefferson knew to have fresh decks of Bicycle playing cards ready whenever the actor complained about his bad luck. He also knew that both Gable and Mickey Cohen showered at least twice a day, so he stocked their compartments with extra towels.

The Hollywood stars treated him with respect and tipped generously. Many, he learned from the tales they told him, came from humble beginnings. The corporate types were a mixed bag. Wealthy men in tailored suits, wives dripping with pearls and diamonds. All white folks, of course. The Negro passengers were usually entertainers. Count Basie once brought his orchestra to the West Coast on the Super Chief. With a piano added to the club lounge, what a dandy trip that had been.

Jefferson delivered the gin and tonic on a silver tray to the man listed on the manifest as Frederick Fredericks. Entering the compartment, he placed the cocktail on the small writing table along with a stainless steel cocktail shaker, brimming with condensation.

"Ah, an extra portion," Fritz Duquesne said happily.

"Lucius tends to do that for drawing room passengers," Jefferson said.

"Because we have so much room to roam we get thirstier?"

Jefferson allowed himself a chuckle. "That might be it, Mr. Fredericks."

They both knew that passengers who paid through the nose for drawing rooms, as opposed to roomettes, expected some perquisites. Duquesne sipped, smacked his lips, and said, "Perfect, as always. We Brits love our G&Ts."

"Yes, sir," Jefferson agreed. "Would you like me to turn down the bed?"

"Not necessary, but thank you. May I buy you one?"

"Sir?"

"A cocktail. Wet your whistle while you work."

"Kind of you, sir. But there are rules and regulations." Jefferson replayed the passenger's words. "Wet your whistle."

The slang sounded forced, as if I'd said, "Blimey, mate."

"If you need anything else, Mr. Fredericks, just hit the buzzer." Jefferson turned to leave, something catching his eye. A shard of adhesive tape attached to the window. He hadn't seen it when he walked into the compartment, but now it caught the light. Perhaps Mr. Fredericks taped a family photo to the window, but if he had, why take it down so soon? Leaving the compartment, Jefferson saw the small reddish-brown suitcase he had carried aboard for Mr. Fredericks.

"Books," Fredericks had said, explaining the hefty weight. "I'm quite a reader."

Perhaps he was, but there were no books on the writing table or the night stand or anywhere in the compartment. A trivial lie, if it was one, but there was something awkward about Mr. Fredericks' affect.

Once in the corridor, Jefferson thought about their conversation. "*We Brits love our G&Ts.*"

Mr. Fredericks indeed spoke with what at first sounded like a British accent. During his years on the rails, Jefferson had conversed with passengers from dozens of countries, and he had a finely tuned ear. Mr. Fredericks trilled his "r's" and spoke in just a hint of a sing-song.

Jefferson had heard all the British accents, from Cockney to the King's English. He remembered a passenger with similar intonation. He was a physician, an Afrikaner, a settler of Dutch descent from Cape Town in the Union of South Africa. The physician also ordered gin and tonics—three a night—and informed Jefferson that he prescribed the drink for patients with rheumatism.

Afrikaner or British, it makes no difference to me. People often pretend to be what they are not, maybe more so when traveling.

But that tape on the window? What was that about?

And when I entered the compartment, Mr. Fredericks' eyes shot to the heavy little suitcase. Why? To make sure he had closed it?

"Evening, Ezra," came the voice from behind.

Preoccupied with his thoughts, Jefferson had not noticed Mickey Cohen approaching. The man moved like a cat.

"Mr. Cohen," Jefferson said with sincere enthusiasm, "I hope you'll be joining us for dinner. As I recall, you're partial to calf's sweetbreads."

"Already ate at the Fred Harvey in the station. LaVonne was starving."

"May I wish you congratulations on your marriage?"

A savvy porter kept tabs on his regular customers.

"Thank you, Ezra. Maybe we'll stop in the dining car for brandy and dessert. Pineapple parfaits on the menu?"

"And green apple pie."

The train rounded a curve, the car leaning just a bit.

"Say, Ezra. You know I'm traveling with Mr. Chaplin and Professor Einstein?"

"Yes, sir."

"I've got their backs, if you follow my drift. You see anything untoward, you lemme know first thing."

"Of course, Mr. Cohen. Are you expecting trouble?"

"Dunno." He patted his suit coat above his holstered revolver. "But I'm always prepared."

Jefferson thought of the little mystery of Mr. Fredericks, but that hardly seemed worth mentioning. He was aware of movement and turned to see two shoes sailing toward him. He caught one, but with his other hand holding the silver tray, the second shoe smacked his shoulder and fell to the floor. A lanky, loose-limbed man of perhaps thirty in gray flannel trousers and a white, V-neck tennis sweater grinned at him. "Hey, George. Shine those tonight, yeah?"

Jefferson picked up the fallen shoe, gritted his teeth, and forced a smile. "Of course, Mr. Lodge."

Harrington Lodge, III, according to the passenger manifest.

Cohen stepped in front of Jefferson, examined the maroon-and-white suede saddle shoes, peered at the young man through narrowed eyes and said, "Sweet shoes. Whadda you, a majorette?"

Lodge took a step toward Cohen to emphasize his greater height and said, "These shoes are quite the rage at the Greenwich Country Club. I don't suppose you're a member."

"And what's with 'George,' huh?"

"They're all called George."

"They?"

"Pullman porters! Because of George Pullman, they're all called George."

"Like slaves taking their masters' names?" Cohen's voice rasped with quiet menace. Jefferson cleared his throat and said, "It's all right, Mr. Cohen."

He appreciated what the pint-sized gangster was doing, but if Lodge complained, it would spell trouble for him. He saw Cohen balancing on his toes, left foot ahead of the right, and feared a hook to the gut would send Harrington Lodge III's toast points and foie gras all over the carpet.

"Cohen," Lodge said. "Your name's Coe-hen?" Chopping the syllables in two with a smirk.

"Yeah, you wanna call me Hymie? See how that goes?"

"Ah, look, fellow. I got nothing against darkies. But there's a pecking order. I've paid full fare for the best drawing room. I spend lavishly in the diner, and I tip handsomely. I unwind in the club lounge and enjoy the views from the observation car. I do all of that, and the porters shine shoes for a two-bit tip. It's the way of the world."

"When I was eight years old," Cohen said, "I shined shoes in Boyle Heights, and I know the likes of you. You give me any more lip, I'll settle your hash and quick."

"How dare you!"

Unruffled, Cohen said, "But I'm gonna give you a pass if you just say, 'Mr. Jefferson, would you be kind enough to shine my shoes?'"

Lodge licked his lips and studied Cohen's face, his bravado deflating like a punctured tire. Maybe he noticed the scar under one eye or the bent nose or maybe the name "Cohen" finally rang a bell. The papers back East occasionally mentioned him in stories about Murder, Inc.

Lodge's tongue flicked out, a harmless garden snake. His eyes, which had managed to smirk nearly as much as his mouth, took on a wary look. With just the hint of a grimace, he said, "Mr. Jefferson, would you be kind enough to shine my shoes?"

"Of course, Mr. Lodge," Jefferson said, exhaling.

"It was a pleasure meeting you, Mr. Cohen," Lodge said, a lie so blatant Jefferson had to clench his jaw to keep from laughing.

Cohen grinned at him. "I'm as pleased to make your acquaintance as the time I had dinner with Al Capone at the Four Deuces. Spaghetti with clams."

Lodge turned and hurried off, as if he had a pressing appointment.

Cohen pulled a wad of currency from a pants pocket, peeled off a twenty-dollar bill and handed it to Jefferson, who tried to turn it down.

"No need, Mr. Cohen, Really."

"Ain't a tip, Ezra. I need your help."

"Sir?"

"You've got eyes and ears on all the passengers, ain't that right?"

"Part of the job, Mr. Cohen."

"Like I was saying before that dumb cluck butted in, I'm looking after Chaplin and Einstein. Anyone give you the heebie jeebies, anyone looks cross-eyed at my two friends, anything just a whisker out of kilter..."

"I will alert you with haste," Ezra Jefferson promised.

THIRTY-NINE
THE DINING CAR CHARADE

The aroma of grilled meat mingled with cigarette smoke. The snowy tablecloths were Irish linen, the finger bowls gleaming silver, the flatware polished to a mirror finish and with a reassuring heft. If not for the Santa Fe's monogrammed drumhead logo on the napkins and the hum of wheels on rails, diners might have thought themselves in Chicago's Pump Room. This was the *Cochiti*, the dining car, with walls of reddish brown bubinga wood and chairs with a lustrous green upholstery.

Enjoying their dinner and each other's company, J. Robert Oppenheimer and Albert Einstein did not pay particular notice to their surroundings...or the eavesdroppers on either side of them.

Brian Sullivan and Milagros Vazquez studied their menus. At the table on the scientists' other side, Fritz Duquesne nursed his third gin and tonic, tilting his head to catch their words with his good ear.

Three tables away, Chaplin dined with Lena Horne, who had found him interesting enough to share a late supper as the Super Chief hurtled through the night. With the train swaying around a curve, graceful as a ballerina's pirouette, Chaplin carefully poured Lena a Château Margaux, its deep crimson catching the light.

"I recommend the lamb chops with Lyonnaise potatoes and French fried onions," he said.

"Sounds fattening," Lena said.

"Good heavens! You're slender, svelte, willowy. You have a figure Venus de Milo would envy."

"It would be hard for her to eat with no arms, Charlie."

Einstein's wild white hair had been tamed for dinner. Beside him, Oppenheimer's intensity showed in every angle of his face, sharp planes like a hatchet blade. He was tackling a Super Chief specialty—the toasted Mexican sandwich, an open-faced concoction of roast beef, hard-boiled eggs, green chiles, pimentos, and celery beneath a mantle of melted cheese. Einstein eyed the towering sandwich with envy as he cut his Lake Superior whitefish into precise bites. They had the table to themselves. Oppenheimer's bride Kitty had retired early, claiming fatigue.

"And how is your son Hans?" Oppenheimer asked. "A civil engineer, if memory serves."

"Hydraulic engineer," Einstein said.

"A practical profession."

Einstein smiled. "He's building a dam in South Carolina. Not like us, searching for a four-leaf clover all our lives."

Duquesne would have savored his oysters Rockefeller—buttered and breaded to perfection—if he hadn't been straining to catch every word. His good ear's tinnitus complicated matters. But so far, only family talk.

He had read Abwehr's dossier on Oppenheimer. Though born in New York, he earned his doctorate at Göttingen in Germany at twenty-three. Beyond English and German, he commanded French, Latin, and Greek—even mastering Sanskrit to read the *Bhagavad Gita* in its original form. Duquesne planned to skip dessert—that damned expanding waistline—but found himself watching a waiter ferry a slice of lemon meringue pie on a silver platter. A distinctly American dish, the combination of tart citrus with airy, sweet meringue. A memory came to him. Heinrich Himmler saying the Americans "were soft as meringue. If they enter the war, we can devour them with a spoon."

Himmler! The four-eyed idiot had never been in the wild. A tiger may be asleep, but it is still a tiger.

Duquesne instructed the waiter to save him a slice of pie, then re-focused his attention on the two scientists. After a moment, he believed he was hallucinating.

They're speaking German!

If they thought that shielded their conversation, Duquesne mused, they were like Roman legions blindly storming the center of Hannibal's forces, only to be enveloped and massacred.

Two geniuses dining together, absent-minded professors of American lore, eccentric and aloof from everyday life, oblivious to lurking dangers.

Straining to hear over clinking flatware and clacking wheels, Duquesne's practiced mind translated their conversation.

Are they talking about nuclear fission? This could be a gold mine!

Speaking German, Einstein said, "How far along do you suppose Heisenberg is?"

"He visited Bohr in Copenhagen but wasn't very forthcoming," Oppenheimer answered in German, "except to say that the complexities of harnessing nuclear fission were even greater than he had imagined."

"Good news, that."

"But they're still ahead of us. The Germans have a unified uranium project, not a gaggle of scientists at a dozen universities, each unaware of the others' work."

"Which is why the President formed the NDRC," Einstein said.

Oppenheimer wiped melted cheese from his upper lip. "Ah, yes. The government's propensity to form committees. And what will those old men do, other than store research papers in file cabinets?"

Einstein, his age about the median of those "old men," chose his words as carefully as a chef chooses fresh pike at the fish market. "That's why Major Groves is so interested in you."

Oppenheimer's gaze drifted to the window, where darkness swallowed the endless cornfields, broken only by occasional farmhouse lights. "Do you think the Major is up to his task? The man's specialty is building barracks."

Einstein nibbled at his whitefish. "I would wager the barracks' roofs don't leak. I would also bet he's inclined to make you head of the bomb project."

"Albert, I'm a scientist, not an administrator."

"Your brain is wired differently. You're like those chess masters who play several boards at once. Or a symphony conductor who directs multiple sections while detecting the tiniest flaw in the brass or woodwinds."

Oppenheimer sipped at his wine, a French Chablis the dining car steward had recommended. "The responsibility, the stress," he said, shoulders slumping. "I am not strong physically." He sighed. "It would probably be better for me to ride horses at a canter in the New Mexico sunshine."

"Please don't take offense, Oppie, but if you are only for yourself, what are you?"

"You goad me by paraphrasing Hillel the Elder."

"Who also said, 'And if not now, when?' To which I would add, if not you, who then?"

His sandwich half uneaten, Oppenheimer lit a cigarette and continued in German. "The best person to run America's atomic program is Werner Heisenberg."

Einstein replied in German, "True, he's a great scientist."

"And not a member of the Nazi party. He caught hell for teaching your relativity, Albert."

Einstein chuckled. "The Nazis called it 'degenerate Jewish physics.' I'm not sure what Protestant physics might be."

Oppenheimer took a long pull on his Chesterfield and said, "Between you and me, Bohr says Heisenberg wants to defect, wants to come to America."

Einstein rocked back in his chair. "*Gotenyu!*" he said, switching to Yiddish. "Have you told Major Groves?"

Duquesne sucked in a breath and held it.

Heisenberg defect!

The old spy would not exhale for fear the sound would interfere with his hearing.

Oppenheimer placed an index finger across his lips as if to say, *hush-hush,* but still spoke loud enough for Duquesne to hear. "When Heisenberg travels to occupied Denmark, the Danish resistance and U.S. Army Intelligence will launch a joint operation to get both Bohr and Heisenberg to our shores."

Duquesne felt the hair bristle on the back of his neck. His lemon meringue pie had arrived and remained untouched.

Food is unimportant. Drink is irrelevant. Information is everything.

Then just as he had done during decades of espionage, he closed his eyes and savored this intelligence bombshell, hardly believing his own ears. He would get a message to Admiral Canaris at Abwehr. What a feat of genius, pulling the rug out from under the SS, which should have had eyes and ears on Heisenberg every moment of every day.

Age be damned, I am Germany's greatest intelligence asset, my exploits the stuff of legend.

At the table on the other side of the two scientists, Brian Sullivan said, "Millie, what are those geniuses saying?"

"Hopefully, what we told them to say," Milagros Vazquez replied. "I thought you spoke German."

"High school German. I can say, 'Which way to the opera?'"

Between whispers, Sullivan and Vazquez pretended to eat, ersatz honeymooners sharing roast prime rib of beef with horseradish sauce and creamed spinach on the side. They started with Romanoff Malossol caviar, Sullivan hoping that J. Edgar Hoover would see their expense reports and have a stroke over the $1.75 appetizer. The splendid dinner, however, was not on the FBI agent's mind. Just hours out of Chicago, the train ride had become a counterintelligence operation. Thanks to Millie, Sullivan had to admit. She snapped the photo of Duquesne in the New Jersey diner then recognized him at the Dearborn Station. She suggested having Chaplin and Oppenheimer plant disinformation with the aging spy and hope the Germans put Heisenberg, their most brilliant physicist, under lock and key. It was a long shot but reflected the kind of ingenuity the Bureau often lacked.

When the hell would J. Edgar Hoover allow women to become agents? The man was a Neanderthal!

At the Kansas City station, Sullivan would call New York and roust the agent in charge from sleep. There was much to report. New York knew Duquesne was on the prowl but not that he'd surfaced on the Super Chief. Once the pharmacist recanted his confession and professed not to know anyone named Fritz, there was no evidence to tie Duquesne to the NDRC espionage case. Perhaps the smartest play was to simply feed him misinformation.

Sullivan had ordered a bottle of a fine red Bordeaux on the Bureau's tab. Now he raised his glass, and when Vazquez did the same, he offered the traditional military toast: "Confusion to the enemy."

Chaplin had reached the conclusion that Lena Horne would not be sharing the tidy bed in his drawing room, but he didn't care. He was enjoying her company. While he worked through his lamb chops and French fried onions, Lena dined on cold shrimp cocktail and aspic salad. As they talked, she spoke of her plans once she achieved success—her commitment to civil rights. "There are clubs that won't hire me, restaurants that won't serve me, hotels where I can't stay."

"That has to change," Chaplin agreed. "The subjugation of Negroes is a cancer on our society."

"If we do go to war..."

Chaplin knew where she was headed. "Yes! Returning Negro servicemen will be the vanguard. How do you deprive people of equality when they fought for your country?"

They fell silent as the Super Chief's air horn shattered the night and the train thundered through a crossing.

"There you are!" boomed a voice. The scent of French cologne—sharp citrus mingled with warm cinnamon—announced Mickey Cohen's arrival before he appeared at the table.

"Evening, Mickey," Chaplin said.

"Yo, Charlie, I'm supposed to keep tabs on you, and you keep disappearing."

"C'mon, join us. Where's LaVonne?"

"Taking a nap 'cause I wore her out, if you take my meaning." He winked at Lena. "Honeymoon, you know."

Cohen sat down, and Chaplin introduced him to Lena.

"Pleased to meet you, Mr. Cohen," she said.

"You're that songbird from New York," Mickey said. "A regular chantoosy."

Chanteuse, Chaplin figured.

"Lena's looking for engagements in Los Angeles," Chaplin said.

"You've come to the right place," Cohen said. "I can book you into Ciro's. Fanciest joint on the Strip."

"Are you sure management will hire a Negro?" she asked.

Cohen barked a laugh. "If they don't, they better have their fire insurance paid up."

"Well, that would be wonderful," Lena said, her voice melodious as a song. "This is so kind of you, Mr. Cohen."

"Hey, coloreds and Jews gotta stick together. Put it to the white man. No offense, Charlie."

Chaplin chortled. "I'm part Romani. My mother claims I was born in a gypsy caravan."

Cohen clapped Chaplin on the shoulder. "You two enjoy your dinner. I'm gonna wake up LaVonne and tell her they're serving those blinis with caviar she eats like jelly beans."

After Cohen left the table, Chaplin said, "What Mickey didn't tell you was that he's a silent partner in Ciro's along with Bugsy Siegel."

"Oh, my. Is that something that should concern me?"

"Not a bit. Ciro's books big-name acts, and every star in Hollywood dines there. You'll meet a lot of people."

"Including Bugsy Siegel?"

"Siegel and Cohen are dipping their beaks into every nightclub and gambling den on the Strip. There's no getting away from them."

She seemed to ponder all of that for a moment, and Chaplin said, "Reading your mind, yes Lena, your life's about to change."

While they ate, the conversation turned to Hollywood. "What I admire about your pictures, Charlie, is your courage," Lena said. "Your pictures reveal universal themes drawn from your most painful experiences."

"Not so. My pictures aren't about me."

"Oh, please." Her laugh sparkled like firecrackers. "In *The Kid*, the abandoned child being sent to an orphanage is you."

He shrugged. "No father around, my mother off to the insane asylum, and yes, they shipped me to the workhouse. But otherwise, it's not my story."

"Otherwise? How about *The Gold Rush*, when you're eating the boiled shoe? That was about your hunger and deprivation. The Tramp who's scorned for his poverty in *City Lights* is you, and *Modern Times* overflows with your compassion for overworked, underpaid laborers, many of whom were Negroes. The lesson for me is that you can go posh and still retain your integrity."

"You may have missed your calling as a headworker or alienist. I can't wait for you to analyze me after you see *The Great Dictator*."

"Caught a matinee at the Astor last week," she said.

Chaplin sliced a lamb chop with a steak knife. Before popping a slice of meat into his mouth, he said, "Did you find it to be an expression of my repressed desire to rule the world?"

"Hardly. It reveals you to be an incurable optimist."

"Most would say the opposite. Europe is run by Hitler and Mussolini, and even though they're buffoons, they're bloodthirsty buffoons."

"That's the background of your story but not your message."

Chaplin raised his eyebrows, as if to say, "Go on."

Lena studied the aspic salad on her plate, the consommé gelatin shimmying like a belly dancer's hips. "You believe your art is so powerful it can change the world. It can turn the masses against totalitarians. Countries will choose brotherhood and peace over hatred and war."

Chaplin's fork stopped in mid-air between his plate and his mouth. "Well, Lena, I can dream, can't I?"

FORTY-ONE
KANSAS CITY CONUNDRUM
Sunday, November 10, 1940

The Super Chief barreled through the night past silent farms and sleeping towns. It swept through railway stations without pause, crossed the Mississippi at Fort Madison, cut through a sliver of Iowa, then thundered past Marceline, Missouri, pulling into Kansas City station at 2:35 a.m.—precisely on time—what railroaders called "the Chief way." The ten-minute stop would allow coupling a new sleeping car, its passengers tucked into their berths hours earlier.

In his drawing room, Chaplin slept fitfully, legs churning as if running. He dreamed of Big Ben tolling midnight, a Luftwaffe bomb striking the great tower, all of London burning, orange flames and oily smoke devouring the night sky.

In his compartment, Einstein stirred, rolled over and drifted back to sleep, snoring as softly as cosmic dust floating through the universe.

Wide awake and still on duty, Ezra Jefferson stood alert on the platform, his white uniform crisp, tunic buttoned, cap and tie precise. The veteran porter watched for wandering passengers while around him the station hummed with activity. Workers loaded fresh produce and topped off diesel tanks and steam generators. A four-man crew of "tonks" rushed through their undercarriage inspections, checking for hot bearings, worn brake shoes, misaligned wheels and axles, searching for any telltale grease or oil that might signal trouble. The burly conductor stood at the rear of the train, eyes scanning the platform.

Only two passengers stepped into the chill night air. Brian Sullivan headed for the Western Union office, its lights burning twenty-four hours a day. Sensing movement, he turned to find Fritz Duquesne twenty yards back. The men locked eyes, motionless. Sullivan tucked his left elbow against his chest, checking that his .38 was holstered, and immediately felt foolish.

For a moment, it seemed as if he were looking down on the scene—the stainless steel locomotive purring, diesel fumes sharp in the air, the conductor with his whistle watching, two men facing off on the platform. Sullivan thought of John Wayne as the Ringo Kid in *Stagecoach*, but that wasn't quite right. Then *Union Pacific* came to mind, Joel McCrea battling corrupt railroad men. Duquesne's right hand slipped under his suit coat, exactly where a right-handed man would carry his weapon.

Sullivan tensed, but Duquesne's hand emerged holding only an envelope. Another man crossed the platform, coming from the direction of the parking lot, striding toward Duquesne. About fifty with brush-cut cornflower hair, he wore bib overalls, a red plaid shirt and work boots.

The men shook hands, Duquesne passed over the envelope, and they exchanged words too distant to hear.

What the hell? Who's the farmer, and what brings him here in the dead of night to meet a German spy?

"Five minutes!" the conductor called out.

Sullivan hurried across the platform, past a dormant popcorn machine and shuttered newsstand and entered the Western Union office. He flashed his badge at a drowsy clerk in a green eyeshade and ordered him out while he used the phone. It was 4:40 a.m. in New York. Sullivan doubted Aidan Murphy would welcome his voice.

"Murphy." The agent in charge's greeting ended in a hacking cough.

"Sullivan here, sir. Sorry for the late call."

"Commies or Nazis, Sullivan?"

"The latter, sir. Fritz Duquesne. On the Super Chief."

"I'll be damned. That old bastard gets around. What's he up to?"

"We don't know yet. But he's shadowing Einstein or Chaplin, or both, and he just met a contact in the middle of the night at the Kansas City station."

"I don't like the sound of that." Static crackled across the long-distance line. "Is he booked through to Los Angeles?"

"That's why I'm calling, sir. Southern California's crawling with Silver Shirts and half a dozen other fascist groups. LAPD thought they were just beer-guzzling loudmouths until—"

"Operation Hollywood," Murphy interrupted. "They knocked over an armory and plotted a couple dozen assassinations. What do you need, Sullivan?"

"Two tactical teams at Union Station. A perimeter on Alameda Street. Four agents on the platform no less than two hours before the train pulls into the station."

"Consider it done. Anything else?"

Sullivan detailed the Werner Heisenberg gambit, explaining how Oppenheimer and Einstein spoke in German, giving Millie Vazquez full credit.

Murphy chuckled. "That was worth waking up for, Sullivan. You think Duquesne bought it?"

"He wants to believe it's true. His history suggests he yearns to be a hero."

"Then he surely chose the wrong profession," Agent Murphy said, hanging up the phone.

FORTY-TWO
A MORAL DILEMMA

After a lousy night's sleep, Chaplin regretted listening to Edward R. Murrow's broadcast before getting into bed.

"Back at headquarters," Murrow began, "I saw a man laboriously copying names in a big ledger, the firemen killed in action during the last month. There were about a hundred names. I can now appreciate what lies behind that line in the morning communiques: 'All fires were quickly brought under control.'"

Fears for his homeland, for London's citizens, haunted him. The real torment, though, was his powerlessness to help. He couldn't win over Lindbergh or Henry Ford or the *Tribune's* Robert McCormick or the great mass of the American people. If polled today, the isolationists would surely prevail.

Just before six a.m., as the Super Chief neared Dodge City, Kansas, Chaplin headed for the dining car, though breakfast service hadn't begun. Surely a cuppa could be had—a full-bodied Ceylon black tea. Walking down the corridor, he smelled cigarette smoke coming from a partially open door in a drawing room near the front of the car.

Charles Lindbergh's compartment.

A woman's hand gripped the edge of the door from inside. It was difficult to tell if she was coming or going or just standing still. Her fingers were long and graceful, the nails painted a bright crimson that reminded Chaplin of Rita Hayworth's distinctive manicure he'd seen up close at a San Simeon party. A puff of smoke wafted out the open door.

Sweet, a little spicy. Not Camel or Chesterfield, both of which Chaplin smoked in his younger days. Then it struck him—Ernst Lubitsch's cigarettes! He'd visited the German director on the *Ninotchka* set barely a year ago. Lubitsch had shared his Overstolz, their aroma unmistakable. German cigarettes.

"I'm sorry, *Liebling. Ich muss los,*" came the woman's voice from inside the room. Telling Lindbergh, "I'm sorry, darling. I must go."

"Until tonight then," came a man's voice, clearly Lindbergh's. "Hug little Otto for me."

The door opened wider, and Chaplin retreated to a spot behind the linen locker at the end of the car. Unseen, he watched the tall, exquisite woman from the Dearborn Station leaving Lindbergh's compartment. She wore a midnight blue satin cocktail dress, one strap slipping off a shoulder, and she carried her black patent leather high-heels in one hand. Her blond hair was mussed, a sparrow's nest after a storm. With her free hand, she straightened a black seamed stocking, which was bunched behind a knee. An Overstolz dangled from her lips, smoke curling upward, making her eyes flutter. No longer so elegant, the woman's heavy-lidded look made Chaplin think of Marlene Dietrich, slouched like a slattern against a street lamp in a von Sternberg picture.

Lindbergh has himself a Teutonic tart, and I have a miniature camera in my compartment, courtesy of Major Groves and Army Intelligence.

The woman disappeared into the gangway, bound for her compartment in the next car.

Chaplin entertained a fantasy of hiding in Lindbergh's wardrobe with the miniature camera, waiting for her evening return. Then memories of his own scandalous divorce from Lita Grey flooded back—the lurid allegations of affairs, the divorce petition's charges of "perverted sexual desires," screaming headlines, and thundering denunciations from Sunday pulpits. One prominent newspaper columnist had posed the question: "Do Chaplin's masterful works of art trump his repulsive moral character?"

Would I really inflict such vicious slander on Charles Lindbergh? I despise his politics, not the man.

People love to tear down their heroes' statues, do they not? Is schadenfreude an even more delicious state of mind than idolization? The bigger they are, the harder they fall...and all that rot.

Something else occurred to Chaplin. It was during his combative divorce in 1927 that Lindbergh completed his historic solo flight across the Atlantic.

He was the "Lone Eagle," the greatest hero in the land, and I was a pariah.

His own career had weathered the storm—the American public's memory, thankfully, lasted about as long as unpasteurized milk. Now, he questioned whether some buried resentment colored his feelings toward the pilot-turned-political-prophet.

No. This isn't personal. This is about rescuing a culture and a people whose very existence hangs by a thread.

The equation seemed simple enough: Britain's survival surely outweighs one man's reputation.

But can I achieve the former by destroying the latter? And even if I could, should I?

Just after 8 a.m., having walked the length of the train several times, Chaplin was still wrestling with his moral dilemma with no resolution in sight. As the Super Chief neared Syracuse, Kansas, the rich aroma of Fred Harvey coffee and sizzling bacon welcomed him back to the dining car. Beyond the windows, a lazy morning sun washed over grassy cattle fields where black Angus and red Herefords grazed in the golden light.

He stopped short at the sight of Lindbergh and Einstein sharing a table, both smiling. "Join us, Chap," Lindbergh called out, patting an empty chair.

Chaplin sat, accepted coffee from a hovering waiter, and Einstein said, "I asked Mr. Lindbergh how he managed to fly thirty-three hours across the Atlantic without relieving himself. On more than one occasion, I engaged in thought experiments all night long and found, by morning, I had wet myself."

Lindbergh chuckled. "I told the professor I had a jar with a funnel to relieve myself, then tossed the contents out the side window to reduce weight."

"If you'd kept it, that jar would be worth a pretty penny," Chaplin said.

Lindbergh's puzzled look prompted Chaplin to add, "Think about it, Slim. All those old inns brag, 'George Washington slept here.' Is that any better than 'Charles Lindbergh pissed here?'"

Their shared laughter filled the car, and Lindbergh said, "The three of us should be friends, regardless of our differences over politics."

The waiter delivered French toast with orange marmalade for Einstein and shirred eggs baked in heavy cream for Lindbergh. Chaplin, the latecomer, ordered wheat cakes slathered in maple syrup.

"I enjoy your company," Lindbergh said, "both of you."

"That's what I hate about you, Slim," Chaplin said, and Lindbergh looked as if he'd been slapped in the face. "You're so damned likable."

All three men laughed.

"The three of us occupy a sacred ground," Lindbergh said. "We're men of the world. Germany, England, America. We've seen things and we've done things no other men have or ever will."

Chaplin thought that crossing the Atlantic, replicated hundreds of times since, probably ought not to be equated with Einstein rewriting the laws of the universe, but chose to keep silent.

"Say, Chap, I caught your new picture in Chicago the other day," Lindbergh continued.

Chaplin waited for a critique, but it didn't come. Unable to resist, he said, "As a man of the world, Slim, how'd you like my final speech about seeking a life where men rise above hate and brutality?"

"Never heard it, Chap. I hit the road when you did that swishy dance with the balloon. You're ridiculing a man millions think is the savior of his country."

"A messiah?" Einstein asked.

"Hitler didn't just build tanks and airplanes," Lindbergh said. "He lifted the spirits of a downtrodden country, gave pride and hope to a devastated people."

"Slim, there's something I can't get out of my mind," Chaplin said. "The sinking of the *Benares*."

"Sure, sure," Lindbergh said. "You made a meal out of that at Dearborn. Seventy-seven British children killed. The gosh-darned arithmetic of war."

"Lenny Grimmond," Chaplin said, echoing Lena Horne's advice: *Save the child.*

"Who's that, Chap?"

"One of those children. He was five years old."

"You're aces at pulling heartstrings, Chap," Lindbergh said, flatly.

"Gussie Grimmond, Violet Grimmond, Connie Grimmond, and another boy whose name I don't yet know."

Lindbergh's expression darkened. "Are you telling me five siblings went down with that ship?"

"The children died horrific deaths, screaming for their mother and father."

"Mother of mercy," Lindbergh whispered.

Are you showing emotion, Slim? At long last, do you have empathy for the pain of others?

"The U-Boat captain didn't know their names," Chaplin said, "but I thought we should."

Lindbergh shook his head sadly. "But Chap, you just proved my point about war. The loss. The heartbreak. We need to stay the heck out of it."

Chaplin was deflated.

I'll never change his mind with logic and reason...or emotion. Must I resort to blackmail?

For a moment, the three men listened to the drone of the diesel engines, the rhythmic *clackety-clack* of wheels on rails, and the soft chime of silverware against fine china. The Super Chief sped along a straightaway, smooth as a toboggan on fresh powder.

Einstein broke the silence. "Mr. Lindbergh, what will you say in your radio address to a spellbound nation?"

"I'm going to talk about the three groups of agitators pushing us toward a disastrous war with Germany."

"I suspect that my countrymen are first on your list," Chaplin said.

"Indeed," Lindbergh said. "Churchill and the Brits are trying to light the fuse."

"That wonderful country took me in when I fled Germany in thirty-three," Einstein said. "I will be forever grateful to the British people."

"The Brits are dang clever," Lindbergh said, "using propaganda to incite hatred of Germany."

"By propaganda," Chaplin began, "do you mean those bomb blasts we hear on the radio, killing women and children every night in London?"

"They're toying with your emotions, Chap."

"True enough. They're hitting my compassion damn hard."

"The second group is, of course, the Roosevelt Administration," Lindbergh said. "Roosevelt has hitched his wagon to Churchill. He's put us on the path to war with lies and subterfuge. Destroyers-for-Bases, Cash-and-Carry, and now Lend-Lease. Each one a closer step to our boys on European soil."

"What's the third group?" Einstein asked.

Lindbergh reached inside his suit coat and pulled out several sheets of paper. Heavy linen stationery, watermarked and embossed with "C.A.L." at the top of each sheet.

Charles Augustus Lindbergh.

Lindbergh's speech was handwritten in bold, black ink with nary a word crossed out.

Chaplin figured Lindbergh considered his first drafts to be the last word on any issue.

Lindbergh turned to Einstein. "This is delicate, Professor. I want to make sure I get every word right so as not to be offensive."

"Ah, so this is where you slander the Jews," Einstein said.

FORTY-THREE
MESSAGE FROM HAMBURG

Breakfast could wait. Fritz Duquesne had a wireless schedule to keep, and that took precedence over bacon and eggs. He unpacked his suitcase with practiced efficiency, attached the cables and headset, and taped the short antenna to the window frame.

By now, the Missouri agent—disguised as a farmhand—would have contacted their Mexico operatives about securing the seaplane and crew, as detailed in Duquesne's hand-delivered letter. He would have relayed the message to East Quogue, where their man would have coordinated with Hamburg for the kidnaping plan's particulars.

Seconds after powering up, Morse code clicked in his ears. It took fifteen minutes to decode the transmission. There were three messages. The first was short and undeniably sweet:

"NEEDLES PREPARED. PROCEED."

Excellent. The chess pieces were in position for snatching Einstein during their ten-minute stop at Needles station. Even at 2:08 a.m., the platform would buzz with activity—crew change, diesel refueling, mail and freight transfers, and redcaps escorting a few late-night passengers aboard for the ride to Los Angeles.

Perfect cover for their plan: lure a sleepy, unsuspecting Einstein from his drawing room onto the platform. The bait: an urgent, confidential War Department telegram. Government instructions would require the station agent to positively identify Einstein before releasing the wire. The real agent would be bound and gagged and replaced by a Bund operative in purloined uniform, who would escort Einstein to the telegraph office. Or more precisely, *near* the office—where Duquesne and the operative would hustle the scientist to the parking lot, into a waiting Lincoln Zephyr, and to the seaplane on the Colorado River less than a mile away.

The second message responded to his query about the blonde registered as Margaret Jones:

"LISELOTTE MULLER. ABWEHR LISTENER, FILE SEALED. DO NOT INTERFERE."

Interfere with what?

So Liselotte Müller had been an Abwehr employee, one of those young women in cubicles wearing headsets, decoding endless wireless transmissions, routing replies from case officers to one desk or another. Then her personnel records were sealed. That ordinarily meant a transfer to a highly confidential position, but what? SS training in Berlin? And why keep him in the dark?

"DO NOT INTERFERE."

That implied an ongoing mission. She could be a full-fledged Abwehr agent or even—*Gott bewahre!*—an SS officer.

The third message was even more troubling:

"ADMIRAL SAW PHOTO ON WIRE SERVICES. SAYS YOU'VE AGED."

Oh, those flashbulbs and the damn American press at Dearborn Station. Admiral Canaris, his longtime patron, was displeased.

"You've aged" has nothing to do with bags under my eyes. It's the Admiral's way of suggesting retirement might be imminent... one way or another.

FORTY-FOUR
RADIOACTIVE MEN

Lindbergh smoothed the sheets of stationery on the breakfast table. Einstein and Chaplin waited for his preview of his upcoming radio address.

"The Jewish race agitates for war when it should oppose it, for they will be among the first to feel its consequences," Lindbergh read aloud.

Einstein chose not to point out that a religion was not a race but did not want to interrupt the flow.

"The greatest danger to our country lies in the Jewish ownership and influence in our pictures, our press, our radio, and our government," Lindbergh continued. "We must limit the Jewish influence for we know that whenever the Jewish percentage of total population becomes too high, a reaction invariably occurs." Lindbergh paused, turned the page sideways, then read a line that appeared to have been added to the speech. "That is regrettable because a few Jews of the right type are an asset to any country."

"I suppose I'm of the right type," Einstein said.

"Of course you are, Professor."

"Did a Jewish friend add that sentence to your speech?"

"No, why would you suggest that?"

Einstein tapped his index finger on the stationery. "It's a different handwriting than yours. The letters are more rounded, the lines more curved, the pen strokes lighter and more delicate. A more feminine hand than yours."

"When I'm tired, my handwriting tends in that direction," Lindbergh said.

"I see," Einstein said.

Chaplin processed that tidbit of information, wondering who would edit Lindbergh's speech to make him seem less antisemitic. The Reich, he concluded. Paradoxically, if Berlin wanted him to run for President in 1944, Goebbels and his propaganda machine would want to smooth out Lindbergh's rough edges. And if Albert was right about a feminine handwriting, could the ghostwriter be the blonde who smokes German cigarettes and hot-foots it from Lindbergh's compartment? Does she write his speeches as well as warm his bed?

Putting aside those thoughts for the moment, Chaplin said, "Slim, you gotta know that William Randolph Hearst has more influence than all the Jews put together. Why aren't you taking shots at the Methodists?"

"Aw, c'mon Chap. That's not a serious question." Lindbergh hastily folded the pages of his speech and tucked them into a suit pocket. "And please don't think for one minute that I'm happy with the way Germany is treating its Jews. Certainly, they have a Jewish problem, but violence is not the answer."

Einstein cleared his throat. "Mr. Lindbergh, do you recall that last year when you were still on good terms with President Roosevelt, I wrote you a letter?"

"Of course. You enclosed a message to FDR, urging him to launch a program to build a new-newfangled bomb. You wanted me to deliver it, probably figuring that coming from me, it would carry some weight."

"Precisely. But you never gave my letter to the President or even acknowledged receiving it."

"Sorry, Professor, but I want Roosevelt to sign a neutrality pact with Germany, not attack her with some whopping big bomb."

"The pact would be the death knell of England," Chaplin said, his voice rising.

"Not our problem," Lindbergh said. "It's America First. Thankfully, God is on our side."

"Oh, for Christ's sake!" Chaplin blurted.

"Precisely," Lindbergh said.

Einstein harrumphed, and Lindbergh continued, "Professor, don't tell me you're one of those scientists who doesn't believe in a deity, even a Hebrew one."

"I don't believe in a God sitting on a throne, listening to our prayers. *Oy*, what a boring job! I believe in pantheism, that the universe, which has existed since the beginning of time, is our supreme divinity."

"So you're not looking forward to an afterlife?" Lindbergh pressed. Einstein shook his head. "One life is enough for me."

"For my part," Lindbergh said, "I'm more worried about the godless Soviets than the Christian Germans. And I fret about miscegenation with a sea of yellow, black, and brown immigrants."

"You're not still harping on eugenics, are you Slim?" Chaplin asked.

"If you'd lived on a farm with barnyard animals, you'd know eugenics is part of nature."

"I'll say this about you," Chaplin said. "You seldom have doubts about anything."

"Thanks, Chap."

"But you're often wrong!"

Einstein, after a contemplative pause, said, "Mr. Lindbergh, in recent weeks, the Nazi occupiers imprisoned half a million Jews in a walled-off section of Warsaw."

"*Ghetto Warschau,*" Lindbergh said with the perfect intonation of a Berliner. "I don't condone such actions, Professor, but considering the hostility between Polish Christians and Jews, perhaps your people are safer there."

Einstein threw up his hands. "What a *bubbe meise!*" The Yiddish slang for "nonsense" cut through the air like a sharp rebuke.

Lindbergh's attention was diverted by the tall, blond woman with the little boy entering the dining car. She wore a small, structured tilted hat in navy blue. The waves of her sunflower hair fell to the shoulders of her matching navy waist-length jacket. Her pencil skirt was knee length, her seamed stockings nude, giving her legs a sleek, polished look. Pearl earrings completed the understated elegance.

Cleans up nicely, Chaplin thought.

The little boy with hair the color of straw wore a double-breasted navy sport coat with gold buttons, gray wool trousers, a white shirt and a striped tie of gray and gold. To Chaplin, who personally supervised the wardrobe department in all his movies, the woman appeared to be a tastefully dressed socialite, Carole Lombard in *My Man Godfrey.* The boy resembled a pint-sized yachtsman or maybe the lead character in *Little Lord Fauntleroy.*

The pair stopped at their table, the woman nodding to Lindbergh. "Good morning, Charles."

"Margaret," Lindbergh said, then turned to the boy. "Otto, what's for breakfast? Kippers?"

"No, sir. Oatmeal for me."

"Good lad." Lindbergh patted the boy on the head.

"Forgive Charles' bad manners," the woman said. "I am Margaret Jones, and this is my son, Otto."

An All-American name, but spoken with an accent, Chaplin remembering her fluent German in her post-coital dishevelment.

Einstein smoothed his mustache with a napkin and said, "And I am Albert."

"Charlie," Chaplin said.

"Oh, I recognize the two of you. Tell me, are you three luminaries solving the problems of the world?"

"Hardly," Chaplin said. "We can't even agree on the problems."

The woman smiled, nodded goodbye, and walked with the boy to a table near the rear of the car.

After a sip of coffee, Chaplin said, "Slim, how do you get away with it?"

"With what, my friend?"

Chaplin raised his fork, laden with a chunk of wheat cake, then pointed in the direction of Carole Lombard and Little Lord Fauntleroy. "Having a spotless reputation as the golden boy."

"Or the golden *goy*," Einstein said.

"While all my indiscretions pop up in Hedda Hopper's column," Chaplin added.

Lindbergh displayed his famous aw-shucks grin. "True enough, Chap. Your conquests are legendary, and mine are politely circumspect." Turning to Einstein, he said, "Professor, if I can get personal, do you have any skeletons in your closet?"

"He means your bedroom, Albert," Chaplin said.

"Well, I hardly think that's a subject for breakfast," Einstein said, reddening.

"The answer is that Albert was unfaithful to both his wives," Chaplin said, "and now, as a widower, he's bedding down a married woman."

"Charlie! Was that necessary?"

"Great men attract women the way flowers attract bees," Lindbergh said.

Or horseshit attracts flies, Chaplin thought.

"I make no such excuses," Einstein said. "I am embarrassed by my conduct."

Lindbergh leaned back in his chair, perhaps contemplating his greatness. "Some of the fairer sex might consider us scoundrels, but gentlemen, are we to blame when women throw themselves at us? It's a fact of nature. Achievement. Power. Prestige. We're each dominant in our fields. The three of us are like...what is it, Professor, the element that emits radiation?"

"Radium, for one. It has an atomic nucleus with too much energy, which it releases as radiation."

"That's us! We're radioactive."

"We leave burns?" Einstein asked.

Barnyard animals and radioactive men, Chaplin thought. *What a bunch of malarkey!*

"Jeez, guys, even your hero FDR has been having an affair for twenty years, and he's a cripple," Lindbergh cracked with a grin.

"I've never heard anything about that," Chaplin said.

"Lucy Mercer, Eleanor's secretary at one time. FDR's been giving her his New Deal 'til it ain't so new. J. Edgar Hoover told me."

Chaplin scoffed. "Then it must be true."

Lindbergh plowed ahead. "I may disagree with Roosevelt's politics, but I understand his biological imperative, just like ours."

"Meaning what?" Chaplin asked.

"Our evolutionary need to spread our seed."

Toying with a thought, Chaplin looked out the window where a wheat field bordered the tracks. The wheat would have been harvested in summer, and now the stalks were short and stubby, yet still danced in the slipstream from the train.

"She's a German national, isn't she, Slim?" Chaplin asked. "This so-called Margaret Jones."

"She is that."

"You crossed the Atlantic alone, but with this woman, you crossed the Rubicon."

"How so? She's just another gal."

"She could be an agent of the Reich. They could blackmail you to do their handiwork." Chaplin heard himself say the word "blackmail" and a sense of shame flooded over him.

That was his assignment for Major Groves and Army Intelligence. Peeping-Tom photos that would humiliate Lindbergh and destroy his carefully pruned public image.

Something I thought I could do but now realize I can't. This debate must be won fair and square.

"No need to blackmail me when I agree with the Reich on basic issues." Lindbergh turned to Einstein. "Not their treatment of Jews, Professor. That's damn excessive. And, of course, I remain patriotic to the U.S. of A."

"Yet, you accepted a fancy medal from Hermann Göring when the Roosevelt Administration asked you not to," Chaplin said.

"The Order of the German Eagle. It would have been rude to refuse."

"With this great power you say we have," Einstein said, "comes great responsibility. Our words, our deeds, must take into account the greater good."

"Precisely, Professor. I believe in the greater good for America. Europe be damned."

The Super Chief's air horn blared, and they were quiet a moment. Outside the windows, automobiles on a road running parallel to the train could not keep up, their windshields winking in the morning sun. Two roadside billboards flashed by:

PALMOLIVE - KEEP THAT SCHOOLGIRL COM-PLEXION

SCHLITZ - THE BEER THAT MADE MILWAUKEE FAMOUS

Einstein cleared his throat and said, "Mr. Lindbergh. Your evolutionary need to spread your seed…"

"Yes, Professor, what about it?"

Einstein couldn't find the words, so Chaplin said, "That little boy, Otto. He's your out-of-wedlock son, isn't he?"

"One of them," Lindbergh said, with no apparent emotion.

FORTY-FIVE
DAGWOOD BUMSTEAD

Freshly showered, shaved, his face tingling with the citrus notes of Eau de Cologne 4711, Fritz Duquesne entered the dining car. He wore a herringbone sport coat in light brown, high-waisted pleated trousers a shade darker, a crisp white shirt, and a dark green knit tie.

He was pleased to immediately spot Liselotte Müller and the little boy.

A grand day for making new friends, he thought. And since Duquesne had not one real friend in the world, what he meant was acquiring an ally, a co-conspirator useful in conquering joint enemies. The table next to Liselotte and the boy was empty, so he headed that way. He smiled at her when taking his seat, but she averted his gaze.

He ordered coffee, scrambled eggs with caviar and a basket of croissants. Liselotte was slicing into eggs Benedict while the boy was pouring milk from a creamer pot into his oatmeal.

"What a corker of a day." Duquesne gestured out the window where sun-splashed prairie grass and sagebrush stretched to the horizon.

Liselotte Müller said nothing.

"But with a nip in the air, I'd wager. Elevation's probably fifteen hundred meters."

Liselotte nibbled at her eggs in silence. Duquesne opened the *Kansas City Star,* brought aboard at the pre-dawn stop. He slipped out the comics section and slid it onto Liselotte's table. "Perhaps your lad would fancy the funny papers."

"What do you say, Otto?" the woman said in a German accent.

"Thank you, sir," the boy said.

"My favorite comic is *Blondie,*" Duquesne said, his eyes on the boy's mother.

Liselotte frowned at her plate as if the Canadian bacon displeased her. "Comics are a waste of time."

A real Miss Grumpy Knickers, Duquesne thought.

"Oh, that Dagwood Bumstead with his bloomin' sandwiches," he said with affected glee. "He's a layabout, constantly late for the tram, snoozes at his desk, in hot water with his boss, Mr. Dithers. I wonder if that's an accurate portrait of the American chap."

"I would not know," Liselotte said without making eye contact. "Alas, it's the way we Brits think of Americans."

"Oh, you're British, then." Her lips parted in faint amusement and obvious disbelief.

"With ancestors back to the days of Edmund Ironside, with perhaps some Viking blood, too."

"I thought, perhaps, Irish, considering your gift of the Blarney." The words smiled while her face remained stone.

A steward wearing a white tunic and a matching apron over dark trousers stopped at Duquesne's table and filled his coffee cup. After he departed, Duquesne said to the boy, "When we cross into Arizona, Otto, we're going to go over a trestle bridge called the Canyon Diablo Viaduct. It's high above a deep gorge, a glorious sight. You'll want to be looking out the window."

"That sounds delightful." Sounding like a polite and pampered child.

"And now," Liselotte said, "perhaps we can enjoy our breakfasts in peace and quiet."

Unperturbed by the brush-off, Duquesne drummed his fingers on the tabletop. To anyone else, it would appear to be a nervous habit. To a former Abwehr listener like Liselotte Müller, it would be instantly recognizable Morse Code. A simple dispatch: "We should work together. I can help you."

He watched her and knew she was getting the message.

At last Liselotte met his gaze, her eyes the frozen blue of an iceberg. "Help me? You? Fritz Duquesne. Peddler of gossip. Vagabond snoop. Washed-up has-been." Her laugh rippled like a babbling brook. "Does a candle offer to help the sun?"

Duquesne's mouth twitched, a greater display of discomfort than he had shown when taking a bullet through the shoulder in the Second Boer War.

She's young. And to her, I'm a dinosaur.

For a moment, he considered snapping his right arm downward and sliding the spring-action sleeve-blade into the palm of his hand. Not to stab the woman, of course. Rather, to slice his croissant and demonstrate...what, exactly? That my tradecraft is not limited to snooping. That I am a man who courts danger.

But she will see a fossil from the age of dueling codes and morning pistols.

He patted his lips with a napkin. "Have you ever been to Africa, Miss Müller?"

"It has not yet been my pleasure."

Duquesne pushed back his chair and stood. "Growing up there, I learned that an old lion may have shed a patch of its mane and lost the grace to ascend a jackalberry tree, but its teeth can still rip a wildebeest to shreds."

"I shall keep that in mind during my travels." She removed a sterling silver compact from her purse, opened it, studied herself in the mirror, smoothing blond strands of hair from her forehead. In a placid voice that she might use when commenting on the weather, she continued, "And I shall keep my Mauser 98 within reach whenever I sense danger."

"*Touché*," he said, but what he thought was, *En Garde.*

Duquesne bowed formally and said, "Good day to you both." He turned smartly and headed toward the vestibule door, sorting which of several plans of attack would be both satisfying and elegant.

FORTY-SIX
SPECIAL RELATIVITY

"Ben's gonna be jealous," Mickey Cohen said, referring to Bugsy Siegel, his sometimes boss and sometimes rival.

"What the dickens for?" LaVonne Cohen said. "You ain't knocked off another of Jack Dragna's bookie joints, have you?"

"Nah. I'm gonna be in pictures."

"Says who?"

The newlyweds sat at a small table in the observation car, absorbed in a game of gin rummy, as the Super Chief wound its way up the Raton Pass through the rugged Sangre de Cristo Mountains just south of Trinidad, Colorado. Beyond the large windows, jagged rock formations and steep canyon walls loomed, a testament to the land's untamed beauty.

"Chaplin. That's who. I asked him, and he says he can tell I got the actor's natural tuition."

Meaning *intuition*, LaVonne knew. She checked her cards. Three runs, spades three through five, hearts, seven through nine, and clubs, ten through queen. Hanging on like an unwanted house guest was the king of diamonds. She just needed one more card at either end of the runs for gin, six possible winning cards in all. She discarded the king of diamonds and drew the two of clubs.

Damn, a two of spades would have been gin.

"Chaplin's probably afraid you'll burn down his studio if he told you to take a hike," she said.

"Anywho, sweetheart, Ben's gonna be jealous. Him being so handsome, all his Hollywood pals telling him he oughta be in pictures. The thing is, I can tell when he's acting, which is all the time, except when he blows a fuse."

"So I've heard," LaVonne said.

"If Ben was on a movie set and got steamed, someone's gonna be pushing up daisies."

"To be an actor, you gotta memorize lines." LaVonne discarded the two of clubs and after Mickey's play, drew the king of hearts and discarded it.

"My memory's locked up tighter than Fort Knox," Mickey said. "I can tell you the finishing order of the Santa Anita Handicap back in thirty-seven. Rosemont, a helluva longshot, nosed out Seabiscuit at the wire, paid $32.40."

"Youse remember that 'cause you had a big bet on Rosemont."

"I had a tip."

"What you had was a hopped-up bay stallion."

"That *was* my tip."

Mickey drew a card, cursed and discarded it. LaVonne drew the ace of diamonds. No help for her hand. "Whadaya gonna play in the pictures, a gangster?"

"Nah. That'd be what they call typewriter casting."

Or something like that, LaVonne thought.

Mickey said, "I got an idea for a picture with me as a rabbi and Paul Muni as a Jewish mobster who's trying to corrupt the street kids in the neighborhood."

"Hold your horses, Mick. I seen that movie, only it was Pat O'Brien as a priest and Jimmy Cagney as an Irish gangster."

"Yeah, yeah. *Angels with Dirty Faces.* This is better."

After Mickey's play, LaVonne drew—oh, joy!—the king of clubs, completing her four-card run from ten to king. "Gin!"

"Aw, nuts!" Mickey groaned, flipping over his cards, more deadwood than a petrified forest, and began counting points. No books, no runs, just ten unmatched cards. "Jeez, seventy-three points."

"Plus twenty-five for gin," LaVonne said. "That's ninety-eight points and if we total all the games on the Capitol Limited, you owe me a shiny new Hudson, preferably the Straight Eight. I'd like maroon. That'll set you back nine hundred smackers, Mick."

"Hell, honey, I'll buy you two!"

Albert Einstein approached their table, and Cohen waved him over. "C'mon, Professor, take a load off."

Einstein nodded thanks and pulled up a chair. "What's today's lesson, Professor?" LaVonne asked.

"We'll talk about Galileo discovering Jupiter's moons and Isaac Newton developing classical physics."

"Classical like music?" LaVonne turned up her nose as if sniffing something putrid.

"Newtonian mechanics, electromagnetism, and thermodynamics. Now, in 1666..."

"So old!" LaVonne whined. "How about something you did?"

"Me? Well, in 1905, I changed everything."

Ten minutes later, Cohen tuned out both his bride and the Professor and was looking at the Super Chief's schedule.

The train would plow through the next two stations without stopping. Raton and Las Vegas, New Mexico. That reminded Mickey of Ben Siegel going on for hours about Las Vegas, *Nevada*, some desert shithole he thought could be turned into a gambling gold mine.

"Casinos, hotels, entertainers, first-rate all the way, Mickey," Siegel would say.

It sounded wacky to Cohen, who was content taking cash from L.A. nightclubs, running bookie joints, and skimming a piece of the racing wire.

LaVonne seemed to be paying attention to the Professor, even asking questions, and Mickey felt a sense of pride that he picked the right tomato to marry.

"So you wrote this paper in 1905?" his bride said.

"Five papers, actually, including one on special relativity," Einstein said.

"What's so special about it, anyhow?"

"Well, we've discussed..."

"I'm joking, Professor. I get it. Mass and energy are sort of the same thing."

"Sort of, yes," Einstein said. "Very good."

"If I'd known that earlier, I woulda said to a masher who pinched my fanny, 'Try that again, buster, and I'll slap you silly at the speed of light squared, and when I'm done, your jaw will have the mass of a stewed prune.'"

Cohen spotted a couple walking past the bar headed toward a table near the magazine rack.

Holy moly!

He instantly recognized the attractive, dark-haired woman. She'd used the restroom at the diner in New Jersey, had been in the audience at the Princeton debate, and was in the passenger seat of the green Hupmobile with U.S. government plates that had passed the limo on the way to Fort Meade. He had pegged her and the driver as FBI. Then the two of them tried to keep Einstein out of the fort and got their asses chewed by Major Groves.

But what the hay are they doing here?

Before Cohen could even speculate, a mustachioed man in his sixties walked into the car, looked around, eyes landing on Einstein, then flicking away. The realization struck Cohen.

I've seen this guy before. Twice!

He'd parked his Packard Super 8 outside the Princeton diner, then taken a table with a clear view of Einstein and Chaplin. A mustache and goatee that day. Later, in the front row at Princeton's auditorium, asking Einstein about splitting the atom, he'd sported a full beard. Today, just the mustache remained, but that was him!

The man approached the two feds at their table, and Cohen felt the hair prickle at the back of his neck. So much for his honeymoon. This was turning into something else entirely. A mystery on a train like in that Hitchcock picture *The Lady Vanishes*. Spies, secret messages, a gunfight in a passenger compartment. And like in the movie, damned if you could tell the good guys from the bad.

Cohen figured he'd handle it the way he did every fight in his boxing days. Nothing fancy. Come in close. Crowd the bastard. Keep throwing leather—or firing bullets—until someone drops.

Only one question…who the hell am I fighting?

FORTY-SEVEN
THE DUEL

Fritz Duquesne approached the table where Brian Sullivan and Milagros Vazquez sat in the Super Chief's club lounge car. The gentle glide of America's most luxurious train barely disturbed the ice in their water glasses as the great engines climbed through the mountains. With a smile as friendly as a golden retriever wagging its tail, Duquesne said, "May I join you?"

Taken by surprise, neither answered, and Duquesne slid into a chair. He scratched his mustache with a knuckle and said, "I love meeting new people on trains."

"Well, then...hello," Sullivan said, puzzled.

Vazquez forced a wary smile and said, "I'm Mildred Dawkins, and this is my husband Bruce."

"We're newlyweds," Sullivan said, a bit too eagerly.

"Sure you are, mate." Duquesne employed a British accent, losing every trace of his natural Afrikaner inflections.

"I sell John Deere farm equipment," Sullivan said, watching a tumbleweed fly past the window.

Slipping into the King's English of an Oxford don, Duquesne said, "I daresay your line of work must be rather perilous, if it requires you to carry a sidearm beneath your jacket."

That left Sullivan speechless. He was used to grilling suspects, not being the one on the hot seat. His hand unconsciously moved toward his holster.

"Oh, let's drop the pretenses, shall we?" Duquesne said.

"Okay, buster," Sullivan said. "You first."

"My name is Fritz Duquesne, but I suspect you know that. I am known as 'the Duke' in international circles." He gave his sobriquet with a note of pride, as if he were a baseball star keen to give his autograph to a 10-year-old fan. "And I'd guess you folks are G-2 or FBI, or Army Intelligence."

Sullivan and Vazquez traded looks and remained silent. No way would they state their real names or occupations. Vazquez interpreted her partner's look to mean, *If the Duke wants to talk, let's just listen.*

Duquesne appeared piqued by their silence. The afternoon sun caught his face, highlighting the web of wrinkles around his eyes. "Perhaps I am giving you too much credit. Maybe you're War Department flunkies, postal inspectors, or just night watchmen at an Anheuser-Busch plant in Newark."

Sullivan spoke up. "What is it you want, Mr. Duquesne?"

"Ah! The newlywed speaks. I couldn't help but notice that the two of you have not so much as held hands, and your wedding band is platinum while your bride's is yellow gold, and quite early this morning, at 2 a.m. or so, you abandoned your honeymoon bed for a trip to the telegraph office in Kansas City. Did a John Deere tractor in Missouri need servicing?"

He's showing off, Millie Vazquez thought. *But why? What's his game?*

"Cut the bullshit," Sullivan said, "and tell us who you met with on the platform in Kansas City."

"A farmer and German American Bund member who thinks he's a Nazi. He's a nobody who knows nothing that would interest you. I have bigger fish for you to fry."

"Meaning what?" Sullivan said.

Duquesne looked out the window, in no apparent hurry. The train rumbled over a bridge, a rocky ravine beneath the trestles. "I come bearing gifts," he said at last.

"And what gifts do you expect in return?" Sullivan asked.

"In due time. Let's bask in the wonderful scenery."

He enjoys controlling the conversation, Vazquez thought. *He's having sport with us.*

"The mountains, the gorges, the great American west," Duquesne enthused. "Do you know we're following the path of the Santa Fe Trail?"

"I've heard," Sullivan said.

"Can you imagine those pioneers in their rickety wagons, braving the elements, beset by desperadoes and Indians, deprivation and starvation? How courageous, how optimistic. That's what I love about America. That, and your glorious Constitution. In Germany, the law of the land is Hitler's latest whim or perhaps his astrologer's latest chart." He chuckled at his own joke. "But here, even though you know I am an intelligence agent for the Reich, you do not arrest me, much less torture me because you have no evidence that I have committed any crimes."

"But the day is young," Vazquez said.

"Hah! Well said. The American wit utterly eclipses the Teutonic variety, does it not? As you probably know, I am responsible for destroying twenty-two British merchant ships off South America in the Great War, not to mention sinking the *HMS Hampshire* and sending Lord Kitchener to Davy Jones' Locker."

"What we know," Vazquez said, "is that you are regarded as a prolific fabulist."

Duquesne smiled at that. A steward in a crisp white jacket stopped at their table and Duquesne said, "This round's on me. Gin and tonics for one and all?" He looked at Sullivan who shrugged. "Three G and T's. Plymouth gin," Duquesne continued.

The steward retreated to the bar, and in a moment, the train plunged into a tunnel, the windows suddenly dark, the only light the subtle illumination from the overhead sconces. Then those flickered and went out.

"Bang!" Duquesne said with a hearty laugh in the dark. He flicked a cigarette lighter, and an eerie orange glow bathed the three of them at the small table. "Blasting holes in mountains. If that's not a metaphor for America, I don't know what is."

A moment later, the Super Chief charged out of the tunnel into the blazing light of day and began climbing the spiny backbone of another mountain.

"This reminds me of a day long ago during the Great War when you two were still in knickers and bloomers."

"Do tell, if you must," Sullivan said. "Then perhaps we can get to the point."

"A snowy day in January 1917, the Metropole Hotel in Brussels. I entered the lobby and who was there but Cavendish, my British counterpart, my enemy. He reached into his suit jacket where he always carried his Luger P08, and I readied the spring-loaded dagger that was up my sleeve. But he pulled out two Cuban cigars, *Romeo y Julieta*, ironically enough. 'Duke,' he said, 'they serve an excellent boeuf bourguignonne in the dining room. Shall we?'"

As she listened, Vazquez took the measure of how much Duquesne seemed to be relishing the moment and came to a quick conclusion.

He's lonely! Forty years as a spy, thousands of nights spent alone. Constantly traveling, maintaining anonymity with dozens of false names and occupations. Does the man even know who he is?

"We made swift work of three bottles of French wine," Duquesne continued, "and after a Cherries Jubilee that could have been crafted by Escoffier himself, Cavendish uttered something rather astonishing."

Sullivan and Vazquez patiently waited for the punch line. The steward brought their cocktails, condensation beading on the tall glasses. Duquesne took a sip and smacked his lips in appreciation.

"Cavendish said, 'We should duel. Shall we say pistols at twenty paces?' Now, I knew he would have won the gold medal at the 1912 Olympics in the rapid fire event had the British security service not nixed his participation."

"So you wisely turned down his offer of a duel." Sullivan took a healthy swig of his gin and tonic.

"I suggested swords. But he knew I was a Paris-trained fencer and had killed three men in duels. He scoffed at me and made another suggestion."

Sullivan shot Vazquez a sideways glance that seemed to say, *Get a load of this guy!* He seemed to be a friendly grandfather telling tales, but Sullivan knew that Duquesne had killed people, perhaps in duels, perhaps not. According to his FBI file, at twelve years old, Duquesne used a sword to disembowel a man who had attacked his mother.

"Cavendish gave a hearty laugh and said, 'We duel with snowballs!' So we went into the street and peppered each other for a few minutes, which Cavendish declared to be 'jolly good fun.' Then he suggested we join forces and knock the top hats off the bankers and lawyers who populated the Place de Brouckère in those days. And that's what we did, *ka-pow,* we sent black silk hats flying."

Outside the windows, a hawk rode a thermal, wheeling above the train as it snaked through a gorge.

"So, Mr. Duquesne," Sullivan said, "are you suggesting we join forces or have a duel?"

"That entirely depends on the two of you," Duquesne said with a smile.

"You have something on your mind, so why not get to the point?"

"First, a word of praise. For about ten minutes, you knocked me sideways. Einstein and Oppenheimer speaking German, a joint American-Danish operation, Heisenberg fleeing Germany to run your atomic bomb program. What an audacious attempt at misinformation. Bravo!"

"I don't know what you're talking about, Mr. Duquesne," Sullivan said.

"Oh, please, sir! It was all smoke and mirrors, or to use the piquant American colloquialism from traveling circuses, a dog-and-pony show."

"If you say so."

"Let me be direct, Mr. John Deere salesman. Werner Heisenberg might not be a member of the Nazi Party, but he is a loyal German who loves his country. He is not a traitor."

Duquesne left a thought hanging in the air, Millie Vazquez thought, as the train wound its way through another series of curves. "Likewise, you are not a party member," she said

Duquesne stirred the ice in his drink with a swizzle stick. "True enough."

"And unlike Heisenberg, you are not even a German citizen. You've spent little time in the country. You have no family there and I would wager few friends."

Duquesne's smile grew wider. "The bride is quicker than the groom. Not unlike Blondie and Dagwood Bumstead. And therefore Mrs. Bumstead...?"

"You're casting about for new opportunities. There's not much use for elderly spies. What are you, sixty?"

"Sixty-three. And unlike those hard-working members of the Brotherhood of Sleeping Car Porters, I have no pension to look forward to." Duquesne paused a moment, then said, "And this leads Mrs. Bumstead to what conclusion?"

"You have an offer for us," Vazquez said. "You'll leave Abwehr, squeal on your confederates, and live out your days in this big, beautiful country you love so much."

Duquesne coughed a laugh and said, "So be it! Look how far we've come without even throwing a snowball."

The three of them remained silent and sipped their cocktails, keeping their thoughts to themselves. Through the window, thin streaks of clouds blanketed the sun, painting the western sky in brilliant oranges and purples. The Super Chief rolled on toward California, carrying its cargo of secrets and lies, truth and consequences.

FORTY-EIGHT
AMERICA FIRST

Chaplin entered the club lounge car hoping to run into Lena Horne. After their dinner one night earlier, she had said, "See you, around," but she hadn't. Now he passed the barber shop, scanned the lounge...and his heart nearly stopped.

I must be hallucinating.

He saw a mirage, an apparition, a delusion. Contentedly standing at the bar, leaning an elbow on the polished mahogany as if he owned the place was a 330-pound phantom.

"W.R., is that you?" Chaplin asked, his voice trembling.

"It's not the Prince of Wales," William Randolph Hearst said. He wore a khaki sack coat big enough to drape a Ringling Brothers pachyderm. His shirt was white, his string tie topped by a turquoise clasp in a sterling silver setting. Chaplin would have cast him as a prosperous saloon owner in a Western.

"But W.R., how...when...?"

"The Santa Fe hooked up my personal carriage in Kansas City. Come back and visit.

Helluva fine custom Pullman with all the bells and whistles, modeled after Henry Ford's, but a damn sight more opulent."

Only now did Chaplin notice that standing next to Hearst, nearly hidden by his massive bulk, was the blond woman with chiseled cheekbones who called herself Margaret Jones. She had changed from her breakfast outfit and now wore a knee-length burgundy wool dress with a fitted bodice, a navy blue felt hat with a white feather, and night-at-the-opera satin gloves that matched her dress. Her makeup was subtle, but for her cherry red lipstick. She could have been a model in a *Saturday Evening Post* advertisement for Cadillac convertibles.

Hearst, a teetotaler, had a cup of coffee in front of him on the bar, and the woman had what appeared to be a martini with two olives. The bartender, a trim man in a white tunic, discreetly left his position and began wiping tables to give the trio privacy.

"Charlie, do you know Miss Jones from St. Louis?" Hearst asked, steam rising from his coffee cup.

"We were introduced at breakfast." Chaplin nodded to the woman who tilted her head noncommittally in return.

Not to mention watching her slink out of Lindbergh's compartment, tousled and mussed. And if her name is 'Margaret Jones,' I'm a monkey's uncle.

"Miss Jones, don't let Chaplin's benign appearance fool you. The man is a rake and a cad."

Chaplin could plead not guilty, but the indictment was obviously true, so he forced a thin smile.

"You must both excuse me," the woman said. "If I don't check on my son, he'll pester the conductor with a hundred questions."

Leaving half her martini untouched by those painted lips, she left the car with a ladylike shimmy of the hips that both men watched.

"Charlie, will we see you at Christmas?" Hearst asked.

By "we," does he mean his wife Millicent or his mistress Marion?

"You banned me from San Simeon until next April," Chaplin reminded him.

"Aw, forget that. The Christmas party will be a knees-up wingding. All your friends will be there. Cary and Gary, Marlene and Myrna, Carole and Claudette."

Meaning Cary Grant and Gary Cooper, Marlene Dietrich and Myrna Loy, Carole Lombard and Claudette Colbert.

"Spencer Tracy will probably empty my wine cellar," Hearst continued, "and it's a damn big cellar."

"Your friendship means the world to me, W.R., and again, I'm sorry about Marion." Chaplin's voice was apologetic, and he wasn't acting. He had few regrets about his philandering, but bedding down his friend's longtime mistress, well that offended even Chaplin's spinning moral compass. "I feel like such a heel."

"Shitheel is more like it. But hell's bells, Charlie. You knew Marion before I did, back when she was a little twist in the Ziegfeld Follies." Hearst chuckled and his belly jiggled. "You probably figured you were grandfathered in."

The Super Chief's horn blared as the train breezed through a crossing. Outside the windows, small wooden buildings of a Western town flashed by, looking like the flimsy facades of a movie set.

Chaplin lowered his voice. "W.R., that woman you were speaking to. She's not what she appears to be."

"Are any of us?"

"I seriously doubt her name's Margaret Jones."

"True enough. It's Liselotte Müller."

"German."

"Right on that account, too, Charlie."

Chaplin took a breath and got directly to the point. "Did you know she's having an affair with Lindbergh and that he's fathered her child?"

"Of course, I know, Charlie. I'm the one who introduced him to that sweet slice of strudel."

For the next several minutes, Chaplin listened in stunned silence as Hearst explained his Machiavellian plan that had all the hallmarks of a Hollywood melodrama. Outside the window, the New Mexico desert stretched endlessly, broken only by jutting rock formations and the occasional cluster of adobe buildings, wispy white smoke curling into the sky.

"Let me get this straight, W.R. You're grooming Lindbergh to run for President in forty-four."

"He would have run this year, but Anne wouldn't let him do it. I came to the conclusion he needed a little female persuasion from under a different set of bed sheets."

"A Nazi agent!"

"Don't get your knickers in a knot, Charlie. She's a lowly junior officer in the *Sicherheitsdienst.*"

"For crying out loud! That's the intelligence service of the SS."

"All she does is write speeches for Goebbels and some lesser functionaries."

"And now for Lindbergh!"

"She's a small cog in the machine, Charlie. Think of her as a liaison for future dealings with the Reich. In forty-four, Hitler will own all of Europe. He'll have bombers that can cross the Atlantic. Japan will have a Navy to be feared. We'll need a president who can keep us out of war."

"That's batty, W.R. We'll need a president willing to fight Hitler, not kiss his ass."

Hearst turned his massive bulk and looked out the window. The train curled through a double horseshoe curve, the craggy, snow-covered peak of Escobas Mountain visible in the distance. "Bluntly stated Charlie, Lindbergh's election will make America great again."

"And you think Americans will vote for someone whose defining achievement is pissing in a jar and not falling asleep in his airplane?"

"You're wrong, my friend. If Lindy had run this year with my support, seventy-five percent of my readers would have voted for him."

"Seventy-five per cent of your readers would vote for Jack the Ripper. Blast it, W.R., Lindbergh's an idiot."

"If I wanted a genius, I'd amend the Constitution and run Professor Einstein. I want a pleasant fellow whose natural instincts align with mine."

"His natural instincts are for fascism."

"Sure, he's mesmerized by der Führer, but I can pull him back. Criminy, Charlie, the Austrian paperhanger hornswoggled me back in thirty-four. He promised to keep Germany out of the beckoning arms of socialism without persecuting the Jews."

Chaplin slapped a hand onto the bar top, making the glassware dance. "And you paid the bastard to write columns for your newspapers!"

"An error in judgment," Hearst admitted. "Kristallnacht showed Hitler's true colors and set me straight. I'm not saying we should get in bed with the son-of-a-bitch, just that we shouldn't go to war against him."

"And you've chosen that simpleton pilot to carry your colors like Seabiscuit for Ridgewood Ranch."

"He was smart enough to take the slogan I gave him."

"'America First!'" Chaplin's voice cracked with anger. "Is that what Lindy was thinking when he accepted that Nazi medal?"

"Lindbergh is straightforward and uncomplicated, and real Americans love him. Lumbermen in the northwest, lobstermen in Maine, merchants on Main Street, auto workers in Detroit, and farmers across the country. In forty-four, when Lindy barnstorms the country, 'America First' will be his clarion call."

Hearst was saying "America First" but Chaplin was hearing "Sieg Heil."

The newspaper magnate cleared his throat, an old Ford grinding its gears. "Lindbergh will have all my newspapers, magazines, and radio stations behind him," Hearst said. "Metrotone News will have two features on him every week in your neighborhood theater. You'll see his face on billboards and multi-page spreads in *Life, Time,* and *Colliers.* He'll have the financial backing of dozens of industrialists whose names you know and whose bank accounts dwarf anything the Democrats can raise. In short, my friend, Lindy will be an unstoppable force."

"You gonna have that Nazi chippy on the barnstorming train with him?"

"She'll be in the background, as will I."

Listening to Hearst, Chaplin's spirits sunk. Not only couldn't he move Lindbergh off his isolationist pulpit, here was Hearst and his multi-millionaire cohorts pulling the strings on their gullible marionette. Chaplin felt helpless. All his fame, his fortune, his art—what did it matter against such ruthless power?

I'm just one solitary man in a world of two billion souls.

A mere player on a stage whose single gift is conjuring laughter and tears. Nothing more than modernity's echo of *Komos* and *Tragos*, the comedy and tragedy of the ancient Greeks. A passing fancy, an entertainer whose words and face will vanish into the ether between evening's dusk and morning's mist. The ferocious tides of history will sweep me aside, and to think otherwise is to embrace both the vanity of Narcissus and the hubris of Icarus.

FORTY-NINE
RAISING PIGS IN PASADENA

With the afternoon sun casting long shadows across the stark New Mexico landscape, Fritz Duquesne, Milagros Vazquez, and Brian Sullivan sat at their table in the observation car as the train roared toward Santa Fe. Outside the large picture windows, the landscape unfolded in a dramatic procession of craggy peaks, each towering higher and more imposing than the last. The steward, a man in his fifties wearing a starched white tunic, delivered another round of gin and tonics, glasses filled to the brim. Flexing his knees as he walked, with tens of thousands of miles on the rails behind him, he did not spill a drop.

When the steward left their table, Fritz Duquesne said, "Shall we talk turkey?" With a smile that curled his mustache, he added, "I so love American idioms. Chew the fat. Bite the bullet. Bring home the bacon."

"Sure thing, Duquesne," Sullivan said. "Now, let's get down to brass tacks."

"Hah! The groom has a sense of humor, too."

Duquesne's laugh seemed genuine to Millie Vazquez, but she told herself the man was a professional liar. She wouldn't believe him if he cheerfully bellowed, "*Guten Morgen!*"

Sullivan said, "Why don't you start by telling us why you're following Albert Einstein from coast-to-coast?"

"Dear me, I thought you knew." Duquesne adjusted his perfectly knotted tie. "I attended his debates with Oppenheimer in New Jersey and Chicago and will do the same at Caltech. My job is to be a whisk broom and sweep up whatever pieces of lint those two drop about America's nuclear program."

Vazquez drilled him with a look. "One would think the Reich would have recruited some bright young physicist for that job."

"Instead of a broken-down old snooper?" Duquesne said with a humorous lilt.

The two FBI operatives stared at Duquesne without saying a word. The oldest interrogation trick in the book. Most people grow uncomfortable in prolonged silences. The only sound was the rhythmic *clackety-clack* of the wheels, the only movement the slight roll of the car as the Super Chief raced through the high desert, a pale November sun highlighting snow on distant peaks.

Finally, Duquesne said, "Don't you trust me?"

"About as far as I can throw a Bradley tank," Sullivan said.

"Why not a Sherman tank?" Duquesne shot back.

"Because there's no such thing."

Duquesne's eyes twinkled with amusement. "I'd be a dismal excuse for a spymaster if I didn't know about the new tank under construction at Lima Locomotive Works in Ohio."

The ring of truth, Vazquez thought. She had no idea whether the U.S. Army was building a new tank, but Duquesne spoke with such confidence that it had the ring of truth.

Sullivan made a scoffing sound. "We know how German spies loiter around defense plants, picking up gossip, taking grainy photos. So sorry, Fritzy, that information ain't worth a bucket of warm spit."

Fritzy? Vazquez wondered what her partner's strategy might be with the insulting rejoinder. Maybe to disguise just how startled he was by the apparently leaked information.

Unperturbed, Duquesne said, "Would you like to know the name of the grease monkey who pocketed the princely sum of three hundred dollars for the tank's specifications?"

"Sure thing. When we get to Los Angeles, we'll take you to the FBI field office, and you can spill."

"And be photographed by an SS agent with a 135 millimeter Leica! Do you want to get me killed?"

"Okay, so talk. What do you have for us and what do you want in return?"

"Our train will go through orange groves in Pasadena," Duquesne said. "If we stood in the mail car's open door, we could smell the blossoms."

"What do you want?" Sullivan demanded.

"A small ranch with orange trees. A new identity, of course, and a reasonable stipend for life."

"You want to grow oranges?" Sullivan's tone reflected more than a smidgen of disbelief.

"And raise pigs," Duquesne said.

"Oranges and pigs." Sullivan let out a sigh.

The steward returned with a silver tray of smoked salmon canapés and cheese and onion puffed pastries. With an air of relaxed casualness, Duquesne popped a canapé into his mouth and chewed contentedly. "My parents had a farm in the South African Republic," he said, eyes distant at the memory. "Quite a nice one until the British burned our barns, killed our livestock, and stole our crops."

"The Second Boer War," Vazquez said.

"Twenty-five thousand Boers perished in the concentration camps, mostly women and children, perhaps another twenty thousand black Africans." He snorted, a contemptuous sound. "All thanks to your friends, the Brits."

"And yet," Sullivan said, "after fighting the British all your life, you want to lay down your arms and raise pigs in Pasadena."

"As much as it pains me to say it, my services are no longer needed. England is done for. Total victory will take a ground invasion, and when it's over, Britain will be left a smoldering husk, its cities reduced to ash."

"You underestimate the pluck and fortitude of the British people," Vazquez said.

"Pluck is dandy, but thousands of Mörser 18 heavy artillery pieces and the greatest infantry in history are something else entirely. England's only hope is that Hitler diverts his attention to the east and does something idiotic like attack the Soviet Union."

"So just what value do you bring to us to justify your retirement as a gentleman farmer?" Sullivan asked.

"To start with, the identities of thirty-three members of my spy ring in the Northeast."

Sullivan nodded and his eyes brightened. As if singing a hosanna, the train's air horn blared. "That's a good start," the FBI agent said.

"To be frank, many are incompetent, but several have produced results. The schematics of the M1 semi-automatic rifle, for one thing. Plans for a new torpedo boat. Layouts of defense installations susceptible to arson. Specifications for a self-sealing airplane gas tank, those sorts of things."

"Tell us more," Sullivan said, managing to keep excitement out of his voice.

"In Los Angeles, my task is to meet with various fascist groups. The Silver Legion of America, the western branch of the German American Bund, the Ku Klux Klan, the American White Guard, and the rather curiously named Black Legion, whose members, I assure you, are decidedly Caucasian. I am quite prepared to furnish you with their identities, as well as their rather unsavory plans for mischief."

"Keep gabbing, Duquesne," Sullivan said. "We're listening."

"Not to brag," Duquesne said, about to brag, "but I also saved the life of one of America's biggest celebrities a few days ago. And I will have to do it again on this very train."

Sullivan took care not to show astonishment.

Vazquez thought, *Oh, how the spy loves to tease, a burlesque performer, lifting the hem of her gown, flashing a peekaboo thigh.*

"What celebrity?" she asked in a neutral tone.

"Charlie Chaplin," Duquesne said. "As you two were there, I'm sure you know that a sniper took a shot at him outside Fort Meade."

"A man with a rifle was found dead at the scene and couldn't be identified," Vazquez said.

"Reinhard Schmidt. A brute lacking in wit and polish, but what can you expect from an SS assassin?"

Vazquez said, "What rifle did he have?"

"Oh, a quiz, how delightful. Herr Schmidt's prized Karabiner 98 sniper rifle."

"Who shot him?" Sullivan asked.

"Hah, Dagwood asks a trick question." Duquesne chuckled. "The *Schweinehund* wasn't shot, stabbed, or strangled, though I dare say I am rather accomplished at all three."

"What then?"

"Given the tread marks that must have been found on his torso, I reckon you already have the answer." He drew the moment out, letting the silence stretch taut. "He was run over by a Packard Super 8 coupe. Whoops, that's what I drive."

Sullivan and Vazquez exchanged looks, then Millie said, "Why would an Abwehr agent kill an SS operative?"

"Without admitting anything, perhaps the Abwehr agent admired Chaplin's films and found the SS assassin to be a disagreeable chap."

"Aw, cut the cabbage, Duquesne," Sullivan said.

"No need to be cheeky, old boy."

"You're implying that you killed this assassin to protect Chaplin. It would enhance your credibility if you gave a plausible reason why you did it."

Duquesne sighed, a teacher exasperated with a plodding student. "In this country, Dagwood, you have your turf wars between the FBI and Army Intelligence, between the Army and the Navy, between state police forces and city departments. I assure you that the tension between Abwehr and the SS makes your intramural squabbles seem like tea parties. That's all the detail I intend to provide."

Vazquez studied the spy across the rim of her glass, weighing each word like a pawnbroker's gold. The old gasbag could be spinning tales, but something in his manner suggested otherwise. "You claim you're going to save Chaplin's life again," she said.

"Yes indeed, but this time, I'll need you two to help," Fritz Duquesne said with an enigmatic smile.

FIFTY
"DARLING, WHAT'S IN THE BOX?"

Brian Sullivan and Milagros Vazquez waited for Duquesne to continue, so he let the pause stretch, heightening the suspense. He had spent a lifetime playing roles, his chameleon act aided by a career that spanned continents and thrived on contradictions. When not spying for Germany, he had been a big game hunter, journalist, movie publicist, soldier, army scout, lecturer, inventor—even an importer of hippopotamuses for their meat.

He was Captain Claude Stoughton, Count Boris Zakrevsky, Major Frederick Craven, George Fordham, Piet Niacud. And of course, Frederick Fredericks.

Today was a novelty. He was playing himself—though a carefully curated version. He had fed Sullivan and Vazquez a string of murky deceptions, each anchored in reality. He truly did admire America and her people. He genuinely believed England would crumble beneath the Wehrmacht's might. He had, in fact, killed Reinhard Schmidt and, in doing so, saved Chaplin's life.

But turn traitor? Name names? Never!

Duquesne wove his intricate web, spinning a tale around Liselotte Müller's supposed mission. Not that he knew her actual orders. But then, neither did the FBI operatives—and they had no way to check his story. And hadn't he built credibility by supplying accurate details about Schmidt's demise?

They want to believe me, because my information, if true, could make their careers!

Duquesne knew the identities and backgrounds of the FBI operatives from a wireless transmission, but there was no need to flaunt his knowledge. Instead, he studied them. Sullivan was trying to conceal his exhilaration, the glow of a man who thought he was on the brink of something monumental.

The hopeful gleam in your eyes gives you away, Agent Sullivan.

This could be the biggest counterintelligence triumph in the history of the FBI, so of course Sullivan's delight was understandable.

But what of the woman?

Vazquez betrayed nothing. Perhaps she knew that if laurels were to be awarded, they would fall like a tailored cloak, covering only Sullivan's shoulders.

Or perhaps she simply sees right through me.

Those dark, bottomless eyes. She is the sharper of the two, though Sullivan is no *dummkopf.* Vazquez, Duquesne surmised, understood the stakes. Letting a German agent bamboozle them would be a one-way ticket to Fairbanks, Alaska where they'd spend their days chasing caribou rustlers. She was cautious, skeptical. He would not underestimate her.

His objective was twofold: distract the FBI from Einstein while signaling to Fräulein Müller that the lion's fangs could still slice through meat and crush bone. Petty, perhaps, to take such umbrage at her insults. But he longed to teach her a lesson.

Duquesne was reasonably certain that Müller was not an assassin but rather a trained counterintelligence agent. He had seen her greet Lindbergh at breakfast in the dining car, and it was obvious the two knew each other and, almost certainly, were lovers. Duquesne lacked access to the extensive files Abwehr and the SS maintained on Lindbergh but was well aware of the rumors. During Lindbergh's visits to Berlin, Hermann Göring, the corpulent head of the Luftwaffe, had provided the American pilot with several German women, and two or more had attained the status of mistress. The chance that any of these *Mätressen* were innocent shop girls or dairy maids was nil. They were intelligence agents of the Reich.

Lindbergh held the rank of colonel in the U.S. Army Air Corps, but that was largely ceremonial, and he was not on active duty. Squeezing him for strategic intelligence was unlikely to be Müller's objective.

But Duquesne knew Göring—knew his long game. With the help of prominent American industrialists, the Reichsmarschall had tried to coax Lindbergh into running against Roosevelt in the recent election. *Klatsch und Tratsch*—what Americans called scuttlebutt—leaking from the Chancellery suggested that a more aggressive effort would be made to recruit him as a candidate in 1944.

Could a man be blackmailed into running for president? Unlikely. Then a more outlandish thought struck him.

Those cunning old English kings.

Their wives would die, and they'd marry a French or Spanish or Belgian princess to cement alliances. Or in the case of Henry VIII, execute one wife to marry another.

If Anne Morrow Lindbergh were to die, would her grieving husband find solace in the arms of Liselotte Müller?

Would sympathetic Americans rally around him as he preached peaceful coexistence with the Third Reich? Would he run for president on that platform? It was precisely the sort of phantasmagoria that Göring, high on morphine, would concoct, and that Goebbels, flaunting his doctorate in literature, would spin into a narrative brimming with noble tragedy.

The train rounded a sweeping curve, and Duquesne refocused. Time to send the FBI on a *sinnlose Suche*—a wild goose chase. Keeping his eyes on Vazquez, he intoned, "Barely out of her teens, Liselotte Müller worked as a listener at *Übersee Funkzentrale*, Abwehr's overseas wireless operation. She received and decoded messages and tapped out replies. Later, she trained as a counterintelligence agent."

So far, the truth. Like any sound structure, the finest lie rests upon a solid foundation of fact.

"And now she's an assassin?" Vazquez said, skeptically.

Duquesne shook his head and continued with his fable. "Her role is to play the lead in an elaborate deception at Union Station in Los Angeles. She'll step off the train quickly, her young son in tow. An SS agent posing as a nanny—who is, in fact, the boy's true minder—will whisk the child into the station. An SS assassin, nattily dressed in a black wool topcoat and carrying a florist's box, will be waiting. He'll pose as Müller's husband."

Always dress your lies with sharp details.

"They'll exchange sweet words and embrace," Duquesne went on, "with Müller turned just so, watching the platform for Chaplin. When he approaches and is no more than ten meters away, she will murmur, 'Darling, what's in the box?' At that signal, the assassin will pull out a tommy gun and rip Chaplin into shreds."

Vazquez raised her eyebrows with suspicion. Sullivan blanched and said, "A tommy gun on a crowded platform?"

"The more mayhem, the better," Duquesne answered quickly. "An easier getaway, and a lesson for the Yanks. Trifle with the Führer and blood will flow. No enemy of the state is beyond the reach of the Reich."

He could read the exchange of glances between the two operatives. They were weighing the risks, calculating the consequences.

Is he selling us a bill of goods?

But could they afford disbelief? Hardly. They would have no choice but to focus all their efforts on protecting Chaplin—leaving Einstein forgotten.

A classic deception! A masterful diversion!

Perhaps not on the scale of Joan of Arc's feint at Orléans, but a masterstroke in its own right. In a few hours, under cover of darkness, his plan would unfold. At the Needles station, Einstein would be spirited off the train, over the border into Mexico, and soon after, across the Atlantic, while these hapless agents scrambled after shadows. They would have a phalanx of agents swarming the platform at Union Station looking for a man with a florist's box. If they found one, he would likely be an affectionate suitor from Malibu or the Valley.

"We could take Müller off the train at Albuquerque and detain her," Sullivan suggested, "and we could pinch the man with the florist box before the train pulls into Union Station."

"Sure you could," Duquesne said easily, anticipating the move and ready to quash it. "But the SS always has contingency plans. Likely, there will be a second gunman, perhaps disguised as a railway policeman. Or a newspaper vendor. Or a pipefitter, a roundhouse man, anyone at all. You'd never see it coming."

The two FBI operatives remained silent another moment, and Duquesne knew they were processing his wild story, sizing up his every word and gesture.

"We'll take under consideration everything you've told us," Sullivan said.

Yes, you surely will.

"To tell you the truth," Duquesne said, a prefix that he only attached to lies, "I feel marvelously unburdened by being forthright with you."

PART THREE

MIDNIGHT PATRIOTS

FIFTY-ONE
KITTY THE COMMIE

The train pulled out of the Santa Fe station where it had made a quick service stop just as the sun dipped behind distant mountains. In his drawing room, Einstein slouched on the sofa, his hands folded over his abdomen, listening intently to the radio. The deep, resonant voice of Edward R. Murrow filled the space, his voice heavy with the weight of war.

"We could hear the drone of a German plane and see the burst of anti-aircraft fire," Murrow said, his tone one of somber gravitas. "Two pieces of shrapnel slapped down in the water, and then everything was drowned in the hum of the pumps and the sound of hissing water. Those firemen in their oilskins and tin hats appeared oblivious to everything but the fire. We went to another blaze, a small two-story house down on the East End. An incendiary had gone through the roof and the place was gutted. A woman stood on a corner, clutching a rather dirty pillow. A policeman was trying to comfort her. And a fireman said, 'You'd be surprised what strange things people pick up when they run out of a burning house.'"

Einstein felt a burning sensation in his abdomen. It wasn't indigestion or an ulcer. No, this was something else. Rage. Grief. Fear.

Will the Nazis burn London to the ground? Will England fall?

Seven years earlier in Germany, the Reich began its campaign of harassment and threats against him. His books were burned, his bank accounts seized, his photograph published in newspapers with the caption, *"Bis Jetzt Ungehäengt."* Not yet hanged.

Targeted for assassination, Einstein had fled to the English countryside, secretly living in a thatched cottage in Norfolk, guarded by villagers with shotguns. Thinking of it now, the whole experience seemed surreal. After months in hiding, he emerged to give a speech at Royal Albert Hall in London. For the first time, he publicly renounced pacifism in the face of tyranny. "The fate of mankind is at stake," he had told the audience.

Long gone were the days when called himself a "militant pacifist," urging young men to resist the military draft.

Sadly, now I am a pacifist in principle only.

Hitler and his *Kriegsmenschen*—war people—changed everything. The world was on the edge of an abyss, and civilization itself hung in the balance. The Nazis were a special case. Western democracies had no choice but to arm and fight to the death.

J. Robert Oppenheimer and Kitty, his bride of nine days, sat in swivel chairs at a small table in the observation car. They paid no mind to the rugged majesty of the New Mexico mountains beyond the windows. They were too busy arguing in hushed tones.

"Dammit, Robert. You can't build some super bomb that FDR will drop on Moscow. I won't allow it." Kitty tapped an unlit Chesterfield on the table for emphasis. At thirty, she had dark curly hair, high cheekbones and intense brown eyes. A slender woman now with a three-month baby bump, she wore a gray dress in lightweight wool that fell to mid-calf.

"The target is Germany, not the Soviet Union," Oppenheimer muttered. He sat, legs crossed at the ankles, his lanky frame hunched over, a lighted cigarette angled in a corner of his mouth. His long, angular face took on a pained expression.

"Sure, Berlin would be first," Kitty fired back. "Or would it? If you took a poll in this backward country of ours, a majority would say that Stalin is a bigger threat than Hitler, that we should kill all the commies and let Europe take it up the ass."

A middle-aged couple at a nearby table shot offended looks at the newlyweds, as if one of them had farted in church.

"Kitty! Please." Oppenheimer pinched the bridge of his nose, his thick brows knitting together.

A voice interrupted them. "Am I intruding on the lovebirds?"

Oppenheimer and his bride turned and saw Einstein, packing his meerschaum pipe, a sly grin under his mustache.

"Albert, please sit," Oppenheimer said, gesturing to an empty chair. "And tell Kitty that FDR won't drop our mythical nuclear bomb on Moscow."

Once seated, Einstein lighted his pipe, inhaled with eyes closed and exhaled a puff of sweet Turkish smoke. "Not Moscow or Berlin, for that matter. The toll of civilian deaths would be intolerable. I think the target would be a German naval port or an army base or perhaps even an uninhabited island, just for demonstration, a warning shot."

"You have more faith in our government than I do," Kitty said.

"What brought on this discussion?" Einstein asked.

Oppenheimer reached inside his suit coat and pulled out a Western Union telegram, which he smoothed onto the table. "Delivered at the stop in Santa Fe." He lowered his voice and said, "From Major Groves."

Einstein listened as Oppenheimer described the message. "In a nutshell, the major wants to know…if FDR authorizes a project to build a nuclear bomb, and if he's in command, and if I can get security clearance, will I run the whole shebang?"

"That's a lot of 'ifs,'" Einstein said between puffs on the meerschaum.

Kitty smirked. "Especially the security clearance when you're married to 'Kitty the Commie,' Fact is, Albert, most of Oppie's friends were Party members at one time or another. Not to mention his brother and wife."

"But you, Oppie?" Einstein asked.

"I'm on the Executive Committee of the American Civil Liberties Union, which J. Edgar Hoover, the troglodyte, considers a communist front. But I've never been a member of the Communist Party."

Kitty exhaled a plume of smoke and said, "In his own mind, Robert isn't a Red, but in his soul, he is."

Oppenheimer shrugged. "Color me pink. I find that communism in theory works far better than in practice, where it's just as inhumane as fascism. As for my security clearance, Major Groves insists he can bypass Hoover by having Army Intelligence handle the vetting."

Einstein took in the vastness of the land outside the observation car windows. The piñon pines and junipers, their dark green foliage contrasting with the dusty tan and rust-red earth, the snow-capped Sandia Mountains in the distance. He wondered if the only peace in the world could be found far from civilization.

Finally Einstein said, "And your answer to the Major?"

"How could I say 'no?' We owe it to America to produce a bomb before Berlin does."

Kitty lit a cigarette, which she pointed at her husband. "Robert should refuse unless FDR agrees to share our research with the Soviet Union."

"A non-starter, to use a horse racing term," Oppenheimer said.

"Dead in the water, to use a nautical term," Einstein agreed, thinking of *Tümmler*, his beloved sailboat confiscated by the Nazis.

Oppenheimer plucked the Chesterfield from Kitty's fingers and used it to light a new one of his own. He exhaled a languid plume of smoke, his breath escaping with the weight of a sigh. "Which brings me to this, Albert. Will you help? I know your moral scruples about war, and I wouldn't ask you to formally join the project, but if I have questions from time to time, may I turn to you in private?"

Einstein realized that Major Groves likely was the source of the request. One which Einstein had already declined. He remembered the phone call from the major the day before the Princeton debate, asking for help.

"I'm a theoretical physicist. I can't build a toy airplane, much less a bomb."

"Your guidance would be invaluable, Professor, and you needn't muscle a wrench."

But world events—on the battlefields and at sea, in capital cities and laboratories—were moving at a ferocious pace and with a complexity that would have baffled earlier generations.

Had it only been six months since Germany invaded France, five months since the British Army's humiliating evacuation of Dunkirk, and four months since Germany began its vicious air bombardment of London? Einstein thought of Winston Churchill's first address to Parliament as Prime Minister: "I have nothing to offer you but blood, toil, tears and sweat." Which made Einstein wonder just how much he could do without violating his deepest principles.

Just how do I reply to young Oppenheimer's request?

"I feel like you're asking me to get a little bit pregnant," Einstein said.

"Which is my condition." Kitty flashed a smile and patted her baby bump.

"Consider the middle ground, Albert," Oppenheimer said. "You wouldn't be in the lab or anywhere near the nuclear plants. This would just be between us, borrowing your brain for answers to pointed questions—scientific, political, even moral. But nothing hands-on. Nothing that could leave fingerprints."

"I see. We work under cover of darkness."

"Midnight patriots, if you will."

"Intriguing," Einstein said. "Any such discrete insights come to mind?"

"Ernest Lawrence at Berkeley began using a cyclotron as a particle accelerator to produce radioactive isotopes for medical purposes," Oppenheimer said. "At first, he thought the equipment might be used to separate U-235 from U-238."

"To create bomb-grade uranium for the core of a fission bomb," Einstein said.

"Precisely. But bombarding uranium with high energy particles is not an efficient way to separate the isotopes."

Einstein noticed the flame in his pipe had gone out but made no move to re-light it. He was intrigued by the issue as it was one of purely theoretical physics. No need to muscle a wrench, as Major Groves promised.

"One answer would be to ionize the uranium atoms and then deflect them into a magnetic field," Einstein said. "The mass of U-235 is less, so those isotopes can be collected separately. But how? Is that your question, Oppie?"

"Again, precisely."

"A lovely problem. I shall give it thought." Einstein struck a match and re-lit his pipe. "How far ahead of us is Heisenberg?"

"I like the fact you said 'us,' Albert."

Einstein shrugged. "For the past five weeks, I've been an American citizen, and in my heart, much longer."

"No way to tell precisely where the Germans are with their so-called Uranium Club, but clearly we have ground to make up."

"Where would you construct such a bomb?" Einstein asked. "Surely not at Columbia or Berkeley in the event of a *Schnellschuss.*"

Oppenheimer chuckled at Einstein's use of the slang term for "premature ejaculation." The younger physicist said, "We'd build a town from scratch hundreds of miles from any city." He looked out the observation window toward the towering mountains. "Perhaps near here."

"But there's nothing here."

Oppenheimer gestured out the window. "I have a cabin on a ranch outside a little town called Los Alamos."

"*Vos ist dos?* Are you a cowboy?"

"I enjoy riding horses on mountain trails. Even more important, the dry climate is helpful for my colitis."

Einstein glanced at Kitty. "And the families? What in the world would they do in this wilderness?"

"Don't worry, Albert," Kitty said with a sly grin. "I'll start a bridge club and a coffee klatsch." She exhaled a long plume of smoke and added, "Plus, of course, a communist cell."

FIFTY-TWO
"I GET A KICK OUT OF YOU"

"Do you believe him?" Millie Vazquez asked.

Brian Sullivan shrugged. "I take every witness' statement with a grain of salt. With a German spy who's a blabbermouth, I'd need all the salt in all the mines in Poland. And yet..."

He let the thought hang, and Vazquez finished it for him. "If Duquesne's telling the truth about a plot to kill Chaplin and we don't act, we'd be like General Custer ignoring the scout who warned about Sitting Bull dead ahead."

They were walking the narrow corridor of their drawing room car, the Super Chief minutes from pulling into Albuquerque. The stop meant a crew change, and passengers would be invited to stretch their legs and browse the stands where Navajo and Pueblo tribe members sold their handicrafts.

Sullivan planned to use the time to place another call to New York, confirming that the Los Angeles office was ready with extra manpower. When the train reached Union Station at breakfast time, a small army of FBI agents, LAPD officers, and sheriff's deputies would have the platform locked down tighter than a cell on Alcatraz.

But first, there was work to do.

"We need to alert Chaplin," Sullivan said.

"And Mickey Cohen," Vazquez added.

Sullivan frowned. "Getting in bed with mobsters doesn't sit right with me."

"Think about it, Brian. If we don't tell him, when we roll into Union Station, Cohen's bound to spot the bulls staking out the platform. Maybe he'll think he's about to be pinched. He'll be armed and unpredictable. Who knows what could happen?"

Sullivan chewed it over. "Okay, okay. Last thing we need is crossed wires and a shootout under the palm trees."

The pair stopped in front of the door to Drawing Room D. From inside came a male voice, the words spoken with a Hudson Valley accent: "Never before since Jamestown and Plymouth Rock has our American civilization been in such danger as now." They both recognized the measured tones of President Franklin Delano Roosevelt.

Sullivan pushed the buzzer, and in a moment LaVonne Cohen opened the door. She wore a bias-cut, flaming red silk peignoir with spaghetti straps and a ruffled neckline and did not seem the least bit shy about it. "Hey, you two are coppers, right?"

"FBI," Sullivan said.

"C'mon in," LaVonne said, "and tell me what J. Edgar wants with little old me."

They entered the compartment. On the radio, President Roosevelt was warning of dire consequences if England fell to Germany. "The Axis powers would control the continents of Europe, Asia, Africa, Australia, and the high seas," he said.

"You're listening to FDR's fireside chat," Vazquez said.

LaVonne jutted out her chin. "You betcha. I can read, too."

"I'm sorry, Mrs. Cohen. I didn't mean it that way."

"No sweat, sweetie. It's just that I get misunderestimated a lot. Sit down, why doncha?" They remained standing, and LaVonne continued, "I'm just doing my nails." She pointed at her feet, cotton balls squeezed between her toes, half her toenails already painted.

"Ruby Red from Cutex," Vazquez said.

"Bullseye, FBI gal. My favorite color."

On the radio, Roosevelt's tone darkened: "The evil powers would bring enormous military and naval resources against this hemisphere. It is no exaggeration to say that all of us, in all the Americas, would be living at the point of a gun."

"We're looking for Mr. Cohen," Sullivan said, sounding very much like a copper.

"Sure you are, handsome," LaVonne said, turning off the radio. "Mick's getting a shave."

Sullivan checked his watch. "Almost dinner time."

"Mick's gotta shave twice a day or he chafes my inner thighs, if you catch my drift."

Sullivan's cheeks colored. He cleared his throat, shuffled his feet, and said, "Thank you, Ma'am. We'll head to the barber shop."

"Mick knows how to treat a lady, I'll tell you that," LaVonne called out as they left the compartment.

The sound was the familiar *swish-whoosh* of a straight razor on a leather strop. The aroma was witch hazel, infused into the hot towel wrapped around Mickey Cohen's face. The barber, a heavyset, fiftyish man with a pencil-thin Errol Flynn mustache, examined the blade of the razor, held a single hair in his left hand, then sliced through the strand with no resistance. He picked up the shaving brush and whisked circles inside the scuttle until the shaving soap was lathered. Then he removed the towel from Cohen's face.

"Got a question for you Wilbur," Cohen said as the barber began lathering his face with the badger-hair brush. "Whadaya suppose is the full cry this time out?"

"If the weather's good, around a hundred-five miles per hour just outside Pasadena."

"Heading through those orange groves?" Cohen asked.

"That's the place." The barber's brow furrowed. "Now, you're not planning to make a book, are you, Mr. Cohen, get all those suckers betting on the full cry?"

"Strictly on the up-and-up, Wilbur. I just enjoy lightening the wallets of rich white men."

"But you're a rich white man, Mr. Cohen."

Cohen laughed and a speck of foam flew from his lips. "To the blue bloods whose kin came over on the Mayflower, I'm a little Jewboy from Boyle Heights."

Just as the barber was poised to make the first pass with the razor, Brian Sullivan and Milagros Vazquez walked into the barber shop from the vestibule, the *clackety-clack* of the train growing louder, then diminishing.

"Officers," Cohen said, nodding. "You got me at a disadvantage."

The FBI operatives both said hello, Sullivan taking in Cohen's worsted wool suit coat with its red silk pocket square, hanging on a rack. The agent noted the absence of a shoulder holster and handgun.

"You packing under that sheet?" Sullivan asked.

Cohen winked at Wilbur and said, "On the advice of my barber, I respectfully decline to answer the question."

"Could you give us a moment?" Vazquez said to Wilbur the barber, who put down the razor, and headed out.

"We're not here to lean on you," Agent Sullivan said.

"No kidding. If you had anything, you'd collar me quicker than a showgirl loses her panties. So what's your beef?"

"We know you're guarding Chaplin on Bugsy Siegel's orders," Vazquez said.

"Yeah, that's a public service, ain't it?" Cohen said.

"We're not entirely comfortable with you packing heat on an interstate mode of transportation," Sullivan said, sounding like a bureaucrat reading the fine print aloud.

"I've ridden the Super Chief a dozen times, and I ain't plugged no one yet," Cohen responded. "And if you're wondering, I got a permit to carry a concealed firearm."

"California must have loosened its standards," Vazquez said.

"Nah. Came with my honorary sheriff's deputy badge, which cost me a cool five grand. Now, what else can I do you for?"

The Super Chief's horn blared as the train sped through a crossing. After a moment, Sullivan said, "As much as it pains me to say it, we need to work together, Mickey."

"Meaning what?" Cohen asked, his tone suspicious.

"Mostly, we just need you to stay out of the way."

Cohen gave a sharp laugh. "And here I thought you wanted to recruit me, even though when I took my physical, the Army told me I was 'morally unfit.' How moral do you gotta be to kill a man?"

Neither agent took the bait. Instead, they spent the next few minutes outlining the threat.

They would take primary responsibility for protecting Chaplin, working in four-hour shifts inside his drawing room, keeping an eye on him all the way to Union Station. Chaplin would remain on board until law enforcement secured the platform and the station entrance, where his chauffeured Rolls-Royce would be waiting.

"Nazis!" Cohen thundered. "Do youse two know me and the boys beat the tar out of those bastards in L.A. a while back?"

"A Bund rally at Alt Heidelberg," Sullivan said. "I saw the report. Pipes and knuckle dusters. A few broken jaws. We know you have nothing but antipathy for fascists."

"Huh? I got no pithy at all for those Jew-haters." Cohen shook his head. "So what's the play at Union Station?"

"We'll be looking for a man in a black topcoat carrying a florist's box," Sullivan said. "Thing is, instead of roses, there'll be a tommy gun inside."

Cohen scoffed. "Jeez, you G-men seen too many movies. That sounds like a load of hooey."

"Maybe," Vazquez said, "but it's a tip we can't afford to ignore."

Cohen wiped the drying lather from his face with a towel. "This got anything to do with that mustached guy I seen you two drinking with?"

Sullivan and Vazquez exchanged glances.

"That information is none of your concern," Sullivan said.

Cohen smirked. "Except you just answered. That guy's your stoolie. I wouldn't believe him if he said the sky was blue."

"Prudence dictates we exercise caution when warned of a credible threat," Sullivan said stiffly.

Cohen rolled his eyes. "I dunno who Prudence is, but if you want, I'll rattle the squealer's teeth with a gun barrel—see if he's telling the truth."

"No." Sullivan's tone was sharp. "Stay away from him. The man is a German intelligence agent."

Vazquez shot her partner a look. *Was that necessary?*

Cohen's eyes widened. "A Nazi spy? Oh, in that case, he's gotta be telling the truth."

Vazquez took control. "Mr. Cohen, just follow our instructions. When we get to Union Station, you'll stay on the train."

"With your honorary sheriff's badge and your revolver holstered," Sullivan added.

"And I'll lead you off when we get the all-clear," Vazquez said.

Cohen smirked. "Ain't my style to hide behind a dame's petticoats."

Vazquez gave him a cool look. "Good, because I don't wear any."

On the radio in Charlie Chaplin's drawing room, Ethel Merman sang that she got no kick from champagne. Chaplin, on the other hand, was delighted to serve the two FBI operatives Moët & Chandon, delivered by Ezra Jefferson, his favorite sleeping car porter. Sullivan and Vazquez sat on the sofa. Einstein and Chaplin faced the two in matching cushioned chairs.

"Let me get this straight," Chaplin said, a note of amusement in his voice. "The FBI has been tailing Albert to see if he's leaking national secrets."

"As if I know any," Einstein said.

On the radio, Ethel Merman complained that alcohol didn't thrill her at all.

"But now, on your own," Chaplin said, "you've decided I'm being led to slaughter by a Nazi Mata Hari."

"Who's also a *shayna maidel*," Einstein said, tossing in the Yiddish for "beautiful young woman."

"Not to mention Lucky Lindy's mistress," Chaplin added.

That caught the FBI operatives by surprise. After a moment, Vazquez said, "No reason she can't be both a spy and a mistress. One role can lead naturally to the other."

"And Hitler's well-documented fury over *The Great Dictator* may well have escalated into an assassination plot," Sullivan added.

On the radio, Ethel Merman dreamily wondered why "*I get a kick out of you.*"

Einstein looked at his friend and said, "Charlie, you need to take this threat seriously."

Then, fixing his gaze on the two federal agents, he added, "You tell Charlie what to do, and I'll make sure he does it."

FIFTY-THREE
"BRING IN THE DUKE"

Fritz Duquesne did not frighten easily. But in this moment, he allowed himself a rare admission—he was afraid. Forty years as a soldier, spy, and saboteur had taught him a simple truth: men in his profession rarely died peacefully. Some might perish in their beds, but not of old age—rather, at the hands of a younger, craftier operative, armed with a stiletto, garrote, or silenced Luger.

Sitting in his drawing room, a gin and tonic in hand, he gazed absently out the window. The bluish-gray silhouette of the mountains loomed closer as the Super Chief neared Albuquerque. The reddish-brown earth slipped past, dotted with sagebrush, cacti, and juniper. Normally, he found the desert's stark beauty mesmerizing. But today his thoughts drifted from the rugged landscape to the dangers closing in around him.

He had read the wireless message multiple times, scrutinizing each word, hoping he had drawn the wrong conclusion.

He had not.

"Take immediate steps to abort Needles mission."

And lose the perfect opportunity to kidnap Einstein? No!

Jolted, he skimmed the remaining instructions. He was to remain on the train until its final destination in Los Angeles, then go directly to the Port of Long Beach. A Spanish freighter with a German crew would take him through the Panama Canal and on to Barcelona where a tri-motor Junkers 52 would fly him to Berlin.

"Upon arrival, report at once for interview at RHSA."

A second jolt. The *Reichssicherheitshauptamt* in Berlin. The nerve center of Himmler's empire, the combined headquarters of the SS, the Gestapo, the Kripo criminal police, and the SD intelligence service. If hell had a home office, it was there. He was not being summoned for coffee and *Kirschtorte*.

Would he even make it to the buildings on Prince Albrecht Street, where an "interview" was often conducted with truncheons and electric currents? Or would he become an appetizer for the sharks before he even reached Germany?

He had never set foot in RHSA headquarters. Abwehr operated from Hamburg where Admiral Canaris shielded him from SS scrutiny. Canaris had a talent for protecting his officers when they worked outside official channels or took actions that Himmler's security apparatus would condemn as insubordination.

He could picture the Reichsführer of the SS, that sallow, moon-faced, thin-lipped, bespectacled bureaucrat, pulling rank, and personally calling Canaris with an unappealable order.

"Bring in the Duke."

Now, either Canaris can no longer protect me, or he believes I am no longer worth the effort.

As Duquesne retraced the events that had led him to this perilous juncture, he had to concede that the past week hardly warranted a banquet at the Hotel Vier Jahreszeiten, let alone the glint of an Iron Cross. The NDRC operation? A humiliating disaster, with the pharmacist and courier arrested. Reinhard Schmidt's death? Under scrutiny by SS operatives in the U.S., no doubt. How long before they dismissed his far-fetched tale of a U.S. Army archery squad wielding crossbows? Ignoring direct orders to steer clear of Liselotte Müller? His most reckless blunder of all. He couldn't resist taunting her, letting her know her cover was as thin as cigarette paper.

Now Duquesne figured Müller had a suitcase wireless of her own and had blown the whistle to Berlin, his insubordination pulsing across the ether like a ripple of dark tidings.

My ego! How foolish to let my pride cloud my judgment.

And there was yet another possibility—one even more foreboding. Had German Intelligence intercepted a message from the FBI operatives on the train? His offer to spill secrets—a clever feint, nothing more—would be taken at face value in Berlin. And with no paperwork to back up his spur-of-the-moment deception, he was, to use the American idiom, a "dead duck."

The Super Chief's horn shattered the desert silence as it approached Albuquerque. The gleaming streamliner slowed, about to ease its well-heeled passengers into the station in cushioned comfort.

Berlin be damned!

He would not abort. He would disembark at the Needles station at 2:20 a.m. His players will be in place, and the Einstein snatch will go off without a hitch. A mere five-minute drive to the seaplane waiting on the Colorado River. Six hours later, as clueless SS agents scoured Union Station in Los Angeles looking for him, his plane would be refueling in Tampico. The fools would realize too late that they had been chasing shadows. His own route to Hamburg would be secure, Einstein in tow, the greatest masterstroke of espionage of his career…or anyone else's.

I will rise from the doomed and be redeemed.

Canaris would have fresh ammunition in his private war against Himmler, whose brazen grasp for authority over the Abwehr would be checked.

Bring in the Duke?

Yes, to be feted.

His mood lifted like a kite on a coastal breeze, and his thoughts drifted to the celebration awaiting him. He could almost hear Canaris toasting his triumph with champagne, likening his victory to the Twelve Labors of Hercules—a treacherous path from disgrace to renown.

And the FBI agents? Thoroughly duped by this old fox. A shame, really, as he rather liked them both. But their naivete, leaping at the bait, was hardly his fault. Should they not have known? Retirement on a pig farm near Pasadena would never be his fate. He was destined for far greater things—and his game was far from over.

FIFTY-FOUR
"THE WORLD AS I SEE IT"
Albuquerque Station, Santa Fe Depot

Chaplin adjusted his 35 mm Leica, focusing on Einstein's face. "Smile, Albert. You look like a cigar store Indian."

Einstein, swathed in a wool serape patterned with red and black geometric shapes, tugged self-consciously at the straw sombrero perched on his head, his wild crop of white hair bristling out like an unruly halo. "I feel foolish," he muttered.

"You look marvelous," Chaplin replied breezily.

The station, part Pueblo Revival, part Spanish Colonial, rose like a sunlit hacienda with creamy stucco walls, red clay tile roof, and archways adorned with wrought-iron lanterns.

At makeshift stands, Native Americans and Mexicans sold turquoise jewelry, leather wallets, earth-toned pottery, beaded moccasins, and feathered headdresses to the disembarked passengers. The air buzzed with conversation and the rustle of goods being examined.

Ten feet from Einstein and Chaplin, Brian Sullivan and Milagros Vazquez stood with their backs turned, eyes sweeping the crowd for threats. Mickey Cohen loitered at a popcorn stand, casually munching but alert for sudden movements.

At a stand near the station's entrance, Liselotte Müller, dressed in a tailored navy suit with padded shoulders and a nipped waist, adjusted a Hopi headdress on her son. The cascade of turkey and hawk feathers trailed halfway down his back.

Taking it all in from a wooden display stand where a tribal woman displayed intricately tooled leather belts was Fritz Duquesne, his gaze cool and calculating. He watched as Chaplin handed the camera to Sullivan. Einstein removed his sombrero, ran a hand through his tangled hair, and looped an arm around Chaplin's shoulders. As Sullivan framed the shot, Einstein suddenly stuck out his tongue, and Chaplin widened his eyes and mouth in exaggerated laughter.

"Goofing around," the Yanks called it.

Movement behind the two friends caught Duquesne's attention. A heavyset man with dark, curly hair hesitated, then sidestepped sharply, an obvious attempt to avoid being caught in the background of the photograph. For a man of his size, he moved with surprising swiftness, slipping out of the frame just as Sullivan adjusted the focus.

Unlike me, caught flatfooted by the wire service photographers at Dearborn Station, hovering like a ghost behind Lindbergh and Chaplin.

The man appeared to be in his mid-thirties, and he wore a freshly purchased serape that sat slightly askew. The neckline of his shirt revealed the collar of a gray suit coat, paired with matching trousers. Most passengers had dressed casually for their souvenir-shopping excursion. More concerning, Duquesne didn't recall seeing the fellow on the train.

The man strolled casually into the crowd of passengers, Duquesne shadowing him at a comfortable distance. The man stopped at a vendor's stand and studied a pair of deer-skin moccasins with blue beads forming a thunderbird across the instep. That prompted Duquesne to glance down at the man's footwear

Boots! Toe-capped, side-laced, black leather boots disappeared into his pant legs.

They looked like Marschstiefel marching boots worn by Wehrmacht troops. Also by Kripo, the criminal police who enjoyed stomping on people's heads with hobnailed soles.

The man turned slightly, giving Duquesne a clearer look at his face. A nose that veered east and west, the unmistakable result of an old break. A jaw like a slab of granite, jutting pugnaciously. A mouth as thin and unyielding as a razor's edge. A brute's face. The kind Duquesne had encountered among countless Kripo thugs over the years.

Suntanned. I hadn't noticed that at first. It's November, and the man is deeply tanned.

With the Gestapo tied up doling out terror in Europe, low-ranking Kripo officers often provided security for German consulates abroad. And the nearest consulate? Likely Ciudad Juárez in northern Mexico—an easy drive to Albuquerque.

But what is he doing here, and why was he in such a hurry that he didn't change out of those boots?

Duquesne would find out. He turned and headed for the entrance to the station, taking care not to look behind him. He entered a large open room, its massive wood beams and wrought-iron chandeliers lending it a rugged elegance. Red and blue tile murals adorned the walls. Passengers sat on wooden benches, reading newspapers, waiting for their trains.

At the far end of the ticket counter, past the gift shop, he spotted a restroom.

As he walked, he heard it—the *click-click-click* behind him. He didn't turn. He knew that sound. Hobnailed boots on terra cotta tile.

Flanked by Brian Sullivan and Milagros Vazquez with Mickey Cohen several paces behind, Einstein and Chaplin continued along the platform, pausing to admire the handicrafts. Chaplin picked up a headdress, a fan of colorful feathers cinched with leather strips and a beaded headband.

"The blue feathers represent the sky and the lakes," Einstein said. "The red ones symbolize life and sacred fire."

"Okay, smart guy," Chaplin said. "How do you know that?"

Einstein fished his meerschaum pipe from the pocket of his sweater, taking his time as he searched for matches. "On my first trip to the States in thirty-one, Elsa and I visited the Grand Canyon. We met some Hopis who initiated me into the tribe as their 'Great Relative.'"

"And a headdress was part of the deal?"

"Plus a peace pipe." Einstein sighed, abandoning his hunt for matches. "If we could only get the nations of the world to sit around a campfire and seal peace with a good smoke."

Chaplin caught his friend's downbeat tone. "What's on your mind, Albert? I know you've been chatting with Oppenheimer, and you just said 'peace' the way a jilted lover says 'farewell.'"

"Young Robert has asked me to help with the bomb project."

"Behind the scenes, I assume."

"Behind. In front. On top. Morally, it makes no difference." Einstein's shoulders sagged as if the weight he carried had grown heavier by the word. "I will always believe that war is a disease, and perhaps one day I will regret urging FDR to build what promises to be an instrument of such destruction."

"But the Nazis, Albert, are an evil the modern world has never known."

"Yes, of course, Charlie. But he who fights with monsters must take care lest he thereby become a monster."

"Sure, Nietzsche's pithy aphorism gets tossed around in all the best salons. But I've got another one. 'Fight fire with fire.'"

"*Yo, mayn fraynd*, "Einstein said, softly in Yiddish, "but who will be left to douse the final blaze?"

Crossing the waiting room, Duquesne calculated quickly. The man would have a gun, likely in a shoulder holster beneath his suit coat. But the added layer of the serape would slow him down, two seconds at most, but enough.

Duquesne slipped into the dimly-lit restroom, then snapped his right arm downward, and the stiletto slid smoothly from his sleeve into his hand. The door creaked open behind him.

The man entered, lifting his serape, his hand darting under his coat—going for a 9 millimeter Luger.

Too slow.

Whirling, his arm a flash of motion, Duquesne slashed cleanly across the man's throat, and the gun clattered to the tile floor. The man's hands shot to his neck, blood spilling through his fingers in dark, pulsing streams.

"Who sent you?" Duquesne demanded, a pointless question. The man could only gurgle in reply, crimson bubbling from his lips.

With all the strength left in his right arm—arthritic elbow and all—Duquesne drove the stiletto deep into the man's abdomen, then twisted it sharply, carving a cruel circle.

Walking the dog, they call it.

The man toppled forward, blood spurting from his abdomen and neck. Duquesne quickly went through the man's pockets. No wallet, no I.D. Of course not. Duquesne quickly washed his bloody hands and knife, grabbed an "Out of Order" sign hanging on a hook, exited the restroom and hung the sign on the doorknob.

He entered the gift shop, then looked out the window, his gaze sweeping the waiting room for any accomplices who might be lingering. His heart was steady, his breathing calm.

This old lion still moves with the unshaken confidence of a king who rules his domain.

Duquesne lingered for a few minutes, concealed between shelves of books. Feigning interest, he picked up *All Quiet on the Western Front.* He had already read Erich Maria Remarque's novel, despite it being banned by the Reich for its anti-war themes and demoralizing portrait of German soldiers.

He moved to the next row and another book caught his eye. Einstein's face stared up at him from the cover. Windblown thistle hair. Whisk broom mustache. Eyes full of distant wisdom. The title: *The World as I See It.*

Oh, shut up and scribble your equations!

He flipped to the table of contents. All pontificating essays.

"Good and Evil."

"The True Value of a Human Being."

And this grandiose gem: "The Meaning of Life."

He thumbed a few pages and read to himself: "We exist for all mankind, in the first place for those on whose smiles and welfare all our happiness depends, and next for all those whose destinies we are bound up by the tie of sympathy. A hundred times every day, I remind myself that my inner and outer life depend on the labors of others, living and dead, and that I must exert myself in order to give in the same measure as I have received and am still receiving."

Einstein the bleeding heart!

Then a thought. He bought the book. Not for himself. For Heisenberg. A gift, delivered along with the author himself. A grand gesture, as befitting the craftiest intelligence agent of his time.

FIFTY-FIVE
A QUIET NIGHT, A LOADED GUN

The Super Chief hurtled through the darkness, cutting across New Mexico and Arizona, bound for California under a moonless desert sky, vast and unbroken. Yet, look upward, and a million diamonds lit the void. In his drawing room, Einstein sat by the window, his gaze fixed on the great misty band of the Milky Way. How many billions of stars made their home in our galaxy? And how many billions of galaxies lay beyond?

How foolish to think we are alone in the universe.

He wondered if distant civilizations had solved the intractable scourges of famine, war, and disease. And if beings from another world ever landed on Earth, would we learn from their wisdom, or greet them with gunfire?

His thoughts drifted again to Oppenheimer, who seemed poised to assemble a brash team of young scientists for the most complicated and dangerous undertaking in human history.

Oppenheimer and Groves and Chaplin have ganged up on me, and I have reached a conclusion. Yes, if asked theoretical inquiries, I shall try to answer, my principles now as flexible as a circus contortionist.

Looking skyward, Einstein easily picked out the star Segin in the Cassiopeia constellation, a faint spark thought to be some four hundred light-years away. If rocky planets like

Earth orbited Segin, could an advanced civilization be peering through their telescopes, studying us at this very moment? If so, they would see our world as it existed in the 1500s. The thought tugged at his imagination. Could they glimpse Galileo, gazing back through his crude telescope with a curiosity as boundless as the stars?

With that whimsical notion, Einstein climbed into bed, his mind alive with cosmic possibilities, but soon the steady purr of the twin diesel-electric locomotives lulled him to sleep.

Charlie Chaplin lay in bed in his black and yellow striped pajamas reading *The Grapes of Wrath*, the travails of the Joad family distracting him from his own tribulations. FBI Agent Sullivan was on the sofa in the drawing room, skimming through the *Saturday Evening Post*. Milagros Vazquez would relieve him at midnight, each taking four-hour shifts.

Chaplin had read his friend John Steinbeck's novel a year earlier and, now that it had won the Pulitzer Prize, was studying the book, rather than reading for pleasure. Steinbeck had accomplished what Chaplin set out to do in *The Great Dictator*.

Deliver popular entertainment layered with lessons of morality, social justice, family, hope, and resilience.

It struck him that the Super Chief's route nearly mirrored that of Route 66, the "Mother Road" that carried the Joad family westward in Steinbeck's novel. The luxurious train and the Joads' battered Hudson, both rolling through or past Gallup, Holbrook, Winslow, Flagstaff, Kingman, and into Needles, California. Oh, the heartbreak of that family and countless others searching for a better life in the darkest days of the Depression.

California. The promised land. A million miles from the Dust Bowl, or was it?

The shotgun-wielding foremen of the San Joaquin Valley were no more compassionate than the bankers foreclosing on farms in Oklahoma.

"There ain't no sin, and there ain't no virtue. There's just stuff people do."

That came from the preacher in the novel who had rejected the black-and-white moralism of his own Sunday sermons. Judgments must be tempered by the human experience. A man who steals an orange to feed his family is not necessarily a criminal.

I am outflanked by geniuses. Steinbeck and Einstein.

Chaplin's mind wandered to the conversation earlier that evening with the FBI operatives. They had confirmed what he already suspected—that the gunshot outside Fort Meade had been an assassination attempt. He remembered the Packard squealing away from the scene, Mickey Cohen firing his crossbow at the fleeing vehicle. The FBI confirmed that the body left behind with a sniper rifle was likely that of an SS assassin. Whether the target was Einstein or himself, or both, the feds could not say.

Word from home was no better. Swastikas had been painted on the walls of his Beverly Hills estate. Stacks of hate mail poured into his Hollywood studio, the common theme being he was a "Jew bastard."

Wrong on both counts! Mum was a gypsy, not a Jewess, and she and Pops were married when I arrived, though the old man took off while I was still in nappies.

Crackpots, Chaplin thought. Real assassins don't send you mail or splash paint. They fire bullets. But when the FBI tells you of a credible threat on your life, you pay attention.

Perhaps, I have been too cavalier about the danger.

"Agent Sullivan, are you awake?" Chaplin called.

"Yes, sir."

"I was hoping for a bedtime companion on the Chief, but you're not what I had in mind."

Sullivan chuckled. "Sorry about that, Mr. Chaplin."

"But what I really wanted to say—I haven't thanked you or Miss Vazquez for taking care of me. Frankly, I'm surprised Hoover approved it."

"Oh, the Director doesn't know, Mr. Chaplin. Our only assignment is to spy on you and Professor Einstein."

Chaplin laughed. "Well, you're in my drawing room, so I'd say you're doing a jolly good job."

Wearing a white silk chemise with lace trim, Lena Horne curled up, feet tucked underneath her, in the lounge chair of her roomette. Compared to the spacious drawing rooms, the roomette was a closet with a fold-out bed, but the accommodations suited her just fine.

Her portable RCA Victor Victrola spun at 78 rpm, the warm tones of Ella Fitzgerald's "Goodnight, My Love" drifting through the small space. Listening wasn't quite the right word. Studying was closer to the truth. Oh, the velvety warmth of Ella's voice, the crystal clarity of her enunciation, the playful sweetness that, in moments of longing, deepened into a heartfelt yearning.

Eyes closed, imagining a nightclub on the Sunset Strip, Lena sang along with Ella. *"Goodnight my love, the tired old moon is descending. Goodnight my love, my moment with you now is ending."*

Both singers were twenty-three years old, but Ella had already made her name with the big bands and was Lena's role model. Perhaps Ciro's, promised by Mickey Cohen and brimming with Hollywood celebrities, would be her ticket to fame and fortune.

Ezra Jefferson lay in his bunk in the crew's quarters, located in the baggage car. He would take a two-hour nap, then rise. There were seven pairs of shoes to shine before breakfast.

In three drawing rooms, sex was on the midnight menu.

J. Robert Oppenheimer and Kitty, married just nine days, went at it with gusto, the sway of the train and the muffled rumble of the locomotives only adding to the rhythm.

A few compartments down, Mickey and LaVonne Cohen rustled the sheets, heaved and humped with abandon.

And in Charles Lindbergh's drawing room, the aviator-philosopher and the Abwehr agent Liselotte Müller thrust and parried in the missionary position, though God's envoys would surely frown upon the extramarital exercise.

Fritz Duquesne sat on the lounge chair in his drawing room, oiling his Luger, then sliding the eight-round magazine into the angled handgrip. He turned over the events of Albuquerque. Why was he attacked when he was going to be taken into custody—there was no other way to put it—at Union Station in Los Angeles? With the Reich's high command fractured into warring factions, the assassination plot could have come from anywhere. But the likely source was the obvious one: the SS, following Himmler's orders.

And Union Station? Just a ruse so I would lower my guard in Albuquerque.

How long before Berlin realized its assassin had bungled his mission? When he failed to report back to Ciudad Juárez, or wherever, a chain of wireless transmissions would ripple across the Atlantic, a back-and-forth of coded inquiries and mounting frustration. No matter. Not with the Super Chief barreling westward, leaving the Chihuahuan Desert of New Mexico, cutting across the Sonoran Desert of Arizona and soon, into California where the Mojave stretched vast and indifferent. Not a single German agent for hundreds of miles.

Ah, the great American West…how I cherish your rugged re-moteness. Let SS assassins crawl all over Union Station. I will be flying high above Mexico, prize in hand.

Duquesne wiped the excess oil from his Luger. If all went well, he would not need to draw the gun, much less fire it. The carefully planned snatch of Einstein from the platform should be quick and painless. Still, one must be prepared. He checked his watch, then looked out the window. The Super Chief was thundering through the Seligman, Arizona railway station. Another ninety minutes or so, and the train would come to a gentle stop in Needles, California.

Sweet memories of past triumphs came to mind, but would any of them measure up to what was to come?

Just after two a.m., as the train crossed the Colorado River on the Red Rock Bridge, Ezra Jefferson worked a horsehair brush across a pair of brown and white saddle oxfords belonging to a corpulent banker from Virginia. Glancing down toward the black water, Jefferson noticed a light. A boat, close to shore.

No! A seaplane, its pontoons nosed against the riverbank in the shallows near the bridge.

He'd witnessed plenty of seaplanes—mostly airmail craft— skim the Mississippi on St. Louis runs, but never one on the Colorado. Engine trouble, maybe. Waiting for a mechanic at first light, he figured.

Once the Super Chief cleared the bridge, the station coming into view, Jefferson saw headlights. A car was tearing along the deserted highway that paralleled the tracks. Nothing unusual there. Over the years he'd watched fools race a ninety-mile-an-hour train, bouncing their jalopies into ditches or sideswiping cottonwoods. And then there were the last-minute travelers, terrified of missing their train.

But no passengers boarded at Needles for the final sprint to Pasadena and Los Angeles. He leaned closer to the window, squinting. A big sedan, that much he could tell. But from this distance, the only clear thing about it was the speed—hellishly fast.

FIFTY-SIX
THE SNATCH

Needles Station, Santa Fe Depot 2:20 a.m.

Seconds after the Super Chief's air brakes wheezed to a stop, the railway platform buzzed with activity. It was the last crew change of the westward journey, and as the engineer, fireman, brakeman, and diesel mechanic stepped off the train, their replacements climbed aboard. The crew of oilers, brake inspectors, and car knockers in denim coveralls swarmed the train, wordlessly going about their work. It was a ten-minute stop with another six-and-a-half hours to the final destination of Los Angeles.

From his perch by the window in the crew quarters' car, Ezra Jefferson snap-shined a pair of black wingtips with a soft cloth, his hands working by rote while his eyes observed the bustling platform. He envied men who went to work at the same place each day and came home each night. The rhythm of their lives had a steadiness his did not.

His thoughts shifted when he noticed a man striding from the Western Union office toward the train. The man wore a crisp white shirt with sleeve garters, a black vest, gray wool trousers with a stripe down each leg and a green eyeshade. He was tall and sandy-haired and walked with an erect posture that was unusual for telegraph operators who sat, round-shouldered, hunched over their teletype machines ten hours per day. Those who worked the graveyard shift like this poor guy usually were old rummies who drank their days away. But this man of about forty looked as fit as one of those tennis players who traveled to New York for the U.S. National Championships each year.

Jefferson kept his eyes on the man.

Petrus Visser embraced his role as a Western Union telegraph operator with theatrical fervor. Before becoming a minor functionary in Abwehr, he had enjoyed a modestly successful career as an actor in Berlin, gaining some notoriety for his performance in Schiller's *Wilhelm Tell* at the Deutsches Theater. In the original production, Tell was the defiant archer battling against tyranny. But in the revised, Nazi-approved version, Tell became a paragon of blind patriotism, with the ideals of personal liberty and universal freedom erased from the narrative. Visser, a born follower, found the revised version fit him like a bespoke tuxedo.

He had met Duquesne, a fellow South African by birth, at a party thrown by *Neues Volk*, the magazine of the Office of Racial Policy, where Visser had been featured as an Aryan ideal—blond, broad-shouldered, handsomely vacant. Duquesne, ever the recruiter, saw his usefulness.

Tonight, Visser had only one line to deliver:

"Dr. Einstein, I regret to inform you—your son Hans has been in a terrible automobile accident in South Carolina. Please come with me at once."

As Visser neared the train, the hiss of its settling brakes still fading, his pulse quickened.

Which car? Which drawing room?
A jolt of panic. He couldn't remember.

Ezra Jefferson watched the Western Union man stop short when he was just steps from the train. He was alongside one of the roomette cars and looked up at the windows, appearing puzzled. Then spotting an oiler who had just crawled from beneath the train, the telegraph man said something. A question, perhaps, as the oiler shook his head as if to say, "Sorry, I don't know."

The Western Union man looked up at the train again, turned left and right, as if trying to decide which car to enter. Jefferson figured he had an emergency telegram to deliver to a passenger. Trained for decades to provide assistance, and it being in his nature to do so, Jefferson would, of course, help the man.

Carrying both the wireless radio case and his suitcase, Fritz Duquesne stepped down from the train onto the platform. He wore a topcoat, his Luger in one pocket, two extra magazines in the other.

Always expect the unexpected.

He caught sight of Petrus Visser thirty yards away, dressed as a Western Union man, obviously adrift, speaking to a railroad worker in dirt-stained coveralls. Duquesne's message had clearly stated, "car six, drawing room D," but he had also told Visser not to write down the information.

You'd think an actor could remember a single-digit number and one letter!

The worker didn't seem to be much help, and Duquesne was on the verge of intervening. His plan had been to head straight for the parking lot, ensuring that Ludwig, the driver, kept the Lincoln Zephyr purring, ready to race toward the river and the waiting seaplane. The 12-cylinder sedan could top 100 miles per hour, but there would be no need for speed. This wasn't a getaway from a bank robbery. There would be no sirens, no gunfire—just a quiet, calculated departure.

Then he saw the old porter step down from the train and approach Visser.

Splendid! Sleeping car porters, the grandsons of slaves, are obedient seeing-eye dogs, trained to serve without question.

If a uniformed Western Union man asked a question, Duquesne thought, there was a greater chance of throwing snowballs in hell than the porter declining to answer.

☞ ☜

"May I help you, sir?" Ezra Jefferson asked.

The man in Western Union garb smiled, displaying two rows of perfect teeth. "I'm looking for Albert Einstein's compartment. Emergency telegram."

The man spoke with a slight accent that Jefferson couldn't decipher. "You can give it to me, sir. Delivering wires is part of my job."

The man hesitated, not expecting the offer. Needing to ad lib, his genial tone became brittle. "Don't trouble yourself. Einstein has to sign for it in the delivery ledger."

Jefferson glanced at the man's empty hands. "I don't see any ledger, or a telegram for that matter."

The man scowled. "They're in the office. The ledger is attached to the counter by a chain." He lowered the tone of his voice in an attempt to sound sinister. "You know about chains, don't you, boy?"

Jefferson had been insulted by far more menacing men in his fifty-two years. Keeping his voice calm, he said, "So you want to wake up Albert Einstein and take him to the telegraph office in the middle of the night?"

"Not that it's any of your business, but his son has been in a terrible motor car accident. He's fighting for his life."

"If that's the case, sir, wouldn't it be simpler to just bring the telegram to the Professor's compartment?"

"Rules and regulations!" the man sputtered. "We Brits love our rules."

That struck something in Jefferson's memory. He couldn't quite grasp it. Then he saw Frederick Fredericks on the platform thirty yards away. Dressed in a topcoat, he carried both his pieces of luggage. Jefferson remembered the heavy reddish-brown suitcase. "Books," Fredericks had told him.

He's booked all the way to Los Angeles, so what's he doing? And why is he watching us?

Then it clicked. When enjoying that gin and tonic, Fredericks had said, "We Brits love our G&Ts." The same clipped rhythm as the Western Union man's "We Brits love our rules." But the accents weren't quite British.

Jefferson's gut tightened.

Both men are liars, but why?

"It's not just the telegram," the man said. "I've got a surgeon on the phone from the hospital. He wants to speak to Einstein."

Jefferson replayed that in his mind because it sounded fabricated, a spur of the moment addition to the story.

"So, are you going to tell me where Einstein is?" the man demanded.

"I'll speak to the conductor and convey your request." Jefferson turned and quickly climbed the steps to the train. He had no intention of speaking to the conductor. The person he hurried to see was Mickey Cohen.

Watching with disgust, Duquesne had no choice. He would lead this numbskull actor to Einstein's compartment and get the plan back on track. He checked his watch. Three minutes had elapsed. Seven minutes to get Einstein off the train and on his way to Berlin.

"No need to apologize, Ezra," Mickey Cohen said, after opening his drawing room door. "I sleep with one eye open. Now what's giving you the heebie jeebies?"

As Jefferson told Cohen about the odd encounter with the Western Union man, Cohen grabbed his Smith & Wesson .38 special, clicked the release, opened the cylinder, and spun it. Six rounds, fully loaded. Still in his silk monogrammed pajamas, he put on his kid leather bedroom slippers, the color of butter, and a navy cashmere top coat, slipping the revolver into one pocket and a handful of bullets into the other.

"You done the right thing, Ezra," Cohen said, heading out of the compartment. "Something ain't kosher in Needles."

Einstein awoke from a fitful sleep, his mind still tangled in the moral dilemma of America's nuclear ambitions. He switched on the reading light and reached for the book on his chest—Ernest Hemingway's *For Whom the Bell Tolls*.

A departure for him. Hemingway's prose was lean and unembellished, stark against the philosophical depths of Dostoevsky or the satirical whimsy of Cervantes, his favorite authors. But just as theoretical and experimental physics were two sides of the same pursuit, so too could literature hold Alexei Karamazov, Don Quixote, and Hemingway's Robert Jordan in the same breath.

Jordan, the novel's protagonist, was doomed—Einstein could sense it. A volunteer fighting fascists in the Spanish Civil War, Jordan was entangled in a tragic cycle of violence. One line spoken by Jordan struck a chord: *"Never think that war, no matter how necessary nor how justified, is not a crime."*

The words gnawed at him.

Hemingway's title had been drawn from John Donne's 17th-century meditation: "No man is an island…every death diminishes me…therefore, never send to know for whom the bell tolls; it tolls for thee."

Einstein pictured church bells tolling not only for the departed but for all, a reminder of humanity's shared fate.

The train's steady rhythm lulled him, the book slipping from his hands as sleep crept in. Then a sharp buzz at his door. His eyes snapped open.

Who the devil could that be at this hour?

Mickey Cohen hopped down from the train and surveyed the platform with the quick and discerning eyes of a predator. He ignored the railway workers and caught sight of Einstein's hair, wilder than usual. He wore a striped bathrobe and was flanked by two men, one in Western Union garb, the other carrying two suitcases. They were perhaps fifty feet from the train, walking in the general direction of the telegraph office. But then the Western Union man grabbed Einstein, pushing him toward the stairs that led to the parking lot.

"Hey youse guys!" Cohen called out. "Stop right there!"

The man with the suitcases turned. It was the mustachioed ratfink who'd had breakfast with the feds.

The Nazi spy!

Cohen waved his .38 in the air. "Step away from the Professor, both of youse."

For a split second, the Nazi hesitated. Then he pulled the Luger from his coat pocket. Cohen ducked, pivoted, moved in a crouch, gripping his revolver. But he didn't dare fire. He'd shot several men, but never at more than ten feet away, and usually less. Einstein was too close to the Nazi bastard to risk a shot.

The Luger barked twice. Sparks flew as bullets *pinged* off the train's metal siding, sending rail workers scattering.

The Western Union man reached for a gun in the back of his trousers, fumbled and dropped it. The weight of cold steel was heavier than the Bakelite prop weapons he used in moving pictures. His actor's hands had failed him, and he dived onto the platform, hands covering his head.

"Professor, *leygt zikh arayn!*" Cohen shouted, ordering Einstein in Yiddish to get down.

Einstein, finally registering the danger, dropped to his knees, then belly-crawled across the platform toward a shuttered magazine stand.

The Nazi scurried behind the concrete pedestal of a lamppost, aimed upward, and fired at the light fixture. The bulb sprayed glass over his head and shoulders but left him in darkness, as he intended. Using the pedestal as cover, on one knee, two hands on his Luger in the combat kneeling position, he fired twice more at Cohen, missing and shattering a window on the train.

Cohen raced six paces to his right, losing one of his kid glove slippers, and dived behind an oil cart, a wheeled piece of equipment with a pair of thirty-gallon drums resting on a metal shelf. The cart provided cover, but Cohen worried—if an oil drum took a bullet, would it explode?

Fritz Duquesne fired again, the bullet *ricocheting* off an oil drum, which did not explode into flames. At least his aim was improving. His nerves tingled, but he was unafraid. He had been in more gun battles than he could remember. Yet his eyesight wasn't what it used to be, and vanity prevented him from wearing glasses.

He had recognized the little thug with the gun. The bodyguard. Out of the corner of his eye, he saw Petrus Visser, the spineless milksop, crawling toward the steps to the parking lot. Two gunshots came from behind the oil cart, the bodyguard firing, both bullets striking the lamppost platform. He was a decent shot.

Duquesne sensed movement behind him, turned and saw Ludwig, the driver, emerging from the lot, Mauser carbine in hand, firing from the hip as if advancing through No Man's Land. Now they had the advantage. Two guns to one, and the thug was pinned down behind the cart while Einstein was trapped behind a magazine stand.

Duquesne allowed himself a grim smile. It would be easy. Kill the bodyguard. Grab the professor. Get out.

Einstein's heart thundered in his chest. First, the horrific news of the automobile crash and his beloved son Hans in a hospital.

A continent away! Is he even alive?

"A surgeon is holding on the phone, says it's urgent," the Western Union man had told him. "Come quick!"

The fear, then utter confusion, as the Western Union man grabbed him roughly and pushed him, but why? They were joined by a man in a topcoat carrying two suitcases. Then Mickey Cohen yelled orders in Yiddish and waved a gun. The man in the topcoat dropped his suitcases and pulled a handgun. Einstein recognized the distinctive German Luger, the sidearm carried by the hated *Kripo* in Berlin.

The night alive with the ferocious crackle of gunfire.

The good news, Einstein now realized, was that Hans was almost certainly not in a hospital. The horrific tale had been a ruse to kidnap him. The bad news was that his own life was in danger.

From his position behind the magazine rack, aware of the cold night air, Einstein saw the muzzle flashes, smelled the acrid tang of cordite, and watched as the light fixture above one gunman's head burst into a shower of glass. A moment later, gunshots shattered two windows in the train. Bullets struck the cart where Mickey Cohen crouched, the impact spitting flecks of fire from the twisted metal. Then—*Gottenyu!*—another man walked across the platform, firing a rifle at Cohen. Each shot cracked through the air, the echoes reverberating across the platform, sparks dancing from metal and concrete like fireflies.

Cohen returned fire, his revolver booming. Suddenly, a figure emerged on the top step of one of the drawing room cars.

The woman from the FBI! Both hands steady on her pistol.

She fired several shots, her rounds ringing out as the chaos intensified. Now the gunfight was two versus two. A bullet struck a lamppost with a metallic *clang,* the vibration jangling Einstein's bones. The scene was surreal—so far removed from anything in his experience that Einstein's mind split between terror and observation. He imagined the bullets as meteors, streaking across the sky in curved paths, subject as they were to gravity. Yet something else caught his attention: the sounds.

The revolvers, Cohen's and the FBI woman's, barking with a deep angry *pop.*

The German's Luger with a metallic *snap.*

The rifle, its shot *cracking* like a whip.

Einstein didn't know calibers, but he understood principles. The heaviest bullet would have the most kinetic energy and the least curvature. The equation was as clear to him as gravity itself: $KE = \frac{1}{2}\ mv^2$

He didn't know the precise speeds of the bullets—those would affect curvature—but it hardly mattered. The critical insight was clear: even if fired from the same position at the same velocity, the bullets, obeying the laws of kinetic energy, would trace distinct paths as they separated.

So too would uranium isotopes of different weights!

A sudden surge of adrenaline cut through his reverie.

Oppenheimer is right. The cyclotron is not suited for separating U-235 from U-238 for purposes of creating nuclear fission. But I know how it can be done!

Milagros Vazquez had never been in a gunfight. She had five days of handgun training before being issued her Colt Police Revolver, which held six .38 Special cartridges in its cylinder. She missed with her first five shots, having little chance of striking the gunman crouched behind the lamppost pedestal. Then she saw the heavyset man calmly approaching from across the platform, firing a rifle, the shots *pinging* off the stainless steel cars. She swept the gun in his direction and fired. The bullet caught the man flush in the throat and he toppled backward, blood spurting from his neck like a fountain as he died without a scream or plea.

Duquesne saw Ludwig crumple, blood pooling at his feet, rifle skittering away.

Verdammt!

It was time to move. As Duquesne had told Schmidt, he knew when to fight and when to take flight. He snapped off two final rounds—wild shots meant to keep heads down—grabbed his suitcases, and bolted, zigzagging toward the parking lot. He prayed Ludwig had left the Lincoln Zephyr idling, ready for a clean getaway. But even if he had, there was every chance the hare-livered Petrus Visser—whose next stage role ought to be Aristophanes' cowardly Dionysus—had panicked and fled, leaving him stranded.

Not that it mattered. The Colorado River lay less than a mile away, just beyond the alfalfa fields.

Only a fool—or an amateur—fails to plan an alternative escape route.

Duquesne cleared the stairs and scanned the lot. No Zephyr. Sirens wailed on the access road, their howls carving through the night. He pictured Visser at the wheel of the Zephyr, pale and sweating, racing for dear life—pursued by cops or wrapped around a tree. Fine with him either way.

Duquesne double-timed for the fields. In less than ten minutes, he'd be aboard the seaplane. But where to after Mexico? Certainly not Berlin. His enemies there would be circling like hyenas over a fallen antelope.

He would lay low south of the border and regroup. Even if Himmler's clique had turned against him, he knew his value. There was no one else with his experience, his cunning, his unshakable instinct for survival. A lifetime as a soldier and a snoop. He wasn't just a cog in the machine of espionage and treachery—he was a linchpin. And he still had his East Coast network. Thirty operatives who would obey him without question.

The war was coming. America's entry was inevitable. And when it did, the Reich would need him. He thought of the great warriors who had rebounded from defeat—King David, Hannibal, Julius Caesar. As he trudged through the dewy alfalfa, the words of Frederick the Great echoed in his mind:

"In every defeat, there lurks the advantage of becoming acquainted with our mistakes."

"Are you all right, Professor?" Milagros Vazquez asked, her voice quavering.

"I'm fine, dear. Thank you." Einstein rose unsteadily, his knees protesting. Vazquez caught him by the elbow and steadied him.

"I'm so relieved you're all right," she said.

"I was *farshrekht,* utterly terrified. The gunfire seemed to go on forever."

"Actually, it was about two minutes," Cohen muttered, joining them.

Agent Sullivan hustled down from the train, checked the husky German rifleman for signs of life, found none, and joined the others. A police siren wailed in the distance.

"Millie, you'll have to stay behind and lay everything out for the locals," Sullivan said.

Meaning the county sheriff's deputies, she knew. "Got it, Brian."

"Not me," Cohen said. "I ain't talking to no San Berdoo coppers."

Vazquez and Sullivan exchanged looks. Like old partners, they had established a method of communicating without speaking. Sullivan nodded, and Vazquez knew what he meant.

"Mr. Cohen, you were never here," Vazquez said, crisply. "Best get back on the train."

"Owe you one, Missy," Cohen said, already headed for his railcar.

"Professor, you must be freezing," she said to Einstein. "Let's get you bundled up and back to bed."

"Bed?" the scientist said, eyebrows raised. "Sleep can wait. I need to talk to Oppenheimer."

FIFTY-SEVEN
SEPARATING ISOTOPES

The San Bernadino Sheriff's Department roped off the platform and delayed the Super Chief from leaving the Needles station. The train's engineer, Thaddeus Gilbert, who had just climbed aboard for the final run to Los Angeles, was not pleased. A tall, large-boned man of fifty-five with the posture of a Buckingham Palace guard and gray mutton chops that clung to his face like storm clouds on a mountain peak, Gilbert had words with the Chief Deputy Sheriff.

Some of those words were "Gosh darn it" and "My train's never late."

The Chief Deputy assured him the delay wouldn't exceed an hour. Muttering under his breath, Gilbert stalked off to the telegraph office to alert his superiors. There he found the real telegraph operator—bound and gagged.

Onboard, the gunfire had jolted passengers awake. They now pressed against the windows, craning their necks to catch a glimpse of the commotion.

Deputies bustled about the platform, erecting portable floodlights, photographing the scene, and collecting spent cartridges. The county coroner crouched over the dead rifleman, performed a brisk examination, then waved for the body to be removed.

A few adventurous souls—still in their nightclothes—clambered down to the platform, eager for a closer look. No one stopped them. Soon others followed, and the crime scene morphed into a carnival. Engineer Gilbert ordered the kitchen crew to serve snacks. Soon, passengers were milling about with Danishes, scones, and steaming cups of coffee, their murmured conversations growing louder as rumors whipped through the crowd.

The wildest theories took hold with the force of gospel. A gang of robbers had attacked the train, aiming to steal millions in gold bars stored in the kitchen cooler. A more imaginative version had New York gangsters ambushing the train to free Louis "Lepke" Buchalter, the notorious head of Murder, Inc. An insurance man from Kansas City swore he'd heard from his wife's cousin's brother that federal agents were transferring Buchalter from Leavenworth to Alcatraz and had slipped him aboard during the quick stop in Topeka.

The truth, as usual, was far less dramatic. The most valuable treasures in the cooler were haunches of Prosciutto di Parma, hanging serenely on butcher's hooks, untouched by the evening's chaos. And Buchalter was still imprisoned in Kansas, though he was scheduled to be returned to New York to be tried for a gangland murder.

Not joining the rubberneckers was Mickey Cohen, who climbed back in bed, spooning with LaVonne and dreaming dreams of the peaceful and content.

Agent Sullivan checked on Chaplin and told him the threat was almost certainly over. The alleged assassination plot had been a diversion concocted by the fleeing Fritz Duquesne. The old spy had been telling tall tales since the Great War, and wasn't this one a doozy? Still, Sullivan would stick close to Chaplin for the rest of the journey.

Einstein, drawing stares as he hurried into the dining car in his bathrobe and slippers, found Oppenheimer sitting alone. A cup of coffee in one hand, a Chesterfield dangling from his lips, Oppenheimer was scribbling equations on a napkin.

"Robert! I think I've got it!" Einstein exclaimed.

Startled, Oppenheimer looked up. "Albert, good heavens! What…?"

Einstein dropped into the seat across from him, breathless. "You need a high concentration of U-235 to achieve a critical mass that can sustain a fission chain reaction. U-238, though much more plentiful, won't do."

"Yes, of course," Oppenheimer replied, setting down his pen alongside an ashtray littered with half-a-dozen cigarette butts.

"But U-235 and U-238 are chemically identical and cannot be separated by chemical means."

"The intractable problem." Oppenheimer drew hard on his cigarette, the ember flaring bright enough to etch his features in firelight, and half the Chesterfield seemed to vanish in a single pull.

"And as you've said, the cyclotron isn't suitable for the task. But I know what is." Oppenheimer's fingers tightened around his coffee cup. "Go on, Albert."

The steward approached and silently poured Einstein a cup of coffee. Rubbing his mustache with a knuckle, Einstein leaned in, lowering his voice as though the steward might be a German spy. "U-235 is slightly lighter than U-238. All you need is a method to separate the isotopes based on their mass."

"Easier said than done," Oppenheimer replied as the steward departed.

"But not impossible. Think of bullets of slightly different calibers—the lighter one will deflect more in a magnetic field." He tapped the table for emphasis. "That's how you separate U-235 from U-238 and voilà, there's your fissionable material."

Oppenheimer pinched the bridge of his nose and squeezed his eyes shut. "A magnetic field," he murmured. "Albert, are you saying to use a mass spectrometer?"

"Did I not say that?" Einstein gave a small laugh, raking a hand through his unruly hair, his fatigue from the sleepless night now plain on his face. "Yes, I should have said that."

Oppenheimer took a slow sip of his coffee, a wry smile forming. "Ingenious, Albert. And once we have enough fissionable material, $E = mc^2$ takes over, does it not?"

Einstein exhaled a long, weary sigh. "Yes, my friend. That is both my fondest hope and my greatest fear."

FIFTY-EIGHT
THE NEW AMERICA
Monday, November 11, 1940

Union Station in downtown Los Angeles was barely a year old, yet its white-stucco walls, red-tile roof, and commanding bell tower gave it the aura of an old Spanish mission. A half-dozen FBI agents from the Los Angeles office swept the platform and declared it clean—no assassins lurking in the shadows—before Sullivan would allow the legendary actor and the brilliant scientist to step off the train.

Moments later, a tight knot of six people moved briskly across the platform toward the arched colonnade leading into the terminal. On this bright autumn morning, Charlie Chaplin, Albert Einstein, Mickey and LaVonne Cohen, Lena Horne, and Ezra Jefferson strode with purpose. At their head, Chaplin halted at a newsstand, plucked the *Los Angeles Times* from the rack, handed the vendor a fiver, and waved off the change.

The front-page headline read: "ARMISTICE DAY." It had been twenty-two years to the day since the Great War had ended, and Europe was once again drowning in blood.

"FDR gave a speech at Arlington Cemetery," Chaplin murmured, scanning the article. The group waited for more.

"Well, Charlie?" Einstein prompted. "What did he say?"

Chaplin, slipping into the President's patrician tones, recited: "I, for one, do not believe that the era of democracy in human affairs can or ever will be snuffed out in our lifetime. I, for one, do not believe that the world will revert either to a modern form of ancient slavery or to controls vested in modern feudalism or modern emperors or modern dictators or modern oligarchs."

Einstein nodded solemnly. "*Fun dayn moyl in Got's oyern,*" he said in Yiddish. "From his mouth to God's ears."

Einstein caught the shadow that crossed his friend's face. "What's wrong, Charlie?"

"I let FDR down. I couldn't change Lindbergh's mind. He's still going to give his isolationist radio address."

"Yet you have the greater stage."

Chaplin looked puzzled, and Einstein continued: "You're speaking at the President's inaugural dinner. The press will cover your every word. Not only that, but *The Great Dictator* will be seen by millions of people. You'll be doing magazine and newspaper interviews. You'll help FDR pass Lend-Lease, no matter what Lindbergh says or does."

Chaplin allowed himself a small smile, clapped Einstein on the shoulder, and turned to the others. "Onward, my friends. Let's get the limo."

Cohen picked up Ezra Jefferson's duffel bag and said, "C'mon, pal."

"Please, Mr. Cohen," Jefferson said. "You're gonna get me in trouble with the union."

"Not unless they wanna deal with me," Cohen shot back. He had insisted on carrying Jefferson's duffel bag off the train, while Chaplin carried the porter's suit bag. Paying their respects.

"Mickey's right, Ezra. You're a real hero and deserve to be recognized," Chaplin said. "Mr. Jefferson, you saved my life," Einstein said. "You and Mickey both."

"I missed the Nazi son-of-a-bitch," Cohen said, curling his hand as if shooting a gun. "Wish I'd had a bazooka."

They entered the waiting room, which resembled a cathedral, a soaring space five stories high with bronze doors, terra cotta tiles, and a ceiling of hand-painted woodwork. A long ticket counter of polished wood and brass ran along one wall. In the center, rows of mission-style wooden benches with supple leather upholstery stood like pews in a grand church.

"Do you have a family, Ezra?" Chaplin asked, as they passed the Harvey House restaurant, the aroma of hot brewed coffee drifting in the air.

"Married twenty-six years," Jefferson said. "Althea teaches European history at Jefferson High."

"Excellent profession," Einstein chimed in.

"Americans have a rather casual relationship with international events."

Chaplin laughed. "That's Albert's refined way of saying that Americans are dumber than dirt about the outside world."

"We have two sons at San Francisco State," Jefferson said, glancing toward a shoeshine stand where a pair of teenage boys were snapping their cloths across the sparkling shoes of two white men in suits. "Isaac's studying business and Freeman's in the dental program."

"If Isaac and Freeman work as hard as their old man," Chaplin said, "they'll both be successes in whatever fields they choose."

"Amen to that," Einstein said.

Chaplin was quiet a moment, working on an idea. Then he said, "Ezra, do you like lobster thermidor?"

"I'm not sure I've ever had it, Mr. Chaplin."

"Charlie, are you thinking what I think you're thinking?" Einstein asked

"Yes, if you're thinking Musso and Frank for lunch," Chaplin replied. "Ezra, is school off for the holiday?"

"It is, sir."

"Wonderful. We'll pick up Althea and all have lunch together if that's fine with you." Jefferson's eyes lit up. "Fine and dandy, Mr. Chaplin. Fine and dandy, indeed."

Exiting the terminal, LaVonne Cohen and Lena Horne were talking nonstop, with Mickey an innocent bystander. "Under no circumstances will you take a taxicab," LaVonne insisted. "Mick's got a block-long Caddy with a chauffeur. We'll drop you at your hotel and pick you up at eight for Ciro's."

"Are you sure it's not too much trouble?" Lena asked.

"Sophie Tucker's appearing tonight. You gotta come."

"The Last of the Red-Hot Mamas." Lena's voice conveyed her admiration. "I love her rendition of *Some of These Days*."

"It's settled then," LaVonne said. "Mick will introduce you to management and set you up for your own show. Ain't that right, honey?"

"Sure thing," Mickey said. "Lena, we got a gal even younger than you opening next week for Mary Martin. The kid's a blonde from North Dakota, of all places. Name of Peggy Lee. You two can alternate days."

"On your days off, you eat dinner for free," LaVonne said, "but you'll be working for me."

"How's that, LaVonne?" Lena asked.

"You'll be keeping Mick away from the cigarette girls."

All three of them laughed, and Lena said, "I'm so grateful to have met both of you."

The plaza in front of Union Station was bathed in California sunshine, the flower beds a riot of bright marigolds, geraniums, and begonias. Three gleaming black motor cars were parked in the semi-circular drive closest to the entrance. William Randolph Hearst's Duesenberg Model J limousine, Charlie Chaplin's Rolls-Royce Phantom III limousine, and Mickey Cohen's Cadillac V-16 Sedan.

The group split up, hugging their goodbyes, the Cohens and Lena Horne heading to the Caddy, the other four to Chaplin's Rolls-Royce.

While waiting, the three chauffeurs busied themselves with their vehicles. Manuel Guerra, Chaplin's chauffeur, buffed the finish of the Rolls. Hearst's longtime employee, Kevin Leary, cleaned the Duesy's headlights, which were the size of manhole covers. And Cohen's driver, Shlomo "King" Solomon, a former heavyweight prizefighter and an ex-con, rubbed French cologne into the upholstery because his boss liked the scent. The three men had something in common. All carried firearms under their suit coats, as they doubled as bodyguards.

When Manuel Guerra saw Chaplin approaching, he hustled to grab the luggage, but the actor waved him off. "That's okay, Manuel. This is my job today."

"If you say so, sir."

"Manuel, say hello to Ezra Jefferson."

The chauffeur took in Jefferson's porter's uniform, shrugged as if nothing his boss did could surprise him, and the two men exchanged hellos. Guerra opened the trunk, then helped Einstein with his bag.

"Manuel, we're picking up Mrs. Jefferson and heading to Musso and Frank."

"Already made the reservation for you and Professor Einstein, sir."

"But...how did you know?" Chaplin asked.

"Whenever you've been gone more than two weeks, you crave Musso's liver and bacon. I'm sure two more at the table won't be a problem."

"Three more, Manuel. You're joining us. It's Monday, and they'll have the sweetbreads you like."

"Thank you, sir," the chauffeur said, beaming.

Watching with amusement, Jefferson asked, "Does this happen often, Mr. Chaplin?"

"What's that, Ezra?"

"That two of the most famous men in the world have lunch with one fellow in a chauffeur's uniform and another in a porter's uniform."

Before Chaplin could answer, Einstein said, "Not often enough."

All four men shared a laugh. Then Guerra held the door for Jefferson and Einstein, and they ducked into the passenger compartment, all saddle brown leather upholstery and mahogany woodwork with silver stringing. Chaplin was about to get in the front with Guerra when he saw Hearst, Lindbergh, Liselotte Müller and little Otto headed for the Duesenberg.

Feeling both chipper and a bit contrary, Chaplin said, "Manuel, isn't that the whitest wagon train you ever saw, right down to the red-headed chauffeur and the Berlin bombshell?"

Guerra didn't think the question actually called for an answer so he kept quiet. Then Chaplin called out, "Say, W.R., you know Duesenberg went bankrupt and is out of business, right?"

"What of it, Charlie?"

"Your Duesy's a symbol of the past. As are you and your precious cargo. You're all whiter than a preacher's collar, whiter than a banker's starched shirt, whiter than a Klondike blizzard."

Hearst strode over to Chaplin and towered above him. "What the hell's wrong with that? White people turned this wilderness into the greatest civilization the world has ever known."

"Ha! The ancient Sumerians thought the same thing. Ain't no place like Mesopotamia. So, too, ancient Egypt, the Persian Empire, the Han Dynasty, the Roman Empire, the Ottoman Empire. All gone, W.R., all these great civilizations turned to dust."

Lindbergh came alongside Hearst and said, "What the heck are you yammering about, Chap?"

"Ah, Lindy, worrying yourself sick about...what do you call it...'the dilution of our northern European blood'?"

"That's a fact," Lindbergh said.

"That's bigotry the Führer would admire," Chaplin said.

"Lindy's a red-blooded American!" Hearst shouted. "We need more like him."

Chaplin gestured toward his group. "Look who's coming to lunch. A Mexican, a Negro, a German Jew, and me...well, I'm a gypsy and a citizen of the world." He gestured toward Cohen's limousine. "And in Mickey's Caddy? Two Jews, a Scotch-Irish gal and a Negro songbird. So you know what you're looking at, W.R.?"

"Not a clue, Charlie," Hearst said.

"Lindy?" Chaplin asked.

"No idea what you're driving at," Lindbergh said.

"The new America!" Chaplin boomed. "You're looking at the future."

#

AFTERWORD

Charlie Chaplin's *The Great Dictator* was both a commercial and artistic triumph, earning a substantial profit and five Academy Award nominations. The film's concluding speech, a denunciation of tyranny and a plea for shared humanity, received mixed reviews—praised by some for its boldness but criticized by others for clashing with the comedic tone of the picture.

In 1952, while Chaplin, a British citizen, was in England promoting *Limelight*, FBI Director J. Edgar Hoover persuaded the Attorney General to revoke his re-entry permit on vague allegations of "moral turpitude" and "political affiliations." Hoover, who had waged a decades-long vendetta against Chaplin and amassed a 2,000-page file on him, finally succeeded in driving the actor into self-imposed exile in Switzerland.

Nine years earlier, Chaplin had married Oona O'Neill, 36 years his junior. The union proved enduring, the relationship devoted. Together, they raised eight children. In 1972, the Academy of Motion Picture Arts and Sciences awarded Chaplin an honorary Oscar, prompting a brief and emotional return to the United States. He died in 1977 at age 88 at his estate in Switzerland, leaving behind a legacy of cinematic genius and unflinching social commentary.

Albert Einstein, a lifelong pacifist, regretted writing the 1939 letter to President Roosevelt, which set the stage for the Manhattan Project by warning of Nazi Germany's potential development of an atomic bomb. The destruction of Hiroshima and Nagasaki deeply troubled Einstein, and he later reflected, "Had I known that the Germans would not succeed in producing an atomic bomb, I never would have lifted a finger."

While the book's conversation between Einstein and **J. Robert Oppenheimer** about uranium isotope separation is fictional, it is rooted in historical fact. When **Vannevar Bush**, Chairman of the National Defense Research Committee, sought advice on refining uranium for use in nuclear fission, Einstein recommended gaseous diffusion, which became critical to the Manhattan Project's success. It is not clear whether Einstein would have agreed to play an official role in the Project or if he would have received security clearance. In any event, he was never asked. After World War II, Einstein dedicated himself to the cause of nuclear disarmament and global peace, becoming a vocal critic of the arms race. He also was a passionate supporter of civil rights for African Americans.

In his later years, Einstein pursued a unified field theory ("the theory of everything") to explain all the fundamental forces of nature. The quest remained unfinished at the time of his death, and the puzzle continues to elude physicists today. Einstein died in Princeton, New Jersey, in 1955 at age 76. He remains the most famous scientist in history.

Fritz Duquesne, the flamboyant South African adventurer turned Nazi spy, was renowned for his charisma, cunning, and ruthlessness. A master of disguise, fluent in multiple languages, he cultivated an air of sophistication while orchestrating daring espionage operations. Over the course of his tumultuous life, Duquesne wore many hats: big-game hunter, journalist, soldier, con man, and counterintelligence agent for Germany in two world wars. Among his endeavors was a bizarre scheme to raise hippopotamuses in the Louisiana bayou for their meat.

He ran the "Duquesne Spy Ring" of more than thirty operatives, mostly on the East Coast of the United States. The espionage network's activities ranged from reporting on Allied ship movements to sabotaging defense plants. In June 1941, seven months after the events depicted in this book, the FBI dismantled the spy ring in a massive sting operation. Duquesne and thirty-two associates were convicted of espionage or related charges, with the spymaster receiving an 18-year prison sentence.

In 1954, in declining health, Duquesne was paroled and lived out his final years in obscurity. He died penniless in a New York hospital in 1956 at age 78.

General Leslie Groves (a major during the time span of the book) oversaw construction of the Pentagon and famously directed the Manhattan Project, which developed the atomic bombs used against Hiroshima and Nagasaki. He personally chose J. Robert Oppenheimer to run the Los Alamos laboratory, overruling objections that focused on the physicist's prior associations with communists. Following his retirement as a lieutenant general, he worked in the private sector. In 1962, he published his memoir, *Now It Can Be Told*, and defended the use of nuclear weapons against Japan. He died in 1970 at age 73.

J. Robert Oppenheimer's appointment as director of the Manhattan Project's Los Alamos Laboratory in 1942 ushered in the Atomic Age. Brilliant and charismatic yet deeply conflicted, the theoretical physicist famously quoted the *Bhagavad Gita* after witnessing the first successful test of the atomic bomb: "Now I am become Death, the destroyer of worlds." After the war, Oppenheimer opposed the development of the hydrogen bomb and advocated for international control of nuclear weapons. These positions, combined with past associations with left-leaning political groups, led to a hearing of the Atomic Energy Commission that revoked his security clearance at the height of the Red Scare in 1954. **Katherine "Kitty" Oppenheimer's** past association with the Communist Party played into the hands of those opposing her husband. Attempts to fire Oppenheimer as director of the Institute for Advanced Study in Princeton, New Jersey were thwarted when fellow scientists, including Einstein, defended him. A chain-smoker, Oppenheimer died of throat cancer in 1967 at age sixty-two. Katherine died in 1972 also at age 62.

A one-time professional boxer and small-time stickup man, **Meyer (Mickey) Cohen** became one of the most flamboyant and notorious gangsters of his era. Known for his lavish lifestyle and ruthlessness, Cohen's reign over the L.A. underworld was marked by feuds with rival mobsters, leading to multiple assassination attempts and sensational headlines. As depicted, Cohen and other gangland associates harassed and beat Nazi sympathizers at German American Bund rallies in the 1930s.

Cohen married **LaVonne Weaver**, a part-time prostitute, in 1940. They were divorced in 1946. Cohen consolidated his power over organized crime on the West Coast following **Benjamin ("Bugsy") Siegel's** gangland slaying in 1947. As depicted, William Randolph Hearst's *Los Angeles Examiner* chronicled Cohen's escapades as if he were a Hollywood celebrity. Florabel Muir, a nightlife and organized crime reporter, accompanied Cohen on his late-night club-hopping on the Sunset Strip. In July 1949, both Cohen and Muir were wounded in a botched attempt to assassinate the gangster outside Sherry's Restaurant.

Cohen served two prison terms for tax evasion, charges he indignantly dismissed as "the only crimes in my whole life of which I can say I am absolutely innocent." Yet he candidly admitted to six killings, saying, "every last one needed killing." He died in 1976 at age 62 following cancer surgery.

Lena Horne rose to prominence as a groundbreaking entertainer and civil rights activist. She first achieved notoriety at nightclubs on Sunset Boulevard. Horne headlined the Little Troc's opening night just weeks after Pearl Harbor, mesmerizing Hollywood celebrities with her renditions of *Stormy Weather* and *The Man I Love*. Overflow crowds followed her to the famed Mocambo nightclub in West Hollywood, where she became the first African American to perform.

Despite her success, Horne faced persistent racial discrimination. Her 1947 marriage to MGM music director Lennie Hayton was kept secret for three years due to anti-miscegenation sentiment. Over her career, she shattered barriers in the entertainment world, appearing in more than twenty feature films and dozens of television shows and creating an extensive catalog of music.

In the 1960s, Horne became deeply involved in the civil rights movement, marching alongside Martin Luther King, Jr. and using her platform to fight for equality. She returned to Broadway in 1981 with *Lena Horne: The Lady and Her Music*, a one-woman show that earned her a Tony Award. Horne died in 2020 in New York City at age 92, leaving behind a legacy as both an extraordinary entertainer and a cultural icon.

Charles Lindbergh, celebrated for his groundbreaking transatlantic flight in 1927, became a controversial figure in the years leading up to World War II. As a leader of the America First Committee, Lindbergh argued against U.S. involvement in the war in Europe. In a 1941 radio address, he claimed that Jews, the British, and the Roosevelt administration were pushing America toward war. He also said that the "greatest danger to this country lies in their [Jewish] large ownership and influence in our motion pictures, our press, our radio, and our government." His remarks drew widespread condemnation for their antisemitic tropes.

Lindbergh's views were shaped in part by his trips to Germany in the 1930s, where he toured Luftwaffe facilities and accepted a medal from Hermann Göring on behalf of Adolf Hitler. His admiration for Nazi Germany permanently stained his reputation.

As portrayed, American isolationists and pro-German interests wanted Lindbergh to run for president against FDR in 1940. Following the war, Lindbergh withdrew from public life and later became an environmentalist, writing extensively on conservation issues. He led a complex personal life that remained concealed for decades. Married to author Anne Morrow, he fathered seven children with three German women between 1957 and 1967. Lindbergh died in Hawaii in 1974 at age 72.

William Randolph Hearst was the most powerful and influential media magnate of the early 20th century. At his peak, he controlled a vast empire of newspapers, magazines, radio stations, and newsreel and film production companies. Actress **Marion Davies** was—using the parlance of the time—Hearst's mistress from 1917 until his death in 1951. As depicted in the novel, Davies and Chaplin were also romantically involved, a fact Hearst was well aware of, thanks to private investigators.

Despite this, Chaplin remained a frequent guest at Hearst's lavish parties at San Simeon.

In the 1930s, Hearst's extravagant spending, combined with the economic toll of the Great Depression, forced him into debt, necessitating the sale of valuable assets. During this decade, as portrayed, Hearst also became a vocal advocate of American isolationism, using his extensive media empire to shape public opinion against U.S. involvement in the war in Europe. His interactions with fascist leaders added to his controversial reputation. In 1934, he met with Adolf Hitler during a visit to Germany, raising questions about his political sympathies. His newspapers later published articles by Hitler and Italian dictator Benito Mussolini, giving these leaders platforms to spread their ideologies to American readers.

After the attack on Pearl Harbor, Hearst's newspapers aligned with public sentiment and supported the U.S. war effort. He died in Beverly Hills in 1951 at 88. Marion Davies died in 1961 at 64.

Ezra Jefferson is a fictional character but represents the thousands of members of the Brotherhood of Sleeping Car Porters, the first union led by African Americans to be recognized by the American Federation of Labor. The life of a sleeping car porter on a luxury train like the Santa Fe Super Chief was a blend of prestige and hardship. Porters greeted passengers, carried luggage, made up sleeping berths, served food and drinks, shined shoes, and kept the cars tidy. Available day and night, porters catered to passengers' every need, from babysitting children to caring for sick adults. They were expected to project cheerfulness and maintain a perpetual smile, leading to the ironic nickname, "miles of smiles."

Before union representation, porters typically worked 400 hours and traveled 11,000 miles per month, sometimes in shifts lasting up to 20 hours. Porters were often called "boy" or even "George" after George Pullman, regardless of their age or name.

Despite hardships, being a Pullman porter was considered one of the best jobs available to African-American men at the time. The work was steady, and sleeping car porters played a significant role in the growth of the African-American middle class.

FBI Special Agent **Brian Sullivan**, Abwehr operative **Liselotte Müller**, and SS Assassin **Reinhard Schmidt** are fictional characters.

Milagros Vazquez is also a fictional character. Women were not hired as special agents during J. Edgar Hoover's reign as FBI director. Women typically worked for the Bureau as secretaries, researchers, file clerks, and typists. It was not until July 1972, two months after Hoover's death, that two women were admitted to the FBI Academy at Quantico, Virginia to be trained as Special Agents.

#

EXCERPT - "MIDNIGHT BURNING"

Named "Best Historical Thriller of 2025" by Best Thrillers Book Reviews

The Genius and the Tramp Fight Fascists in 1930s Hollywood

Before World War II began, the battle for America's soul was already underway.

It's 1937, and as war clouds gather over Europe, fascists march in America. When real-life friends Albert Einstein and Charlie Chaplin uncover a Nazi plot to assassinate Hollywood's biggest stars and ignite an insurrection, they strike back with nothing but their ingenuity, raw courage, and the fierce resolve of Georgia Ann Robinson, LAPD's first Black female officer. In a race against time, the trio must outwit and outfight their enemies before America veers toward an unthinkable future. Inspired by a true story. Read an excerpt below:

ONE
WHO WE GONNA KILL?
May 4, 1937 – Santa Monica Mountains

The sign on the sheriff's office read, DUSTY CREEK, ARIZONA. True, there was plenty of dust but no creek, and Arizona was three hundred miles away.

The saloon, hotel, and general store were flimsy wood facades. The town was as phony as a politician's promise, a gigolo's smile, a mortician's sympathy.

Welcome to the Paramount Movie Ranch in the Santa Monica Mountains north of Malibu, California. A forlorn and forgotten donkey stood in the street outside the make-believe assayer's office, as if waiting to be loaded with saddlebags of gold. Otherwise, the mythical town was empty and as silent as the films shot there.

Half a mile up a gentle slope, a dozen men huddled in a clearing behind a stand of laurel bay trees. In the center stood William Dudley Pelley, a former screenwriter who had penned two Lon Chaney pictures but whose career had stalled like traffic at Hollywood and Vine.

Pelley appraised the men like an auctioneer at a cattle sale. They were tall and short, fit and fat, smart and *dummkopfs*. All were Caucasian and untrained as soldiers, except for a few of the older ones who'd fought in the Great War. No obvious losers, misfits, or poseurs. Or FBI agents, not that J. Edgar Hoover gave a hoot, as long as Pelley's troops targeted communists and not Republicans.

"Welcome to the new world order," Pelley said to the group. "Not the world of Franklin Delano Rosen-*stein*. Or the Wall Street bankers or the Brits, or the scum-of-the-earth immigrants who infest our cities, despoil our daughters, and steal our jobs."

The men mumbled their agreement. They wore corduroy trousers, blue ties, and silver shirts with epaulets. Sewn over the heart on each shirt was a large, embroidered *L*, the color of blood, signifying the Silver Legion of America, Pelley's homegrown paramilitary. "Silver Shirts," the newspapers called them.

Two men stood out among today's recruits: Skowron and Zorn.

Skowron was in his late thirties. Thick neck. Hands like grappling hooks. A scarred face, as if he'd escaped prison headfirst through barbed wire. A prizefighter's smashed nose and the tattoo of an anchor on his neck.

About forty, Zorn was a husky, scowling fellow with one cauliflower ear, two missing front teeth, and the neck of a Brahman bull.

Pelley sensed that both men had moxie to spare.

A thousand like Skowron and Zorn. Oh, the torches I could light!

At forty-seven, Pelley had a gunmetal gray mustache and Vandyke beard that was trimmed to a sharp point, giving him an unfortunate resemblance to popular images of Satan. In his white jodhpurs tucked into knee-high black leather boots with a riding crop in one hand, he might be taken for an English gent, readying the hounds for a jolly good fox hunt.

"Some call you the 'American Hitler,'" a newspaper reporter had baited him several weeks earlier. "Are you comfortable with that?"

"I stand deep in the Führer's shadow," Pelley answered, "but if others should say it, I shall not tell them nay."

The *Los Angeles Times* headline had read, AMERICAN FASCIST RECRUITS WHITE CHRISTIANS FOR HIS CAUSE. Other than the phrase "Nazi copycats," which Pelley found insulting, the story was dandy and brought several hundred new men to the meeting hall at Alt Heidelberg.

Now Pelley jabbed his riding crop into the chest of a pudgy man in his late twenties with a receding blond hairline. "Eckart!"

"Yes, sir!"

"Eckart, can you kill?"

Theatrics, a tactic of the Führer himself.

"I…I can kill," Eckart squeaked.

"Have you killed?"

Eckart grabbed the seat of his pants and pulled his undershorts out of his butt crack, nervous as a schoolboy facing a bully. "I've shot rabbits, sir."

"Rabbits one day, Eckart. Rabbis the next."

So much work to do, but Pelley was undeterred. The strength of his will, unyielding as a slab of granite, could shape this butterball into a fighting machine. He believed that a man with unbridled self-confidence could leap any boulders that life had strewn in his path. Hadn't he risen from deprivation to become a Hollywood storyteller and now the leader of a movement that would revolutionize the country?

Revolution! The ultimate goal.

It would take years, of course. But as he liked to say, Rome wasn't sacked in a day. Now, he smacked his thigh with his riding crop like Charlie Kurtsinger whipping War Admiral at the clubhouse turn.

"You wanna be Silver Shirts?" he yelled to the group.

"Yes, Mr. Pelley, sir!" came the robust replies.

"Can you kill?"

"Yes, Mr. Pelley, sir!" Louder this time.

"As the Führer has instructed, 'The first essential for success is a constant and regular employment of violence!'"

Oh, the strength of the Führer! No feeble notions of the brotherhood of man.

Three years earlier, Pelley had attended the Nuremberg rally where Adolf Hitler preached the gospel of fascism to three-quarters of a million followers. Pelley could still feel the electricity coursing through him, could hear the staccato *clip-clop* of goose-stepping soldiers, the music of victory.

"Who we gonna kill?" Pelley sing-songed to his men.

"Com-mu-nists!" the men sang back.

"Who we gonna kill?"

"Jews!"

"Who are we?"

"Pa-tri-ots!"

Pelley noticed that Skowron hadn't joined in the chant and was about to call him on it.

But before he did, the man said, "Talk's cheap."

"How's that?" Pelley asked.

Skowron scratched at his chin stubble, which ran jagged thanks to his scar, the wound apparently stitched by a blind doctor or a drunk sadist. "How 'bout some shootin'?"

Pelley didn't regard this as insubordination but rather an eagerness to engage the enemy. "Grab your weapons!" he shouted.

The men scrambled for their 1903 Springfield rifles. Hurrying faster than his fingers could manage, Eckart stabbed himself trying to attach his bayonet. He yelped and stuck his bleeding hand into his mouth.

"Eckart, jam that thumb up your ass!" Pelley waggled his riding crop. "Hit the dirt, men! Low crawl to the perimeter." The men belly flopped to the ground and wriggled up an incline toward a ridge, where they jammed together, as close as peanuts in a Baby Ruth.

"Spread out, dammit!" Pelley ordered, and the men repositioned themselves into a prone firing line.

Twenty yards away were half-a-dozen makeshift targets, sheets of plywood nailed to trees. Each sheet had a crudely drawn body in black paint with a large photo of a man's face on top. Six targets, six different men.

"I wanna shoot FDR," Eckart said. "Knock him out of his wheelchair."

"I got Joe Stalin," another man said. "Commie scum."

"What's Groucho Marx doing up there?" a third man asked.

Pelley did not say that the target was supposed to be Karl Marx, but the lad gathering the photos did not know the difference between the revolutionary socialist and the mustachioed comedian.

"Why are we shooting King George?" asked another. It didn't take an Anglophile to recognize the monarch, as he wore a crown.

"Pipe down!" Pelley demanded. "Two men to a target. Sort it out."

The men debated distances, traded targets, shifted around and—other than Skowron and Zorn—took so long to get ready that a Civil War cavalry officer on horseback could have slaughtered them.

"Hell's bells," Pelley whispered to himself. He drew a silver flask from a pocket and took a long pull, a warm cascade of Old Quaker whiskey sliding down his throat. He knew that Hitler suffered many failures before spending a full year preparing for the Night of the Long Knives.

"Fire when ready!" Pelley ordered. "Kill them all!"

In a moment, the hills were alive with the sounds of gunfire. Stalin and FDR took several flesh wounds in the plywood, but nothing near their heads. Pelley grabbed his flask and knocked back another two slugs of the whiskey.

"Scope's cloudy," complained one man.

"Don't worry, fellow," Pelley said. "New weapons are on the horizon. Browning Automatics."

"US Army rifles?" He sounded skeptical. "How's that possible?"

Pelley gave him a crooked smile. "You'd be surprised how many friends we have in the American military."

As the firing continued, Groucho took one in the mustache and His Royal Highness one in his diamond-studded crown. Eckart missed Roosevelt with his first two shots but then nailed his forehead with his last three.

"Attaboy, Eckart! I knew you had it in you."

A body like a bowl of pudding but a steady hand.

Skowron was teamed with Zorn, the two bruisers even more fearsome with rifles in their meaty paws. They fired ten rapid blasts at the sixth target, a square-jawed, handsome, silver-haired man with a cocky smile. Every shot true, shredding the photo.

"Great work, men," Pelley said.

My squad leaders.

Maybe it was the warmth of the whiskey in his belly or the sweet smell of cordite in the air, but Pelley's mood became positively buoyant.

I have found my cause. A fascist America.

"Who's that guy we just plugged?" Skowron asked.

"That bastard's Charlie Chaplin," Pelley said, spitting out the words.

"Didn't recognize him without the mustache and stupid hat," Zorn said.

"Chaplin's got more money than God and gives a lot of it to a commie front called the International Relief Association." Pelley hawked up a wad of phlegm and spat onto the ground.

"Never heard of it," Zorn said.

"It was started by that so-called genius Albert Einstein. They're bringing Jews and gypsies and what-not into the States to replace white Christians. I've got my eyes on them, and one fine day I'll reward you boys with the chance of putting bullets in both their head."

TWO
TWO MEN, TWO SECRETS
Chaplin Estate, Summit Drive, Beverly Hills

Twenty miles to the southeast, at the same moment that his photo was being blistered into confetti, Charlie Chaplin—garbed in white linen trousers and a matching long-sleeve cotton shirt—bounced a tennis ball several times, preparing to serve. The tennis court was located on Chaplin's ritzy estate, as befitted a multimillionaire. His opponent was Albert Einstein¾two geniuses, one of the arts, one of the universe. With thunderclouds of war gathering across the globe, the newspapers had stopped calling them "the two most famous men in the world." The burden of fame now rested on the shoulders of men named Hitler and Stalin, Chamberlain and Roosevelt.

After traveling from England as part of a vaudeville troupe at age twenty-one, Chaplin knew, early on, that he'd be more than a comedian playing music halls in the red-light districts of midwestern America. He spent those days polishing his visual comedy and bedding down a legion of young women who sprouted like wildflowers on the prairie.

Now, at forty-eight, as writer, actor, director, and producer of his films and co-owner of the studio that distributed them, he was at the pinnacle of the world's most glamorous industry. He was still an accomplished athlete, still a master at physical comedy, still heartthrob handsome and well aware of it.

Chaplin looked across the net at Einstein, a man he admired for his intellect, his charm, his passion for social justice…for everything other than his lousy tennis game. Something was bothering Chaplin, a conversation he needed to have with Einstein but didn't know quite how to approach. Without consulting his friend, Chaplin had accepted an invitation for both of them—a reception at the German consulate, the heart of darkness.

Research for a motion picture, but Albert's gonna be peeved.

Chaplin tossed the tennis ball over his head and hit a graceful serve.

Albert Einstein loved the time spent with his friend. Today was California bright, neither warm nor chilly, Chaplin's estate dotted with rose bushes of a dozen hues, while overhead and red-headed finches perched in the palms. Having fled Germany when Hitler came to power, Einstein, now fifty-eight, lived in Princeton, New Jersey, where he pursued his research at the Institute for Advanced Study.

He watched the fuzzy white ball cross the net and bounce, taking an elongated hop that reminded him of the puzzling elliptical orbit of Mercury. Remembering how general relativity solved that little cosmological puzzle might have caused Einstein to slap the ball into the net. More likely, it was his herky-jerky swing, as if he were swatting pesky houseflies.

"Thirty love, mate!" Chaplin called out.

Einstein also had a secret to share with Chaplin, something that perhaps he should tell the War Department or even President Roosevelt himself. Charlie, who had been in the States for twenty years, would know what to do, he thought.

Chaplin hit a powder-puff serve, and Einstein's return sailed six feet beyond the baseline. "Forty love, Albert. Try hitting with topspin to keep the ball in."

"Who knew that gravity needed my assistance?" Einstein said with a shrug.

Fifteen minutes later, Chaplin and Einstein sat at a courtside table, where a uniformed houseman had placed a pitcher of lemonade and a silver platter of cucumber and egg salad sandwiches, their crusts surgically removed by Chef Maurice in the kitchen. The world was a powder keg, insurrections were brewing, American fascists were arming, but life was tennis, lemonade, and finger sandwiches in Beverly Hills…for now.

Chaplin sipped his lemonade and studied a photograph Einstein had placed on the table. It showed two men in lab coats, their backs to the camera, staring at a blackboard with a mathematical equation partially visible:

$$^{238}_{92}U + n \rightarrow$$

"So, who are they and what are they doing?" Chaplin asked.

"German chemists who've been working with radioactive isotopes," Einstein said. "Otto Hahn and Fritz Strassmann."

"And those numbers…"

"An unfinished equation related to the alpha decay of uranium."

"That would've been my guess," Chaplin cracked.

"They're bombarding uranium with neutrons, attempting nuclear fission."

Chaplin popped a cucumber finger sandwich into his mouth. "Okay, I'm stumped. Nuclear *fiction*?"

"Fission! A chain reaction that would unleash a staggering amount of energy."

"An explosion?"

"A Nazi bomb, the likes of which the world has never seen."

"Sodding hell!" Chaplin shouted. "I'm going to need something stronger than lemonade."

Unseen by the two friends, perched twenty feet above the ground in an oak tree on the estate's property line, a pencil-thin man in his thirties aimed his Leica 35 millimeter at the courtside table. Klaus Spengler was on special assignment for the Reich's Ministry of Public Enlightenment. Today's target was Charlie Chaplin, though Spengler had no idea why the propaganda branch gave a tinker's damn about the actor.

Albert Einstein's appearance in the viewfinder surprised Spengler. Any number of magazines would pay top dollar to have candid photos of those two celebrities, but Berlin would have even greater interest. The Reich had declared Einstein an "enemy of the state" with a bounty on his head.

Through the long lens, Spingler focused the crosshairs on Einstein. It occurred to him that it was the same view he'd have if he were looking through the G98 scope his father, a German Army sniper, had used in the Great War.

Spengler watched Einstein pull a paper from his pocket and place it on the table.

No, not a paper. A photograph!

He adjusted the focus.

"Was ist das?"

Two men in lab attire stood at a blackboard. Do they know they're being photographed?

No, I think not. This is Spitzel und Spione. *Spies and snitches, or as the Yanks say, cloak and dagger.*

Professor Einstein, what mischief are you up to?

The Leica *click-click-clicked* as Spengler snapped photos, certain he would receive a substantial bonus when he delivered the negatives to the German consulate at tomorrow night's reception.

#

If you enjoyed this excerpt, you may purchase the Midnight Burning paperback at Amazon, Barnes & Noble and Bookshop.org. The ebook edition is available at Amazon, Barnes & Noble, Apple, Google Play, and Kobo. The Brilliance audiobook is available at Amazon. Visit Paul Levine's website at www.paul-levine.com for more information. Kindle Unlimited members always read free.

"LASSITER'S GHOST" — SNEAK PREVIEW

In *Early Grave*, an aging Jake Lassiter sues to abolish high school football as a dangerous "public nuisance after his godson Rodrigo Pittman suffers a catastrophic injury in a game.

Fighting a devious and well-heeled New York City law firm, and with his personal life in tatters, Lassiter is in couple's therapy with fiancée Dr. Melissa Gold and vows to live long enough to fix his relationship and achieve justice for his godson.

LASSITER'S GHOST: (COMING SOON) Eight years after *Early Grave*, Rodrigo Pittman is a newly minted lawyer in need of clients. Penelope Claypool, a Miami television personality, wants him to overturn her father's murder conviction on the ground that Lassiter, suffering from CTE, botched his case. Rodrigo gets advice from the spirit of his deceased godfather...or are those just voices in his head?

For more information, please visit the Paul Levine's website at www.paul-levine.com and sign up for Paul's newsletter at www. paul-levine.com/newsletter/.

-1-

Lassiter and the Layabout

Eight years ago...

With tinnitus whistling in my ears like wind across razor wire, woozy with vertigo and wincing through a migraine, I grip both sides of the lectern and, voice rattling, grumble at the jury, "Ladies and gentlemen, if you think the prosecutor painted a vile portrait of my client, you ain't heard nothing yet."

A buzz ripples through the packed gallery. Like spectators in a circus tent, the journalists, lawyers and courtroom regulars expect a show. What tricks does this wily old lawyer have up his sleeve? Will he make the triple somersault on the trapeze or plunge to his death? Will he tame the roaring lion or be eaten alive?

"C'mon, Jake Lassiter's closing! Let's see how many clowns fall out of the little yellow car."

I'm a broad-shouldered, shambling storyteller, tie at half mast, collar bursting, silvery hair shaggy as a sheepdog. Older folks remember my checkered career with the Dolphins. Second-string linebacker. Slow afoot but a sure tackler. Nothing fancy then, nothing fancy now. Just an old war-horse trial lawyer in an era of supersonic missiles and short attention spans.

"You've watched Archibald Claypool sitting next to me for the last three weeks," I say to the jury, nodding toward the defense table.

Claypool sits with perfect posture, a handsome, fifty-something, shinily manicured, well-tailored aristocrat. His salt-and-pepper hair is swept straight back with a widow's peak suggestive of a 19th Century European prince or a Transylvanian vampire.

"You've listened to him testify," I continue. "What did you see and hear?"

I let the jurors ponder a beat, then answer my own question. "You saw a man in a fifteen-thousand dollar Savile Row suit of the finest Vicuña wool. A Patek Philippe Nautilus watch in 18-karat white-gold with the blue sunburst dial. Seventy-five grand easy."

I amble to the defense table and squint at Claypool's glimmering watch. "Two twenty-five p.m." I look at the watch on my wrist. "Yep, same time on my thirty-two dollar Casio.

Which says a lot about Archie Claypool's values, but not a damn thing about whether he murdered his wife."

I let that settle. The jurors appear curious.

What's this guy selling?

"The suit. The watch," I continue. "A man who'd rather be caught dead than underdressed." I address him the way a jailer might address an inmate. "Archie, shoot your cuffs."

Claypool winces as though I'd asked him to remove a kidney. "Please don't call me 'Archie.'"

Nevertheless, he extends his arm toward the jury.

"Check out the diamond pinky ring and onyx and diamond cufflinks," I tell the jury. "The day we met, I told him, 'Archie, before I pick a jury, you better lose the bling.' And you know what he said?"

I walk to a spot three feet from the rail of the jury box, moving cautiously, as I have the balance of the town drunk on roller skates. Then I lower my voice to a whisper as if conveying a secret. "'I shan't stoop to conquer,' he said. "That's from an eighteenth century play. Archie would know that. He's well read. You have a lot of time for books when you haven't done a lick of work in your entire life."

In the gallery, the spectators titter. At the defense table, Claypool smirks. His polished nails drum on the scarred walnut, his prominent chin jutted out and tilted up.

He's the most exasperating client I've ever represented, a guy who could win Olympic gold in narcissism. Before trial, with charges pending, he posed aboard his yacht for a lifestyle magazine, all suntan and smiles, hoisting a flute of champagne. Not a trace of grief for his dead wife. Against my explicit instructions, he held press conferences, answering reporters testily, apparently insulted by the inconvenience of being charged with murder. And this very morning, he flashed a slow, lascivious grin at a female juror thirty years his junior.

I let my gaze sweep across the jury box. "Do you remember my client's testimony? I asked him how he spent his time. His answer?" I thumb through the daily transcript, then read aloud. "'I'm something of a layabout. It's all I was ever trained to do. Eat fine food, drink fine wine, wear majestic clothes, romance beautiful women, and generally lay about.'"

Three jurors nod their heads while two others look as if they want to spit. All keep their eyes on Claypool, who has a remarkable ability to peer down his nose—literally—at them.

"I asked if he had any particular skills. And he answered, rather proudly, 'Cribbage, croquet, and contract bridge. And I have an excellent nose for French wines.'"

I shake my head sadly, trying to look embarrassed to be the mouthpiece for such a reprobate. "No, you won't run into Archie Claypool having a Death Dog and a brewski at Keg South on Dixie Highway."

In other words, he's not one of you good folks.

I carefully move back to the defense table and point an accusing finger at my client. It's usually what the prosecutor does when reciting the perpetrator's evil acts. I've never given a closing argument where I attack my own client as if he just kicked my pet dog. Maybe no one ever has. But Claypool's antics give me no choice.

"So what do you think of Archie Claypool as a man?" I ask. "I'll help you out. He's an arrogant, egotistical, narcissistic twit. An unfaithful husband. A professional loafer. Snobbish, supercilious, and haughty. What he is not, however, is a murderer. Archie may be a louse, but he did not kill his spouse."

In case they missed it, I repeat, "Archie may be a louse, but he did not kill his spouse."

Yeah, yeah. "If the glove doesn't fit, you must acquit."

A buzz runs through the gallery, a hive of excitable bees. Spectators exchange incredulous looks that seem to ask, "Has Lassiter lost his mind?"

My migraine shifts gears, thudding hammers sharpening into ice picks.

"If she'd known him," I continue, "Granny Lassiter, the woman who raised me, would have said, 'That piece of work is so high and mighty he thinks he's looking down on the Lord.'"

I pause again, not for effect, but because the ringing in my ears has reached bells of Notre Dame proportions. Deep in my skull, steel strikes flint, and sparks shoot into flames.

I have chronic traumatic encephalopathy, the industrial disease of pro football. Better known as CTE, it will kill me. I just don't know when. Half a dozen of my Miami Dolphins teammates already have succumbed.

Just not today, I whisper to myself.

"Your job, your sworn duty," I tell the jurors, "is not to decide whether my client is a good man, a kind man, or a faithful husband. He is none of those. You are to determine the truth of the state's allegations that he is a murderer." I point to the sign above the judge's bench and read aloud, "'We Who Labor Here Seek Only the Truth.'"

I don't tell them that years ago I suggested adding a footnote:

"Subject to the truth being ignored by lying witnesses, concealed by sleazy lawyers, excluded by inept judges, and overlooked by lazy jurors."

These days, I think the inscription from Dante's *Inferno* might strike the correct note: *"Abandon all hope, ye who enter here."*

I turn around, careful not to fall, and scan the gallery.

Spectators sit on oak benches that resemble pews in the Church of Bad News. Melissa Gold, my doctor, and more important, my fiancée, sits in the front row, her gold-flecked green eyes following me, worry etched across her face.

No problem, Mel. Win, lose, or draw, it's stone crabs and Key lime pie for us tonight.

Tank Pittman, my old Dolphins roomie, sits next to Melissa, his 300-plus pounds threatening to topple the pew like an overloaded rowboat. He's brought his son, Rodrigo, my godson, who's playing hooky. The kid's an eleventh grader at Saint Frances Academy and has been watching my closing arguments since he was twelve years old. I've made him a promise. Once he graduates from law school, I'm changing the name of the firm to Lassiter and Pittman.

I walk behind the prosecution table so the jurors will focus their attention on State Attorney Raymond Pincher and the three young prosecutors arrayed around him. The flunkies are grinning like kids with cotton candy at the county fair. It has to be fun watching a defense counsel set himself on fire.

I've been sparring with Sugar Ray Pincher—in boxing rings and courtrooms—for twenty-five years. Pincher is scribbling something on a legal pad in big block letters.

I feel my heart race, then slow, then race again.

Damn, my ticker has the flutters.

Atrial Fibrillation. The drummer has lost the beat, and yet the song plays on. My heart is arguing with itself over whether it should stop beating.

"Day after day, you've heard what a rotten scoundrel Archie Claypool is," I say, breathing hard. "What you haven't heard is evidence that he planned and carried out the cold-blooded murder of his wife, Gabriela. The state presented a case of suspicion but not evidence. It built a pyramid of innuendo with a rumor on top, but that, ladies and gentlemen, is not proving guilt beyond a reasonable doubt.

I'm rolling now, working through the pain, chugging along, an old freight train lugging a hundred tons of boxcars up a steep incline.

"Premeditated murder? You've seen him. You've heard him. Archie Claypool couldn't plan a picnic without his valet, butler, chauffeur and caterer."

At the prosecution table, Pincher stifles a smile and angles his legal pad so I can see what he's written: "Jakester, you're still the guy who took the shy out of shyster and put the fog into pettifogger. Genius or madman?"

I roam the well of the courtroom, gathering my thoughts, stopping in front of the empty witness stand where generations of perjurers have spun their tales. Vertigo settles in like an unwelcome trespasser. I brace myself against one of the ancient armrests, home to a million sweaty palms.

"I generally don't make personal comments in closing argument," I say. "In fact, it's not really proper." I shoot a look at the prosecution table where Pincher raises his eyebrows but keeps quiet. On the bench, Judge Melvia Duckworth clears her throat, a friendly warning I'll ignore.

"I'm just an aging linebacker-turned-lawyer, and I've been stomping through Dade County courtrooms for a helluva long time," I say, refusing to use the newer "Miami-Dade" name. It just seems silly to me.

"It's time to hang up my spikes. I hope I'm not such a lousy lawyer that my last official act is to let an innocent man be convicted of murder. And how could that be? The state's case has a fatal flaw, and that is..."

The courtroom seems to whirl around my head. The judge, the jurors, the court reporter, the clerk, the bailiff, Pincher, Claypool, Melissa, Tank, Rodrigo, and a merry-go-round of startled faces in the gallery. All spinning as if they're planets and I'm the sun. Then like a star that has spent its last spark, I faint dead away.

-2-

Penelope's Game

Today...

Rodrigo Pittman skimmed the two-page Complaint for Damages and said, "A man named Boris Petrovsky claims you ruined his picnic. Potato salad and all."

"All the upper-air observations and satellite imagery pointed to a hot, humid day with no rain," Penelope Claypool said in the calm, reassuring tone she used delivering the weather on Miami's Channel 10.

August in Miami, Rodrigo thought. Predicting the weather should be about as difficult as predicting rush-hour gridlock on I-95. It was pretty much the same every day.

"High in the low nineties. Gusty winds from the southeast with afternoon thunderstorms."

Except Penelope had predicted no rain, and gushers had drenched Crandon Park, washing away the Petrovsky clan's dreams of rare burgers, short ribs, and matching sunburns.

"Weather forecasts, like lawsuits, are as much art as science," she said. "And just

because a storm messed up the guy's picnic, how does he make a federal case out of it?"

Technically a *state* case, Rodrigo thought.

"He's a *pro se* plaintiff," Rodrigo said. "No lawyer. Looks like the complaint was typed on an old manual typewriter."

"So his case is weak?"

"You didn't guarantee sunshine any more than a sportscaster guarantees you'll win money betting his picks."

A smile flickered across her face. "I like that."

Rodrigo smiled back. Even a rookie lawyer could drop-kick this lawsuit out of the courthouse on a ten-minute motion calendar.

He turned back to the complaint, wanting to sound more experienced than he felt. Still, he couldn't help noticing her. She was maybe thirty, a few years older than him. Chestnut hair to her shoulders. Wide-set brown eyes. Far less makeup than she wore under the studio lights. A turquoise blouse tucked into high-waisted jeans, tan boots, ankles neatly crossed. At close to six feet tall, she had the kind of presence that made people look twice.

Rodrigo forced his eyes back to the complaint. He intended to keep the conversation strictly professional. His godfather would have laughed at that. What had the man he called "Uncle Jake" told him years ago?

"It's no sin to date a client, kiddo, but I'd draw the line at fleeing felons."

Rodrigo wore an off-the-rack gray pinstripe suit, pale blue shirt, and striped tie. For a guy who preferred cutoffs and a Duke T-shirt, it felt like dressing for his own arraignment. At twenty-six, he was still growing into the role of lawyer. Dark hair and a neatly trimmed mustache. The fine-boned features came from his mother, Liliana Santiago. So did the burnt cinnamon complexion. The height, six-feet three, came from his father, Langston "Tank" Pittman. That's where the physical similarity ended, as his father was about twice as wide as his rangy son. Tank had spent his working life flattening running backs as a defensive tackle, first in college, then in the NFL. Built like a concrete bunker, he made Rodrigo feel positively delicate. Long before Rodrigo was born, Tank and Uncle Jake had been teammates, roommates, and best friends on the Dolphins.

"Weather forecasting has too many variables to be one hundred percent accurate," Penelope said. "Two-day forecasts are about eighty percent correct. Go out ten days? Down to fifty percent. South Florida's ocean convection throws it all off."

"You know your stuff."

"Meteorology degree from Penn State and a master's in atmospheric science from Cornell."

Rodrigo smiled. "Then you and my godfather have something in common."

"What's that?"

"Penn State."

"Jake Lassiter," she said.

"You've heard of him?"

"Famous in his day. Died too young."

Rodrigo looked toward the window, hoping not to show his emotions. "If Jake were here, he'd say he lived a full life."

"*Not full enough*," came the husky rumble in Rodrigo's ear.

Jake's voice.

The voice of a dead man.

Rodrigo didn't acknowledge the intrusion. When other people were around, he treated Jake's voice like a spam call. Don't answer and move on.

He turned back to the lawsuit and opened a browser window on his desktop. "Give me a second." A moment later, he grinned. "As I suspected, Petrovsky's a vexatious litigant. A frequent filer. He sued Budweiser because two six-packs failed to attract women on the beach. He sued a Chinese restaurant because a fortune cookie promised great business success that never materialized. And he sued a movie theater because the popcorn bucket wasn't truly bottomless."

"What a jerk."

"It's a shakedown. He's looking for a nuisance settlement."

"You want me to pay him off?"

"No way. I'll move to dismiss and seek fees for a frivolous lawsuit. The only way to stop people who abuse the system is to make it expensive."

Rodrigo delivered the advice with the confidence of a seasoned trial lawyer rather than a guy who'd been a member of the Florida Bar for eleven weeks.

"Sit tall in the saddle, kid. Your client has to believe you're untarnished and unafraid, even when you're outgunned, outspent, and outmanned."

Jake had drilled that lesson into him years earlier, during Rodrigo's lawsuit against his high school football coach, the school, and the state athletic association. Sent back into a game while concussed, he'd suffered a broken neck, partial paralysis, and a future that nearly disappeared.

A limp remained. So did weakness in his left arm. The rest was a miracle.

"Coaching malpractice," Lassiter called it, establishing a new tort under Florida law. He defeated an army of New York lawyers financed by a consortium that broke every rule in the book.

Bravado came easy to Lassiter. Rodrigo had to fake it, at least for now.

He tapped an index finger on the complaint. "Petrovsky sued both you and Channel 10. Won't their lawyers defend you?"

"Shutts and Bowen. They said they'd represent me, but I

could hire independent counsel if I wanted."

"Happy to take your money, but you don't need me. They're a deep-carpet firm, and they won't cost you a dime."

She gave him a curious little smile. "I know. But I had another reason for wanting to meet you."

"*Hey, kiddo,*" Jake said from somewhere behind Rodrigo. "*This is where you ask her to dinner. I'm thinking Prime 112 on South Beach. A 35-ounce ribeye if you've got two hundred bucks to spare.*"

"Hush," Rodrigo whispered.

"What?" Penelope asked.

"Sorry." Rodrigo cleared his throat. "Just...thinking."

They both sat quietly for a moment. All three of them, if you counted Lassiter.

Rodrigo looked up. Uncle Jake—or the image of him—stood by the dirt-streaked window. Faded jeans, black Chuck Taylors, and a T-shirt that read: "A friend will help you move. A good friend will help you move a body."

Thick-necked and still in decent shape, with shaggy hair once the color of beach sand, now flecked with silvery gray. He looked to be in his late forties. Not bad for a guy who'd died in his sixties. It was the way Rodrigo preferred to remember him.

"What's the other reason you wanted to meet me?" Rodrigo asked.

Penelope cocked her head and gave him a small smile, as if deciding how much to reveal.

"*Penelope Claypool,*" Lassiter muttered. "*Claypool! Think about it.*"

The answer hit Rodrigo. "Was Archibald Claypool your father?"

"Still is," she said evenly. "Serving life. But very much alive."

"Jake represented him. A murder trial."

"Which he bungled, likely due to his deteriorating mental condition."

Her tone had sharpened from inquisitive to accusatory.

Lassiter leaned over Rodrigo's shoulder. *"So much for martinis, steaks, and an after-dinner romp."*

"So why are you here, Ms. Claypool?" Rodrigo demanded. "What's this really about?"

"I needed to size you up. I know your credentials. Summa cum laude from Duke. Harvard Law Review. But diplomas only tell part of the story."

"She's right, pal," Lassiter said. *"I graduated in the top half of the bottom third of my law school class. Night division."*

"You're a newbie," Penelope continued. "Never handled a felony, let alone a murder. Though you did beat a sidewalk roller-blading ticket and a leaf-blower noise violation."

"Okay, you've sized me up," Rodrigo said. "So what's your game?"

"My father would be summering in the Hamptons and skiing in St. Moritz if Lassiter hadn't botched the trial."

"Let's say that's true. Just where do I fit in?"

"I want you to overturn the conviction. Prove that your beloved godfather was incompetent. Do what Lassiter couldn't. Prove my father is innocent."

-3-

Dead Men Don't Drink

"You came here under false pretenses," Rodrigo said. "You misrepresented your intentions."

He heard Lassiter snicker behind him. *"When did you start talking like Masterpiece Theatre, kiddo?"*

Penelope Claypool reached into the oversized purse at her feet and withdrew a file nearly four inches thick. "Before you turn down the case, would you at least look at this?"

Rodrigo shook his head. "No way I'm taking the case. You had to know that."

The mournful blast of a boat horn drifted through the open window. Rodrigo welcomed the distraction. His office occupied a weather-beaten bungalow overlooking the Merrill-Stevens shipyard on the Miami River. Mega-yachts cruised upriver from Biscayne Bay to have barnacles scraped, blisters repaired, and mahogany polished. The bungalow itself had seen better decades. Its cedar siding was more mildew than wood, and the clapboards curled like stale toast. Out front, a small sign hung crookedly from a post:

LASSITER & PITTMAN
ATTORNEYS AT LAW

Rodrigo had been a high-school senior when Jake died, so they had never practiced together. The name wasn't a partnership. It was a tribute.

He turned back to Penelope.

"Ms. Claypool—"

"Penelope," she said.

"Ms. Claypool," he repeated, "I'm sorry, but I can't help you. Maybe somebody else can, but you're talking to a guy who idolized Jake Lassiter, as a lawyer and a man."

"Would you agree that it's a defense lawyer's job to humanize his client, especially if he puts him on the stand?"

"Of course."

"My father's testimony was a disaster."

Rodrigo glanced over his shoulder. Jake was still there. Only now he'd shed the jeans and T-shirt for blue boxing trunks and eight-ounce gloves. He danced in the corner of the office, working an invisible heavy bag.

"*True*," he said between breaths. "*Worst witness I ever put on the stand.*"

That gave Rodrigo pause. His godfather had an almost inviolable rule: never let a defendant testify if State Attorney Ray Pincher was prosecuting the case.

"On cross-examination," Jake liked to say, "Sugar Ray can turn Mother Teresa into a madam in a Delhi brothel."

"I'm sure your father appealed his conviction to the Third District," Rodrigo said.

"Affirmed, two to one. Rehearing en banc granted, then four to three to affirm."

"And the Florida Supreme Court?"

"Cert granted, but conviction affirmed, five to two. Rehearing granted, and we picked up a vote, but still lost, four to three."

"Two rehearings," Rodrigo said.

"Unusual, isn't it?"

"As rare as an honest politician in Miami City Hall. Sounds like some serious backroom politics. Then what?"

"Petition for certiorari to the U.S. Supreme Court denied."

"When? That started the clock ticking."

"Twenty-three months and two weeks ago."

Rodrigo nodded. "So you have two weeks to file a claim of ineffective assistance of counsel."

The Hail Mary for overturning a conviction, the last gasp for a defendant who has exhausted his appeals, Rodrigo knew.

"There are several prominent lawyers in Miami who specialize in post-conviction relief," he said. "I'd recommend Marcia Silvers for starters."

"A few months ago, you finished first on the Florida Bar exam out of 687 applicants. You turned down a federal clerkship for this." She waved vaguely at the stained wallpaper, threadbare rug, and streaked window overlooking a dry dock where yachts were pampered more than their owners' mistresses.

"*Shithole*," Rodrigo thought she was about to say.

"Solo practice," she said. "Just like your godfather."

Penelope held his gaze and flashed her television smile. A slight tilt of the head. Warm. Approachable. Stopping just short of flirtatious. It was her expression when forecasting a perfect March weekend or apologizing for an August so humid that only mosquitoes, alligators, and Ponzi schemers could stand it.

From the corner, Uncle Jake, now skipping rope, huffed, "*Another shift in the weather, Rod. Hard to tell for sure, but I think she's hitting on you.*"

Penelope dropped the folder onto the desk. "If you examine the file," she said, "you'll conclude that your godfather was grossly negligent and that my father was wrongfully convicted."

Rodrigo slid the folder two inches back toward her. "In a county with seventeen thousand lawyers, I'd have thought you'd try someone else."

Jake stopped skipping rope and perched on the corner of the desk. "*Think Rod, and you'll figure exactly why you're the perfect lawyer for this. But first, breathe.*"

Rodrigo fell back on the box-breathing routine Jake had taught him years earlier. Before kickoff, Jake used to say, everybody's heart is pounding like a jackhammer in a phone booth. Inhale four seconds. Hold four. Exhale four. Hold four. Then buckle your chin strap and knock somebody out of his jock.

Rodrigo took a slow breath and waited.

"I thought you might have potential," Penelope said.

"I'm not buying it."

"*Think about it, Rodrigo,*" Jake whispered. "*You. Me. Tank. History. C'mon, kiddo.*"

His pulse slowing, Rodrigo finally saw it. He turned to Penelope. "You want to use me, and not for my legal talent You think that if Jake Lassiter's godson—the guy who worshipped him—claims he bungled the case, the judge will believe it. It's like hiring the judge's brother-in-law to sit at counsel table, and it's dirty pool."

Penelope was quiet a moment, her silence a tacit admission he was correct. "The case could launch your career," she said finally. "It could establish your reputation."

"As a traitor."

Rodrigo pushed back his chair and crossed to a side table, trying to hide his limp.

"*Never do that in front of a jury,*" Lassiter said. "*Exaggerate the limp. Go for sympathy.*"

"Leave me alone," Rodrigo muttered.

"What?" Penelope asked.

"Nothing."

Rodrigo picked up an old chrome coffee percolator that was gurgling. The vintage machine had belonged to Jake, a bourbon-neat, coffee-black kind of guy. He poured himself a cup without offering her one.

He returned to his chair, favoring his left leg despite his best efforts not to. "Do I have to show you out," he asked, "or can you find the door?"

A shadow of sadness crossed her face. "Are you really that callous? My father is serving life without parole for a murder he didn't commit."

Rodrigo took a swallow of coffee. Something Jake had said

about Archibald Claypool drifted back to him. What was it?

Jake leaned close. *"Archie Claypool was a pompous ass. But I never thought the state met its burden of proof."*

Which wasn't the same thing as saying Claypool was innocent. And it certainly wasn't proof Jake had screwed up. Lawyers lost righteous cases every day. Weather forecasters missed storms. Life was imperfect.

Rodrigo realized Penelope was still talking.

"Lassiter was known for courtroom theatrics," she said. "So when he broke all the rules, people assumed it was part of the act. But he was fading. It wasn't strategy. It was dementia."

"And yet a few months later," Rodrigo said, "Jake whipped the smartest, nastiest New York lawyers on the planet when they had him outgunned, outspent, and outmanned."

Repeating Jake's words, his mantra of confidence in the face of long odds.

"Your football injury case," Penelope said.

"Watching Jake was better than law school." The memory left a bittersweet ache. "He'd burst through the swinging gate into the well of the courtroom like a cowboy entering a saloon. And he was every bit as smart as he was tough. Sure, he had symptoms of CTE during the trial, but he fought through them. And he won, but he worked himself to death…literally."

"Obviously he still had moments of lucidity," Penelope said. "But his blunders in my father's case were startling."

She dangled that like live mackerel on a forty-pound test line, but Rodrigo refused to strike. He didn't ask, "What blunders?"

He wanted to say, "Goodbye and good luck."

And he almost did. But there was something in her eyes. Not manipulation. Not calculation. A plea. The look of a daughter who genuinely believed her father was innocent.

He relented. "Skip the bill of particulars. What's the worst mistake Jake made?"

"I'll give you two. He pushed my father to be as obnoxious as possible on the witness stand. To create a role that was false. A caricature of a man who's rich and spoiled, arrogant and immoral."

"Jake coaching your father to alienate the jury? You've got nothing but a convict's word, and I'm not buying it."

"Your godfather videotaped every client meeting. He said he couldn't trust his memory and couldn't read his own handwriting. The proof must be on those tapes. Find them. Watch them."

That jolted Rodrigo. Part of him wanted—needed—to know if Jake had blown it. But Jake had been his warrior, his sword and his shield. Rodrigo would defend his memory with his last breath.

"Then there's the closing argument," Penelope continued. "That alone would warrant a new trial. Lassiter called my father every name in the book and ended with: 'Archie Claypool may be a louse, but he did not kill his spouse.'"

Rodrigo chose not to reveal that, as a high-school student, he'd sat in the courtroom and watched Jake deliver that closing. Wild? Absolutely. Crazy? Who knows? Rodrigo had assumed it was part of a larger strategy he was too young and inexperienced to understand.

Now he just wanted Penelope Claypool out of his office and out of Jake's past. "You're wasting your time and mine," he said. "Go peddle your story somewhere else."

She scooped up the folder and slid it back into her purse. "Not until you turn over the videos."

Rodrigo gave her his not-a-chance look. "You can't have the videos. They're Jake's work product."

Lassiter whistled. *"Look who aced Evidence."*

"The attorney-client relationship has become adversarial," Penelope shot back. "Work-product protection no longer applies, at least not when the client seeks the documents."

"Whoops," Jake said. *"You might have cut class that day. I'm pretty sure I did."*

"They teach work-product exceptions in meteorology school?" Rodrigo asked.

"My lawyers say they can compel production."

"Your lawyers? Then you damn sure don't need me."

Penelope rose. "Now that I've taken your measure, I sure as hell don't want you."

She marched out without a goodbye, thank you, or see-you-later. The office door slammed behind her, rattling the bungalow's walls.

Rodrigo slumped into his chair and closed his eyes.

"Do you need my help, partner?" Jake asked.

"Yeah, could you stick around for awhile?"

"I'm all yours 'til 6 o'clock. Then it's Texas Hold'em with my old teammates."

"Where are you? Heaven?"

"Doubt it."

"Hell?"

"Maybe. It's as hot as Miami but less humidity."

"I don't know what to do, Uncle Jake."

"Why? You have a problem with the weather gal?"

"Meteorologist," Rodrigo corrected him. "Her lawyers are going to rake you over the coals. Win or lose, that's what people will remember."

Jake snorted. *"Lighten up, Rod. Maybe we oughta head over to Keg South. Brewskis and a heart-to-heart about the case."*

"You think that'll help?"

"*The talk? Sure thing. The beers, maybe not. Dead men don't drink.*"

###

For more information, please visit the Paul Levine's website at www.paul-levine.com and sign up for Paul's newsletter at www. paul-levine.com/newsletter/.

BOOKS BY PAUL LEVINE

EINSTEIN-CHAPLIN SERIES

This much is true: Albert Einstein and Charlie Chaplin were friends in real life; Sgt. Georgia Ann Robinson was the LAPD's first Black female officer; a homegrown fascist militia plotted to kill Chaplin and 20 other celebrities and overthrow the U.S. government. That's the setup for the first two novels, which are stand-alones and need not be read in order. Both are Kindle Unlimited titles.

MIDNIGHT BURNING: When American Nazis conspire to assassinate twenty celebrities and ignite an insurrection against the U.S. government, Einstein and Chaplin fight back, armed only with their ingenuity, raw courage…and the iron resolve of the LAPD's first Black female officer.

MIDNIGHT PATRIOTS: German spies scheme to kidnap Einstein while SS assassins target Chaplin for his blistering lampoon of Hitler in *The Great Dictator*. The final reckoning—a clash of Nazis, FBI agents, a German mystery woman, and our heroes—erupts aboard the luxury Santa Fe Super Chief on its run from Chicago to Los Angeles.

PRAISE FOR "MIDNIGHT BURNING"

Named "Best Historical Thriller of 2025" by Best Thrillers Book Reviews

"Aside from Einstein, the genius in this book is Paul Levine, who uses real people and true events to weave an intricate thriller tapestry [and] to enhance a tale that has more plot turns than a spiral staircase." —*Bookreporter*

"Inspired by historical events and the real-life friendship between Chaplin and Einstein, Levine, has carefully crafted an intriguing and in many ways timely historical thriller that immerses readers in the world of 1930s Los Angeles." —*Booklist*

"Levine's latest will appeal to fans of historical mysteries, especially ones with real-life protagonists. Levine does an excellent job capturing the atmosphere of Golden Age Hollywood as well as the spirits of two of the most important figures of the era." —*Library Journal*

"This series promises to mix fun capers with serious societal commentary and is one to watch out for." —*First Clue Reviews* (Book of the Week)

"Einstein and Chaplin are phenomenal main characters... The cast of characters is rich and varied, and the author easily blends fiction with fact to create a compelling, well-researched novel." —*Historical Novel Society*

"Paul Levine brings the snappy humor of his terrific Jake Lassiter series to the ingenious pairing of real-life friends Charlie Chaplin and Albert Einstein on a roller coaster ride to save America from a fascist threat within its borders." —Jacqueline Winspear, *New York Times* bestselling author of the Maisie Dobbs series

"Einstein and Chaplin put everything on the line—not just for survival, but for the American ideals of justice and freedom. Takeaway: Gripping, cinematic ride through one of Hollywood's most turbulent chapters. —*Booklife* (Editor's Pick)

"A captivating narrative filled with richly developed characters who evoke powerful emotions...a compelling story set against a backdrop of intrigue and suspense that is truly unforgettable." —*Coffee Pot Book Club* (United Kingdom – Highly Recommended)

"Despite the fun, the story is eerily and frighteningly relevant today. This may be Levine's masterpiece." —Lee Goldberg, #1 *New York Times* bestselling author

"Takes you on a wild ride through a dark chapter of American history, shining a light on the bravery of some unexpected heroes. Highly recommended for anyone who loves historical thrillers or believes in the power of art and intellect to fight against the shadows." —*Bookpleasures*

MEET JAKE LASSITER

Jake Lassiter, a second-string NFL linebacker turned night-school Miami lawyer, is a throwback. Frequently in trouble with the law himself, he's a "brew and burger guy in a paté and Chardonnay world." He can be cynical, saying, "I always assume my clients are guilty. It saves time." Still, he believes in righting wrongs, no matter the obstacles: "If your cause is just, no case is impossible." Each book is a "stand-alone," so they need not be read in order. In fact, they can be read in reverse order! All books in the series are Kindle Unlimited titles.

PRAISE FOR THE "JAKE LASSITER" SERIES
Nominated for the Shamus Award
Named to "Best Legal Thrillers of the 21st Century"
by Best Thrillers Book Reviews

"Jake Lassiter is great fun." —*New York Times Book Review*

"Lively entertainment. Lassiter is attractive, funny, savvy, and brave." —*Chicago Tribune*

"One of the most entertaining series characters in contemporary crime fiction." —*Booklist*

"Mystery writing at its very, very best." —*USA Today*

"Clever, funny and seriously on point. Top-notch stuff from Paul Levine. His Jake Lassiter is my kind of lawyer." —Michael Connelly

"One of the best mysteries of the year." —*Los Angeles Times*

"Jake Lassiter has a lot more charisma than Perry Mason ever did." —*Miami Herald*

"The ending courtroom battle sears with intense and realistic turns and builds to an unforgettable closing scene." —*Kirkus Reviews*

JAKE LASSITER SERIES

TO SPEAK FOR THE DEAD: Linebacker-turned-lawyer Jake Lassiter begins to believe that his surgeon client is innocent of malpractice...but guilty of murder.

NIGHT VISION: After several women are killed by an Internet stalker, Jake is appointed a special prosecutor, and follows a trail of evidence from Miami to London and the very streets where Jack the Ripper once roamed.

FALSE DAWN: After his client confesses to a murder he didn't commit, Jake follows a bloody trail from Miami to Havana to discover the truth.

MORTAL SIN: Talk about conflicts of interest. Jake is sleeping with Gina Florio and defending her mob-connected husband in court. Then the hubby gets homicidal.

RIPTIDE: Jake Lassiter chases a beautiful woman and stolen bonds from Miami to Maui.

FOOL ME TWICE: To clear his name in a murder investigation, Jake follows a trail of evidence that leads from Miami to buried treasure in the abandoned silver mines of Aspen, Colorado.

FLESH & BONES: Jake falls for his beautiful client even though he doubts her story. She claims to have recovered "repressed memories" of abuse...just before gunning down her father.

LASSITER: Jake retraces the steps of a model who went missing 18 years earlier...after his one-night stand with her.

LAST CHANCE LASSITER: In this prequel novella, young Jake Lassiter has an impossible case: he represents Cadillac Johnson, an aging rhythm and blues musician who claims his greatest song was stolen by a top-of-the-charts hip-hop artist.

STATE vs. LASSITER: This time, Jake is on the wrong side of the bar. He's charged with murder! The victim? His girlfriend and banker, Pamela Baylins, who was about to report him to the authorities for allegedly stealing from clients. Nominated for the 2014 Shamus Award.

BUM RAP: Lassiter defends Steve Solomon in a murder case...and tries not to fall for Victoria Lord.

BUM LUCK: After clearing a guilty client, a despondent Lassiter threatens to kill the man. Did Jake suffer one too many concussions playing football? All signs point to the fatal disease CTE.

BUM DEAL: With his CTE symptoms growing worse, Lassiter switches teams and prosecutes a murder case. There's just one problem…or maybe three: no evidence, no witness, and no body.

CHEATER'S GAME: Lassiter matches wits with the mastermind behind the college admissions scandal in an effort to keep his nephew Kip out of prison.

EARLY GRAVE: When his godson suffers a catastrophic injury in a game, an aging Lassiter sues to abolish high school football as a dangerous "public nuisance" and becomes the most hated man in Miami. With his personal life hitting a rocky patch, he reluctantly begins couples therapy with fiancée Melissa Gold.

LASSITER'S GHOST: (COMING LATE 2026): Seven years after *Early Grave*, Lassiter's godson Rodrigo Pittman is a newly minted lawyer in need of clients. Penelope Claypool, a Miami television personality, wants him to overturn her father's murder conviction on the ground that Lassiter, suffering from CTE, botched his case. Rodrigo gets advice from the spirit of his deceased godfather…or are those just voices in his head?

MEET STEVE SOLOMON
AND VICTORIA LORD

Meet the mismatched legal team Steve Solomon and Victoria Lord. Solomon considers ethical rules as mere suggestions and lives by his own code: "When the law doesn't work, work the law." Solomon is ethically-challenged and a rule breaker. Lord is a straight-laced Coral Gables blueblood who does everything by the book. In four gripping legal thrillers, the duo battles and banters in the jailhouse, the courtroom…and sometimes the bedroom. All the novels are Kindle Unlimited titles.

PRAISE FOR THE "SOLOMON vs. LORD" SERIES

"Remarkably fresh and original with characters you can't help loving and sparkling dialogue that echoes the Hepburn-Tracy screwball comedies. A hilarious, touching and entertaining twist on the legal thriller." —*Chicago Sun-Times*

"One of the best legal thrillers of the 21st Century." —*Best Thrillers*

"The barbed dialogue makes for some genuine laugh-out-loud moments. Fans of Carl Hiaasen and Dave Barry will enjoy this humorous Florida crime romp." —*Publishers Weekly*

"Some of the juiciest and funniest lingo I've read in a thriller in a long time." —*Connecticut Post*

"The writing makes me think of Janet Evanovich out to dinner with John Grisham." —Mystery Lovers

"The repartee between Solomon and Lord is some of the greatest dialogue I have read in years, and is reminiscent of the very best of what we heard from Dave and Maddie of *Moonlighting*." —*Bookreporter*

"A refreshingly delightful mystery. The scene at the nudist colony alone in *The Deep Blue Alibi* is worth the price of admission." —*Bookloons*

"Paul Levine has written a terrific courtroom drama that's also funny as hell." —Dave Barry

"Paul Levine writes some of the funniest—and most wickedly accurate—courthouse dramas you'll ever read."—Carl Hiaasen

"SOLOMON vs. LORD" SERIES
Nominated for the Edgar, Macavity, International Thriller and James Thurber Awards

SOLOMON vs. LORD: Trial lawyer Victoria Lord, who follows every rule, and Steve Solomon, who makes up his own, bicker and banter as they defend a beautiful young woman, accused of killing her wealthy husband.

THE DEEP BLUE ALIBI: Solomon and Lord come together – and fly apart – defending Victoria's "Uncle Grif" on charges he killed a man with a speargun. It's a case set in the Florida Keys with side trips to coral reefs and a nudist colony where all is more –and less – than it seems.

KILL ALL THE LAWYERS: Just what did Steve Solomon do to infuriate ex-client and ex-con "Dr. Bill?" Did Solomon try to lose the case in which the TV shrink was charged in the death of a woman patient?

HABEAS PORPOISE: It starts with the kidnapping of a pair of trained dolphins and turns into a murder trial with Solomon and Lord on *opposite* sides after Victoria is appointed a special prosecutor, and fireworks follow!

STAND-ALONE THRILLERS

IMPACT: A commercial jet crashes in the Everglades. Is it negligence or terrorism? When the legal case gets to the

Supreme Court, the defense has a unique strategy: Kill anyone, even a Supreme Court Justice, to win the case.

BALLISTIC: A nuclear missile, a band of terrorists, and only two people who can prevent Armageddon. A "loose nukes" thriller for the 21st Century.

ILLEGAL: Down-and-out lawyer Jimmy (Royal) Payne tries to re-unite a Mexican boy with his missing mother and becomes enmeshed in the world of human trafficking and sex slavery.

PAYDIRT: Bobby Gallagher had it all and lost it. Now, assisted by his 12-year-old brainiac son, he tries to rig the Super Bowl, win a huge bet…and avoid getting killed.

BOXED SETS

SHATTERED JUSTICE: Four of the author's best-loved bestsellers: "Solomon vs. Lord," "The Deep Blue Alibi," "To Speak for the Dead," and "Illegal."

MIAMI LAW: The three "Bum" books that bring together Jake Lassiter with Steve Solomon and Victoria Lord: "Bum Rap," "Bum Luck," and "Bum Deal."

3 DEADLY SINS: Wrath, Lust, and Greed are at center stage in three of Jake Lassiter's greatest adventures: "Flesh & Bones," "Lassiter," and "Cheater's Game."

Kindle Unlimited members always read FREE.

For more information and to purchase Paul Levine's novels, please visit his website, www.paul-levine.com.

\#

NUMBER ONE BESTSELLING AUTHOR
PAUL LEVINE

The author of twenty-five novels, Paul Levine won the John D. MacDonald Fiction Award and has been nominated for the Edgar, Macavity, International Thriller, Shamus, and James Thurber prizes. A former trial lawyer, he also wrote twenty episodes of the CBS military drama *JAG* and co-created the Supreme Court drama *First Monday* starring James Garner and Joe Mantegna.

To Speak for the Dead, an international bestseller, introduced readers to linebacker-turned-lawyer Jake Lassiter and was named one of the best mysteries of the year by the *Los Angeles Times*. Levine is also the author of the critically acclaimed *Solomon vs. Lord* series of legal capers. *Bum Rap*, the novel that brought both series' characters together, was the Number One bestselling book in the Kindle Store upon its release. The Best Thrillers Book Review named *Early Grave*, *Solomon vs. Lord*, and *State vs. Lassiter* to its list of "Best Legal Thrillers of the 21st Century." Additionally, it named *Midnight Burning* the "Best Historical Thriller" of 2025.

Levine is a member of Penn State's Society of Distinguished Alumni and graduated, with honors, from the University of Miami School of Law. He lives in Santa Barbara, CA. Visit his website at www.paul-levine.com or follow him on Facebook at www.facebook.com/PaulLevineAuthorPage/ or on X @Jake_Lassiter

For information, contact:
Kimberley Cameron
Kimberley Cameron Associates
kimberley@kimberleycameron.com

Published by Herald Square Publishing
Cover design by Asya Blue Design, asyablue.com.
Interior Design by Steven W. Booth, GeniusBookServices.com
Author Photo by Doug Ellis, DougEllisPhoto.com
ISBN: 979-8-9942630-1-3